WHEN SPRING MEANT GOODBYE

WHEN SPRING MEANT GOODBYE

A Novel

She was too young to carry a child. But she did. And when he left with the blossoms, she carried him still.

ZANNE PASCALE

ISBN: 979-8-9930291-0-8

Published by Zanne Pascale.

Dedication

For Dave, who didn't try to rescue me, you just stood close enough that I remembered I could rescue myself. You found me in pieces and never flinched. You stayed while I rebuilt. *This story is stitched with that kind of faith.*

For Lillie and Noah, who arrived after I thought nothing else could bloom. I was so scared to try again. But you are my world, and I would choose you a thousand times.

And for Truffles, Cloud, Princey, and Flippers, because sometimes love comes with paws, whiskers, or webbed toes. You make the quiet moments brighter.

And always, for God, who held me through every season, who carried what I could not, who planted hope where I thought nothing would grow again.

May every cherry blossom carry what was lost, and all the wonder of what still came after.

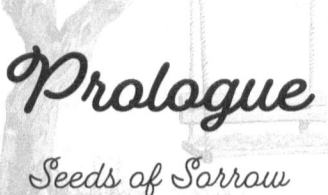

Prologue
Seeds of Sorrow

I blinked against the harsh fluorescent glare, my vision swimming as I fought to orient myself. For a fleeting moment, I clung to the hope that it had all been a dream, that I would wake up in my bed, wrapped in warmth, safe in the familiar cocoon of home. But reality settled in quickly, heavy, and unrelenting.

The couch beneath me was a battlefield of lumpy springs and worn fabric, pressing into my back like a punishment. A dull ache throbbed in my neck, a reminder that I hadn't been asleep long, just long enough for the rhythmic hum of nearby equipment to pull me under.

The room was sterile, drowning in white, the sharp scent of disinfectants clinging to the air. Someone had tried to soften the edges: a throw pillow here, a lamp in the corner but it was a poor disguise. The emptiness seeped in, curling around me like a shadow.

I was alone. And there was no escape from it.

I pushed myself up from the couch, my muscles stiff from hours of restless waiting. The old, dingy curtains I had pulled shut earlier hung limply, their fabric heavy with dust and time. I hesitated before peeling them back, letting the light spill in.

Below, the lobby buzzed with movement, people rushing in and out, grabbing breakfast, lost in their routines. I still couldn't wrap my head around the idea that a McDonald's sat just a few floors beneath me, tucked inside the facility like it belonged there. The scent of coffee and fried food must have drifted through the halls, though I couldn't smell it from here.

I watched strangers sit in chairs, eating, talking, even laughing. They carried an ease I couldn't understand. How could they be here, in this place, and still look so content? Their happiness felt almost offensive, starkly contrasting the weight pressing down on me.

My gaze wandered past the lower lobby and towards the other part of this facility: the windows. Dozens of curtained windows, protecting rooms just like mine, each holding their own story, their own quiet grief. Then, finally, my eyes landed on the one that held my heart.

I was going to have to walk back into that room today. And I was going to have to make the hardest choice of my young life.

Chapter One 1988
Seeds Of Adolescence

I burst through the front door, escaping yet another torturous day of eighth grade. My backpack, weighed down with textbooks and crumpled worksheets, landed on the floor, with a heavy thud, mirroring my exhaustion. School had become unbearable, but home had not been much better lately.

Middle school felt like a downgrade from elementary school; the magic had faded and so had the cookies and milk that used to make the day bearable. That small moment of comfort had once been the highlight of my afternoons. Now, the only positive aspect was the fact that I could make it home in less than two-minutes flat, a blessing on rainy days.

My mom lounged on the couch, lost in the drama of her favorite TV show, while my grandmother animatedly shared her latest adventure. Her voice carried through the room like clockwork, part of our daily ritual. My dad had built her an extension to our house an "in-law suite" just for moments like this, so she would never miss a visit.

Since my grandfather's passing from lung cancer three years ago, my grandmother had made it her mission to never let time slip away. She visited often, determined to hold onto whatever was left, but the visits weren't the same anymore.

My mother spent most of them tending to my nephew, a tiny, wriggling bundle only a few months old, swaddled in soft fabrics and the scent of baby powder. My grandmother sat stiffly across the room, her eyes locked onto him, sharp and unreadable. She never smiled, never cooed the way she had for the rest of us as babies.

Instead, she watched.

Her hands rested motionless on her lap, fingers curled just slightly inward, like she was resisting the urge to grip something. A thought, an old regret? The air was thick with something unsaid that hummed beneath the ordinary sounds of the house, tangled in the quiet rustle of her shifting seat, in the clipped way she spoke when my mother lifted the baby into her arms.

It felt like waiting.

Waiting for her to acknowledge him.

Waiting for her to say something.

Waiting for an explanation.

Yet neither of us was brave enough to ask for it.

The phone was already ringing as I swiftly maneuvered over the couch to answer it.

"Hello?"

"Hi, is Ellie there?"

"This is me."

"Hi, my name is Jennifer, and I'm calling to tell you to leave Rob and Mike alone."

For a moment, I thought I must have misheard her. The words seemed too absurd to be real. I didn't even know Jennifer; who did she think she was, calling my house and making demands? She had the wrong number, or this was some kind of prank.

"Um, excuse me, but who even are you?"

"I'm a very good friend of theirs, and they asked me to tell you to leave them alone."

Her voice carried a quiet menace, but it was the next words that hit me.

"If you refuse to do what I say, I am going to hurt you."

I must admit that scared me. I had no idea who this girl was, no clue what she even looked like. What if she was some towering force, a female Goliath, one swing away from knocking me down. The whole situation made no sense. Why would they tell her that they wanted me to leave them alone? I had known those boys since kindergarten. We had history.

So why was she suddenly in the middle of it? After careful consideration, I realized the only way to get real answers was to face this head-on.

"Meet me behind the school," I told her. "Out by the baseball field."

If they had put her up to this, if this was all some ridiculous joke, I needed to know. I wasn't about to let my imagination run wild, picturing threats that might not even exist. I had to see for myself. I had to ask.

I told her I'd be there in ten minutes; just enough time to steady myself, gather my thoughts and head out.

I stepped onto the field, my stomach fluttering with nervous anticipation as my eyes scanned the horizon, eager for the first glimpse of her. Then I spotted her, striding up the hill with effortless confidence.

She wore torn leggings; the fabric slashed in multiple places to reveal glimpses of her sun-kissed skin. Over them, a short, flowing skirt swayed with each step. A crop-top clung to her frame, accentuated by a pair of bright-colored Chuck Taylors, each sneaker covered in inked doodles like miniature works of art. Black lace fingerless gloves adorned her hands, adding to the rebellious aesthetic.

Her hair was asymmetrical shaved over one ear while cascading long over the other. A single dangling earring graced one side, while a shorter stud balanced the other. Dark, smoldering makeup framed her eyes and lips, enhancing her striking features.

There was no doubt she wasn't from my school. No one there carried themselves quite like this girl. She was bold, unmistakably different, and undeniably captivating.

I imagine she had been in more than a few fights—and won her fair share. Calling a stranger and issuing a threat takes a certain kind of boldness. As she approached, a snarl played at the edges of her mouth, her body language broadcasting an unmistakable message: I am not someone you want to mess with.

She moved with a guarded coldness, her demeanor calculating, as if she wanted me to feel intimidated. And that was the whole point.

She wasted no time explaining why she was there; the boys asked her to scare us off. Rob, it turned out, is beyond tired of Mel and her relentless flirting and swooning.

Mel, my best friend, has been hopelessly in love with Rob since she first laid eyes on him in kindergarten. Every day, we would ride bikes through town, chasing the boys, and her infatuation grew each year. She would pour her heart out, professing her undying love for him, only for Rob to roll his eyes and take off, never once showing the slightest interest in her.

We had spent countless summers caught up in our version of cat and mouse. Whether we set out for 7-11 or the cemetery, it always seemed inevitable we'd run into the boys, and they would taunt us just enough to spark the chase. Often, they let us catch them. We had to believe they enjoyed the game as much as we did, otherwise why keep playing?

So, when I found out that Rob and Mike had enlisted this punk rock stranger to threaten us, I was completely blindsided.

"Rob said rumors are going around at school that he's dating Mel," Jennifer explained.

Mel had been telling everyone they were together. And because of that lie, Rob and Mike had decided Jennifer was the perfect person to send a warning our way.

The more we talked, the more absurd the whole situation seemed, and soon we found ourselves laughing about it. What started as a tense encounter had unexpectedly turned into something almost amusing.

We both agreed that Mel was the real issue here. This was not a conflict for both Mel and Ellie; it was simply a Mel problem.

I promised to talk to Mel and convince her to ease up on Rob, to give him some space. Meanwhile, Jennifer would report back to the boys, letting them know she had delivered their message and that we would not bother them anymore.

It was a strange resolution, but somehow it worked.

The next day, I asked my new friend to meet me at the corner after school since she finished earlier than I did. I was surprised to learn that she attended a private Catholic school--her punk-rock style did not exactly scream traditional. Even more surprising, she lived just two minutes from my school.

As I stepped out of the building and hurried to the corner, I spotted Jennifer standing there, looking completely out of place yet somehow perfectly herself. We exchanged small talk for a few moments before Rob and Mike rolled up on their bikes.

The looks on their faces were priceless. They had thought they'd created enemies, solved their problem, and yet here we were standing together, smiling.

"Hey boys, I'd like you to meet my new friend, Jennifer."

"What?" Rob blurted, his confusion written all over his face.

Jennifer smirked. "Yes, thanks so much for giving me Ellie's number. I think we have a wonderful friendship ahead. Who knew we had so much in common?"

I will never forget that moment. They had tried to be cruel, to shut us down over Mel's harmless infatuation, and now their plan had completely backfired. Justice had been served. We had not set out to humiliate them, but we could not deny the satisfaction of watching their scheme unravel before their eyes.

As the eighth-grade school year neared its end, the days stretched longer, and the air grew thick with summer's sticky warmth. The school was buzzing with plans for the middle school graduation dance; a milestone I was not sure I wanted to be part of. I had never been to a dance before, let alone learned how to dance. Given how shy I was, I expected to do little more than watch from the sidelines, if I even decided to go. The thought of standing there, watching everyone else have fun while I wrestled with nerves and the fear of embarrassing myself was hardly appealing.

Mel, on the other hand, was determined to go. She had built up a fantasy in her mind; Rob would see her standing alone, finally notice her, and, in a grand romantic gesture, sweep her into his arms as they danced the night away.

I had never told Mel the full truth about Jennifer's call. She was supposed to call Mel too, but I had convinced her not to. Instead, I had simply told Mel that the boys were trying to stir up trouble. I could not bring myself to be the one to shatter her hopes.

Since no one had asked me to be their date for the dance, Mel and I decided we would go together. If luck was on our side, she would get her long-awaited dance with Rob, and I would dance with Mike. I did not have a crush on him the way Mel did on Rob, but dancing with a boy even just once felt like something worth experiencing. After all, we had been friends forever. One dance did not seem like too much to ask.

On the night of the dance, Mel and I got ready together, carefully coordinating our matching outfits. Our hair had to be exactly right: big and bold, which meant an excessive amount of Aqua-Net hair spray and teasing to achieve the perfect look.

By the time we arrived, nerves had fully set in. The school gym was decorated with balloons and streamers, and popular radio hits filled the air. The cool kids clustered on one side, while we found ourselves on the other. I spotted a few teachers I was not particularly fond of, along with several familiar classmates.

We were relieved to see that Rob and Mike had shown up, though we had never actually asked if they were coming. Since becoming friends with Jennifer, I wished she could be there too, but she was not a student at our school, so she wasn't allowed.

Mel and I danced and giggled, keeping an eye on the boys to see if they were watching us. We had no idea how to dance, but that did not stop us from jumping and moving to the beat, caught up in the excitement of the night.

Rob and Mike had been watching us on and off throughout the dance. Every time I glanced over, I caught them whispering, covering their mouths so we would not know what they were saying.

Then, Mel made up her mind. She was going to ask Rob to dance. No matter what his response, she was convinced that one day she would win him over. I admired her courage, even as my stomach twisted with nerves on her behalf.

I watched as she walked straight up to him, looked him in the eye, and asked him to dance. His reaction was immediate—an emphatic no. He turned his back on her, shutting her down completely.

Mel walked away in tears and my heart ached for her. It was painful to watch her hopes crumble right there on the dance floor.

Just then, I noticed Mike heading towards me. My stomach dropped—was he about to scold me for not stopping Mel? I braced myself, expecting the worst. Instead, he surprised me.

"Hey, Ellie, would you like to dance?"

I froze. Was this a joke? Was he serious? My nerves skyrocketed, and I felt like I might throw up.

He looked at me expectantly. "Well?"

I hadn't expected this. I had always been shy, and after witnessing what had just happened to Mel, I wasn't sure I could handle the pressure.

But somehow, I managed to say yes.

We walked to a clear space on the dance floor, and I placed my hands on his shoulders while he rested his on my waist. We swayed to the music, awkward but laughing every time our eyes met. I wasn't sure which of us was more nervous.

From a distance, I saw Mel watching, tears still in her eyes. For her sake, I should have said no. But I didn't have time to process what was happening. I was shaking, sweating, and completely overwhelmed.

I worried about stepping on Mike's feet, about making a fool of myself. But after a moment, I decided to say what was on my mind.

"I was wondering why you and Rob asked Jennifer to threaten me and Mel," I finally said, my voice tight with nerves. The silence between us felt unnatural, and I needed to fill it. I had a general idea of the answer from Jennifer, but she was still a stranger—there was always the chance she had twisted the truth.

Mike didn't hesitate. "Rob is just sick of Mel always saying she likes him and trying to hang out with him. He doesn't like her at all. He's just not attracted to her and thinks she's ugly."

Wow. That was brutally honest, crude even.

I swallowed hard. "I'm sorry to hear that. She's in love with him."

15

Mike shrugged. "No, he doesn't even want to be her friend. He thinks she's super annoying."

Embarrassment burned through me—not for myself, but for Mel. She had convinced herself she had a chance with Rob, that if she kept trying, he would eventually come around. He was her kiss and marry. But now, hearing the truth, I knew I could never tell her how he felt. I would have to soften the story and make it kinder to her heart.

Mike continued, "Anyway, that's why we asked Jennifer to threaten you guys. It wasn't about you. Rob is tired of Mel and wants to be left alone."

I finally saw my chance to ask something that had been nagging at me. "How long have you and Rob known Jennifer?"

"Maybe two years now."

"How did you meet?"

Mike chuckled. "It's crazy. One day, we were riding our bikes and saw this girl sitting on the grass by a tree. We started talking to her, and we dared her to show us her boobs. She did it; they were huge! We couldn't believe it. Now, every time we see her, we ask her to do it again, and she always does. We don't think she's hot or anything, but her boobs are just massive."

I stared at him, stunned. That was their connection to Jennifer?

"Anyway," Mike continued, "we told her how you and Mel are always chasing us on our bikes and asked her to call you guys to get you to stop. Rob is just sick of it."

I hesitated before asking the question that had been sitting in the back of my mind. "So... you don't mind me?"

I held my breath, bracing for the answer.

Mike glanced at me. "No, we like you."

The song ended, and we let go of each other. Without another word, I walked back to Mel, and Mike returned to Rob.

Mel wasted no time. "Well? What did Mike say? Does Rob like me?"

I hesitated, knowing I couldn't give her the full truth. Maybe, after Rob had refused to dance with her, she would finally start to realize he wasn't interested.

"Mike said that Rob isn't looking for a girlfriend right now—he just wants to be friends."

Her eyes lit up. "So, he's willing to be my friend?"

"Yes, but he doesn't want to be chased around or asked about dating. He'd rather you just be cool around him, not so lovesick."

Mel nodded, determination flickering in her expression. "Okay. I think I can do that. If I'm his friend over time, I can wear him down, and then he'll see we're meant to be."

I sighed inwardly. She was a hopeless romantic, unwilling to let go of the idea that Rob might eventually come around. If she gave him enough space, he'd at least start to tolerate her.

For the rest of the dance, we watched everyone else twirling across the floor. Mel's eyes stayed fixed on Rob from across the room, already plotting her next move. I wasn't thinking about boys anymore, not really. My mind had drifted somewhere else.

That night, after the dance, I ended up at Jennifer's house again. We sat at her dining table for hours, just talking—about music, about ourselves. She loved The Cure; I was all about Mötley Crüe. She was punk, I was hard rock. She was fearless, while I was shy. Her parents were split, mine were still together. She had MTV. I didn't.

She showed her boobs. I never had.

"Mike told me you flashed your boobs. Is that true?"

"Yup," she said, like it was no big deal.

I couldn't understand it. I'd be mortified. Hers were round and full, like cantaloupes. Mine were barely anything—practically prunes. I had nothing to show.

"Don't you feel weird about it?"

"Not at all. It makes them happy, and I love the attention. Plus, why not give them a thrill?"

Jennifer was unlike anyone I'd ever known. She smoked openly, even shared cigarettes with her mom. She went to private school because she'd been expelled from public though she never said why. Her dad had a new family, and no room left for her. And besides me, she had no other friends.

I often wondered what her life had been like before I came along.

I loved being at her house. There was a weightlessness to it. Her mother let us drift from room to room like air—no rules, no shame. It was everything my house wasn't. Growing up, our rules were ironclad. Modesty wasn't just expected it was doctrine. Sundays meant sitting in front of the television, watching solemn men preach salvation through flickering screens. Sex wasn't discussed. Not even hinted at. It hovered like something dangerous and forbidden; unseen, a word we'd swallowed whole before it could reach our lips.

Only recently things began to shift. My sister, brave or reckless, or both, had pushed back hard against these rules, and the rebellion left its mark. The rules didn't vanish, but they softened, dulling a once sharp edge. Even so, freedom was relative. What passed for leniency in our house still felt like a leash when I stepped into Jennifer's.

At her place, I saw a different kind of living. She could light a cigarette in the kitchen and talk to her mom about anything—boys, body image, dreams, fears—and no one flinched. There were no hushed silences or sharp glances. Just openness, raw and unapologetic. For a long time, I thought that kind of freedom only existed in movies.

Looking back, it wasn't just Jennifer's house I longed for, it was how light I felt inside it. Like I could finally exhale.

"Jennifer don't forget we have an appointment at Planned Parenthood tomorrow morning. We can't be late," her mom reminded her.

"I know, Mom."

Wait. Planned Parenthood?

"Why are you going there?" I asked, the words rushing out before I could stop myself.

My sister had gone there once for birth control pills. When I found them, I ratted her out. My dad was furious. He gave her a bloody nose and grounded her for a month. To my parents, the pill meant sex, and sex outside marriage was a sin. My parents would never allow even a hint of intimacy with anyone before marriage. But that beating didn't stop anything and she got pregnant soon after.

"My mom doesn't want me getting pregnant. She had me when she was nineteen, and she doesn't want me to make the same mistake."

So, was Jennifer having sex?

18

"I'm still a virgin," she said knowingly, reading my mind, "but my mom wants me prepared."

Jennifer's mom was nothing like mine. She worked, she drove, she moved through the world like it belonged to her. My mom stayed home, scrubbing already-clean counters, the television muttering in the background like a tired preacher. Once, she tried to learn to drive but ran a bicyclist off a bridge. She came home pale and shaken and never tried again. After that, the world outside became a place for other people.

She didn't want to go anywhere. Not the mall, not restaurants, not even out for a coffee. It wasn't just that she was introverted; it was like she had stepped out of the flow of life, like joy was something that happened to other people. She made a few efforts at friendship over the years, but they never lasted. Instead of going out to dinner or watching a movie like you would with a friend, my mom would start talking about salvation, calling people sinners, and warning them about hell. You could watch the warmth drain right out of the room. I used to wonder if she was lonely, or if she honestly believed that being alone was more righteous.

At Jennifer's house, I felt accepted. I could be honest about what I did and didn't do. It was another universe. Jennifer could talk about anything—love, fear, bodies, even death—and her mother listened, unflinching. No topic seemed off limits. That house wasn't simply different. It was oxygen.

I hadn't been spending much time with Mel lately, and honestly, I didn't mind the break. No more Rob drama. No more pretending to care about who danced with whom or what came next. I just wanted to be here, in this other world, where the air felt lighter and the rules didn't press against my skin. I wanted to see life through someone else's eyes— Jennifer's eyes. Eyes that didn't flinch. Eyes that had already seen too much and still stayed open.

Jennifer walked everywhere, so my bike started collecting dust. However, when she mentioned visiting her cousin on the opposite side of town, I hesitated. That was a place I wasn't supposed to go.

My dad, being a police officer, knew every corner where trouble lurked. His warnings echoed in my mind, cautioning me about the areas with the highest crime. The opposite side of town was filled with those troublesome corners. But there was something exhilarating about defying his advice, about stepping into unknown streets just to see them for myself. So, I went.

We walked, her boombox blasting at full volume, the music weaving through the humid air like a declaration of freedom. We didn't care who was listening. We talked, we laughed, we dreamed aloud, letting every word bounce off the pavement and float into the summer sky.

I loved being with her. There was something easy about it, something unshakeable. At that moment, the neighborhood didn't matter, the rules didn't matter. It was just us and the rhythm of our footsteps against the concrete, carving our adventure, one song at a time.

Jennifer's cousin Gene was nice, sweet even, and undeniably cute. She had this idea that we might become something, though I suspected it was less about romance and more about easing her guilt when she inevitably ditched me for her latest fling.

This side of town was different from mine. Here, life spilled onto the front steps. Toddlers wobbled outside after baths, their diapers sagging as they toddled through the evening air. Mothers stood in doorways, smoking with their hair still wound in tight curlers, chatting like sentries overlooking the neighborhood. Privacy was a luxury no one had. Everyone knew everyone—and their business, too. Before long, this became our usual hangout, a place where summer stretched lazily into the night.

I never quite hit it off with Gene, but Jennifer made the most of the season, cycling through three different boyfriends before summer's end. She would vanish for long stretches with whoever she was dating at the time. When she returned, she'd swear they had only been making out. I wasn't sure I believed her, but I never saw anything beyond heated kisses with my own eyes.

And, despite the fun we had on this side of town, a lot of my dad's warnings turned out to be true. Life here had an unfiltered edge.

Arguments flared between couples, raw and public, sometimes escalating into shoving matches right there on the pavement. Some girls carried the evidence of those fights; black eyes and bruises that spoke louder than words.

On the corners, people took slow sips from bottles tucked into crumpled paper bags, their movements practiced and casual, as if secrecy was just another part of survival. The thick, pungent smell of weed drifted from open windows, curling into the humid air.

Police cars cruised through often, not with sirens, but with silent curiosity, their headlights sweeping the streets like they were waiting to see what trouble would unfold next.

Then, one evening, a police car rounded the corner, its presence sharp and sudden. My stomach dropped. Even before I saw his face, I knew—it was my dad. Panic jolted through me, and I darted toward a nearby alley, but it was pointless. He had already spotted me.

The car door slammed.

"Ellie! What are you doing here? You know you're not allowed in this part of town." His voice cut through the quiet hum of the neighborhood. Before I could protest, he yanked open the back door and shoved me inside as if I were just another suspect hauled off for questioning.

Humiliation burned through me. Jennifer, her latest boyfriend, and half the neighborhood stood watching. I sank into the seat, my face hot, my pulse hammering. Whatever reputation I had built here evaporated the moment the police car touched the street.

When we got home, my dad wasted no time. He told my mom where he had found me, his voice clipped, firm like he was reporting a crime instead of talking about his daughter. Then he turned to me.

"Bend over."

The words landed with a finality that made my stomach twist. I watched as he reached for his nightstick, the same one I had seen him carry every day, the one that meant authority, control. I had never imagined it being used on me.

"Pull down your pants."

I hesitated. He wouldn't go through with it. He would see the fear in my eyes. But when I obeyed, the first strike came fast. A sharp, burning pain shot through me, stealing my breath. The second hit sent tears spilling down my cheeks before I could stop them. By the third, I was openly sobbing. I ran to my room the moment it was over, choking on my anger, my humiliation, my betrayal.

"You're punished for the rest of the summer," he called after me. "No phone and no going out."

I slammed the door behind me. I had gotten in trouble before...but this time was different. I wasn't used to being hit. I watched it instead. My brother and my sister took the brunt of it. The crack of the stick. The sharp intake of breath. The way they learned to stiffen their bodies just in time, like it might soften the blow. In the past I was spared, not because I was good, but because I broke easily. Raised voices were enough. I'd dissolve in tears before the punishment could begin, unraveling myself as if to say, "See? I've learned already."

My parents believed in discipline, the kind you could hear from the next room. It started with the usual tools: a ruler, a hairbrush, something nearby. But those things snapped and wore down. Eventually, my father turned to what wouldn't. A police nightstick, heavy and sure. He'd brought it home years ago, and it stayed. Not on a belt, but in our hallway closet. Always within reach.

I hated him at that moment, with everything in me. Summer had barely been mine to begin with. Now, he had taken what little remained.

Chapter Two
Seeds Of New Beginnings

Two weeks had passed, each day stretching into the next with unbearable monotony. I had never been more bored in my life. There was only so much I could do in my bedroom, and I refused to linger where my parents might try Conversation. Instead, I immersed myself in music; songs that throbbed through my chest, songs that made me feel something beyond this suffocating silence.

I transformed my space into something of my own, covering every inch of my walls and ceiling with posters ripped from my favorite metal magazines. The room became a shrine dedicated to a world where lyrics and heavy bass drowned out my thoughts.

At night, my anger found reckless outlets. I would spray hairspray along the side of my dresser and flick a lighter, watching the flames surge and vanish, burning off in a brief, rebellious moment. The destruction felt good, if only for a second. And yet, nothing could touch the ache of not knowing.

Was Jennifer still heading downtown without me? Was Mel still trailing after Rob, caught in her orbit of infatuation? I missed everything. The summer…the life I had carved out for myself was slipping away beyond my reach. No one could understand the torture of being locked away, severed from the streets that had become my home.

One evening, swallowed by restlessness, I picked up a razor and drew it across my skin. A cross; simple, deliberate. My mark. If I weren't old enough for a tattoo, I'd make my own. I told myself it was just a symbol, just a phase. But something calmed me in the sting and my control over it. I carved other things too; symbols from album covers, the initials of boys I barely spoke to but somehow swore I'd never forget.

The pain was never the point. It was the permanence. The ritual. The way it gave shape to everything swirling inside me. As the blood surfaced, something in me settled. The pain was real. Visible. A reflection of everything I carried inside.

With only a week left of summer, I could tell something had shifted. My dad carried it in his posture; in the way his words didn't land as firmly as they used to. He started to crack jokes around me, fishing for a reaction, for something.

Guilt. Maybe he regretted what he had done, maybe he didn't. I wanted to laugh. I wanted to let it go. But that would mean absolving him too easily. So, I kept my jaw tight, my silence was deliberate, refusing to let him off the hook.

It wasn't until a few nights later that he finally relented. "There are only a few days left before school starts," he said. "You can go out."

And just like that, the sentence was lifted. Freedom, handed back to me like it was some kind of favor. I didn't say thank you. I just walked out the door and walked to Jennifer's house.

Jennifer opened the door, her eyes wide with surprise. Before I could say anything, she pulled me into a hug so tight I could feel the lingering shock in her grip.

"How are you here? I thought you were still punished. What happened?"

I pulled back, swallowing hard. "I think my dad finally felt bad." The words tasted bitter, hollow. "I just walked out. I want nothing to do with him."

Her expression shifted, and her concern settled deep. "Wait, what do you mean?"

"My dad beat me," I said, my voice quieter now, like admitting it made it more real. "With his nightstick. The one he carries for work. Can you believe that?"

Jennifer's breath hitched. "Oh my God. That's abuse. You should report him."

I let out a hollow laugh, one that didn't hold any humor. "My sister tried once. He almost broke her nose, but when you're a police officer, you can get away with that kind of stuff."

Jennifer's face tightened with anger, her fingers curling into fists at her sides. "That sucks. I'm so sorry." And for the first time, someone said the words I hadn't let myself admit I needed to hear.

"I want to go out. Let's go for a walk."

Jennifer lit up at once, already buzzing with plans. "Yes! Let's go. I need to see my boyfriend."

Of course. While I'd been grounded, watching the summer leak away through a cracked window, she'd already moved on to the next boy in town.

"I don't want to go downtown," I said quickly. "I can't risk my dad seeing me. I'm not about to get punished again with only a few days of freedom left."

It hit me then how much life had happened without me. Relationships had started and ended; friendships had twisted or vanished. All of it unfolding just beyond reach. When you're locked away, time doesn't stop. It rushes on, indifferent. And when you finally step back into the world, it takes a minute to recognize yourself in it again.

Jennifer sighed. "Fine. Where then?"

It had been so long since I had gone out that I didn't really know where to go. We were too old for a simple 7-11 run for candy. Before I could think of an idea, Jennifer blurted, "Let's go to my dad's neighborhood."

I blinked. "Wait. You know where he lives?"

"Not exactly," she admitted. "But I know the general area. We can explore."

I shrugged. "Okay, as long as we get far away from my house."

"That works for me."

And just like that, we had a plan.

We walked past my old elementary school. The playground was deserted, the swings creaking gently in the breeze like they still remembered the laughter, the shrieks, the unfiltered chaos of recess. It all felt strangely familiar but distant, like revisiting an old injury long after the bruises had faded.

As we walked, I remembered what that school was like, what I was like: I was smaller in every way, surrounded by people that knew just where to wound. They teased me about things I didn't even understand yet, words and judgments handed down before I could name them. I didn't have language for what made me different, only the feeling that I was. Out of place. Marked. Alone, even in a crowd.

Noticing me stare at the school in silence, Jennifer wasted no time filling me in on what happened over the summer. Her words came fast, a blur of names and fallouts: who was together now, who had drifted, who had betrayed whom, and why. I tried to keep up, nodding in all the right places, but it all felt like a show I'd missed too many episodes of.

"And Mike and Rob are still annoyed about Mel riding her bike up and down their street," she added with a laugh, rolling her eyes.

I could picture Mel quiet and determined, looping the same block repeatedly like it meant something. Like it might bring him back.

"I feel bad for her," I said. "It must be awful to love someone that much and never have it returned." Jennifer nodded, but we left it there. She had stories. I had silence. And some feelings were too big for words.

We rounded the corner and spotted a group of kids clustered on the sidewalk; their ages scattered like mismatched puzzle pieces. Some stood chatting while others kicked at loose gravel. The younger ones weaved in and out of the crowd with restless energy. Jennifer and I kept walking until we were close enough for her to recognize one of them instantly.

"Hey, Steve! What's up?"

Steve turned, his face breaking into a familiar grin. "Jen! Good to see you. How are you?"

"I'm doing okay." She glanced around. "What's with all these kids?"

Steve let out a half-laugh, gesturing toward the group. "Oh, these? They're my siblings."

Jennifer's eyebrows shot up. "All of them?"

Steve sighed, nodding his head with exaggerated exhaustion. "Yup. Every single one."

Jennifer blinked at the swarm of kids, then let out a low whistle. "Damn."

Steve just shrugged. He'd clearly made his peace with it.

I recognized him from school, but only vaguely. A face that lingered in memory without a name to attach to it. His light brown hair feathered at the sides, long bangs framing those striking blue eyes. He walked with a strut, owning the pavement like the neighborhood itself belonged to him.

He tried not to smile, keeping his cool, but when he did, I caught a glimpse of his buck teeth, a quiet imperfection in his effortless swagger. He looked like a young Tom Petty, all sharp angles and understated charm.

Jennifer introduced us, and we decided to stay for a while. The yard buzzed with movement, kids darting in all directions, their voices overlapping like tangled radio signals.

They kept running up to me, firing off questions with relentless curiosity, their excitement bubbling over. I stood in front of the small Cape Cod house, studying it, wondering how a space so compact could hold all of them. Steve appeared to be the oldest.

I had only ever known life with one sister and one brother, and even then, my brother was only a half-brother and had already moved out. The thought of growing up surrounded by that many siblings felt almost unfathomable, so much noise, so much energy, so much shared space.

And yet, they were happy. Even when their bickering flared up, it was lighthearted, woven into their play like an unspoken rhythm. I liked being with them. But more than that, I liked being with Steve. He wasn't the cutest boy I had ever seen, but his blue eyes were striking, impossible to ignore. More than that, he was kind.

When his little sister stumbled, he moved instantly, scooping her up, brushing off the dirt from her knees, pressing a quick kiss to her forehead. It was such a simple act, but it left an impression. Wow. He was sweet.

Jennifer sighed, glancing around, clearly losing interest. "I think I'm ready to head out."

But I wasn't.

There was something about this place, the chaotic energy, the easy laughter, the unspoken closeness between siblings that held me here.

"You can go, Jen," I said. "I want to stay. I don't want to go home yet."

She raised an eyebrow. "Are you sure? I mean, you don't even really know Steve."

"I know," I admitted. "But I'm having fun, and I want to stay longer."

Jennifer studied me for a second, then shrugged. "Okay then. See you later."

"Bye."

And just like that, she was gone, leaving me in the middle of someone else's world, a world I suddenly wanted to understand. I wanted to know everything about Steve. Had he been here all along, unnoticed in the blur of school hallways? How had I never really seen him before?

Did he genuinely love his siblings this much, or was it just something he performed as an unspoken duty rather than genuine affection? And what about *his* favorite music?

We sat on his front porch, and I tried to dig into the pieces of his world. But the noise around us swallowed our whole conversation. His siblings ran past, shouting, laughing, pulling at his attention, their energy relentless.

Finally, he leaned closer. "Why don't we sit in my dad's van? We can lock them out and hear each other." I hesitated for only a second before nodding. It sounded like the perfect escape.

We walked over to the van and climbed in, shutting the door behind us, sealing ourselves inside a space where the rest of the world couldn't reach us.

We sat in the back seat together, the sun slipping below the horizon, casting everything in muted shadows. I could barely make out Steve's face, just the occasional glint of his eyes when he turned toward me.

His little brother tried the van door a few times, rattling the handle, but after realizing it was locked, he gave up. Outside, the noise of his siblings continued, but here, it was just us.

We talked, throwing questions back and forth, pieces of ourselves revealed one answer at a time. He loved The Beatles and classic rock. He wrestled and ran track. He was in my grade, meaning in just a week, we'd both be walking into high school. And he was quiet. Shy.

"I can't believe you're here," he admitted suddenly.

I glanced at him in the dim light. "Why?"

He hesitated before answering. "I just wouldn't have imagined a girl like you spending time with a boy like me." I wasn't sure what he meant by that, and before I could figure it out, another thought surfaced.

"So, how do you know Jennifer?"

He leaned back against the seat. "We dated last summer."

I blinked. "Really? She never mentioned that." Then again, I shouldn't have been surprised. Jennifer had dated half the town.

"How long?" I asked.

"About a month. If even."

"Why'd you break up?"

He let out a short laugh, shaking his head. "I don't know. I mean... she's Jennifer."

I frowned. "What's that supposed to mean?"

He shrugged, searching for words. "It's just... well, she's Jennifer."

I wasn't sure what he was getting at, but I decided not to push. Instead, I let the silence settle between us, filling the space with that unanswered question. The moon hung high now, its pale glow stretching across the street, marking just how late it had gotten.

Steve's mom had already called his siblings inside, their laughter fading into the house one by one. The world outside had quieted, but I wasn't ready to go home yet. Still, I knew I was pushing my luck.

"I should go," I said softly.

Steve turned to me, his expression shifting, something reluctant, something heavy in his eyes. "Don't," he said. "Stay a little longer."

There was something about the way he looked at me, something in the way he hesitated, half-smiling before quickly looking away.

"Why do you keep doing that?" I asked.

He exhaled, shaking his head like he couldn't believe his own words. "I just can't believe you're here."

"Why not?"

He hesitated. "I don't know… you're just not the type of girl I'd ever expect to be sitting here with me right now."

I frowned. "What does that mean?"

Another pause. Then finally, "You're beautiful." The words landed softly but carried weight. I had never thought of myself as anything but less than average. I was taller than most of the other girls with emerald-colored eyes and blonde hair. I had very pale skin and lots of freckles. Other than my mom I had never been complimented for my looks.

"I saw you at the graduation dance," he continued. "I wanted to ask you to dance, but I was afraid you'd say no. You were dancing with Mike, and I figured he was your boyfriend. I thought I didn't have a shot." I let out a quiet laugh. "Oh no, Mike and I just shared a dance. We've been friends forever. He's not my boyfriend."

Steve looked away, then looked at me. And before I had time to process, before I could even think about what would happen next, he leaned in. I had only kissed a boy once before, and that was just for practice. But this? This was different. This was real. And I wasn't expecting it.

"I should go," I told Steve quickly. "If I don't, I'll end up punished again."

"Can I walk you home?"

I nodded. "Of course. Thank you."

We walked hand in hand through the back field behind the school, our steps light, almost hurried, but still lingering just enough to stretch the moment. When we reached my house, he paused.

"Good night."

Then, as if he wasn't quite ready to let go, he asked, "Can I call you later?"

"Of course." I gave him my number. He repeated it back, memorizing it, locking it away in his memory before leaning in again for one last kiss.

I ran inside, breathless, knowing I was late. Knowing there was no way I was getting away with it. My mom and dad were both on the couch, the flickering glow of the eleven o'clock news washing over them.

"Ellie," my dad said, his tone sharp but tired. "You're late."

"I know." I swallowed hard. "But it was my first day out after being stuck inside for weeks. I was excited to see my friends."

My mom glanced at me. "Where were you all this time?"

"Jennifer introduced me to some friends of hers."

My dad narrowed his eyes. "What street do these friends live on?"

I forced a casual smile. "Don't worry. Not downtown. Actually, the opposite direction. West side."

"What street?"

"Oak Street."

His posture eased a little. "That's a nice area. That's where all the little Cape Cod houses are, right?"

"Exactly."

"Okay. Well, glad you had fun."

And just as I started to breathe again, the phone rang. I already knew who it was.

After we talked, I couldn't stop thinking about him. The way his whole face softened when he mentioned his sister, the quiet protection in his voice. He had a big family, noisy, close, full of teasing and loyalty and he loved being part of it. He talked about his mom's fried chicken like it was sacred, how fishing with his dad before sunrise was his favorite kind of silence. What he had wasn't just love. It was belonging. He had a place, and he knew it.

And then there was the way he looked at me, like he didn't quite believe I was real. He told me I was too pretty to like someone like him, and I wanted to tell him that wasn't it--that it was the way he made the ordinary feel steady, safe.

He played sports, dreamed big, and stayed clean because he wanted to, not because someone told him to. He said his body was something he hoped would carry him forward, not something he needed to punish or escape. There was a kind of reverence in the way he spoke about life. About his family. About the future

31

And all I could think was how different we were. How foreign that kind of closeness felt. My family was tight-fisted with affection, tangled up in silence and sermons. Love didn't taste like sacred fried chicken or come packaged in a tackle box prepared for early morning fishing trips, it came with conditions.

His world felt sunny and open. Mine was full of shadows I hadn't even named yet

Chapter Three

Seeds Of High School

The past few days had been a blur of time spent with Steve. He occupied every corner of my thoughts. Each morning, I found myself walking to his house as soon as I woke, spending the entire day either there or out with him and his friends.

And when night fell, our conversations continued over the phone, stretching well into the quiet hours of the night. His family welcomed me with warmth, their home always alive with movement and noise. Privacy was scarce, a rare commodity in the constant bustle, but we found our moments, sneaking away when the need arose, carving out our own spaces in chaos.

I was smitten in no time at all. Not because he said the right things or looked a certain way, but because for the first time, I felt seen. Wanted. My parents had never asked about my day, my dreams, or my thoughts. They didn't make room for who I was becoming. But he did. Just by listening, by reaching for my hand like it meant something, he gave me a sense of being real.

When he held my hand, my heart fluttered like it had just remembered how to fly. I loved seeing our fingers interlaced together. When he looked at me, the rest of the world blurred. It was possible with him. Like I could become anything. Like I could finally exhale.

But summer doesn't last forever.

The warmth of his gaze, the lazy afternoons, the feeling that absolutely anything was possible, all of it began to fade as the first day of high school crept closer. Excitement was nowhere to be found. The building itself felt daunting, its sprawling halls, endless rows of lockers, and even an Olympic-sized swimming pool made it seem more like a college campus than a place for freshmen. I wasn't ready to trade freedom and possibility for fluorescent lights and bell schedules.

To make things bearable, I signed up for a few electives that seemed fun, sewing and cooking. Cooking especially felt like an adventure waiting to happen. At home, the kitchen was off-limits, a space reserved for special occasions like Easter and Thanksgiving when my mom prepared elaborate meals. We were never allowed to cook, and my mom did not make daily meals. This class will finally give me the chance to learn, to create something of my own.

Taking the bus to school is a new reality, no more morning walks for me. At least I had Mel on the ride with me, and we always sat together.

"Hey, Mel, what's up?" I said as we settled into our seats.

Mel smirked. "Oh, so can I talk now? I thought you forgot all about me since you met Jennifer and Steve."

I rolled my eyes. "Forget about you? Never. I've just been busy."

"Glad we get to sit together every day," Mel said.

"Yeah, me too."

I leaned against the window. "How was the rest of your summer?"

"Nothing special. I'm ready to be back at school."

"Really? Not me. I never wanted summer to end."

Mel laughed. "That's because you're in love."

I scoffed. "In love? Nah. Just having fun."

This new school felt like a maze, an endless stretch of unfamiliar faces and confusing hallways. I caught glimpses of a few kids from middle school, but none of them are in my classes, not Mel, not Steve, not even Mike or Rob.

The only bright spot in my day? I had lunch with Steve. We sat at a small round table, and he wasn't alone. A guy I didn't recognize was with him.

"Hey, Ellie." Steve grinned at me. I love it.

"This is my best friend Clay," he continued. "He's in tenth grade and lives just up the street from me."

Clay offered a polite smile. "Hey, nice to meet you. How are you liking high school so far?"

I shrugged. "I hate it. I don't know anyone in my classes, I keep getting lost, and I still have no clue where my locker is. Honestly, I don't even know how to find the right bus to get back home!"

He smirked, shaking his head with a laugh. "Give it a couple of days and you'll know this place like the back of your hand."

I figured out how to get through most of the day. The hallways didn't swallow me, at least not completely. Here and there, I spotted familiar faces from middle school, people whose names I didn't always remember but whose presence felt like a kind of anchor. But there were so many new kids, too. Faces I'd never seen, clustered into laughing groups, shouting across hallways like they already owned the place.

High school pulsed with a different kind of energy. It was louder, sharper, heavier somehow. Like everyone was being sculpted into someone else and pretending they were already there. I could feel it right away; this wasn't going to be anything like before.

Math was my last class of the day, and the one I dreaded the most. I barely scraped by last year, so now I'm in a remedial class. Two teachers facilitate the class. One teacher would lecture while the other assists students and honestly, I could use all the help I can get.

As I settled into my seat, I noticed a boy I hadn't seen before. His eyes kept drifting toward me, holding just long enough that it's obvious. A shy, almost guilty smile played on his lips, like I've caught him doing something he shouldn't.

I raised my hand to go to the bathroom, and as I passed by, it hit me. He's fully checking me out. Not subtle at all. Steve officially asked me to be his girlfriend, so I'm taken. But a little harmless attention during the worst class imaginable? I don't mind it one bit – the new hip-hugging skinny jeans I bought were definitely worthy of attention. Maybe math won't be as miserable as I thought.

After school, I managed to find the right bus and sank into the seat next to Mel.

"Guess who I saw today?" she asked, her voice full of excitement.

I smirked. "Hmm, let me guess… Oh, I don't know was it, Rob?"

Her grin widened. "Yes! We have the same lunch. I love high school. I get to see him every day now! This is going to be the best year ever!"

I nodded, trying to match her enthusiasm. It's not that I wasn't happy for her. But I hated school. I'd rather spend my days with Steve or riding my bike around town, feeling free. I didn't like the kids who could be so cruel. There were bullies everywhere, hallways thick with them, especially if you weren't popular or didn't wear the right brands. They sniffed out differences like blood in the water. If your jeans weren't the newest cut, if your backpack was the wrong color, if you raised your hand too much, or not, they'd find it and twist it into something laughable.

What made it worse was how much they fed off your reaction. If they sensed it stung, they doubled down. Laughing louder. Making sure you know they weren't done. Showing it hurt only gave them more pleasure. The way I saw it, this wasn't going to be the best year ever. It wasn't even going to be a good one.

As soon as I got home, I called Steve to see if he wanted to hang out. Luckily for me, he had wrestling practice and dinner first, but after that, he could come over. I hated waiting, but I was relieved he still wanted to see me.

Dinner was never much of a tradition in our house, regularly or otherwise. My dad's police schedule kept him out most nights, and my mom never saw the point in cooking for just the two of us. She'd tell us that my dad's first wife, my half-brother's mom, had been a phenomenal cook. Everyone in the family said so. That's why my mother never tried. She didn't want to feel like she was competing with a ghost. So, she didn't cook at all. We finally had a microwave now, which opened a few more options, but nothing substantial. Not that it changed much.

Even back when my siblings still lived at home, we mostly fended for ourselves. Cereal, peanut butter, crackers. Sometimes it was just a matter of opening the fridge and hoping something could pass for dinner. One night, my sister showed me how to make 'butter balls'; just a spoonful of butter rolled in sugar. No measuring, no recipe, just instinct. We sat cross-legged on the kitchen floor, whispering and laughing like we were getting away with something we shouldn't be. And those little balls tasted like childhood joy: sweet and full of endless possibilities. We didn't have much, but for a minute, we had that and each other. Most nights, we ate what we could find, or we held out hope that someone, somewhere, might invite us over and offer us a plate. It wasn't always hunger, exactly. It was the absence of something else. The table was never set. The chairs never filled. The silence, always there. The saddening feeling like you weren't worth the effort.

After school, I had nothing to do; no sports, no clubs, nothing. I never played any sports, mostly because I was terrible at all of them. Gym class was the worst. I was always picked last, and everyone knew that if I ended up on their team, they were going to lose. I wanted to try, but my shyness held me back, trapping me in hesitation. Since sports weren't for me, I tried to play guitar once as a kid, under my grandfather's strict instruction. But his relentless drills, hours of practice, calloused fingers, and tear-filled frustration drove me away from music entirely. I swore off all instruments after that. As a child, I dreamed of joining the Girl Scouts, of wearing the uniform, of being a Brownie. I would have given anything for it. But my mom didn't drive, and my dad's odd work hours meant I had no reliable way to get to meetings. Eventually, I just stopped trying. If I couldn't do that, I figured, I wouldn't bother with any extracurriculars at all.

While waiting for Steve, I had to admit I was jealous. Steve had activities, commitments, and an entire world outside of school that I wasn't a part of. He had friends beyond me, a schedule that didn't revolve around just us. I guess that's what people would call well-rounded. And then there was me. I just had school, a random hang-out here or there, and Steve.

I'd given up so much of my free time just to be near him, shaping my days around him, like maybe if I stayed close enough, I'd matter more. But even with all that, he was still being pulled in every direction, each piece of his life calling him back, none of them me.

So many of the things that first drew me to him--his close family, his love of sports, his friendships. I used to admire all of it. Now, they felt like obstacles I couldn't compete with. His mom still wanted him home for dinner. His dad had planned several weekend fishing trips. His parents checked on his homework to keep him eligible for sports. His friends called after school to play touch football. And his younger siblings still wanted their big brother to be available for them.

And me? There was no one waiting at home. No one was wondering where I was or who I was with. It was easier for everyone if I stayed out of the way. That's the part that hurt the most, that he had so many people who wanted his time, but that I didn't feel like one of them. Not really.

Chapter Four

Seeds Of Threats

I Waited for Steve for three hours. Three long, dull hours. Bored out of my mind. The only thing I'd managed to do was cover all my textbooks in paper grocery bags, just like school required. Hardly thrilling. Finally, there was a knock at the door.

"Mom, I'll get it."

I swung it open, and there he was at last.

"Mom, can we go down to the basement to work on homework together?"

"Ellie, you can, but you have to leave the basement door open."

I frowned. "Why?"

"Because he's a boy, and I don't feel comfortable otherwise."

I sighed. "Okay, Mom, but that's seriously so stupid."

I turned to Steve, rolling my eyes. "Come on, let's go."

I wasn't thrilled about leaving the basement door open, but at least my house offered more privacy than Steve's. Not that we had homework to do, I just needed something to say.

My basement was 'finished' with a couch, a TV, and a bathroom. Since it was partially above ground, it even had a separate entrance. Steve talked about wrestling practice, how much he liked lifting weights, and how focused he was on his health. He loved flexing in the mirror, showing off his muscles. But beneath all that, he was insecure. He told me he didn't think he was extremely attractive, especially because of his teeth. I guess he felt that building the perfect body would make up for whatever flaws he thought he had.

I agreed silently that his teeth were large, not the most attractive feature, but that wasn't what mattered to me. What I cared about was how he treated me. I wanted someone who prioritized me, who respected me. I had seen how some boys treated girls like trophies, like objects, and I knew I didn't want that. And even though he had so many other priorities in his life, he still found time to spend with me, and that meant the world.

Steve had been taking things slowly with me, and I was grateful. So far, we have only kissed. Those quiet, careful moments felt like more than enough. But lately, with more time alone and the air shifting between us, I couldn't help but wonder if things might change. If we'd take that next step.

I'd never really let myself go *there* before. Growing up, the rules were clear and absolute: **you didn't cross that line until marriage**. It wasn't just discouraged; it was unthinkable. I'd absorbed it all without question, like gospel sewn into my skin. But now… now, it felt more like a question than a commandment.

Afterall, my sister had broken those rules, and she hadn't been struck by lightning. She wasn't swallowed up by shame or banished from the family. She just lived her life—still standing, breathing. That realization settled inside me, quiet but insistent. The world wouldn't end. It was okay to want, to wonder, to feel.

Steve and I had quickly settled into a routine; school, lunch together, then "homework" at my house. I loved having that break in the middle of the day, a moment to look forward to amid the monotony. After school, we'd head to my place, where we'd pretend to study, but mostly just enjoy each other's company. We watched lots of TV together and listened to all our favorite bands. While I enjoyed harder rock, Steve liked classic rock, so I tried to enjoy classic rock, like the Beatles.

Many nights, my dad surprised us by ordering pizza from our favorite shop. Steve loved it. His mom always cooked, and takeout was unheard of at his house. But thanks to my dad's recent pay raise, he treated us more often, and I wasn't complaining!

However, there was one person who seemed to not want me to be happy. Even pizza couldn't seem to appease my grandmother. One afternoon, as Steve and I walked through the door, she was visiting my mom, perched in her usual spot. The moment she saw us, her expression darkened. We greeted her politely, but she barely acknowledged us. Instead, she locked her eyes with Steves.

"You better not do anything with my granddaughter," she said, her voice sharp.

Steve and I exchanged confused glances. "What are you talking about, Grandmom?" I asked.

"I mean it, boy. You better not touch her. Don't try to have sex with her. I wouldn't let any boy or girl alone together in my basement. You're just asking for trouble!"

Looking back, it was true that my grandmother saw something. She noticed things other people missed, especially when it came to my step-brother. She'd warned my mom about the way he looked at me, how something in his gaze wasn't right. But my mom brushed it off every time. Said she was overreacting, being dramatic. So eventually, I stopped hoping people would notice. And eventually, like my mom, I stopped wanting to hear her crazy ideas about boys in general. Steve wasn't like my step-brother, and he deserved better than to hear her pestering comments. Heat flooded my face; embarrassment, anger, frustration, all tangled together.

"Grandmom, you're so ignorant! How dare you talk to him like that?" I grabbed Steve's arm. "Come on, let's get out of here."

As we left, I shook my head, my mind still replaying the moment. What a weirdo! I apologized to Steve for my grandmom's outburst. I still couldn't believe she had acted like that. We found the humor in it, though, replaying her words in exaggerated voices, cracking up until we were laughing so hard, we could barely breathe.

The thing was, I had never even thought about having sex with Steve. We had only kissed. My parents had always taught me that sex was something to wait for until marriage. My sister had been raised with the same belief, but she still ended up pregnant at seventeen. And even then, she managed to graduate. My parents had tried to push her into marrying the father of her child, but she wasn't ready. Instead, they just moved in together. My parents didn't believe in living together before marriage, but since my sister was older now, and already a mother, she made her own choices.

That's why my grandmother worried about me. She had seen how things turned out for my sister and assumed I'd follow the same path. But I wasn't her.

Chapter Five

Seeds Of Jealousy

Jennifer called me. Ever since school started, we have only been able to see each other on the weekends.

"I miss you, Ellie," she said, her voice tinged with something more than just distance. "I'm glad you like Steve so much, but ever since I introduced you to him, it's like I don't even exist."

"Oh, come on, that's not true," I protested. "Remember all those times downtown when I was alone while you were making out in the alley?"

"Yeah, but that was different."

"How so?"

"Because you were still with me. We were still hanging out."

I sighed. "Yeah, I get it."

I felt bad, but I couldn't help how I felt about Steve. "I'm just so happy," I admitted. "We have so much fun together, and I love his company. He's so good to his brothers and sisters. He treats the little ones so sweetly. He wants to teach me to hunt and fish. When I'm with him, I feel special, like he's honored to be with me. He doesn't think he's good enough for me, but I mean, come on he's on the wrestling team, and what do I have?"

"Oh, come on, Ellie, you're super-hot," Jennifer scoffed. "I mean, Steve isn't all that great looking."

"I know, but that's not the most important thing to me."

Her tone turned mischievous. "Have you kissed him yet?"

"Yes," I admitted, my cheeks turning red.

Jennifer burst into laughter, the sound deafening on the phone speaker. "Isn't it hard since his teeth are so big? I mean, they would always cut me."

I paused as the weight of Jennifer's words settled in. I hadn't known she and Steve had kissed. Sure, I knew they had dated briefly, but I never thought much of it. And yet now, something sharp and uneasy twisted inside me. Anger. Betrayal. Confusion. I don't know why, but for some reason, I had just assumed I was his first kiss. Someone should have told me this sooner.

I cleared my throat, cutting off her laughter. "Um, no, I haven't had any of his teeth cut me."

"Oh, well, that's good," Jennifer casually said, oblivious to my sudden shift in mood. "I always found that to be a problem." She paused briefly, then, in the most casual manner, blurted

"So, have you seen how big he is?"

I blinked; my fingers twisted the phone cord. "Um... what do you mean?"

"You know, his stuff. It's huge, isn't it? Biggest I've ever seen."

Just when I thought I couldn't get upset any more, a fresh wave of fury washed over me. She had seen his penis.

"Uh, yeah, it's huge," I said, forcing my voice to stay casual. There's no way I'm admitting I haven't seen it—not when she has.

"So, what were you doing when you saw it?" I asked, trying to sound uninterested while also trying to get information out of her.

"Oh, you know, just fooling around and stuff."

My fingers tightened on the phone cord. "Jennifer, sorry, but my mom's calling. She needs to use the phone. I gotta go."

"Okay, bye," she said.

I quickly put the phone on the receiver and sank to the floor. A sudden wave of jealousy crashed through me, sharp and unexpected. She was with him before me, and I knew it shouldn't matter. None of it changes what he and I have now. But still... it lingered, like an unpleasant aftertaste.

It's not that he cheated. He didn't. I know that. But something about it feels like a betrayal anyway. Like they lived out this story, shared glances, moments, even feelings and left me outside of it. And worse, they decided I didn't need to know.

Now there was a space between us that hadn't existed before. And I'm angry. At Jennifer for being part of something unspoken. At Steve for not saying anything sooner. At both of them, for making it feel like there was something to hide. It's not about what happened, but about what didn't; the honesty, the choosing to tell me before I had to figure it out in pieces.

I immediately called Steve, but his dad answered. "He's at practice," he says.

Ugh.

I need to ask him; did he and Jennifer have sex? How else would she know what she knows? I dialed again, hoping he's back. His dad answered. I hung up.

Steve finally called me back.

"Did you hang up on my dad earlier?" he asked.

I hesitated. "No, I only called once," I lied.

"Okay, well, someone did," he says, brushing it off. "So, what's up?"

I took a breath. "Well, I was talking to Jennifer tonight, and she said some things that made it seem like maybe you and her did more than just date."

"Like what?"

"I don't know. More."

Steve lets out a short laugh. "I don't know what she told you, but we barely dated it was, like a couple of days."

"Did you kiss her?"

"Yes."

"Was that it?"

He sighed. "What are you trying to get at?"

I pressed forward. "Did you do anything else with her?"

"No, not really."

"So, you're a virgin?"

"Yes, of course."

I studied his words, searching for any hesitation, any sign he's not telling the truth. I have no real reason to doubt him…but then why would Jennifer say that?

"You know what?" I said, shifting my frustration. "She's probably jealous. She feels like you're taking me away from her, so now she's trying to ruin it for me." I let go of the telephone cord, my fingers relaxing slightly at the idea that maybe I had worked myself up for nothing.

"Sorry, Steve. Jennifer was just making stuff up."

Steve laughed a little, "Yeah, well, you know Jennifer."

"Yeah," I murmured. "At least I thought I did." I looked down at my feet and then muttered into the phone, "Can I come over?"

"Of course, but I'm playing tackle football with the neighbors," Steve says.

"Oh, okay, that sounds fun. I'll be right over."

I walked to his house and saw the chaos unfold. Children everywhere. Children running, laughing, tumbling into the grass. Steve's siblings were all playing, along with Clay, Steve's other friend Mac, and two of the popular girls from school, Amy R and Amy P. I hadn't realized they were all Steve's neighbors. Both girls played softball and ran track, and both were effortlessly athletic and beautiful. Steve asked if I wanted to join in the game, sweat beading on his hair. I shook my head instantly. "No way, I'm not running with a football."

Instead, I took a seat on the porch, watching the game play out. Everything seemed fine, until I caught Steve tackling Amy P.

And I saw it. I saw him.

Not just an accidental grab, not a fleeting mistake. While tackling her, his hand deliberately caught her chest, lingering in a way that made my stomach tighten. A "whoops" moment? No. This felt more like taking an opportunity, like 'grabbing a feel' the first chance he got. I waited, the weight of my thoughts pressing against my ribs, until the game ended and everyone had finally cleared out and went home. It was just him and me now.

"Steve," I said, my voice tight. "I saw you grab Amy's breast."

He froze, his expression a mix of confusion and defensiveness. "What? I didn't do that."

"Yeah, you did. You can't deny it; I was right here. I saw you."

His jaw clenched. "Ellie, I swear to God I didn't. I don't know what you think you saw, but that didn't happen, and if it did, it was an accident."

But I did see it. I knew I did. And it didn't look like an accident.

Later, Clay approached me, his expression tense.

"Ellie, I hate to admit it, but I saw Steve grabbing Amy's boob. No doubt about it: it was clear as day. I also know he did it on purpose. That's the only reason he plays with those girls."

I swallowed hard. "I know," I said. "He denied it, of course, but I know what I saw."

Clay shook his head, frustration flickering in his eyes. "I can't believe he did that. I'd never treat a girl like that. And if you were my girlfriend, I would never do anything to hurt you."

I met his gaze. "I appreciate that, Clay." We stood for a moment, the weight of what just happened in the air, but seeing the sun beginning to set, I knew it was time to go home. The weight of yet another betrayal settled in my chest, making it hard to breathe as I began my trudge home.

Was Steve really the person I thought he was? I'd always assumed he was just as inexperienced, just as unsure as I was when it came to the opposite sex. But now doubt seeped in, whispering that he might have more experience, more desire, than I ever realized.

That thought twisted inside me, stirring something ugly, something I didn't want to acknowledge. Insecurity. Jealousy. And suddenly, I wasn't sure if I was more upset with him or with myself.

I'd never been in a relationship before, so I didn't know what kind of person I'd be, the jealous type, the anxious one, the girl always waiting by the phone. And honestly, I didn't think I *should* be jealous. I was a decent-enough-looking girl. People told me I was pretty. But still, I never quite believed it.

Insecurity clung to me like a second skin, even if I couldn't always trace where it started. Maybe it was the way my dad used to call me "backwards" whenever I was shy around strangers. Maybe it was because

I'd been too thin as a child, all elbows, and hollow cheeks, and now that I was older, my body hadn't caught up to the girls around me. They all had flat stomachs, curves, and confidence they wore like perfume, and boobs that Steve seemed to like so much.

And I didn't have any of that. And I didn't feel wanted. I felt like an afterthought. Like a consolation prize someone might settle for if no one better came along.

I didn't know if I trusted love yet.

I wasn't even sure I trusted *myself* to be worthy of it.

Chapter Six

Seeds of Gossip

It had been a few days since I'd spoken to Steve. The silence between us felt heavier now, laced with doubt and disappointment.

Clay had told me something I didn't want to believe, that after I left the football game, Steve had bragged about Amy. About how big her chest was. About how he got a handful. I didn't think he was like that. I thought he liked me.

A pit formed in my stomach. I looked at myself in the mirror, scanning my reflection with new uncertainty. My shape was cute, but my chest was small. I tried my best to look good, styling my hair carefully, picking out makeup that felt cool and confident. I even tried to get new clothes to fit me just right. My jeans were my favorite. I wore them just like my sister, tight, hugging every curve. Most girls wore them that way now, and I saw how guys noticed the way their eyes lingered. However, Jennifer had borrowed my favorite jeans last week, and when she wore them, they looked better on her. Everything looked better. I just wish I were a bit thinner. I need to go on a diet.

Some girls seemed to flirt effortlessly, like it was just a language they'd always known. I wasn't one of them. I tried now and then, especially with Steve, but it always came out feeling clumsy, like wearing a pair of shoes that didn't quite fit. There was a kind of confidence to flirting that never sat comfortably with me. While others sparkled and drew attention like fireflies in summer, I often lingered on the edge of the glow, wondering if I was missing some secret. It just wasn't my way of being seen.

Was I attractive? I wasn't the prettiest girl in school, but I wasn't at the bottom either. A solid 7 or 8, maybe? But none of that seemed to matter. Guys our age weren't looking for sweet, smart, or interesting people. They wanted it to be easy. And that wasn't me.

When I first met Steve, one of the things I liked most was that he hadn't pressured me into anything that night in the car. It was refreshing, different.

A year ago, things hadn't been so simple. I'd been asked out by a boy from school, and I was excited, it was my first real date, my first chance at something that felt special. We met one evening under the bridge in town, and he asked if he could kiss me.

I was so excited. No one had ever shown real interest in me before, not like this. The popular girls had already claimed their place in the world of dating, effortlessly gliding through hallways with boys trailing behind them. I wasn't part of that orbit. I heard what the boys talked about: who was pretty, who wasn't, who looked good in what and the works. Sometimes it felt like they were handing out invisible ranks. I'd listen, quietly, pretending not to care.

But that night on the bridge, something shifted. For once, the spotlight tilted my way. I felt lucky. Seen. I was one of the pretty ones. One of the selected. And for someone like me, who had always hovered on the edge of everything, that feeling was its own kind of magic. I hesitated, nervous. I had never kissed like that before, never felt the weight of expectation pressing down on me. He told me he'd show me how. So, we kissed.

I was grateful for the darkness, for the way it hid the embarrassment warming my cheeks. His tongue felt moving against mine, unfamiliar and overwhelming. Then, suddenly, the moment shifted. He started unzipping his pants. I jolted back, confusion knotting in my chest. "What are you doing?"

"Well, now I want you to do it here," he said, gesturing to the bulge beneath his zipper.

Revulsion surged through me. I told him to fuck off and quickly walked away, my heart pounding, fear creeping in. Would he twist the story? Would he tell everyone at school that I *had* done it?

I never would.

But I had learned earlier in life that some boys lie, spinning stories about what they wished had happened instead of the truth. When I was in third grade, walking home from school one afternoon, a group of boys started shouting at me.

"Ellie Keen, the blow job Queen!"

I didn't understand what they meant, but the way they said it mocking, teasing made my stomach twist with embarrassment. Their laughter was sharp, their gestures exaggerated, something about it all felt wrong, even if I didn't fully grasp why. I ran home, heart pounding, tears burning my eyes. As soon as I stepped inside, I turned to my mom.

"Mom, what's a blow job queen?"

She looked at me, startled. "Ellie, why would you ask me that?"

"Some kids were calling me that on the way home, and they were doing this." I mimicked their motions, the way they had twisted their hands and mouths.

"Ellie, stop that. It's dirty."

I hesitated. "But...what does it mean?"

"It's something only married grown-ups do," she said, her voice tight.

"Oh." My chest felt heavy. "Then why would they be yelling it at me?"

She sighed. "I don't know, honey."

But even then, I understood that sometimes, people say things not because they're true, but because they want power over someone else. And that day, it had been me.

That night, I overheard my mom telling my dad about our conversation. My sister chimed in, her voice tight with frustration. I listened from the hallway, my stomach twisting as I pieced it together. It had happened to her too.

Years before, when I was still just a little kid, a group of kids started calling my sister the same thing. She said it was all lies, a nasty rumor that spread like wildfire. The thought made my skin prickle. Those kids had older siblings. They knew we were related. And now, it was happening to me. Every time a boy showed interest in me, I assumed he had only one reason, to see if the rumor was true.

And when that boy had put me in that position under the bridge, that fear was further ingrained in me. Because even though we both knew I had refused him, he lied about it. Told people his lies. And just like my sister, it spread like wildfire. Ever since, I'd carried the weight of that story, the worry that any attention I received wasn't real, it was just curiosity wrapped in manipulation.

I had been called by that name for years. By girls and boys. By kids I didn't even know. It spread like wildfire, passed down like some cruel tradition, like they had a right—no, a duty—to say it. To remind me.

They wrote it in bathroom stalls, carved it into desks, Graffitied it on garage doors in back alleys. Some even etched it into the pages of my yearbook, permanent, like they wanted to make sure I never forgot.

It was disgusting. A word I hadn't even understood when they started saying it, before they crowned me with it, before they twisted it into something degrading. A 'queen' they called me. But it wasn't admiration. It was mockery, something meant to strip me bare, to make me ashamed, to make me small. And it worked. I wanted to hide. To disappear. To scrub it from walls and memory, but no matter how much I wished, the name stayed.

My mom said it was dirty. That word clung to everything. If I ever, did it, I'd be dirty too. And if a boy asked, then he was already tainted, someone to stay away from. I didn't know much; only that desire was dangerous and shame clung easy.

So, I didn't want any part of it. Not because I understood what it was, but because I had already been harmed by it and stained by it. Guilty by association, I figured. A girl marked by implication.

When I met Steve, I thought he was different. And that night in the car, I felt that he had proven his difference. He hadn't pushed me or asked me to do anything for him. In fact, he even told me he had never heard me referred to by that name. I had believed, hoped even, that he wasn't dating me to dig up the truth behind a reputation I never asked for. But now doubt was creeping in, whispering the one thing I never wanted to question.

Had I been wrong about him? He was closer to Jennifer than he let on; I could see it in the way they leaned into each other, the way she laughed a little too easily at things he said. But that wasn't the worst of it. I had seen him during the football game; his hands too familiar, grabbing at Amy like it was his right.

A chill settled in my stomach.

Maybe he knew the rumors about me. Maybe he believed them. He was just waiting to find out if they were true. I hadn't meant to inherit it— the weight of whispers, the name passed down like an unwanted heirloom. At first it felt like a link between my sister and I; something that tethered me to her in a way I hadn't expected. But beneath that was anger. If not for her, none of this would have reached me. I hadn't earned the reputation, hadn't lived it; yet here it was, shaping my world all the same.

The more I learned about our 'earned' title, the heavier it became. My sister had endured this for years, quietly, without me knowing. She had begged our parents for help, urging them to intervene. There were conversations, school meetings, and promises of change. And yet, nothing. Just more of the same, the whispers slipping through the cracks, the injustice lingering long after it should have disappeared.

I wondered if she wanted to shield me from it. Or had she wished I had understood sooner, so she wouldn't have been alone in it for so long?

Chapter Seven

Seeds of Self Doubt

Steve cornered me in the hallway, his voice low but insistent.
"Why have you been ignoring me?"

Students passed by, laughing and talking loudly about whatever they found important that day. I tried to focus on the scuffed tiles beneath my shoes, but Steve's presence pressed in; familiar, and yet suddenly foreign.

"I just want to be left alone," I mumbled.

"Why? What's wrong?"

His tone held a softness I didn't expect, so different from the usual bravado he wore around his friends. I hesitated, my heart a trapped bird fluttering in my chest. I looked at my shoes and spoke quietly, "I just... I feel like you're lying to me about things."

His brows furrowed, confusion and concern mingling in his gaze. "Like what?"

"Like grabbing Amy's chest. And you never told me about kissing Jennifer. She seems to know things about you that I don't, things she shouldn't." My voice was a whisper, nearly lost beneath the echo of slamming lockers and distant shouts.

Steve stepped closer, closing off the noise. His tone shifted, pleading now. "I promise I haven't hidden anything. What happened with Amy was an accident. And yeah, I kissed Jennifer, but it didn't mean anything. It's nothing like when I kiss you." He reached for my hand, his palm warm and trembling.

I blinked, fighting the urge to withdraw. "What do you mean?"

"When I kissed her, it was just... something that happened. But when I kiss you, I feel it everywhere. In my entire body." He exhaled, running a hand through his hair in that way he did when he was nervous. "I've missed you these past few days. I love spending time with you. I've never been this happy before." His voice grew quieter, more certain. "I would never do anything to ruin that."

A part of me wanted to believe him. To let those words smooth over the jagged edges of doubt.

But the other part of me, the one that remembered all the ways I'd been let down, all the things whispered in locker rooms and hallways, held back. That part of me always felt the truer version of me, the one I grew up as and the one I learned to trust the most. My dad used to call that part of me "backwards." He'd say it with a crooked grin, like my shyness was a puzzle or a punchline. I didn't speak up. I didn't stand out. I moved through life like I didn't want to leave footprints. And for a long time, I didn't. I was always the quiet one; the girl people leaned on, borrowed from, and passed over. The one who got asked for favors but never the dance. Love was something that happened to other girls, louder ones, brighter ones; girls who didn't have to try so hard just to feel seen. Eventually, I learned to listen more than speak, learned to hope quietly and hurt quietly too.

But Steve looked at me like no one ever had. There was something electric in the silence that stretched between us; longing, hope, fear, all tangled together. Then he paused, his eyes holding mine.

"I think I might be falling in love with you."

My breath caught. "What?"

He smiled, nervous and earnest at once.

"Can you say that again?"

"I love you."

The words felt weightless and heavy, both. They filled the hallway, the empty spaces I thought I'd never escape. And then we kissed, right there in the swirl of after-school chaos, for everyone to see. And I didn't care. I didn't care who was watching, who might whisper, who might spin it into something ugly. Let them. Because at that moment, I finally felt chosen. I was his. He was mine. I had never felt anything like this before.

After a lifetime of feeling invisible, of being an afterthought, of being used and passed over, this was different. This was real.

In that moment, I would've given him anything, even my virginity, if he asked. He hasn't. But there's one thing I'll never, ever give. Because of the rumor. The one they've been whispering about for years. It can never be true. Because if it is, all the times I fought it, denied it, swore it wasn't me, every wall I built to keep it out, would mean nothing. And I'm not ready to lose that part of myself. Not yet. Maybe not ever.

Later that night, as I lay in my bed listening to the hum of my radio vibrate through the speakers, I replayed every moment with Steve. The way he held my hand, the way his thumb traced tiny circles on my wrist. The way his eyes flickered between hope and uncertainty. I thought too about the way Jennifer's voice sounded when she said his name, too familiar, too bright. I thought about Amy's laughter at the neighborhood game, sharp and ringing in my ears long after the lights went out.

I wondered what would be left of me if I gave in; if I let go of the part of me that clung so tightly to innocence, to the idea that I was still untouched by the worst things people said. If I let, go of my "backward" ways and lived in the confidence I had felt earlier that day. The uncaring, shameless way of life. And yet in the back of my mind, I still wondered if Steve saw me, really saw me, or if he was searching for the girl from the rumors; the one I was never allowed to be.

I watched the shadows on my ceiling and tried to imagine a world where I could be loved without fear, without the weight of shame. But even in the quiet, the echoes of old wounds lingered. The whispers, the laughter, the stains that never quite faded. And as I drifted toward sleep, I promised myself that night that I would not be undone by the stories others told about me.

I would write my own story, even if I had to do it in the margins, even if my voice shook every time I tried.

Chapter Eight

Seeds of First Love

I had settled into a routine; school and Steve. That was my life. He still had his family, his wrestling, his track meets. But me? I hadn't spent much time with my other friends. I didn't care. I just wanted to be with him, always. People said I was obsessed. That I should make time for other relationships, keep my options open, even date other boys instead of locking myself into something so exclusive. But they didn't get it. By this point, I wasn't just in love, I was planning an entire future. If Steve asked me to marry him today, I wouldn't hesitate. I would say yes in a heartbeat.

My dad told me we were going away for a week to the mountains. *Again.* We always went to the mountains. It was a four-hour drive to our trailer, tucked deep in the woods, miles from the nearest town. No running water. No sewer. Just isolation. I had been going there my entire life. My mom loved it. She thrived in the quiet, the way the world felt far away. She was a recluse at heart. But my sister and me? As we got older, we hated it. No phones. No kids our age. Nothing to do except the occasional trip to the mall, a movie, swimming in the mountain lakes, or ice cream. And the rest of the time? Just stuck in that trailer, waiting for the week to be over.

And now, the thought of leaving for an entire week away from Steve, with no way to call him, was unbearable. It would be like when I was punished and cut off from the outside world.

What if he spent time with Jennifer? Or Amy? What if something happened between them while I was gone? I wouldn't know if he was feeling people up or keeping other secrets.

No.

There was no way I was going without him. It took a lot of begging, crying, and convincing, but in the end both our parents agreed. Steve could come on the trip. I was honestly surprised. My parents were more lenient than I expected. Their only big rule? We had to sleep in separate bedrooms. That wasn't a big deal.

We'd still get to spend every waking hour together, every meal, every quiet morning, every late-night talk before bed. I'd get to see his routine, the way he started and ended his days. We could swim, explore, and I could finally show him all my favorite places in the woods. We'd hike, spot deer, even see a bear or two.

Steve was thrilled. He loved hunting and fishing with his dad and the idea of spending time in the true wilderness excited him. And honestly? The idea of sharing this experience with him, just the two of us, away from everything else excited me too.

I packed everything I needed in a backpack and threw it in the trunk of my parents' station wagon. Steve, excited to get going, showed me his packed bag, double-checking that he had everything he needed. At the bottom, tucked away, I spotted a familiar foil packet.

I picked it up, holding it between my fingers. "What's this for?"

Steve glanced at it and sighed. "My dad gave it to me."

"Your dad?" I blinked. "Why would he give you those?"

He rubbed the back of his neck, looking more uncomfortable by the second. "He came into my room last night and gave me... the talk. The birds and the bees."

I stared at him. "No way."

"Yeah. Can you believe that? So awkward." He shook his head, exhaling. "Anyway, he said he figured we might decide it's time and wanted to make sure I was prepared." Then, as if that wasn't bad enough, Steve groaned, his face twisting in embarrassment, his eyes unable to meet mine. "And before I left, he growled, patting me on the back, and said, 'Go get her, tiger.'"

I gaped at him. "Are you serious?"

He nodded, finally looking back at me, eyes wide. "I know. Weird, right?"

So far, I'd only allowed Steve to get to 'second base'. After what happened with Amy, I felt like I needed to let him get a good 'feel' or he might make a habit of "accidentally" grabbing other girls. The last few times we made out, he got on top of me and started grinding his bulge in his pants against my pelvis. He would rub and grind me so hard that the next day my bones would be sore. He would start breathing hard and get into it so that it almost seemed like I disappeared, and he was hypnotized. I didn't understand what he was getting out of it, but it made him happy, so I let him do it.

That being said, I wasn't exactly comfortable. The whole thing felt strange, oddly lopsided. He was enjoying it so much, completely immersed in whatever *this* was, while I just sat with the quiet hum of discomfort pressing against my ribs. I didn't feel much of anything during it at all. I knew I should say something, shift the moment, pull away, but that would mean disrupting his happiness, and the last thing I wanted was to embarrass him or say something that made me look foolish. So, I stayed. I went along with it, despite the way my skin prickled with unease, despite the small voice in the back of my mind whispering that I didn't belong here at this moment, not really.

In fact, it felt wrong.

The whole thing, the way he moved, the expression on his face reminded me too much of something I had tried to push away.

Mark used to do this. My half-brother. When I was younger, he would sit me on his lap, hold me there too tightly, and grind himself against me as if I belonged to him. I would squirm, try to pull away, but his grip was firm, unyielding. I never liked it.

His mother died when he was young, and that left an emptiness no one tried to fill. But grief doesn't explain what he became. He was a thief. An alcoholic. He hurt girls. And he hurt me when I was five. He was fifteen. I only wanted someone to spend time with me, to be seen. Not to be used. Eventually, I told my parents. My grandmother had already warned them. She'd noticed how Mark's eyes lingered too long, how he shouldn't be left alone with me or my sister. But no one listened until it was too late. My father confronted him, and then Mark was gone. But the blame stayed behind. My father said I'd tempted him. That walking around in pajamas, or just underwear, was enough to make a boy lose control. As if I should've known what my body would provoke. As if it were my fault for being visible.

I was a little girl, and somehow the shame landed on me.

Mark's obsession with sex didn't stop there. Pornography, strip clubs, pushing boundaries until they shattered. He raped a woman later in life and ended up in jail. When I confronted him about what he'd done to me, he said I wanted it. That we were "just playing." And my father still agreed. Said it was just puberty. As if desire was justification. It twisted the way I saw everything; myself, my worth, and every boy who followed. I was taught that if I didn't disappear, I deserved what happened when I was seen.

And now, years later, I found myself with Steve, feeling his hands on me, his body pressing close, and a flicker of that old panic rising in my chest. I had to remind myself this was different. He was not Mark. I was not five. But my body remembered, and the past didn't care how much time had passed.

Still, the moments with Steve held something else, too. Something tender. Something real. He loved me. I loved him. And even if no words were spoken, something in that silence offered comfort. This wasn't about being taken, it was about being chosen. Being wanted for who I am, not for what someone thought they could take. We could carry that with us forever. Just him and me. Me and him. And eventually I decided that…if Steve wanted me, chose me…I would let him.

The drive to our place in the mountains was long but Steve made it fun. We watched the trees and scenery change as my parents drove. We sang some songs and enjoyed each other's company. It was nice. Perfect, even.

When we finally arrived, we unloaded all our things from the car and headed inside the trailer. My parents, again, reminded us of the rules regarding our sleeping arrangements and made sure to watch us put our things in separate rooms. Once everyone was settled in, we managed to sneak out for a walk in the woods, the thing I was looking forward to the most in all of this. Alone time with Steve.

The sun was high in the sky as we walked, blinking through the trees of the woods and lighting our path. I watched the ground, being sure not to trip on any large rocks or sticks as I led the way through the familiar woods. "So, do you think we're ready for this?" I asked. My voice was steady, but my heart was racing.

"I mean, I am," Steve replied, his confidence unwavering. "I've been ready."

I swallowed hard, unsure if my certainty matched his. "I'm nervous. I don't exactly know what to do, but I know we'll figure it out." I let out a breath, trying to ground myself. "I mean, you're prepared, thanks to your dad." Still, doubt lingered, the weight of my parents' beliefs pressed against my thoughts. They said it was a sin. I could already imagine the disappointment in their eyes.

They would never forgive me.

"But we love each other," I said, more to convince myself than anyone else. "We'll probably get married anyway, so... what's the difference?"

Steve nodded, his gaze steady. "Yeah, that's true. We do love each other. And I would love it if we got married."

A small smile broke through my uncertainty. "Since we're going to the mountains, let's pretend we already are. Let's act like Mr. and Mrs. Jones."

His fingers brushed mine, a quiet agreement. "That sounds like heaven."

I laughed softly, my anxiety slipping away. "I would love to be Mrs. Jones for the week... but forever sounds even better."

We had planned everything perfectly, the timing, the way we would slip away unnoticed. Our picnic was simple, hastily thrown together with what we could grab without suspicion. A blanket, some Pop-Tarts, and juice. It wasn't romantic, but it was enough.

The clearing in the woods was farther than I had expected, at least a ten-minute walk from the trailer. I had imagined soft, plush grass, but the ground was uneven, littered with tree roots and stray debris. It wasn't ideal, but it was ours for the moment. Steve spread out the blanket, smoothing the corners before we sat down.

I pulled out my radio and pressed the play button. Never Say Goodbye by Bon Jovi crackled through the speakers, one of my favorites. The melody settled between us like an unspoken promise.

Steve turned to me, his voice gentle but sure. "Are you ready for this?"

He said he was nervous, but it didn't show, not in the steady way he looked at me, not in the quiet certainty of his words. I, on the other hand, felt every bit of my hesitation, like an unspoken weight settling in my chest. It must be a guy thing, maybe he was just more confident, or maybe, just maybe, he knew more about all this than he was letting on.

I hesitated, nervous energy tightening my chest. "Yeah, I think so," I said, though my voice betrayed me. "I mean, I'm super nervous.

Because I was. And I still wasn't sure. I knew it went against everything my parents had taught me about what a girl should do. But I was terrified that if I didn't, he'd find someone else who would. After all, girls at school talked like it was normal. Like it was something expected. I didn't want to be left behind. I didn't want to lose him just because I was too afraid to try. I had no plans to be with anyone else. Not ever. In my mind, this was it; me and Steve. One boy. One love. One forever. And if giving myself to him meant we'd stay together, maybe it was worth the risk.

He smiled, reassuring and patient. "That's okay. We'll take things slow."

I nodded, the world narrowing down to just him, just us. The first kiss was soft, tentative. Then it deepened, his breath growing heavier, familiar. The rhythm of it, the urgency reminded me of the time in the basement, of the way he had pressed against me before. The forest around us blurred into nothing, leaving only the feeling, only the moment. I pulled off my bottoms and lay there, waiting, watching, my breath uneven. Steve slid his pants down to his ankles and fumbled with the condom. He hadn't practiced opening one of them before, and the first one broke in his hands. A quiet curse escaped his lips before he grabbed another, carefully trying again. He hovered over me, his warmth pressing against mine, and kissed me again, soft at first, then deeper, more certain.

"Are you ready?" he murmured.

I nodded, though the uncertainty still sat heavy in my chest. "Yeah," I said. Slowly, he pushed forward, but it wasn't as natural as I had imagined. The pressure, the unfamiliar sensation, it felt like resistance, like something wasn't quite fitting the way I expected. He hesitated, then pressed harder, and suddenly there was a sharp break, a moment of something different. I had never watched pornography or knew exactly what the scene should look like, but I had seen some things on TV and knew there was usually an intense amount of movement and sweat, grunts and sighs, like a full-on workout. Three movements, then stillness. He collapsed against me, his head resting on my chest, his breath slowing.

"Wow, that felt amazing," Steve said.

I lay there, staring at the sky, feeling the weight of silence settle between us. The blanket was tangled around my legs, warm and slightly damp. My heartbeat, once rapid, had already slowed, leaving behind an odd emptiness, like stepping off a rollercoaster and realizing the thrill had faded too fast.

"I guess I'm not a virgin anymore," I murmured, my voice quieter than I expected. The words felt flat, too small for the moment. Beside me, he shifted, sitting up and running a hand through his hair. His breath was steady, his skin glowing faintly in the sunlight. "Me neither," he said, his tone unreadable.

I searched his face for something, acknowledgment, excitement, reassurance. But there was none. Just the same boy as before, now changed in a way that neither of us seemed ready to define. I had imagined it would be so much more. That there would be this grand emotional shift, some revelation. Instead, it was just... this.

I wasn't disappointed, but it was far less than I had imagined. On TV, the girl usually gasps, sighs, melts into it, overwhelmed by some grand, all-consuming pleasure. Sometimes, she even screams, a sound of undeniable certainty, of pure, dramatic bliss. But I felt...almost nothing. A slight pain at first, sharp enough to register, but nowhere near scream-worthy. And after that? Nothing close to pleasure, just an odd space where I thought something more would be.

Did we do it wrong? Miss some essential step no one ever talks about. Or was it always like this, and I had simply expected more? The silence stretched, heavier now. I turned my head to the side, trying to absorb the feeling, waiting for it to mean something more. That's when he looked down.

His expression shifted, his face growing pale and nervous. "Where the hell is it?"

"Where is what?" I sat up, trying to look around for what he could possibly mean.

"The thing." He patted the blanket hastily. My stomach tightened when I found 'the thing'. The condom. It had slipped off, and no longer where it should have been. We stared at each other, shock and fear flashing across both our faces.

"Oh, shit," he breathed.

I swallowed hard.

"Don't worry," Steve said, his face still white as a ghost, trying to reassure me. "You never get pregnant the first time."

I didn't answer. My mind was already spinning.

The walk back to the trailer felt different, like the air had thickened somehow, every sound too sharp, every step too loud. Leaves whispered beneath our feet, and somewhere in the distance, a bird sang happily, oblivious to the new weight we carried. Steve walked beside me, close but not touching, and I couldn't figure out if I wanted him to or not. My skin still remembered his weight, but my heart felt further away than it had before.

In my head, I started talking to myself like I always did when things got too loud inside. *You wanted this, remember? You said yes. You laid down. You let it happen.* But another voice, the quieter one, the smaller one— whispered back: *Did I say yes because I wanted it, or because I didn't want to lose him?*

I glanced at him. He looked the same. Calm. Maybe even content. And that stung. Because everything inside me felt rearranged, like I'd opened a door I couldn't close, and he was already walking past it.

Does he think I'm different now? Easier? More grown up? Does he love me more... or less?

I rubbed my arms. I wasn't cold, but I felt like I should be. Like I had stepped out of something and left part of myself behind. The way he'd said *"Wow, that felt amazing"* kept looping in my mind, and I wanted to believe it meant something. But if it had meant something to *him*, why did I feel so… alone? I tried to picture myself back in the clearing, on the blanket, saying yes. My face tilted just enough to avoid his gaze. My breath trembling. And underneath it all, a voice that wasn't mine but sounded like me saying:

> *Be what he needs.*
> *Don't ruin this.*
> *You can't go back now.*

We reached the edge of the clearing, the trailer's roofline just visible through the trees. I heard the tinny echo of the TV through the walls before I saw the glow of it in the window.

I wanted to stop walking. Just for a second. Just to breathe. But instead, I kept going, one foot in front of the other. Like maybe if I didn't look too closely, I wouldn't feel the shift that had already begun. We pushed the door open, stepping inside the trailer.

"How was the picnic, guys?" my mom asked casually.

I forced a smile. "It was nice. We had an enjoyable time."

"Oh, great," she said, her attention flicking back to the screen. "It's supposed to rain soon, so you're back just in time."

I nodded, but my stomach twisted. *She knows.* The thought hit me like a whisper in the back of my mind, growing louder with each passing second. She can see right through me. She knows what I've done. It was irrational, but I couldn't shake the feeling. Almost as if God Himself had told her, as if the weight of my sin was written across my face. Could she smell him on me? Could she sense the change? Was there some invisible mark that gave me away? I shrank into myself, trying to seem small, unnoticeable. I didn't want to take any chances, didn't want to say or do anything that might betray the secret now forged between Steve and me like a fragile, unspoken truth.

I felt different around Steve after what happened in the woods, exposed in a way I couldn't take back. A part of me had been given, shared, and now there was no way to bury it again, no way to pretend it hadn't changed something inside me. It was a new kind of vulnerability, sharp and lingering.

I had given something away, and I could never have it back.

Would he still love me, still want me the same way? Or had I just become another mark, another name added to a quiet, invisible list? The thought tightened in my chest, edged with uncertainty. I had to trust him in a way I hadn't trusted anyone before. And that scared me more than anything. Would he see me differently now? Would others find out? I didn't want to be labeled or judged for something that felt deeply personal.

But Steve… he seemed lighter, more at ease, like something had shifted between us, deepening his affection. And even though I didn't quite understand why, I liked it more than I wanted to admit. I liked being seen. I liked being wanted. I liked being cherished. There was something intoxicating about it. And even though I was unsure about it all at first, whatever had changed between us, I wasn't sure I wanted to let it go.

The rest of the mountain trip went as good as I could have expected. We spent so much time together, caught up in a world that felt entirely our own. I taught Steve how to drive my four-wheeler, guiding him until he could manage the sharp turns and bumps with ease. We roamed across every road within reach, chasing nothing but the feeling of freedom. The wind whipped through my hair, laughter spilling from both of us, unfiltered and easy. No school, no younger siblings, no whispers of bad nicknames, just us, weightless in the moment.

Each morning, we hiked as the sun rose, breathing in the crisp mountain air, letting it wake us in a way no alarm ever could. We swam in the lake, the ice-cold water shocking our skin, making us gasp before we adjusted to its bite. At night, we crept along dirt roads, searching for deer, hoping for a glimpse of a bobcat or a bear, the thrill humming beneath our quiet anticipation.

And we talked. Really talked. About what we loved, about the moments that shaped us, about why we believed what we did. I opened myself fully, stripping away hesitation, exposing my truth without reservation.

With him, I held nothing back.

Our week in the mountains had ended, and it was time to return home to the familiar routines, the competition for Steve's attention, the unspoken battles with girls like Jennifer and Amy, and the distractions of wrestling and track. I had loved having Steve all to myself, away from everything that pulled him in different directions. I didn't miss home at all, not like I usually did. There was no ache for what I was missing, no need to check in or catch up with friends. With Steve here, none of that seemed to matter. The world could have gone quiet, and I wouldn't have noticed. Because *he* was my world.

I never thought the mountains would be a place I'd want to escape too instead of from. But now, they hold something of ours, something we could never take back. We left our virginity there; tucked away in the quiet wilderness, a gift exchanged between us.

We fooled my parents. They thought separate beds would keep us apart, as if love could be contained by walls or rules. But they didn't really understand. They didn't know the depths of teenage love, the way it defies logic, the way it feels inevitable. I was going home, a different version of myself. Changed. And I wasn't sure yet what that meant. I still couldn't fully process what we had done. There was no immediate reckoning, no lightning strike, no cosmic punishment; a strange contrast to the warnings that had once felt so absolute. Had my mom been exaggerating all those things just to scare me?

And really, for all the nerves leading to it, the anticipation crackling like static beneath my skin, the actual moment left me feeling... nothing much at all. He was practically glowing, treating it like some monumental milestone, but for me, it felt like stepping through a door into a room I already knew too well. A little bleeding followed, which unsettled me at first, though I vaguely remembered reading about it in a Cosmo article.

What worried me more was the condom. How it had slipped off so easily, like it had never quite fit in the first place. Were they supposed to be that unreliable, or had he missed some crucial instruction? They really should make those things foolproof.

I decided Jennifer and maybe Mel would be the only ones I told. I trusted them to keep it to themselves, to not let whispers slide between locker doors and ripple through the hallways. As soon as I got home from the mountains, I called them to share everything.

Still, even with their silence, part of me felt tainted, as if I had been marked with a scarlet letter, branding me in a way I couldn't shake. I already had a bad reputation; one built on lies I had never deserved. But this…this was different. This could carve out a new reputation, and this time, it wouldn't be false.

I loved Steve. I saw a future with him, marriage even, so I shouldn't feel this shame. But I did. The burden was heavy, pressing into me as if my parents already knew, even though I knew they didn't. And maybe that was the worst part. Their judgment hung in the air, unspoken yet present. My father's harsh reaction when he caught my sister with birth control, the way my mother always spoke of sex outside of marriage as a sin; it all lingered, shaping the guilt I wish I didn't carry.

I wish I could share these moments with my mom. It felt like a milestone; awkward, nerve-wracking, but full of meaning. I wanted to tell her everything... how unsure I was, how much I loved him, how I was doing this not just out of pressure, but out of something that felt deeper. I wanted her to know me.

But I couldn't.

She would've been disappointed. Angry. She would've told me I was ruining myself, that I was a sinner, that I'd broken something sacred. And that's what hurt the most; not just the shame I knew was waiting, but the silence I had to live in instead. This was a moment that truly mattered. And I had no one to share it with within my family.

Chapter Nine

Seeds of Punishment

Returning to school, everything felt off, disjointed, unfamiliar, like the rhythm of my life had shifted and I wasn't quite in step with it anymore. All I really wanted was to be with Steve.

School had never felt like home to me. It was a place divided by invisible lines, sporty kids, popular kids, the rich, the struggling, each locked in their own world. I didn't belong to any of them. I wasn't sure I belonged anywhere. The subjects bored me; the classrooms suffocated me. Most days, I either slept with my head down or escaped to the bathroom, skipping classes just to avoid the monotony.

Once, I had been a straight-A student, back when learning felt natural, effortless. But that changed when my parents moved me to a private Christian school for three years—years that threw my entire foundation off balance. They were ahead of my old school, and I fell behind, missing out on things like multiplication tables and the basics of drafting a paper. When I finally returned to public school, my grades had plummeted, but worse than that, I had lost time. I had lost connections. Life had moved on without me.

My old friends had changed, grown into different people, while I felt stuck somewhere between the past and present. Even Mel, even Rob, and Mike, at one point, they had been my world. But I had drifted, and now, I wasn't sure where I fit anymore.

School wasn't about learning, not for me. It was just a place I endured. I couldn't even tell you what I was supposed to be absorbing in any of my classes. All I did was write Steve love letters, my thoughts tangled in him, and stayed up all night on the phone, chasing the only thing that made me feel alive.

I called Steve's house before school, and he answered.

"Steve?"

"Yeah."

"I'm going to be late today."

"Oh, okay."

"Wanna be late with me?"

"Why? I've got plenty of time to get ready."

"So, do I. That's the point, I'm choosing to be late. I hate my morning classes. Sewing isn't until after lunch, so let's just show up then."

He hesitated.

"I don't know…"

"Oh, come on. It'll be fun."

A pause, then the answer I wanted.

"Okay."

We agreed to meet halfway between our houses in fifteen minutes. As far as my parents were concerned, I had left at the usual time to catch the bus. My mom wouldn't notice; she never did. She'd been taking sleeping pills my whole life, always more than prescribed. Most days she slept until noon, so sneaking around in the morning wasn't difficult.

Steve and I met with our backpacks slung over our shoulders, still planning to make it to school by midday.

"Where should we go?" I asked. "I don't want my dad spotting me in the cop car, or another officer reporting us for truancy. We need to go somewhere no one will see us."

Steve thought for a moment. Then, his eyes lit up.

"I know. Let's go to the state hospital."

"The state hospital?" I hesitated.

"Yeah, one of the abandoned buildings. No one will see us."

"We must be careful. We can't get caught."

"Trust me," he said. "No one will ever know."

The state hospital was practically in my backyard, sprawling across a massive property. The other entrance sat right across from our high school. Several buildings were still in use, housing patients, though only one kept them locked inside. Another was used for drug and alcohol rehab.

It wasn't eerie to me; it had always been there, just another part of the landscape. I have walked around the area plenty of times. There was a popular stream at the back of the property where locals fished, and two of the unused buildings had even been repurposed as training grounds for new firefighters years ago. Their hollowed-out frames stood with missing windows, boarded doors, and layers of graffiti. But they also had easy access.

Steve and I made our way over, slipping through a window that once had been boarded up but had long since been pried open by others before us. He helped me climb through, careful to keep shards of glass from catching in our sneakers.

Inside, the darkness swallowed us. Only slivers of light from the broken windows cut through, illuminating dust swirling in the chilly air. The chill was sharp; no heat, no electricity, just the hollow echo of a place long forgotten. Scorch marks stained the walls, evidence of old fires, but what caught me off guard was the furniture. Papers scattered across the floor, hospital beds lined up against one wall, fragments of lives that had once occupied this space. I found myself wondering about them. Who slept in these beds? What had landed them here? Where had they gone?

We moved cautiously toward the stairs. The steps creaked beneath us; some boards missing, the railing long gone. At the top, light poured into a gaping hole in the ceiling letting the outside seep in.

Discarded beer cans and empty bottles littered the floor, remnants of parties held in secret. I wandered to a window, gazing out at the world beyond. From the outside, no one would ever know we were here. It was the perfect place to disappear, just for a little while.

Despite my better judgment, we decided to curl up on one of the broken beds. It had a mattress at least, which was better than the cold floor. Still, the thought of how many others had been here, doing who-knows-what, made my skin crawl.

Steve kissed me hard, like he always did. Softness had never been his style, and by now, I was used to it. It was familiar. Then he shifted, climbing on top of me, and I knew exactly what he wanted next.

"I don't know if I want to do this here," I muttered. "That mattress is full of germs."

"It's no big deal," he said. "You don't even have to take your clothes off, just slide your pants off your one leg."

"Oh. Yeah, I guess."

This wasn't romantic. It wasn't about whispered promises or tenderness. It was just about squeezing it in whenever we could, same as before. Except this time, there wasn't even the presence of a condom.

"You know, Steve," I said, trying to keep my voice even, "I know this wasn't planned, but you really should start carrying protection. Just in case."

"I know, but I was going to school. Why would I need one? I was worried about getting caught, not about that."

"Well… in the future, we need to plan better."

Steve was different this time than in the mountains.

"Wow, this just feels so incredible. I think I can feel all of you."

He seemed to finish even quicker this time, maybe only two thrusts.

"I never want to wear protection again. That was so much better. You can't even imagine how much better that was."

I mean it didn't feel much different to me, besides maybe it slid in a little easier without the catching of the rubber on my delicate skin.

"It's a horrible idea, Steve. I don't want to get pregnant." "You're not going to get pregnant."

"But why risk it, Steve? I mean, anything can happen."

Steve said he felt like we would be safe and to not worry. Steve asked if we could do it again because it happened so fast, but it felt so amazing. We ended up doing it two more times after that.

He shifted closer, wrapping his arms around me, holding me like I was something fragile and precious. I loved this, the way he made me feel safe, like nothing outside this moment mattered. His heartbeat was steady beneath my ear, his breath warm against my skin. This was home.

"I want this forever," I murmured.

Steve's voice was soft, questioning. "What do you mean?"

"Just this," I said. "To be held like this. To be with you."

For a while, we lay there, talking about school, about the future. Steve told me he planned to go to college, hopefully with a scholarship.

I laughed, shaking my head. "I'm never going to college," I said, not even hesitating. "I just want to be like my mom; a stay-at-home wife and mother."

"But I want to drive," I added quickly. "I don't want to be stuck in the house all day. I want a partner forever. Someone who's honest and trustworthy. Who makes me feel like I'm the most important thing in the world."

Steve looked at me then, his expression was serious. "I can do that."

His words settled deep in my chest, wrapping around my heart like his arms around me. I let myself believe him. I let myself dream. We lay there together, and I imagined the future waiting for me.

After we were together, something shifted in Steve. He was softer, more open in a way I hadn't seen before. He held me closer, lingered in touches that felt more intentional, and words spilled from him easily, dreams, hopes, fragments of thoughts he hadn't shared before. Vulnerability suited him, and I liked this version of him.

That was when I decided giving something of myself was worth it if it meant receiving this in return.

I blinked awake, the sky stretching endlessly above me blue and cloud-scattered, impossibly bright. Confusion settled in. Where was I? Beside me, Steve lay still, his chest rising and falling in deep, steady breaths.

"Steve, wake up," I whispered, shaking him lightly. His eyes fluttered open.

"We must have fallen asleep," I said, sitting up. My stomach lurched as I checked my watch. "Oh no, it's 1:30. We missed school."

Panic sparked in his expression, and we scrambled to our feet, grabbing our backpacks.

"It's too late now," I muttered. "We just have to get home like nothing happened."

We tore down the steps, each thud echoing in my ears, the rush of cool air hitting my skin as we burst through the door.

"I love you, Steve. Call me when you get home."

"Okay. Love you too."

Then I was running fast, slower, my breath sharp, my legs burning. The weight of the day still clung to me, wrapping around me like his arms had moments before. By the time I made it home, I forced my breathing to even out, stepping inside with careful ease.

Mom glanced up. "How was school?"

"Same as yesterday," I said smoothly.

"Any homework?"

She never asked me that. My pulse stuttered.

"No, no homework." I was already retreating. "I'm going to my room."

Collapsing onto my bed, I exhaled sharply. I got away with it. The best day ever. I lay there, staring at the ceiling, reliving every second the sky, the warmth of his arms, the quiet promise in his voice.

Dad was home, grabbing a quick dinner with Mom. He did that sometimes--coming in while still on duty, catching a meal, watching football. Being a Corporal meant he could get away with things like that.

The phone rang. Normally, I'd answer, but I was still in my room. I heard Dad pick up. "Hello?"

Silence.

That was odd. He wasn't talking, just listening. Then, the click of the receiver.

"Did Ellie go to school today?" he asked Mom.

"Of course," she said.

Then his voice sharpened. "Ellie, get out here. Now."

Oh no. I stepped into the living room, my stomach twisting.

"Did you go to school today?"

"Yes."

His jaw tightened. "The school just called. Said you were absent. Explain that."

I swallowed hard. "It must be a mistake. I was there."

His eyes narrowed. "So, you're lying too."

The disappointment in his voice hit harder than the anger.

"Who were you with?"

I hesitated. "Steve."

"Where did you go?"

"We just walked around."

"Walked around." His teeth clenched, his jaw grinding. His voice rose.

I felt the sting behind my eyes. I always cried when Dad yelled; not because I wanted to, but because I couldn't help it.

"Ellie, you're punished. Straight to school, straight home. No phone. No friends. And no Steve."

"But—"

"I think he's a bad influence."

I turned and ran to my room, slamming the door behind me. I collapsed onto my bed, tears spilling over. How could they do this? It wasn't even Steve's idea, it was mine.

I needed to call Steve.

I had promised I would when I got home, and now he was probably wondering why I hadn't. Worse, his parents might get the same call mine did. He needed to know.

But I couldn't.

I stared at the phone, knowing it was useless now. No calls. No friends. No Steve. Tomorrow, I'd have to wait until lunch to tell him everything. I sank onto my bed, frustration boiling inside me. Punished. Again.

It felt like I was always being punished. Always being told what I couldn't do, where I couldn't go, who I couldn't see. I hated this house. I hated these rules. I just wanted out.

Chapter Ten

Roots of Rebellion

L unch couldn't come fast enough. The moment I saw Steve, I rushed to him. "I'm so sorry I never called last night. The school called my parents; they found out we skipped."

His expression darkened. "Yeah. My dad got the same call."

"I got punished. No phone, no friends, no you."

Steve sighed. "My dad was pissed. I have to stay home and babysit my little sister all weekend."

"At least you're allowed out. At least you can be on the phone. I'm stuck in the house all week."

I lowered my voice, frustration bubbling up. "Steve, I can't go all week without seeing you. Over the weekend, I won't even get to see you at lunch. I won't be able to stand it."

He thought for a moment, then his eyes lit up. "I know. Sneak out your bedroom window and meet me behind the school."

I blinked. "What? You want me to climb out my window?"

"Yes. Didn't you say your sister used to do that?"

"Well… not exactly. Her boyfriend snuck in, but he got caught because he left footprints in the snow."

Steve grinned. "Well, it's not snowing. But you know it's possible."

I hesitated, then nodded.

"We'll meet on the field at 2 AM tomorrow morning," he said. "I'll bring a blanket."

A thrill ran through me.

"Okay. Let's do it."

I couldn't wait. The alarm buzzed at 1:45 AM. I blinked awake, my heart already pounding. Sliding open my window, I climbed out; careful, quiet. I had gone to bed dressed, ready for this. The night was deep and dark, but the moon cast just enough light to guide me. Mom and Dad's fan hummed inside, drowning out any small noises I might make. That gave me confidence; I wouldn't wake them.

I sprinted across the lawn, my breath sharp in the frigid air, then down the street toward the school. The fear crept in as I ran. It was late. Too late. What if someone was out here? What if some weirdos saw me, followed me? By the time I reached the field, I was breathless, my pulse hammering in my ears. Steve wasn't there. I swallowed hard. Had I been stood up?

For a moment, I thought about turning back, slipping home before anyone noticed. But then, movement. A shadow stretched across the field. I stiffened, fear spiking in my chest. Then I saw it; the familiar way he walked, the easy sway of his shoulders. Relief flooded through me.

"What the hell took so long, Steve?"

"Sorry," he said, catching his breath. "I woke up my brother and had to wait for him to fall back asleep. It's not easy sneaking out when you share a room with three other people, ya know."

I huffed, nodding my head. "I guess that's true. I hadn't even thought about that." I was grateful Steve had remembered a blanket as the night carried a slight chill, and the grass was damp with early dew. We lay down together, staring up at the vast sky; stars scattered like tiny diamonds across the darkness.

"There are so many out tonight," I murmured. "It's beautiful."

Steve turned his head, his gaze locking onto mine. "Not as beautiful as you," he said softly.

Warmth spread through me, deeper than the blanket, deeper than the night air. I knew the risk. I knew I could get caught. But right now, none of that mattered.

We made love right there under the moonlit sky. The adrenaline and rush of sneaking out and being out in the open made the entire moment so intoxicating. I knew I couldn't stay long. Dad's shift started at 4 AM, and I had to be back in bed before he noticed I was gone.

I knew our time together was precious, and I would do anything to have it. Every moment we shared felt like a stolen treasure, a secret world where only we existed. The thrill of sneaking out, the quiet whispers under the stars, and the warmth of Steve's presence made everything else fade away. I cherished these moments, knowing that they were fleeting but incredibly valuable. Our connection was something I held onto tightly, a beacon of light amid the restrictions and punishments. I would do anything to keep this feeling alive, to hold onto the magic we created together.

"I'm so glad I got to see you tonight," I whispered.

Steve smiled. "Me too."

Then his eyes lit up. "How about tomorrow night? But this time, I'll climb in your window."

I blinked. "Really?"

He nodded. "Yeah. This way you won't feel scared?"

I laughed softly. "Thank you, that's so sweet."

I hesitated for only a second before nodding.

"Okay. Let's do it."

Chapter Eleven
Roots of Shame

I set my alarm for 1:45 AM again. As soon as it went off, I slid my window open and waited, heart pounding. Right on time, Steve appeared from the shadows. I reached out, gripping his arms to help pull him inside. He climbed onto my bed and a loud crash followed. My stomach dropped.

Fluffy exploded into barking. Oh no. She needed to shut up. Right now. My parents would wake up. The sharp creak of a door. Footsteps. Slow, deliberate. Oh, shit.

"Steve, hide!" I hissed.

There wasn't much time. I scanned the room wildly, my mind scrambling for an answer. The closet? Too obvious. Under the bed? He'd never fit in time.

"Get under the blanket," I whispered. "Hurry."

He hesitated. "Ellie—"

"Just do it!" I pleaded.

Steve dove beneath the blanket as I fluffed it up to make it look lumpy, masking his shape. I threw myself onto the floor and shut my eyes, breathing as steadily as I could. The bedroom door swung open, a blast of light illuminating the space.

Blinking slowly, I forced myself to look drowsy. "Dad? What are you doing?"

He crossed his arms. "Fluffy's been barking like crazy. I wanted to make sure everything was okay." His gaze flicked to the open window. "Why is this open?"

My pulse thundered in my ears. Stay calm. "It's so hot in here, Dad. I couldn't sleep, so I opened the window to cool off. The floor's cooler too, so I decided to lie down."

"You can't just leave the window open," he scolded, moving toward it. "Bats could fly in. Bugs. Here—let's put the fan in the window so you don't have to open it again."

No. No, no, no. He was right over Steve.

I clenched my fists as he braced himself against the bed, placing his knee down—right next to Steve's elbow. My breath hitched. I felt sick. If he realized Steve was there, he might shoot us both.

"Alright." He stepped back, satisfied. "That should help. Keep it in place, alright?"

I exhaled shakily. "Yeah... sorry, Dad."

He smiled at me. "Get some sleep, Ellie. Night."

The door shut. A pause. Silence.

Then I ripped the blanket back.

Steve was drenched in sweat. "Ellie," he breathed, eyes wide, "I almost peed my pants."

I let out a short, hysterical laugh. "You and me both."

We lay still, afraid even to breathe, waiting for Fluffy to settle down. After what felt like forever, the house was finally silent again.

That was when we made love; quietly, urgently, the weight of danger still lingering in the air. Afterward, I whispered, "Just leave by the front door. I can't risk removing the fan."

Steve nodded, slipping away.

We got away with it. Somehow.

Monday rolled around, and the second I approached the lunch table, I heard Steve's voice loud, animated.

"...And my knee was right next to her dad's elbow, man. I thought I was going to die."

Clay burst out laughing. "Wait, hold up. You were in Ellie's bed when he walked in?"

Mac shook his head, grinning. "Dude, her dad's a cop. And he didn't notice? That's unbelievable."

The air in my lungs evaporated. Heat flooded my face. My stomach twisted painfully.

Steve laughed, oblivious. "Yeah, I mean, for a cop, that was pretty dense."

Clay whistled. "Damn, sneaking into a girl's room in the middle of the night? That takes balls."

Laughter erupted around the table. My pulse thumped in my ears. It was obvious Clay knew we were having sex. They all knew.

I swallowed, trying to keep my expression neutral, but I felt like I was shrinking. The moment wasn't private anymore, it was out in the open, dissected, retold, turned into entertainment. And Steve wasn't even realizing what he'd done.

I wanted to disappear.

My punishment was finally over, and I had been looking forward to seeing Steve after school. When he showed up though, Clay was with him.

I wasn't upset; I was just surprised. We hadn't talked about him coming either.

Down in the basement, we settled in like always, flipping on the latest WWF match. I wasn't a fan of wrestling, especially this kind, but the boys were engrossed. An hour passed.

I felt Steve's hand brush my side. At first, I thought it was accidental. Then, his fingers trailed higher, slipping beneath my shirt. My breath hitched.

"What are you doing?" I whispered, darting a glance at Clay. He was right there.

Steve smirked. "Oh, he doesn't care."

I pulled his hand away. "Well, I care. Come on, not with him sitting right next to us."

Steve shrugged, unfazed, and instead grabbed a blanket, draping it over our laps. Before I could protest, he whispered, "I want to do it anyway."

"No." My voice was firm, but my pulse quickened.

He didn't listen. I froze. His hands were on me, moving despite my refusal. A cold wave of realization tightened around my chest. He knew I wasn't comfortable.

I sat rigid, heart pounding, staring at the TV screen but not seeing anything at all. Clay didn't seem to notice. Or maybe he did—and just chose not to say anything. But how could he not? The blanket shifted with every movement.

I felt sick. I wanted to scream. To shove him away. Instead, I just sat there. And Steve didn't care. I sat frozen, my skin crawling. I had let him do it, but I hadn't.

Why did Steve think that was okay?

I felt used and dirty. Like Clay was there to watch us, like we were some kind of show. Humiliation burned through me, hot and suffocating.

To me, intimacy was meant to be a sacred, quiet, deliberate exchange; something meant to be held close. It wasn't supposed to be rushed; squeezed into stolen moments or careless places. It wasn't meant to be something you tossed into any corner, in front of anyone, as if it were nothing at all. It was supposed to mean something.

Then—my dad's voice.

"Ellie, come here."

I jolted upright, my heart hammering. Was I in trouble? Did he know?

I scrambled up the stairs, my pulse pounding in my ears. But when I reached the doorway, my dad stood there, holding my favorite pizza and a two-liter bottle of soda.

"Thought you guys might like some dinner."

I blinked. "Wow… thanks, Dad. This is great."

He smiled. "Since Clay's here, you guys can shut the door."

I nodded, numb. "Okay. Thanks."

I carried the food downstairs, my hands trembling. The boys tore into it, devouring slice after slice, eyes glued to the wrestling match.

I sat still. Silent. Staring at nothing. The shock of what had happened clung to me, heavy and suffocating. And no one noticed.

After dinner and wrestling were over, Clay and Steve got ready to head home. I kissed Steve goodbye, shut the door, and retreated to my room.

I collapsed onto my bed, staring up at Steve's picture, the one I had pinned on my Motley Crue poster. Did he genuinely love me? The thought gnawed at me, relentlessly.

It felt like all he wanted was to squeeze in sex whenever possible, no matter where we were or who was around. There was no self-respect. No respect for me.

I replayed the moment in the basement; the way he had ignored my discomfort, the way he had acted like it didn't matter. Like I didn't matter.

Why wouldn't he care that something so intimate, so private, had been shared with someone else sitting right there? Why didn't he stop when I said no? Would someone do that if they absolutely loved you? The question sat heavy in my chest, pressing down like a weight I couldn't shake. This wasn't sitting right with me.

I had never doubted us before. But tonight, for the first time, I did. I went to bed with that doubt curling around me, sinking into my bones.

Chapter Twelve
Roots of Deceit

I didn't understand why I needed him so much and why just hearing his voice could loosen the knot in my chest. Maybe it was because, for once, someone had chosen *me*. Or maybe it was because I didn't know how to feel whole unless someone else was holding the missing pieces. It wasn't just love, not entirely. It was feeling needed. It was fear. It was the hope that if I could just be wanted long enough, maybe I'd forget the parts of myself that still felt broken. I didn't trust it, but I clung to it. Because the girl inside me, the one who always faded into the background, was starving. And Steve made her feel full, even if it never lasted long.

"No. I don't believe you love me at all."

The words spilled out before I could stop them, sharp and final.

"If you loved me, you would never have treated me the way you did the other night." My voice shook, but I didn't care. "I feel used. That's all I ever feel with you."

Steve sighed. "Ellie, calm down. You're being so dramatic."

Dramatic.

I clenched my jaw.

"It wasn't a big deal," he continued, his tone dismissive. "Clay didn't even know what we were doing. Trust me."

I let out a bitter laugh. "I don't care if he knew. I knew. And I wasn't comfortable. And you didn't care."

Silence. My pulse pounded in my ears.

"You're such a jerk," I whispered, my throat tight. "I don't want to be your girlfriend anymore."

The words felt like steel, solid and unbreakable.

"We're over."

I hung up.

The phone felt heavy in my hand, like it carried the weight of everything I had just let go. I stared at it, breathing hard, my chest tight. Then slowly I set it down.

Later in math class, I felt it again- Ed's stare. He was always watching me.

Last week, he slipped a note onto my desk as he walked by. A confession. He liked me, thought I was cute, wanted my number. I shut it down at once. "I have a boyfriend," I had written back. But things are different now. So, this time, I stared back.

I asked to go to the bathroom, and when Mr. Fritch dismissed me, I left a note on Ed's desk with just my number, scrawled in quick, slanted handwriting. Call me. When I returned, Ed was grinning, his expression sharp, knowing. I swallowed.

I didn't find him particularly attractive. He wasn't ugly, but he wasn't someone I had ever wanted. And yet, his attention was addictive. The way his eyes followed me, tracking my every move sent a thrill through me. I started getting up more often than necessary, just to feel them on me.

That night, Ed called me.

"Hey, Ellie! How are you?" he asked.

"I'm doing great. What's up?"

"Not much. My mom said she could drive me over if you wanted to hang out."

"Really? Okay, let me give you my address."

"She said it'll take about ten minutes."

"Sounds great! See you soon!"

I slipped into my favorite pair of skin-tight jeans, spritzed on a hint of perfume, and hurried downstairs. When I told my mom that a friend, not a boyfriend, was coming over, she gave a knowing nod but didn't press further.

The knock came sooner than I expected. I took a steady breath and opened the door. There he stood, holding a single rose, the kind sold at the 7-Eleven counter.

"Hi, Ellie. This is for you."

I blinked, caught off guard by the gesture. "That's so sweet... I don't know what to say." Steve had never given me flowers.

Stepping aside, I motioned for him to enter. "Please, come in."

He turned to my mom with a polite smile. "Hello, Mrs. Keen. It's a pleasure to meet you."

"A flower and good manners." My mom returned the greeting, her expression unreadable.

"We're going downstairs," I informed her.

She nodded but didn't budge. "Okay, just leave the door open."

"I know."

I led Ed through the house, showing him around before stopping in front of my wall of board games.

"Want to play something?" I asked.

He scanned the options and pulled out Connect Four. "I'll be red, you be yellow."

We played several rounds, and he won every time. I hadn't gone easy on him; he just had some serious skills. Afterward, we sank onto the couch and flipped through the channels.

"Ellie, I thought you had a boyfriend," he said.

"I did. We just broke up."

"What happened?"

I hesitated. "I guess we just weren't meant to be."

He smirked. "Too bad for him. Good for me, though because now I'm here."

As we talked, he kept inching closer. His thigh brushed against mine, lingering there. When I turned to look at him, he was already leaning in. His lips met mine in a soft, hesitant kiss, so light it barely registered.

When we pulled apart, he grinned. I mirrored the expression, but something inside me didn't feel right. Even though Steve and I had technically ended things, this felt wrong. The kiss didn't stir anything in me. At that moment, I knew Ed wasn't going to get into my heart. But I couldn't say that out loud.

He leaned in again, this time with more urgency. His hands roamed, pressing closer.

"Ed, stop."

He froze. "Ellie, what's wrong?"

"It's too fast. I'm just not ready for this." I swallowed, forcing a smile. "I mean, I'm glad you came over and I do like you…" A lie. "But I don't want to do all that right now."

He sighed, then pulled back. "Sorry."

Relief flooded through me.

We played one more round of the game before he checked his watch. "My mom's on her way."

He stood, and I followed him to the door. We exchanged goodbyes, but the air felt thick, like we'd argued, though neither of us said anything. And now, I knew one thing for sure, I didn't want to be with Ed.

Maybe he had heard the rumors whispered that painted me as something effortless, something to take without consequence. Perhaps he thought I would be easy, carefree; something handed over without hesitation.

He was wrong. I missed Steve.

Chapter Thirteen

Roots of Guilt

Monday at school, Ed was grinning like he'd just won something. As I walked past him in the cafeteria, he leaned toward his friends, whispering. Their laughter came a moment later; too loud, too obvious. My stomach was clenched.

At our usual table, Steve and Clay sat talking, but I turned away. We weren't a couple, so why sit with him? I slid into the seat next to Mel instead. She barely looked at me. Just a quick glance before focusing on her tray.

I cleared my throat. "Haven't seen you much lately."

She shrugged. "Yeah."

Silence stretched between us. The kind that said more than words. She knew why I was sitting there. So did I. I forced myself not to glance over at Ed, but my mind was already there. The whispering. The smirks. What was he saying?

Mel let out a sharp sigh. "He's probably bragging."

I was tense. "Bragging about what?"

She finally met my gaze, leveling me with an unreadable look. "You tell me."

My pulse stammered. "He just came over. That's it."

She picked at her food. "Mm."

I swallowed hard. Was Ed telling them that? Or was he saying more? Twisting the truth?

The thought sank like a stone in my chest.

The bell rang, signaling the end of lunch. I waited, watching as Steve and Clay left the cafeteria, then Ed and his friends. Only then did I step out, making my way toward my next class.

The stairwell was packed, voices overlapping in a chaotic hum. Then, shouting. I craned my neck, trying to see past the heads in front of me, when suddenly, Steve swung. His fist connected with Ed's face.

Shock jolted through me.

I shoved my way through the crowd, grabbing Steve's arm. "Stop! What are you doing?"

Ed staggered back, blood trickling from his nose, his face was flushed red with anger, pain or humiliation; I couldn't tell. The crowd buzzed, eyes locked on the scene.

"Ed, walk away," I said firmly.

He hesitated, then turned and did just that.

I exhaled, still gripping Steve's arm. "There's nothing to see here, move along." Slowly, the crowd dispersed, their murmurs fading.

I faced Steve, my pulse hammering. "What were you thinking?"

His jaw was tight. "I heard Ed's been telling everyone he was at your house over the weekend saying you guys had sex and are dating now."

The words crashed into me.

"He said what?" My voice was sharper than I intended.

Steve nodded. "That's what I heard."

"That's not true," I snapped. "Yes, he came over, but we didn't do that. And we're not dating."

Steve's expression didn't soften. "Well, that's not what he's telling everyone."

Ed had wanted more from me, I knew that much, but I didn't feel the same way. And now, watching the way Steve clenched his jaw, the way his fists hadn't fully relaxed, I realized something else. He was jealous. The thought hit me harder than I expected. He honestly believed I was with someone else. And he cared enough to throw a punch over it.

I was glad I'd stepped in when I did because if I hadn't, Steve would have done a lot more damage. He lifted weights. He wrestled. Ed wouldn't have stood a chance.

Steve exhaled, shaking his head. "I was really hurt when I thought you were with another guy."

His words were quiet, but they carried weight.

"Is that why you broke up with me?" His gaze searched for mine. "Because you wanted to be with him?"

"No," I said quickly. "Not at all. I don't even like him."

His expression softened just a fraction.

"I just…" My throat tightened. "I don't want to feel used."

Steve studied me for a long time. Then finally his shoulders eased, his features gentled.

"I love you," I whispered.

His lips parted, hesitation flickering across his face before vanishing.

"I love you too."

Later in math class, I spotted Ed at his desk, his eyes already on me, just like always. I slid into my seat, pressing my lips together as I scribbled a note.

I can't believe the lies you made up about me. I don't want anything to do with you.

That felt too harsh.

I hesitated, then added, *Steve was really upset, and I just think it's best if we don't talk anymore.*

I didn't want to hurt him, despite everything. But this needed to end. I asked to go to the bathroom, using the moment to pass his desk. As I walked by, I slipped the note onto his stack of papers quickly, unseen.

When I returned, I stole a glance at him. His face had changed. The usual cocky energy was gone. Instead, he wore something unfamiliar or something heavy.

Sadness. A flicker of guilt rose in me, but I swallowed it down. He had lied. He deserved this.

Chapter Fourteen

Roots of Betrayal

Steve and I were back, stronger than ever. When he invited me over for dinner with his family, I hesitated. My family never ate together unless we were on vacation, but his family did every single night. And somehow despite their size, they all managed to be home at the same time.

Tonight, even his older sister Joanne, the one who had already moved out, was here. I hadn't even known he had an older sister until recently.

I took my seat, nerves twisting in my stomach. Around me sat his mom, his dad, his sister, her boyfriend, Steve, and his six younger siblings.

The food smelled good, but I couldn't shake my apprehension. Steve's dad had joked earlier that he was going to make me try venison. He hunted. He fished. They ate what they caught; things I had never imagined on a dinner plate.

I had spent hours riding through the mountains with my family, spotting deer. The idea of eating one felt impossible.

A plate was set in front of me; a dish with chunks of meat smothered in light-colored gravy over white rice. It looked safe. I picked up my fork and took a bite. The flavor was odd. It was definitely not chicken.

"Well, Ellie?" Steve's dad asked, watching me closely. "What do you think?"

I swallowed, searching for an answer. "Umm… the rice is great."

He chuckled. "And the meat?"

I hesitated. "It's, uh… kind of… not like chicken?"

Laughter erupted around the table.

Steve grinned. "Ellie, you just ate squirrel."

My stomach dropped. A squirrel. A sweet, innocent yard squirrel. I wanted to cry. I forced a smile, shifting the food around on my plate, trying to make it look touched. The rice was manageable. The squirrel... not so much.

Despite my awkwardness, conversation flowed; the family chatting easily, welcoming. Even though I was still shy, I began to feel something I hadn't expected. Like I was part of them. Like they were bringing me into their world.

After dinner, we had plans to hang out near the cemetery. Steve had asked Clay to convince his older brother to get us some beer. He agreed, which meant Clay would be tagging along.

We walked down the dimly lit path, hiding the beer in a couple of bags. I had spent hours in this cemetery, so I knew it like the back of my hand. At the far end stood a baby section; rows of tiny graves marked with single dates, babies born and gone on the same day. Little lamb sculptures rested on top, their heads missing. Vandalized. Forgotten. It was always unsettling, always sad.

Beyond that, a massive mausoleum loomed; its doors locked tight. But behind the bushes lining the baby section, there was a crawl space low, ground-level opening beneath the structure.

We met up with everyone and slid inside, the dirt crunching beneath us. A flashlight flicked on. And then, the Ouija board. What better place to mess around with the supernatural than a cemetery?

The beer was warm and cheap. We drank anyway. The cold seeped through our jackets, the dampness of being half-underground pressing in.

When it was my turn, Mel sat across from me.

"Ask it if you cheated on me," Steve muttered, his words slurred.

I stiffened. Still dwelling on that?

Fine. I set my fingers on the planchette.

"Did I cheat on Steve?"

The pointer drifted.

Slowly.

Then, yes.

I sucked in a breath. "Mel, you pushed it."

"No, I didn't."

"Yes, you did."

Her face was unreadable, but suspicion curled inside me. Was she trying to make me look guilty?

Steve saw. His hands curled into fists. "I knew it. I knew you cheated on me."

Frustration boiled over. "That's not true!" I stood and started pacing, my voice sharp, my heartbeat louder than anything else in the space.

Mel crossed her arms. "The board did it."

I whirled on her. "You did it! Why would you do that? Do you see what's happening?"

Steve wasn't listening anymore. He was muttering about lies, about trust, about me. His breath was thick with beer, his words sticky with spit. His hands pressed against me, his body leaning in.

I recoiled. "Stop."

He didn't.

"Clay."

I turned; my voice was urgent. "Will you walk me home?"

He glanced at Steve, then back at me.

"Sure."

The dizziness came in waves, blurring the edges of the world around me. The beer was wearing off, but my body hadn't caught up yet. I could barely walk straight. Clay steadied me, his hand firm around my arm as I stumbled.

"I swear, Clay, I didn't cheat on Steve," I mumbled. My words felt thick in my mouth, tumbling out before I could think. "We weren't even dating back then. And I didn't sleep with Ed. I don't know why the Ouija board said that."

I hesitated, the truth pressing against my ribs. "I did kiss him, though. But it was a mistake. It wasn't cheating." My chest tightened. "Just... don't tell Steve, okay? He's already so mad."

Clay let out a breath. "Don't worry, I ain't gonna say nothing to Steve."

Relief washed over me, but before I could fully sink into it, Clay turned to me, his eyes steady, serious in the dim glow of streetlights.

"If you were mine, Ellie, I'd never treat you like Steve does," he said. "He doesn't appreciate what he's got. You're beautiful." His voice softened. "I'd treat you like a queen."

Something in his gaze flickered, but I shook it off. Clay and Steve were friends. He would never cross that line. And I didn't think of Clay in that way; he felt more like a big brother, someone safe, someone steady.

We kept walking, my head spinning, the laughter coming in bursts between my drunken ramblings. I barely recall my words—only that it was a crisp night, the stars were hazy, and Clay got me home safely.

I stumbled through the front door, my head still buzzing from the night's events. My parents were waiting, their expressions tight with frustration.

"Ellie, where have you been? It's way past curfew."

I blinked, my vision swaying slightly. I hadn't even realized how late it was.

"You smell like beer," my mother said, crossing her arms. "Have you been drinking?"

"No, of course not," I said quickly. "Some kids were drinking, and one of them spilled it on my jacket."

Their eyes narrowed, unimpressed.

"We don't want you around kids who drink, and we certainly don't want you to stay out this late," my father said firmly. "So, we've decided—an impromptu trip to the mountains this weekend. You're officially grounded."

"What?" My stomach twisted. "No. I can't go. I won't get to see Steve or my friends. I'll have no way to talk to them".

"Maybe some time away will help you remember how to follow the rules," my mother interrupted.

"I hate the mountains! I miss everything that happens at home when you drag me up there. I don't want to go!"

"It's not up for discussion, Ellie," my father said, his tone final. "You're going."

The next day at lunch, I sighed, pushing my food around on my tray. "I'm punished again," I told Steve. "My parents are forcing me to go to the mountains for the weekend."

"That's okay," Steve said casually. "I made some plans with a few friends anyway."

I blinked. "Oh. I didn't realize. What are you doing?"

"We're going to walk around the mall looking for girls."

I froze. "Looking for girls?"

"Yeah, Clay doesn't have a girlfriend, so I thought we'd help him find someone."

I stared at him, my stomach twisting. "Don't you think that's weird? You already have a girlfriend, so why would you be helping to look?"

Steve rolled his eyes. "Ellie, I'm not going to be looking. I'm just helping him."

I scoffed. "Seriously? Of course, you're going to be looking."

He sighed, clearly annoyed. "Why are your parents even dragging you to the mountains, anyway?" He was trying to change the subject.

I clenched my jaw. "Because you acted like a jerk at the mausoleum, and I went home drunk. They smelled beer on me, and I was super late." I narrowed my eyes. "Don't try to change the subject, Steve. I don't want you going with them."

"Ellie, I spend all my time with you. I want to hang out with my friends too. I don't appreciate you telling me what I can do."

I stared at him, my chest tightening. "I can't believe this." My voice was quieter now, but the anger still burned. "You know what? I'm glad I'm going away for the weekend. I need a break from you anyway." I grabbed my tray, standing abruptly. "Have fun at the mall looking for girls."

Chapter Fifteen

Roots of Destruction

I got home from school and threw a few things into my bag for the weekend; my movements stiff, mechanical. I refused to speak to my parents. They weren't ready yet, so I retreated to my room, shutting the door behind me.

I sat on my bed, the radio humming softly in the background, but my mind was elsewhere at the mall, with Steve. I imagined him and his friends scanning the crowd, their eyes trailing girls in tight jeans and crop tops, their laughter easy, their attention fleeting. I could see them leaning against storefronts, watching, waiting. My stomach twisted.

I reached for the pin on my nightstand, turning it over in my fingers. The sharp edge glinted in the dim light. Without thinking, I pressed it against my skin, carving a fresh cross into my arm. The sting was immediate, grounding. I traced the same spot again, deeper this time, as the images in my mind grew sharper Steve laughing, flirting, slipping into the car with some girl. My breath hitched.

I barely noticed how deep I had gone until my mother's voice cut through the haze. "Ellie, it's time to go."

I stared at the mark on my arm, the raw redness of it, then pulled my sleeve down. Without a word, I grabbed my bag and walked out the door.

We arrived at the trailer, and I stepped inside, the familiar scent of old wood and stale air wrapping around me. Relief flickered through me—it was only a weekend. But at the same time, a weekend without any way to communicate felt like a lifetime.

I sank onto the bed, staring at the ceiling but my mind was elsewhere at the mall, with Steve. I could picture him, his easy smile, his eyes scanning the crowd. Girls flirting and gesturing, their laughter ringing through the air. I imagined him and his friends watching, waiting, sniffing after them like dogs.

I thought he wanted to be with me. Marry me. Loved me. So why was he out there looking at other girls? The answer hit me like a weight in my chest. Because all he cares about is sex. That's all he ever wants to do with me anymore. It's impossible to spend time with him without it creeping in, no matter who's around. He doesn't care. He's just using me. And if he can't use me, he'll find someone else.

I swallowed hard, my throat burning. Does he even love me at all? The thought made my stomach twist. I wasn't the thinnest or the prettiest. It wouldn't be hard to find someone else to tempt him away. I had tried losing weight, but it was so hard. Maybe if I had a flatter stomach. Bigger boobs. Maybe if I had sex more often. How do I keep his attention? I wasn't sure I could. I felt like such a loser.

This is all my parents' fault. If they hadn't dragged me away, I could have convinced Steve not to go. Or I could have asked Clay to keep him in line. Worst case, I could have gone myself, pretended to help, and made sure Steve didn't do anything.

But no.

I was stuck in the mountains, cut off from everything, surrounded by people who didn't understand anything about my life. I came to the crushing realization that Steve had been using me. Maybe since the beginning. He probably heard the rumors and thought I'd be easy. I had been manipulated, strung along by sweet words and empty promises. The lies, the inconsistencies, nothing ever made sense. He was just waiting until he found something better.

I loved him with everything I had. He was all I cared about. I barely focused on school and barely spent time with my friends. My parents felt like strangers.

I still don't know why I clung to him the way I did. Maybe I just wanted to feel chosen by anyone. Even if deep down I knew I was being used, I stayed. Because what if that was the best I could get? What if this was as close as I'd ever come to love?

We never did anything couples were supposed to do; no dates, no dinners, no memories stitched into photos or ticket stubs. We just… existed in this gray space. And when I wasn't with him, I didn't feel real. Like I was orbiting Earth from some far-off place, watching everyone else live while I floated further away.

A weekend could rearrange the entire ecosystem of high school; friendships could bloom or vanish; rumors could flare and fade. And me? I'd come back to school on Monday with the sinking feeling that life had moved on without me. I just hadn't missed out. I'd been erased.

I wished I was dead. The thought settled in my chest, cold and certain.

I walked to the kitchen cabinet, my fingers trembling as I opened it. My mom's prescription bottles lined the shelf. Sleeping pills. She always took too many. I picked up the bottle, turning it over in my hands. 'Take two at bedtime.'

I did the math in my head. Twenty should be enough. Enough to make me sleep forever. Enough to make Steve realize what he had done. I poured them into my palm, the small white pills stark against my skin. Then, without hesitation, I washed them down with a gulp of Coke.

I put the bottle back exactly where I found it. Then I went to my room, laid down and let the exhaustion take over.

I dozed off, drifting in and out of consciousness. My body felt weightless, yet heavy at the same time. My mouth was dry, like cotton pressing against my tongue. My arms tingled with numbness, and my heart beat slowly, sluggish, as if struggling to keep up.

Darkness. Then light.

I wasn't sure if it was still the same day or if I had been in bed for days. Time felt warped, slipping through my fingers like sand.

"Ellie, do you want something for breakfast?" My dad's voice cut through the haze.

I didn't answer. I let sleep pull me under again.

Hours passed—maybe minutes, maybe days.

"Ellie, are you hungry yet? We have some dinner," my mom said.

Still, I said nothing.

The sun was up, but I couldn't move. My eyelids felt too heavy to lift, my thoughts too scattered to make sense of anything. Had I died? Was I still in the mountains? Had Steve gone to the mall yet? Was there time to stop him?

I felt nauseous, my stomach twisting violently. A sharp buzzing filled my ears, drowning out everything else. I lurched forward, gagging, but all that came up was stomach acid; bitter, burning, useless.

I needed to go to the bathroom. Slowly, painfully, I managed to sit up. My limbs felt like lead, my mouth sour, like rotten orange juice. I had no idea what time it was. I forced myself to stand, gripping the edge of the bed for balance and stumbled toward the bathroom.

"Ellie, it's nice to see you finally awake—just in time to pack up," my mom said casually.

I blinked at her, my mind struggling to catch up.

"It's Sunday?"

"Yup. I guess you were so mad you decided to sleep the entire weekend away. Get your stuff we're headed back home."

I couldn't believe the pills had only made me sleep. Maybe it wasn't meant to be. Still, the time had passed so quickly. A whole weekend gone in a blur of exhaustion.

I was disappointed the pills hadn't worked. Disappointed and honestly scared. Scared of what might've happened while I was gone, of the silence I'd left behind and the silence I came back to.

And then there were my parents. They barely checked on me. It was like I'd disappeared for the weekend, and no one noticed. No questions, no conversations, just a hollow space where care should've been. It felt like they didn't want to see how much I was unraveling, like trying to understand me was already too much work.

Their distance made everything worse. Not because I needed them to have all the answers, but because I just needed them to try.

The drive home stretched endlessly; the road winding on and on, but my mind was elsewhere. All I could think about was Steve; what had happened at the mall, who he had looked at, what he had done.

I needed to know.

As soon as we got home, I walked straight to Steve's house. I wanted to surprise him, catch him before he had time to prepare for me.

I knocked on the door, my heart pounding. His dad answered.

"He's not home," he said. "Up the street, hanging out with the boys."

"Thanks," I muttered, already turning away.

I spotted Steve up the street, tossing a football with the neighborhood kids, both Amys, Clay, and a few others.

"Hi, Steve. I'm back."

Steve caught the ball, held it for a beat, then walked over to me, pulling me into a hug. His lips brushed mine.

"I missed you."

"I missed you, too."

I didn't bring up the mall right away. I didn't want him to think that was the only reason I was here.

Clay and the guys kept talking, their laughter filling the air.

"Hey, Ellie," Clay said.

"Hey, Clay."

I hesitated, then asked, "So... how was it? The mall, I mean."

"Oh, you know. No big deal."

No big deal?

I studied him. Clay wasn't the type to hold back details. He had been told not to talk about it.

Steve slipped his arm around me. "I missed you so much, Ellie. Let's go to your house and hang out."

"Okay."

Of course, Clay joined us.

It didn't take long for what I knew would happen to happen because it always did. And Clay was there the entire time. He had to know. He had to hear. Maybe he just didn't care. Or maybe he liked knowing.

Afterward, I was still insistent on finding out what had happened at the mall. Steve and Clay gave me just enough details to paint a picture, but only one that made Steve look innocent, like he had only been there to support their friend.

I didn't buy it. But I had no proof. So, I had to accept it. I didn't tell them about the pills I took in the mountains. I didn't think anyone cared much anyway.

Chapter Sixteen
Roots Of Devastation

Weeks blurred into months; the school year slipped past in a haze. I still spent time with Jennifer or Mel occasionally, but most days belonged to Steve. Once we cracked the system—intercepting automated calls, forging notes—we started skipping school more often. The world outside didn't notice. We spent entire days tucked away in the forgotten corners of the state hospital, lost in the dim solitude of my basement, wrapped in the secrecy of his bedroom. No one came to look because no one knew we were gone. And when no one knows you're hiding, it's astonishing how easy it is to disappear.

Clay's presence became an unspoken part of life; always there, always included. The only time he wasn't hovering in the background was when Steve and I skipped school. Otherwise, he was a fixture in my basement, where beer and pizza were practically tradition. Steve trusted him with me, but sometimes that trust felt more like surveillance. There were no private moments, no deep conversations unless Clay were part of them too.

At one point, I even tried to set him up; if he had someone else to focus on, I'd get some breathing room. But teenage girls could be shallow, and few saw past the fact that Clay didn't fit their idea of the perfect boyfriend. He was a good guy though. Too good. He'd do anything for me; like the time I casually mentioned craving my favorite candy bar. Without hesitation, he jumped on his bike and pedaled through the pouring rain just to get it. Steve would never do that, especially over something so small.

Clay was loyal, maybe too much so. His presence, once familiar, was becoming suffocating. I finally told Steve I needed space. Just one day, when it was just the two of us. No third wheel. My request was met with frustration; a fight that stretched into days of silence. That's when I realized that they weren't just friends. They were a package deal, and I had no say in the matter.

Even though I knew summer wouldn't bring much change, I was still excited to be done with another school year. There was a sense of relief in closing that chapter; a small hope that maybe things could shift. I wanted more time with Jennifer; time to reconnect and recapture what had been slipping away. And most of all, I wanted things with Steve to feel like they had in the beginning; back when our conversations stretched for hours, when we could lose ourselves just by looking into each other's eyes. Back when it all felt simple.

My sister burst through the door, barely stopping to catch her breath as she dropped off her son. She had to work and with daycare out of reach, my mom had been watching him every day. At eighteen, she was juggling a live-in boyfriend and a child; her life felt miles away from mine. At least she had managed to graduate just weeks before giving birth. Otherwise, she might not have pulled it off.

"Hey Ellie, did you hear about the accident last night?" she asked, her voice edged with urgency.

"No. What accident?"

"Some of the guys were drag racing. One of the cars lost control. I think Rob's in the hospital; he might not make it."

My stomach tightened. "What? Was Mike with him?"

"No, but I think Mike's brother was driving."

"Oh my God," I whispered, the words barely forming. "I can't believe this. I must call Mel."

I picked up the phone, cutting through the quiet.

"Mel, it's me Ellie."

"Oh, hey Ellie! How are you?"

I hesitated. "I was wondering if you'd heard the news."

"No… what news?"

"It's about Rob."

Her voice sharpened. "What's wrong with Rob?"

"There was an accident." I tried to explain, but I didn't know much more than what my sister had told me. Silence stretched between us. I could feel her heartbreak through the phone, the weight of it settling in.

"I wish I didn't have to tell you this," I murmured. "But I didn't want you to hear it from someone else."

A pause. Then, softly, "Thanks, Ellie."

"I'll let you know if I hear any updates."

The line stayed quiet for a moment longer before she finally whispered, "Okay."

Time seemed to freeze as we waited for updates; each passing hour stretching unbearably. We already knew the truth that Rob was brain dead and survival was unlikely. His fate rested in his parents' hands, a decision no one should ever have to make.

Two days later, the news came. Rob was gone. The damage to his brain had been too severe.

Mike's brother had been behind the wheel that night; choosing to race, choosing recklessness. He lost control, crashing head-on into a telephone pole. He survived; his leg broken, his hip shattered, requiring multiple surgeries. But he would live. And that fact sat heavy in my chest. Clark had chosen to race. He was the driver. Why did Rob have to die? How was Mike supposed to survive without his best friend?

I had to call Mel. The weight of it pressed down on me—it was the hardest call I'd ever made. The moment she answered, I could hear the hope in her voice; the expectation that this was just another conversation. And then I told her.

She broke. Sobs tore through the phone, raw and unfiltered. She was shattered, and I wasn't sure if she could ever be whole again.

Mel asked me to go with her to Rob's house. We had always known where he lived; years of bike rides had made his neighborhood familiar. She wanted to offer condolences; to tell his parents how sorry she was. I agreed.

We knocked, and his mother answered.

"Hello, Mrs. Reed. I'm Mel, and this is Ellie. We were friends of Rob, and we just wanted to say how sorry we are. He meant so much to us."

Mel's voice cracked, and then the tears came again. Mrs. Reed stepped aside, inviting us in, offering us something to drink. We sat at the kitchen table, the weight of grief pressing down on all of us. She tried to comfort Mel, but Mel was too shattered to be soothed.

I felt guilty, watching her pain spill into a home already drowning in sorrow. I tried to explain to tell Mrs. Reed how much Mel had loved her son, how she had spent years hoping they might one day be something more. I saw something shift in her expression, a quiet understanding. Rob had never mentioned Mel, but that didn't matter. Mrs. Reed could see it now; the depth of feeling, the quiet devotion Mel had carried all this time.

Then, Mel asked if she could have something of Rob's to remember him by. Mrs. Reed disappeared for a moment, returning with his favorite Guns N' Roses shirt. He had just been to their concert last month and had the time of his life. That same album had been playing on the CD player when the accident happened.

"I feel like Rob would want you to have this," she said.

Mel took the shirt, pressing it to her face, breathing it in like he was still there. We thanked Mrs. Reed, grateful for her kindness during her grief. Before we left, she asked if we would be at the funeral. We assured her we would.

The viewing and funeral arrived faster than I could process. I still couldn't believe that Rob, my fifteen-year-old friend, the boy I had known since kindergarten, was gone. I had never lost someone so young, someone still in the prime of their life.

I remembered all the times we chased each other on our bikes, them chasing us, then us chasing them, a rhythm that felt like it would go on forever. We shared crayons in elementary school, then in middle school shared science notes like quiet secrets passed between old friends.

There was a kind of soft, steady love I had for both boys; not the dramatic kind, but something built over years of being woven into each other's lives.

Sometimes we pretended I married Mike and Mel married Rob. Best friends tangled up with best friends, destined to grow old in the same neighborhood, still riding bikes, still laughing.

It would be hard to imagine a world without Rob in it. A world with no more bike rides at dusk, no more chases that turned into joy. And honestly... how could there even be a Mike without a Rob?

Mel was inconsolable, trapped in her grief, and there was nothing anyone could say to ease it. The funeral was held during the school day, so not everyone could attend, but more people showed up than I expected. Familiar faces from school filled the room, their expressions heavy with sorrow.

Then I saw Mike. He sat in the corner, slouched so low it was as if he were trying to disappear. I hadn't spoken to him yet. He and Rob had been inseparable—always together, always a pair. Rob and Mike. Mike and Rob. I couldn't imagine one without the other. How was he supposed to go on without his best friend?

I hesitated, then slowly walked up to him. His eyes lifted, meeting mine, and I felt the weight of everything in that single glance.

"Mike, I am so incredibly sorry. I'm just... so, so sorry."

He stood, his eyes brimming with tears, and I didn't think I just hugged him. He didn't pull away. He let me give him that moment and I was grateful for it.

Later, we gathered at the cemetery; the same one where we had spent summers riding bikes, chasing each other, laughing under the sun. Now, we were here to say goodbye.

I knew that every time I rode past this place, I would stop. I would look toward Rob's resting place and whisper, *See you later, my friend.*

I tried not to fixate on the fact that Steve hadn't come to the funeral with me. He wasn't close to Rob or Mike, but he knew I'd grown up with them. That alone should've been enough.

But instead of offering comfort, he accused me of using the funeral as an excuse to get close to Mike. As if mourning the loss of someone I'd known all my life could somehow be reduced to a scheme. As if grief were some kind of manipulation.

He thought I had feelings for Mike, and I knew if he'd seen us hug, he would've lost it. But it wasn't like that. I wasn't crossing lines. I was holding space for someone whose world had just fallen apart. For someone who used to chase me on bikes until we couldn't breathe from laughing.

Steve made it seem like I'd done something wrong. Like being kind, being human was a betrayal. But what hurt more than the accusation was the absence. The silence where his support should've been.

I understood why his mom wouldn't let him miss school, but I had expected him to at least *want* to be there for me. A funeral wasn't the place for anything but mourning, and I had no interest in Mike beyond wanting to be there for him.

I couldn't shake the disappointment. Steve hadn't even said he was sorry for my loss. Lately, it felt like he was becoming someone I didn't recognize.

Mel drifted away after that, as if grief had carved out a part of her that she couldn't get back. She always looked distant, weighed down by something too heavy to shake. Every time I reached out an invitation, a simple attempt to reconnect, she turned me down. It was like she had retreated into a world where sorrow was the only thing that made sense.

Chapter Seventeen

Roots of Fear

Summer had arrived, bringing with it a sense of long-awaited freedom. School was behind me, and the weight of grief, though lingering, had begun to loosen its grip. It had stretched across a season, shaping the days in quiet ways, but bit by bit, life found its rhythm again.

I welcomed the warmth, the open sky, and most of all, the time with Steve. There were moments when uncertainty clouded things, but together, we navigated them. He was a constant, and I never imagined love could feel this whole, this consuming, yet effortless.

The plan was to meet up with everyone, and Steve would get alcohol. Of course I was going, and I asked Jennifer to come along. Mel hadn't been herself since Rob died, so I wasn't expecting to see much of her. We decided on an old, abandoned house not far away; the perfect place to gather without worry. The anticipation bubbled inside me I was ready to unwind, let go, and soak in the ease of summer nights.

The night was warm, carrying the unmistakable scent of summer in the air. The abandoned house stood silent; its walls still intact, though its windows had long since vanished. Time and neglect had worn it down, leaving behind signs of those who had passed through; graffiti covering every surface, remnants of past visitors scattered across the floor.

Among the debris were tattered porn magazines, their pages splayed open as if frozen in time. My eyes flickered to the images, unwilling yet drawn in, each picture exposing everything the women had to offer. The contrast between the evening's carefree energy and the unsettling remnants of the past lingered in the space around me.

Clay showed up with Steve, and I brought Jennifer. A few of the other neighborhood kids arrived as well. We brought a radio and played some music. Everyone was laughing and drinking and just having a great night. It didn't take long before Steve came up and started kissing me. I loved it when he showed me affection, but sometimes I just wished he would hold my hand or put his arm around me instead he always wanted to get right to business.

Sometimes being with him felt like I was holding my breath. Like I was shrinking to fit into a space that was never mine to begin with. He could be sweet, but there were moments when it felt like I wasn't there. Just a prop in whatever version of himself he wanted to show the world. And yet... I still stayed. I still wanted him.

Maybe it's because I'd gotten used to being let down by the people who were supposed to protect me. My parents barely saw me. My brother had taken things I was too young to name, and they never noticed. Or maybe they did and just looked away.

So, I learned to settle. To survive in places that made me feel small, because "wanted" even the distorted kind was better than being invisible.

Steve pulled me away from the crowd, his grip firm but familiar. The distant hum of laughter and music faded as he led me into the adjacent room, its silence pressing in. Against the wall, the air was cooler, and the rough texture of peeling paint was beneath my fingers. The moment was quick, urgent and before anyone could wonder where we had gone, we were already slipping back into the noise unnoticed.

Clay sat quietly, a shadow of his usual self, and I could tell something was weighing on him. I made my way over, nudging him gently. "What's wrong?"

His voice was low, heavy with something deeper than just words. "I just wish I could find a girl like you. Someone special. I see how you look at Steve, how much you love him. I want that." His eyes flickered with something unresolved. "I still don't get it, though. I don't think he treats you right. But I guess I just don't have what girls are looking for. I mean, I don't wrestle, I don't run track, and I don't work out. I'm overweight."

I met his gaze, firm but kind. "Clay, a lot of those things don't matter. What's important is how you treat a girl, that's what counts. One day, you're going to find your person."

His expression softened for a beat, but then he looked at me; too long, too intent. The air between us shifted, and I realized, too late, that he was leaning in. My pulse quickened.

Before I could react, Steve was there fast, forceful, and then his fist connected with Clay's face. The impact was sharp, sending Clay stumbling back, shock splashed across his features.

"What the hell, Steve?" Clay sputtered, holding his jaw.

"You were about to kiss her," Steve snapped.

"No, I wasn't. I would never do that, man, you're my best friend!" Clay protested, fear in his voice.

"Steve, why did you do that?" I said, anger rising in my chest. "We were just talking. Everything was fine. He was sharing something with me."

Steve's glare didn't falter. "Ellie, we're leaving. Right now."

Clay blinked, still stunned.

Steve's voice was cold, final. "Don't ever talk to me again. If you even look at her, I'll kick your ass."

He grabbed my hand, pulling me away before I could speak.

I was frustrated about what had happened, but a part of me felt warmed by the fact that Steve still got jealous enough to hit his best friend over something like that.

"Steve, I wasn't going to kiss him," I said, my voice softer now. "I think he just had too much to drink and was being vulnerable. I love you and I would never do that."

Steve exhaled, rubbing the back of his neck. "Maybe I reacted too quickly. I saw him leaning in and I just saw red. Then it was too late."

The tension between us lingered, but the night still felt alive; the buzz of alcohol making everything softer, slower. "I don't want to go home yet," I said. "How about we hang out behind the school for a bit?"

Steve nodded. "Yeah, that sounds nice. Just the two of us."

We walked over, settling onto the swings; the quiet hum of the night wrapping around us. The air was warm, carrying the scent of summer grass, and the stars stretched wide above us.

"It's such a beautiful night," I murmured.

"Not as beautiful as you, Ellie," Steve said, his voice low.

We sat there for a while, talking about the future. "What do you want to do after high school?" I asked.

"My parents want me to go to college," he said. "But I'd love to do something with special needs kids. Since my brother has a disability, I see how hard he must work and how kids treat him. I have a soft spot for that. I think I could make a difference."

I smiled. "Yeah, you're good with all the kids, especially Joe. He's lucky to have a big brother like you."

I hesitated, then admitted, "I only ever pictured myself as a mom. I hate school, so I can't imagine doing more of it voluntarily. Honestly, I have no idea what I want to do. Maybe a hairdresser or something."

Steve nodded. "Yeah, I can see that. You'd be good at that."

We lay in the grass, the night folding gently around us. The stars blinked overhead like they were holding their breath, and for a moment, the world felt impossibly quiet.

It always stunned me how I could be wrapped in frustration or hurt, and then, just like that, fall into love with him all over again.

We made love under the open sky, nothing between us and the universe. And at some point, lulled by the warmth of the night and the weight of each other, we drifted to sleep, limbs tangled, hearts a little less heavy.

We woke up to a sky still draped in darkness, though the hush of early morning lingered in the air. My pulse quickened as I checked the time—5 a.m. "Steve, I need to get home. I missed my curfew. My dad's gonna kill me."

Steve sat up, rubbing the sleep from his eyes. "Okay, I'll walk you back. Just sneak in and get in bed—pretend you were there all night. Maybe they didn't even notice."

I nodded, pulling myself up, the cool dew from the grass clinging to my skin. The walk back was quiet; the kind of silence that felt stolen, like the world wasn't meant to be awake yet. When we reached my house, Steve kissed me goodbye, the moment quick but lingering.

The door wasn't locked. The house sat in perfect stillness, wrapped in darkness, as if nothing had changed. I moved carefully, my breath shallow; every creak beneath my feet feeling impossibly loud. Slipping into my room, I eased into bed, the sheets familiar, safe. I shut my eyes and willed myself into stillness, pretending just for a moment that I had been here all along.

I stayed in my room, waiting, hoping my parents would come in and see me, believing I had been there all night. But the minutes stretched on, and no one came. Eventually, impatience won over and I stepped into the kitchen.

"Good morning, Ellie," my dad said, his voice even.

"Morning, Mom. Morning, Dad," I replied, forcing casualness into my tone.

Mom's expression was unreadable. "It's nice to see you finally decided to come home last night."

My stomach tightened. "I—"

"We waited until two a.m.," Dad continued, "then decided to go to bed. Where were you?"

I swallowed. "Oh, um. I was with Jennifer. She wasn't feeling well, and I couldn't leave her. I stayed until she felt better. Sorry, I didn't call, there wasn't a phone nearby."

Mom's eyes narrowed. "That's odd, because Jennifer called here last night looking for you."

My breath hitched.

"And Clay showed up, wondering if you were home," Dad added. "He said he saw you last with Steve."

Heat rushed to my face. "Oh, yeah, well—Steve walked me home to be safe. It was late, and—"

"Ellie, you're lying," Dad interrupted, his voice sharp. "We're tired of the lies. We don't want you to spend time with Steve anymore. You're grounded."

"For how long?" I asked, panic starting to creep in.

"All summer."

"What?" My voice cracked. "You can't ground me for that long, that's three months!"

"We can, and we will," Dad said, his tone final. "Now go to your room. Or I'll get the nightstick out as well."

Fear shot through me. "No, Dad, no!" I gasped, turning and running to my room, tears burning in my eyes.

There was no way I was going to be punished for an entire summer. Three months? That was impossible. Could parents even do that? There had to be some kind of rule against it somewhere. But then again, they had tried it once before with my sister. She ran away.

That was it. That was my way out.

I couldn't go the entire summer without seeing Steve. My dad didn't understand; none of them did. They didn't see how much I loved him, how much I needed him. Without him, I didn't want to exist. I'd rather be dead than be without him.

I was leaving tonight. I didn't know where I would go or what I would do, but I wasn't staying here. Not trapped. Not cut off from the only person who made me feel whole.

After my dad left for work, I seized my chance. My mom was in the shower, and I snuck in a call to Steve; my hands shaking as I dialed. I gripped the phone tightly, my pulse hammering in my ears. "Steve, my parents caught me. I tried so hard to convince them I was helping Jennifer, but Clay had been to the house."

"Did you get in trouble too?" I asked.

"No. No one even realized I was gone," Steve muttered, frustration curling in my chest. "You're lucky. Me? Not so much. I got grounded for the entire summer. My parents don't want me to see you anymore."

"What?" His voice sharpened.

"Yeah. Can you believe that?" I exhaled, my mind racing. "Anyway, I decided I'm leaving. I can't live like this. My dad even threatened to get his nightstick out. I hate it here. They don't understand. They want to end us."

Steve was silent for a beat. "Ellie... where are you going to go?"

"I have absolutely no idea," I admitted. "But as far away from here as possible."

He hesitated, then said, "Grab some money and meet me in two hours behind the school. I think I have an idea."

Relief flooded through me. "Okay."

I met Steve behind the school, his knapsack slung over one shoulder, his expression steady but charged with quiet determination.

"Listen," he said, voice low. "I have some family on the other side of Philly. We can take the train and try to find my uncle. He works at the bus station. If we can track him down, maybe he'll take us back to his place and let us stay for a while. Give your parents time to cool off. Maybe they'll regret your punishment."

I nodded, the idea slowly settled in. "Okay… but how will we find your uncle?"

Steve shrugged, a small grin tugging at the corner of his mouth. "I'm not sure. But it'll be a fun adventure."

I exhaled, glancing at him. "You don't even have a reason to run away. Your parents didn't even notice you were gone."

"Exactly the point," he said, his voice edged with something unreadable.

I hesitated for only a second before answering. "Okay."

Chapter Eighteen

Roots of Adventure

We walked to the local train station; the early morning air was thick with the scent of asphalt and lingering exhaust. The station was quiet, except for the occasional shuffle of tired commuters, their movements practiced, routine.

Buying our tickets felt surreal, like we were stepping into something bigger than ourselves. The train arrived with a low rumble, its doors sliding open with a mechanical hiss. We climbed aboard, settling into vinyl seats that were cracked and worn, their surfaces sticky from years of use.

I had only ever taken the train once as a kid with my grandmother. My parents never used public transportation. This world, the hum of the tracks, the muted conversations of strangers felt foreign, yet thrilling.

Around us, passengers sat in silence, their faces blank with familiarity. They were heading to work, returning home, moving through their daily routines. But we were running away. We were stepping into the unknown, chasing something uncertain.

A grand adventure.

The train rattled beneath us, the rhythmic hum of the tracks filling the space between conversation and quiet thoughts. I shifted in my seat; the worn vinyl sticky against my skin, my nerves buzzing with a mix of excitement and unease.

It was just me and Steve running away together. No rules, no restrictions. My parents couldn't stop us now. Instead of tearing us apart, their punishment had only pushed us closer.

I glanced out the window, watching the city blur past in fleeting moments; life moving forward, indifferent to our escape. The passengers around us sat in silence, their faces blank with routine.

We stepped off the train into the heart of the city, swallowed by its vastness. Neither of us knew where we were just that we weren't home anymore. The streets stretched endlessly, unfamiliar and unwelcoming. We weren't city people. We were small-town kids, out of place in the rush of strangers and towering buildings.

The heat pressed down, thick and suffocating, carrying the scent of asphalt and sweat. People stared as we wandered, unsure of where to go. A man approached, his voice rough, asking for money. I couldn't say no; I handed him five dollars.

Steve frowned as the man walked away. "You can't just give away our money. We might need it."

I shrugged. "He looked like he needed it more."

We walked for what felt like hours; the sun dipping lower, casting long shadows across the streets. The polished business suits and casual wear faded, replaced by torn clothes and weary faces. The city shifted around us, revealing a different side; one that felt forgotten.

People huddled under blankets on the sidewalks; bottles tucked into paper bags. A man sat against a wall, drinking straight from a bottle of green aftershave. My stomach twisted. Why would anyone drink that?

Panhandlers lingered on every corner, their voices blending into the hum of the city. Eyes followed me hungry, assessing. I felt exposed, vulnerable, like prey in the wild.

"Steve," I whispered, my pulse quickening. "I think we need to get out of here. I'm afraid."

He nodded, his expression tight. "Yeah. I'm starting to feel uneasy, too."

I saw in his eyes the same fear creeping in. We didn't belong here. We needed to get back to the train station, find the bus station and get somewhere safe.

"I saw signs earlier with directions to the bus station," I said. "Let's circle back and find them before anything happens."

"Yeah. We need to get out of here."

As we hurried back, the city pressed in around us. A man sat on the ground, a needle hanging from his arm. Another stumbled, tripping over his own feet. Voices called out, asking for money.

Then a man flicked his tongue at me, his gaze sharp, predatory.

Steve grabbed my hand, and we started walking faster, almost running.

Eventually the streets began to look familiar, more like the place where the train had first dropped us. Relief settled in as I spotted the signs for the bus terminal, guiding us toward something solid or something known.

Inside, the terminal was dimly lit, humming with the quiet energy of late-night travelers. We approached the employee's window and Steve leaned in. "Is Guy Salam working?"

The man nodded. "Yeah, hold on. I'll go get him."

A few moments later, Guy appeared, his eyes bright with recognition, a smile stretching across his face. "Steve! What are you doing here? And at this time of night?"

Steve shifted his bag on his shoulder. "Ellie's having some trouble at home and we needed a little getaway. We were hoping maybe we could stay at your place for a few days."

Guy scratched his head, considering. "Well… maybe. I'm not sure. How about you guys sit out here while I finish my shift? Then we'll head to the house and talk about it in the morning."

Steve nodded. "Okay."

We settled into the worn seats of the terminal, waiting as the hours stretched on. The hum of distant conversations, the occasional shuffle of footsteps, is all blurred together in the quiet weight of exhaustion.

Finally, Guy's shift ended, and he drove us to his house; the city fading behind us as we disappeared into the night.

"Thank you so much, Guy, for letting us come with you tonight," I said, relief settling into my voice. "I don't think we would have lasted long in the city."

Guy nodded, his expression serious. "No, it's not a safe place for kids like you, especially not young girls. I'm glad you came to me for help."

His house was small, a Cape Cod-style home nestled on a quiet street in a town that felt worlds away from where we had just been. The air was calmer here; the streets lined with trees instead of towering buildings.

Inside, the house was still; the kind of silence that comes when everyone else is asleep. I had assumed Guy lived alone, but apparently not. He led us down the hall, stopping at a door.

"Sorry, it's not much," he said, pushing it open. "I didn't know I'd have company tonight."

The room was bare, with just four walls, a floor, and a sliding glass door leading outside. No furniture, no bed. Just space.

"Sorry, you'll have to sleep on the floor," Guy added. "But it's got to be better than the streets."

"Definitely," I said, grateful despite the circumstances. "Thanks for helping us and letting us stay here."

Guy gave a small nod. "We'll talk more in the morning."

Steve's excitement was contagious. "I loved this place—every summer, like clockwork, I escaped here for a week or two. It was tradition, a rhythm I never questioned. My mother grew up here, and her sister and two brothers had never left. This was their home."

"Oh, so that's who else lives here?" I asked, scanning the quiet surroundings.

"Yeah. My two uncles and my aunt," said Steve.

I smiled, but something in my chest felt unsettled. This place was carefree in ways that made me both comfortable and cautious. Steve's uncle—charming, reckless, forever surrounded by women—had always been someone he admired. But why? Because he drank freely? Because he smoked and laughed like the rules never applied to him? I didn't say anything, but my thoughts sat heavy.

Steve pulled open the sliding glass door and stepped outside. I followed, stepping into the warm night air. The patio stretched out beneath us, leading to the pool; vast, pristine, almost glowing under the moonlight.

"Wow," I whispered.

Steve grinned. "Amazing, right? It's my favorite part. I get so tan just hanging out here all summer."

"I wish we could go in, but I didn't bring a bathing suit."

"That's okay. We don't need them."

Before I could react, he peeled off his clothes and dove in, slicing through the water with ease. He surfaced, laughing, shaking droplets from his hair.

"Come on! It feels incredible."

I hesitated. We had been very close before, but this was different. Exposed. Unfiltered. The nerves tingled in my fingertips, but there was also something exhilarating about it—about us, about now. Without thinking any further, I stripped down as fast as I could and jumped.

The water wrapped around me, warm and smooth, different from the mountain lakes I'd always known. Chlorine clung to my skin, mixing with the scent of night air, of summer freedom. We floated, drifted, savoring the silence; the untethered feeling of being young and reckless under the stars.

No one was watching. No one was telling us what to do. We were just *being*.

In the quiet corner of the pool, our bodies pressed together, lips meeting in a slow, certain kiss. The world shrank, leaving only this-this moment, this closeness, this certainty that stretched beyond words.

For the first time, I felt completely seen. Bare and free. Vulnerable and raw. And in that instant, I knew this was the man I would spend the rest of my life with.

We had so much fun until we were both exhausted and ready to sleep. We climbed out and dried off and then cuddled on the hard floor and eventually drifted off. I never once worried or thought about the consequences of running away or what my parents might be thinking.

They couldn't understand that Steve wasn't just a boyfriend; he was the only person who made me feel like I existed.

At home, I was invisible. My parents didn't listen, didn't ask, didn't *see* me. Their disapproval only pushed me closer to him, because at least with Steve, I felt chosen. Even when it wasn't perfect, it was *something*. And the truth was, I was more afraid of being alone than being hurt.

Every time they tried to pull us apart, I clung tighter. Not because I didn't see the cracks, but because walking away meant facing the emptiness that waited for me on the other side. And I didn't think I could survive that silence.

The next morning, the kitchen was filled with the scent of freshly cooked breakfast pancakes stacked high, eggs perfectly fluffy, golden toast waiting beside a pitcher of orange juice. It was the kind of meal that felt like home, even though my parents never made breakfast.

Steve and I sat down, the weight of the previous night still lingering between us. His two uncles and aunt were gathered around the table, their presence both welcoming and unfamiliar. I fidgeted slightly, unsure of my place among them, but they were kind, making casual conversation, asking if I'd slept well.

Then the doorbell rang.

Guy got up to answer it, and I barely registered the muffled voices until a familiar one cut through the morning haze. My stomach twisted.

Steve met my gaze, his expression mirroring my disbelief.

How? How did he know where to find me?

And then my father stepped into the room.

"Come on, Ellie," he said, his voice heavy with controlled frustration. "It's time to go home."

Heat rushed to my cheeks. My father turned to Steve's family, offering them a curt nod. "I appreciate you calling and letting me know where she was."

I barely heard the rest. My feet moved mechanically toward the door, toward the waiting car, where my mother sat stiffly in the passenger seat.

Betrayal burned in my chest. I turned back just once, to Guy, standing there like nothing had happened. So that was it. He hadn't helped us. He had sold us out.

"Ellie, why in the world would you run away?" My mother's voice cracked, frustration laced with hurt. "What is so terrible about our house? About the way we treat you? What have we ever done to make you hate us this much?"

I clenched my fists. "Mom, I don't hate you guys." The words rushed out, tangled in frustration. "I'm just so tired of you always telling me what I can and can't do your constantly in my business, always punishing me."

My father exhaled sharply. "Well, guess what, young lady? You're punished again."

Figures. My stomach tightened. "See? That's exactly why I hate being at home."

My parents exchanged a glance. "Steve probably won't even get punished," I shot back.

Dad's response was immediate, cool, and matter-of-fact. "Steve's parents decided he's going to stay at his uncle's house for a couple of weeks, so the two of you can have a break from each other."

The words hit me like a slap.

"Oh, great," I scoffed. "So, he gets a vacation, swims all day, and enjoys life while I'm stuck locked in my bedroom? How is that fair?"

Silence stretched thick between us. I turned toward the window, jaw clenched, swallowing the bitter resentment burning inside me.

"I hate my life."

Chapter Nineteen

Roots of Shock

The weight of my punishment had finally lifted. I didn't know if my parents had let me out early or if my mom had just grown tired of watching me drag myself around the house like a ghost.

Whenever I tried to spend time with her, she got annoyed. She had her favorite shows to watch, floors to clean; no time to entertain a restless daughter. She'd suggest things for me to do, but they never included her. It was always something that would keep me out of her way.

I was happy to finally be free.

Steve was still at his uncle's, and when I called, his voice was bright, full of excitement. "I'm having so much fun," he said, launching into a rundown of his week—his siblings visiting, long afternoons swimming, nights filled with beer and laughter. He told me about the different women who had come by the house to see his uncle, how the energy was electric, how effortless it all felt.

With every word, my stomach twisted.

I had spent two miserable weeks locked in my room, drowning in silence, my only companion, the same songs played repeatedly. I had been aching for him, counting down the days, picturing our reunion. But now, I couldn't shake the image of him sun-kissed, effortless, flirting, having the time of his life without me. Had he even missed me?

The phone suddenly felt heavy in my hand. I opened my mouth to say something, anything, but the words refused to come. It had been so long since I'd talked to Jennifer. I missed her, so I finally picked up the phone.

The moment she answered, it was like no time had passed at all. "You should come over," she said, laughter in her voice. "Just like old times. Sleepover?"

"Let me pack. I'll be right over."

But as I tossed clothes into my bag, a thought crept in an uneasy weight I had been avoiding. I hadn't had my period in months.

I never tracked it like some girls did, never circled dates on a calendar, so maybe it had been a month...or two? My stomach flipped at the possibility. No. I wasn't pregnant. I couldn't be.

Could I?

I needed a test. But I had no money, and asking for one was impossible. If I went to buy one, what would the store clerk say? Would they judge me? Would someone recognize me?

On my way to Jennifer's, I stopped at the pharmacy; the fluorescent lights humming overhead as I walked down the aisle. My breath felt too shallow, my fingers ice-cold as I scanned the shelves. So many different boxes. Digital, lines, words, symbols. None of it made sense.

Finally, I spotted one with a simple check or minus sign. Easy enough. My heart pounded.

Before I could second-guess myself, I grabbed the box and slipped it into my purse. Then, panic.

What if the test didn't work? What if I messed it up? I needed backup. I grabbed another, this time moving even faster, shoving it deep into my bag. I didn't look at anyone.

I forced myself to wander toward the makeup aisle, pretending to browse, my fingers tracing lipstick tubes absently while my mind screamed at me to just leave.

Minutes stretched endlessly.

Finally, I turned, walking toward the doors, my breath caught in my throat as I crossed the threshold; one step, two, until I was outside.

Whew. I made it. I had stolen something for the first time in my life, and no one knew. And no one ever could. I tightened my grip on my purse and kept walking.

Jennifer was waiting.

Jennifer and I fell into our usual rhythm catching up on gossip, eating cookies, laughing like no time had passed.

At some point, she asked me to cut her hair. "I want a shaved checkered pattern on one side," she said, grinning.

I hesitated. "I've never done anything like that before."

"So? Just try."

That was Jennifer; bold, unapologetic, always reminding me of Cyndi Lauper with her wild style. We didn't ask her mom. We just did it.

As I worked, she shared. "Things at home have been rough," she admitted. "Mom's boyfriend thinks I am too much trouble. He wants me to stay with my dad for the rest of the summer."

I paused, the clippers humming in my hand. "But your dad never wanted you there."

She shrugged, but her voice was tight. "Yeah. He has a new family now."

Jennifer felt unwanted.

I understood that feeling more than I wanted to admit.

So, I told her about Steve; how he was always flirting, always getting himself into situations that didn't make sense. And then, hesitantly, I told her about my period. Or rather, the fact that I hadn't had one in months.

"I don't think I'm pregnant," I said quickly. "But I got a test just in case."

Jennifer didn't ask how I got it, and I didn't offer it. I wasn't about to tell her I had stolen it.

"Let's do it now," she said.

I nodded, grabbed the box, and read the directions. Then I went into the bathroom, my heart pounding, and peed on the stick.

I didn't want to watch. It would be like waiting for water to boil— it never happens if you stare at it. So, we put on the newest Cure song and agreed not to look until the last note played. The music filled the room, but I barely heard it. My pulse was too loud, my thoughts too tangled.

Finally, the song ended. We walked into the bathroom. I looked down. Positive. Jennifer's mouth hung open.

"It's a mistake," I whispered. "Let me do the other one."

I peed again. This time, we watched. The second test confirmed it. Positive again. I stared at the test in disbelief. My chest tightened as I read the result again, as if trying to change it.

"I feel fine. This can't be right," I murmured, shaking my head. "My parents will kill me."

Jennifer sat beside me, arms folded, eyes wary. "You should've just given him blowjobs like I did."

I blinked. "What?"

Jennifer shrugged. "Then you wouldn't be dealing with this."

I swallowed hard. "Wait, are you saying you did that with Steve?"

Jennifer rolled her eyes. "Yeah. Ages ago, way before you ever even knew he existed."

The room felt smaller. The air was still. "You never told me."

"I'm sure I did," Jennifer said, but the indifference in her voice only made the betrayal cut deeper.

"No. I'm certain you didn't." My voice cracked, my stomach twisting. "And he told me he was a virgin. That he had never done anything with anyone else before."

Jennifer sighed, tapping her nails against the desk. "Technically, that's not sex. So, he didn't lie."

I clenched my jaw. "No, he definitely lied. He made me believe I was the first. The only one."

Silence stretched between us. The weight of reality was sinking in, Steve's deception, the pregnancy, the uncertain future.

I felt betrayed. Not just by him, but by her too. My best friend and my boyfriend; two people I trusted to be honest with me, to keep me safe. How could they both lie?

It wasn't even about when it happened. I knew it was before he and I were together. What hurt was the silence. The half-truths. I'd asked them, separately, if there had ever been anything between them. Both times, they looked me in the eye and told me it was just a kiss.

But it wasn't. And they knew how sensitive that was for me; how much that kind of secrecy could shatter me. Why not just tell the truth? Why not give me the dignity of knowing instead of finding out like this?

Maybe it wasn't just a lie. Maybe it was the kind of truth they chose to hide. Because it wasn't just a kiss, they both knew that. They knew it was more, and they knew that kind of intimacy was complicated for me. Sensitive. Loaded with memories I didn't ask to carry.

I asked them directly. Trusted them with the question. And still, they offered me the sanitized version, as if I couldn't handle the truth or didn't deserve it.

So, it wasn't just about what happened between them. It was disregard. The choice to protect themselves over me.

Jennifer finally spoke, her tone oddly detached. "So, what are you going to do?"

I inhaled sharply, gripping the edge of the table. "I'm going to pretend the test is wrong. That's what."

Jennifer scoffed. "Yeah, good luck with that."

We went to bed soon after that, but sleep didn't come easily. My mind churned with anger, disappointment, and the dull ache of betrayal. Jennifer had lied. Steve had lied. The two people I trusted most had been keeping secrets from me, and now everything felt tainted.

Lying in the dark, I stared at the ceiling, listening to the steady rhythm of Jennifer's breathing. It felt wrong; how could she sleep so peacefully when she had just shattered so much? The room, once familiar and comforting, now felt suffocating; the walls closing in around me.

I just wanted the sleepover to end. The excitement, the laughter, the ease gone. All I could think about was leaving, putting distance between myself and the weight of these lies. I made up my mind. First thing in the morning, I was going home.

I couldn't stop thinking about it. The lies. The betrayal. The fact that Steve and Jennifer had been together. It was so obvious now—the way she casually mentioned his size before, like it was common knowledge. And of course, it was. She had firsthand experience. How had I not seen it before? How could I have been so naïve?

And the worst part? I couldn't shake the feeling that maybe, just maybe, the only reason he wanted me was because of that ugly label people used against me. Because he assumed, expected, maybe even hoped I'd do it. If that was the reason he liked me, then had I ever even mattered at all?

A bitter wave of nausea curled in my stomach. And now, on top of everything, I am pregnant. I had to tell Steve. He had to know. But what then? What were we supposed to do? My parents could never find out. Absolutely not.

Chapter Twenty

Buds of Change

Steve was finally back from his time at his uncle's, and after spending some time at home with his parents, he came over to see me. Relief washed over me when I saw that Clay wasn't with him.

He talked animatedly about his trip; how much fun he had, the places he went to, and the things he did. His excitement was contagious, but I couldn't shake the unease lingering in the back of my mind. He looked different too; tanned, refreshed, and sporting a new haircut.

I hesitated before speaking, but the words tumbled out anyway. "Steve, I was worried about you out there. The drinking, the girls... all of it."

He smiled, shaking his head. "Oh, Ellie, I love you. You never have to worry about stuff like that. They just like to flirt, but it's nothing to worry about."

But I did worry. The thought of him being surrounded by temptation, of him slipping away from me, gnawed at my chest. "I do worry, though. I'm afraid you're going to cheat on me."

His expression softened, and he reached for my hand. "I would never cheat on you. I love you."

I wanted to believe him. I needed to believe him. But the doubt still lingered, quiet but persistent.

"We need to talk." My voice was steady, but my hands trembled. "I found out something while you were gone. I don't know how to say this."

Steve pulled back slightly, his expression shifting. "What is it?"

I swallowed hard. "I'm pregnant."

His arms dropped from around me, his body stiffening. "What?"

"Yeah," I whispered. "I realized it had been some time since I had my period, so I took a test. It was positive."

Steve stared at me, then down at my stomach, as if expecting to see some kind of proof. "That doesn't mean you're pregnant. Those tests are wrong all the time."

"I thought the same thing," I admitted. "That's why I took another one."

"And?" His voice was tight.

I exhaled slowly. "That one was positive too."

"Oh."

Silence stretched between us, thick and suffocating.

"So," I said, searching his face for something.

"So," he echoed, his gaze darting away. "Well… that one could've been wrong too. If you got them at the same time, they probably came from the same batch. If one was defective, they all were."

I stared at him. "Steve—"

"I mean, do you feel pregnant?" he interrupted.

I hesitated. "No."

"And you don't look pregnant," he added quickly. "I think it was a mistake. I wouldn't worry about it."

His words settled over me like a weight, pressing down on my chest. He wanted this to disappear. He wanted me to believe it wasn't real.

But it was. I felt confused. Maybe he was right. Tests could be wrong. I didn't have any morning sickness, and I felt fine. Maybe it was a mistake. But what if it wasn't?

"What will we do?" I asked, my voice barely above a whisper.

"If it's true, we'll love it," Steve said simply. "But I'm not going to worry about it."

His certainty unsettled me.

"Well," he added, a small grin tugging at his lips, "this means we can have sex all we want and not have to worry about protection."

I blinked. "I mean… yeah, but that assumes it's true."

"Yeah, I guess," he said, shrugging. "But I don't think it is."

"So, you don't think we should tell anyone?"

"No. Definitely not. I have no idea how I'd ever tell my parents."

I swallowed hard. "At least your dad knows you're having sex. Mine still thinks I'm a virgin."

"Yeah, but my dad gave me condoms and told me to protect myself. He'd still be pissed."

Silence stretched between us.

"Let's just assume you're not pregnant for now," Steve said finally. "See if you get your period next month."

I knew it was a dumb idea. I knew it was just avoidance. But I agreed anyway. Then he kissed me, his hands moving with a new kind of certainty one that came from knowing he didn't need protection.

Chapter Twenty-One
Buds of Secrets

Summer had wound down too quickly, and before I knew it, back-to-school shopping was here. My mom told my dad to take me to the mall to pick out a few outfits. We never spent time together, so the idea of shopping with him felt strange.

"You can pick out five or six outfits," he said as we walked in.

I headed straight for my favorite store, the Deb Shop. They always had the latest styles, and I knew I'd find something I liked. My dad gave me space, letting me browse and take my time, which I appreciated.

After walking around, trying things on, and narrowing down my choices, I started to feel hot, too hot. My skin was clammy, and a wave of dizziness crept in. I hadn't eaten all day, hoping to shed a few pounds before shopping, but now I regret it.

I handed my dad the clothes and asked him to check out while I sat down, explaining that I felt overheated. As I stepped out of the store toward the lobby, everything started to blur. My ears rang, my hands shook, and my vision darkened. I barely made it to a seat before everything went black.

I don't know how long I was out, but when I came to, a man was standing nearby. "Are you okay?" he asked.

I nodded weakly. "Yeah. My dad is coming."

When my dad arrived, his face tightened with concern as he saw me sitting on the dirty ground.

"Are you okay, Ellie?"

"I think I might have passed out," I admitted.

"That's not good. Maybe you need something to eat." He reached down to help me up. "Come on, let's grab something at the food court."

He guided me to a table, then went to get us lunch. As I ate, he watched me carefully. "Your color's coming back," he said.

I felt the shakiness fade, the heat slowly released. Relief settled in.

"Thanks, Dad. I feel better now."

"Good," he said, standing up. "Let's head home."

We didn't go home. Instead, my dad pulled into the emergency doctor's office.

"What are we doing here, Dad?"

"I need to get a refill on your mom's meds, and I figured the doctor could check you out too just to make sure you're okay."

Oh yeah, great. My heart pounded. The doctor was going to find out I was pregnant. Or maybe not. This wasn't a real doctor's office, at least, not in the traditional sense. It was the kind of place you went to when you didn't have a primary physician and just needed a quick check-up, a required work physical, or a drug test. My dad liked it for its late hours and because the doctor handed out refills even when the required days hadn't passed. My mom didn't even have to come in, so my dad could pick up her pills for her, no questions asked.

That was the arrangement. My dad, a cop, had found a doctor willing to bend the rules so my mom could keep overdosing on her sleep meds.

Would this doctor figure out I was pregnant? Absolutely not.

My dad explained to the doctor what had happened at the mall.

"Yeah, it's never happened before, but I hadn't eaten anything all day."

The doctor frowned slightly. "And why is that?"

I forced a shrug. "I just want to stay thin, ya know?"

"Teenagers," the doctor muttered, shaking his head. "You still need to eat, though. Just make good choices; fewer chips, more fruit. Does that make sense?"

I nodded quickly, eager to end the conversation. "Yes, of course, doctor."

His verdict was exactly what I had hoped for. "I think Ellie will be just fine. Just make sure she eats."

That was it. No further questions. No suspicion. I had escaped.

Relief surged through me as my dad picked up my mom's medication and we headed home. I could hardly believe I had gotten away with it. My hands were clammy, my heart still hammering in my chest. The weight of paranoia sat heavy in my stomach, but it was finally fading.

I hadn't been caught. I let out a slow breath, sinking into the passenger seat. I was safe. For now.

We arrived home, and my dad told my mom what had happened. She barely reacted; this was familiar territory for her. My mom had been on and off diets for as long as I could remember. She'd starve herself for weeks, then binge on her favorite foods, only to purge when she thought no one was looking.

Once, while grocery shopping, a stranger walked up to her, touched her stomach, and asked when she was due. I don't think I'd ever seen her more humiliated. She talked about it for weeks; her voice edged with quiet devastation. I watched as she slowly stopped eating, as weight-loss pills appeared in the medicine cabinet, as laxatives became her routine until they led to accidents she couldn't control.

I knew she could relate to what had happened to me at the mall. But even if she offered advice, it wouldn't be helpful.

"It's okay," I told her before she could say anything. "I know I need to eat. I was just in a hurry this morning and didn't think about it. I'll be fine, honestly."

She nodded absently, accepting my words without question.

I grabbed my shopping bags and carried them to my room, putting each item away. The mindless act felt grounding, pulling me back to something normal. But as I smoothed a shirt over the hanger, the weight of another thought settled in.

Another year of school. Tenth grade.

I failed math last year, and my parents didn't let me take summer school; we took too many trips to the mountains. So now I had to retake ninth-grade math, stuck in a class without any of my friends.
The only good thing? It happened during Steve's lunch.

I could just skip class and sit with him every day. I didn't need an excuse to miss math class, but this seemed like a pretty good one to me.

Chapter Twenty-Two
Buds of Growth

Mel and I were back on the bus together, but it didn't feel the same. We never hung out anymore. Everything had changed. She didn't know the secret I was carrying. The whole summer had passed, and I still hadn't gotten my period.

We barely spoke now. We had no shared friends, no common interests. The connection we once had built around Rob and Mike had faded. After Rob died, it was like everything else we shared died with him.

We still sat together, but it wasn't the same. Mel kept her headphones on, lost in her music, and I just stared out the window, watching the world blur past.

Clay sat with me at lunch, like always. He never failed to bring me a peanut chew, something I had been craving every day for reasons I couldn't quite explain. He never questioned it, never hesitated, just handed it over like it was nothing. But to me, it was everything. It was better than the school lunch I was finally able to buy.

I had never bought lunch as a kid. We couldn't afford it, but we made too much for a free lunch. My dad always said we were just a hair over the allowed income. So, from kindergarten through eighth grade, my mom packed the same thing every day a peanut butter sandwich and a thermos of water.

I grew to hate peanut butter. Some days, it was so thick that you could see my teeth marks in every bite. Other days, it barely coated the bread. The worst days were when she used an end piece or didn't wrap it properly, leaving one side rock hard. So, finally being able to buy lunch felt like being rich.

My dad's promotion to Corporal meant we had just enough room in the budget for it. Not for daily candy though, which made Clay's generosity even more meaningful.

Steve never had money, and if he did, he saved it for beer. But Clay? He never let me go without. I made sure he knew how much I appreciated it, saying thank you ten times over.

I still hated school with every ounce of my being, especially this year, because I didn't have lunch with Steve. Sitting with Clay was fine, but it wasn't the same. I barely saw Steve during the day.

He, on the other hand, was thriving. He had friends in his classes, hadn't failed any, and was still on the wrestling, track, and cross-country teams.

Sometimes, he'd tell me about the kids on his cross-country team. But instead of talking about how well they ran or where they placed, he'd mention what they wore, how they complimented his running, and how amazing his scores were. It felt like he was testing me; trying to make me jealous, waiting to see how I'd react.

And I did get jealous. I hated picturing him running alongside girls in tiny shorts, their legs moving in front of him for miles while I was struggling with my own body. My pants were getting tighter.

The other day, I couldn't even zip them. My fingers ached from trying, so I grabbed a wire coat hanger and used it to pull the zipper up. It worked. But barely.

It didn't take long before I started skipping classes again. Some days, I went to all three lunch periods instead of going to lessons. Other days, I showed up late or left early. I wanted something exciting to do. I wished I could drive somewhere, anywhere, but my only real goal was avoiding class. There were still kids who called me that awful nickname, like I was a joke they decided I'd never outgrow.

Some days, it felt easier to skip it all and just be with Steve. At least with him, I didn't have to pretend I was okay. School was overwhelming. The lessons blurred together, and no matter how hard I tried, I couldn't concentrate. I was failing almost everything, even gym, which sounded impossible, but I stopped changing for class.

I couldn't stand the thought of anyone seeing my body. I'd always been ashamed of it. Some girls walked through the locker room like they had nothing to hide, laughing, tossing their hair like they didn't care who watched them. But me? I just wanted to disappear. I didn't want anyone to see the parts of me I hated; the ones I couldn't figure out how to hide.

I could still convince Steve to skip sometimes. Sneaking into Steve's house that morning felt like a small adventure; a fleeting moment of excitement amid the weight of everything we were avoiding. I pressed myself into the closet, finding the perfect hiding spot behind the rafters, waiting for his dad to leave for work. Once we knew the house was ours, the day unfolded in a way I hadn't expected. Steve, always full of surprises, made an incredible breakfast, something I never thought he could do. My mom never let us use the stove, so watching him cook felt like witnessing a skill far beyond anything I knew.

We spent the morning playing Mario Kart, laughing, and even playing hide-and-seek, finding joy in the simplicity of being alone together. But what made that day unforgettable wasn't just the games or the quiet house, it was the conversation. For the first time, we allowed ourselves to talk about the possibility of a baby, something we had been avoiding. We shared name ideas if it were a boy; tradition would have us name him after his father. If it were a girl, we both loved Samantha and would call her Sammy. It felt good to acknowledge the reality ahead of us instead of pretending it wasn't there.

Steve had always loved babies. His family had plenty of experience, especially since his mom had just welcomed her eighth child. I had seen the way he cared for his baby sibling; gentle, patient, filled with warmth. I knew he would be a great father, even if I wasn't sure how to be a mother. My family dynamics were different. I had always been the youngest, and even though my mom babysat my nephew, I had never taken care of a baby before. I was relying on Steve to guide me, to show me the way.

We talked about our future that day; how if I were pregnant, we would keep the baby, and how abortion wasn't a possibility we could consider. And more than that, we decided we would get married. We would build a life together, raise our child, and become a family. Sitting there with him, talking about something so real and adult, felt more important than anything school could have taught me. At that moment, discussing our future felt like the only lesson that truly mattered. Eventually we decided to head to school; late, but early enough to avoid a call home. It was a small loophole; late still meant present and present meant no trouble. So, we started walking over.

We were nearly at school, just a block away, when I caught sight of a police car from the corner of my eye. Something in me hesitated, but I already knew. It was my dad. He saw me before I had the chance to duck; before I could slip away unnoticed. There was no time to hide. It was too late.

I froze. Steve saw him too. In an instant, my dad double-parked his patrol car right in front of us, got out, and walked toward me with a purpose that made my stomach drop. He didn't stop. Didn't hesitate. He raised his hand and slapped me across the face.

The shock hit me before the sting did. I had never been hit like that before, never by him. But I had seen him do it to my sister, so even as the moment stunned me, it wasn't entirely unexpected.

He demanded answers about why I wasn't in school, what I was doing, why I was running around with "riff raff." I scrambled for an explanation, crafting a lie that would make him believe I wasn't skipping; that I had only woken up late and asked Steve to walk me to school. I wanted him to feel guilty, to recognize that I was headed to class. But the lie wasn't for him, it was for me, to hold onto some semblance of control.

It didn't matter. He grabbed me by the scruff of my neck and shoved me toward the patrol car, leaving Steve standing there, stunned and silent. As I was being forced inside, a woman, just some stranger passing by paused long enough to ask if I was okay. I guess a cop smacking a teenager in the middle of the street wasn't something you saw every day.

My dad drove me home in silence, the weight of what had just happened pressing down on me. When we walked inside, my mom and grandmom were sitting on the couch, laughing as they played with my nephew. The warmth of their moment felt completely disconnected from the storm brewing inside me.

Without hesitation, my dad announced that he had found me skipping school. He made it clear that he wouldn't write me a note, meaning I'd have no excuse and would have to face whatever punishment the school decided. I already knew what that meant: In School Suspension. I had never been before, but I wasn't upset about it. If anything, it meant I wouldn't have to sit through classes, which felt like a relief.

Maybe I should've told the lady on the street I wasn't okay. But how do you start that kind of sentence with a stranger?

Steve just stood there, frozen. But then again, what could he really do? My dad was a grown man. A cop. That kind of power makes people look away, even the ones who care about you.

Still, I couldn't believe Steve saw him hit me. Right there, out in the open. And nobody did anything. Not even me.

But none of that mattered compared to the anger still burning inside me. My face stung where he had slapped me, and the humiliation of it lingered. I wanted to call child services to file a report, to make someone listen. But I knew better. My sister had tried before, and because he was a cop, nothing had come of it.

So, I just sat there, crying, feeling the injustice of it settle deep into my bones.

Chapter Twenty-Three

Buds of Resilience

My punishment was set for three days in In-School Suspension. That was the price for not bringing in a note after an absence. I wasn't sure what lesson I was supposed to take from it; how sitting in silence for hours was supposed to make me more likely to have a note next time. It felt less like discipline and more like senseless bureaucracy; an empty rule enforced simply for the sake of enforcing something.

In-School Suspension wasn't what I had imagined. The room looked more like a college lecture hall, with sloped rows of desks descending toward the front. A teacher sat at the head of the room, overseeing about ten students, each spaced far enough apart to prevent talking or passing notes.

I scanned the room, my eyes landing on a familiar face, Ed. I hadn't seen him since last year. He smiled, and I smiled back, a small moment of recognition in an otherwise bleak setting.

The realization struck me with unexpected weight; three whole days without seeing Steve. No glances across the lunchroom, no casual hallway conversations, no lingering moments by his locker. The absence felt tangible, as if the rhythm of my routine had been quietly disrupted.

We were given work, but most of us just sat there, staring at nothing. If you dozed off, you'd be woken up. The rules were simple, sit still, stay quiet, endure the hours. Lunch was dropped off, a quick twenty-minute break, and then back to silence. No snacks, no distractions.

The hours stretched endlessly, each minute dragging into the next. I wasn't sure if I preferred this over regular classes, but at least in class, I could sleep. This was something else entirely; a slow, suffocating kind of punishment. A living hell.

On the third day of In-School Suspension, I noticed a girl who had been there the entire time with me. She had jet-black hair and dramatic winged eyeliner; she looked like someone I'd probably get along with. I imagined she was a Metallica fan.

Curious, I decided to write her a note, asking what had landed her in ISS. I asked to go to the bathroom, and on my way out, I casually dropped the note onto her desk. When I returned, she had already written a reply and handed it off to me. I unfolded the paper and read her answer: she had been caught smoking in the bathroom.

That one exchange opened the door to an entire day of passing notes back and forth. We talked about music; it turns out, she did like Metallica, but her favorite band was KISS. She told me about her boyfriend; how he was older and had his own apartment. She was a grade ahead of me, but still technically a minor.

The day flew by in a way the others hadn't. I wish I had written to her on the first day. By the end, I had saved all our notes, including the one where we exchanged phone numbers.

When I got home, I told my dad about Michelle Florence, the new girl I'd met in detention, and how her dad was a cop. His face lit up at the name he recognized instantly.

"Oh, yeah. Good guy. We worked the beat together for years." There was admiration in his voice, but then a pause. "There were… rumors, though. About his wife. I never knew if they were true."

I nodded, letting that linger.

Still, my dad seemed eager for me to befriend her. "She's probably a good kid," he said. "Might be a better friend option than Jennifer."

I didn't mention that Michelle had been caught smoking, and he didn't ask why she'd been in ISS. It felt naïve to assume she was a "good kid" based on her father's reputation, considering where I met her. But I decided to take it as a win.

That night I called Michelle, and we talked for hours. She was different; more mature than I'd expected. She could already drive, had a lot of freedom, and her life seemed miles ahead of where I was.

Her boyfriend was twenty-one. That alone surprised me, but the real shock came when she told me why her parents had forbidden them from being together; it wasn't his age, but his race. So, she snuck around, determined to make it work; convinced that love mattered more than their approval.

As we talked, I learned more about her world. Her mother had been an alcoholic for years, drifting in and out of facilities. On one of those visits, Michelle had lost her virginity in her parents' car to a patient.

She was nothing like my other friends. She had lived on the edge, seen more, done more. There was confidence in the way she spoke, an unshaken certainty. I still had so much to learn, and I knew without her even saying it that she was about to teach me.

Michelle and I became fast friends. If Steve had plans, I was at her house. It became a routine place, her world, her stories. I loved her mom, even though she usually was passed out on the couch. There was something oddly comforting about her presence, even in her absence.

Steve, though, wasn't thrilled. He didn't like Michelle's boyfriend, especially because he was older and lived in an apartment with three other guys. He was convinced Michelle was trying to set me up with one of them. I would never cheat on Steve. But again, he was the jealous one, and I couldn't deny it felt good.

I still preferred being with Steve. Even with all his commitments, all the hours he gave to everything but me, I would've chosen his distracted presence over his absence every time. Still, I hated how often I found myself alone, quietly aching for him more than I cared to admit.

When he wasn't around, Clay would stop by. He'd made it clear he liked me, and that made things... complicated. I didn't feel as comfortable around him anymore, not like before, when we were just friends and that was enough. There was tension now, unspoken but heavy, and I wasn't sure how to move through it.

But then there was *her*. A new friend that brought a kind of light with her. Her home was dysfunctional in its own way, but it let me breathe.

It let me step outside my life for a little while and pretend things didn't weigh so much. Being with her felt like slipping into someone else's story for an afternoon; one without all the pressure, all the silence.

Chapter Twenty-Four

Buds of Truth

Jennifer told me she had an appointment at Planned Parenthood. "If you're on the pill, you have to get an exam every year to keep the prescription."

I hesitated before asking, "Do you think I could go with you?"

"To my appointment?" she asked.

"I mean… do you think I could get seen by the doctor?" My voice was quieter now. "I haven't been feeling great, and my clothes are getting tighter. I think I might finally need to see if I'm pregnant."

Jennifer nodded. "Yeah, let me ask my mom if she can take you too."

I exhaled, relieved. "Okay. Thanks."

A few minutes later, she came back with an answer. "She said yes."

The next day, I told Steve I was going and walked over to Jennifer's house. Her mom grilled me on the car ride about what I was going to do if I were pregnant. I told her I would get married and take care of it. She didn't look very convinced and told me to consider all my options.

We arrived at the office, and I filled out the paperwork. The first thing they asked me to do was pee in a cup. Jennifer had already gone back, and now I was just waiting; nervous, restless, trying not to overthink. I knew what they were looking for. A plus sign on the dipstick. A confirmation of what I already suspected.

Finally, the nurse called me back. She gestured for me to sit. I hesitated for a moment, eyeing the bed; it was only half a bed, with strange metal leg-like structures jutting out from the bottom, footrests attached. I had never seen one like it before.

I sat down.

"Well, you're pregnant," she said, matter-of-fact. "Now we need to determine how far along you are."

She started asking questions. When was my last period? Had I had morning sickness? Cramping? Spotting? Tenderness?

I didn't have any answers. Not really. I had spent weeks ignoring every signal my body had been sending me, pretending they weren't there. But now, there was no more pretending.

The smell of antiseptic clung to the air as I sat stiffly at the examination table, my hands gripping the edge like a lifeline. The nurse flipped through paperwork, her voice steady, clinical, as if she were asking about allergies or past surgeries.

"How many sexual partners have you had?"

The words hit me like a slap. My stomach twisted.

"And have you ever had any sexually transmitted diseases?"

Heat rushed to my face, my pulse hammering against my ribs. I had no idea how to answer. No one had ever asked me about these things before; not friends, not family, and not my mother. In our house, those conversations simply didn't happen. If you talked about it, it meant you were doing it. So, we never talked about it.

I swallowed hard, fumbling for words. The nurse waited; patient but expectant, unaware of the panic rising inside me. I answered her questions; my voice was steadier than I felt, willing myself to push through the discomfort. When she handed me a thin paper gown, I hesitated.

"I'll be back in a moment to do an internal exam," she said.

I nodded, unsure of what that even meant, but I didn't ask. Instead, I took the gown and waited, my pulse a steady drumbeat in the silence, the freezing air of the exam room settling around me.

"Hello Ellie, my name is Dr. Den, and I will conduct your examination today. I need you to please lie back on the examination table, which is upholstered in clean, crisp white paper, and scoot your bottom to the edge. Once you're comfortably positioned, please place your feet in the stirrups."

I followed her instructions, feeling a swirl of nerves and a flutter of anticipation in my stomach. "Ellie, are you still wearing your underwear?" she asked, her tone calm yet professional, making it clear she was there to help.

"Um, yes," I replied, with my voice slightly shaky.

"I need you to go ahead and take them off," she instructed gently. "Have you never done this before?"

I felt my cheeks flush with embarrassment. "No, I have not. This is my first time," I admitted, my heart racing.

"That's understandable. Just remove them and scoot to the edge of the table," she encouraged, her demeanor reassuring and compassionate.

Taking a deep breath, I followed her guidance, removing my underwear and shifting to the edge of the table, which felt cool against my skin. "Now, I need you to relax your knees and let your legs flop open," she continued, her voice steady and calming.

At that moment, I thought to myself, "Oh my God, I can't believe this is happening right now." She was positioned on a stool, and her focus was intense as her face settled directly between my legs. A bright spotlight illuminated the area, contrasting the bright whiteness of the exam room with shadows that danced in the corners. The warmth of the light contrasted sharply with the coolness of the air, heightening my awareness of just how exposed I felt.

"Okay, Ellie, you need to scoot down a bit more and try to relax. The more you relax, the easier this will be," she advised, her tone reassuring me that everything was normal and routine.

"Now I need to apply some cold gel," she said, squeezing a thick, translucent substance from a tube onto her gloved fingers. The gel felt icy against my warm skin, sending a shiver down me. She then picked up a metal tool that looked stark and foreign; something I couldn't fathom wanting inside my body.

With slow, deliberate movements, she gently inserted the tool into my vagina. The sudden cranking sound it produced filled me with dread, and I felt uncomfortable pressure. My mind raced, bound by anxiety and self-consciousness, and all I could think about was why I hadn't done something as simple as spraying perfume beforehand.

"Alright, Ellie, I am going to remove the clamps now and use my two fingers to check your ovaries and feel your stomach. Then you'll be done, okay?" she reassured me, her professional tone grounding me amidst my rising apprehension.

"Okay," I managed to say, my heart pounding in rhythm with my anxiety.

As she inserted two fingers, I gasped involuntarily, a wave of awkward discomfort washing over me. "You have had sex before, Ellie; I mean, you are pregnant," she noted, her observation ringing in the air, infusing the moment with an odd blend of professionalism and intimacy.

"Yes, but it's always been the really simple way. I have never had fingers inside before," I confessed, my feelings of exposure mixing with a sense of vulnerability.

"Do you use tampons?" she asked, her brow slightly furrowed in concern as she looked up at me, trying to gauge my comfort level.

"No," I replied softly, my voice barely above a whisper.

"Okay, well, I am all done. Please get dressed, and I will be right back to talk with you," she said, offering a small, reassuring smile that made me feel a bit more at ease.

A few moments later, she returned. Now that I was dressed, I felt steadier, more myself again.

She sat across from me, flipping through her notes. "So, based on the examination, we believe you're about twenty-three weeks pregnant."

Twenty-three weeks. The number hung in the air, unfamiliar yet massive. She met my eyes. "Do you know if you want to keep this baby? You have a small window if you'd like to consider an abortion. We can help you with that."

The words made my stomach twist. "No," I said quickly. "I don't want an abortion. My boyfriend and I are keeping it."

She studied me for a moment, then nodded just barely. "Are you sure? If you wait much longer, it will be too late, and you'll have to go through with the pregnancy. Adoption is always a choice, but right now, we can still schedule you for the procedure within a few days."

"No, I don't want an abortion." My voice came out steadier than I expected, but inside, everything twisted, tightening, unraveling, rebuilding around this decision. The air in the room felt heavy, thick with unspoken tension. My pulse thudded against my ribs, a restless rhythm, while a sharp chill prickled across my skin despite the warmth pressing in from outside.

I had seen the videos. The stark, sterile room, the mechanical hum of medical instruments, the clinical precision of movement. The thought alone made my stomach clench. I imagined the cold metal against bare skin, the invasive sensation of something foreign shifting within, and the unbearable emptiness that would follow. The images replayed in my mind, vivid and relentless, until I had to squeeze my eyes shut, as if that could erase them.

I really couldn't go through with it. The fear wrapped itself around my spine, not just because of the procedure but because of everything beyond it. Of what it would mean to undo what had already begun. Of the weight of carrying something forward when I wasn't sure I had the strength.

She sighed and slid a few pamphlets across the desk. "Take these with you. If you change your mind, they will explain the process. It's quite simple."

I hesitated but picked them up anyway. "Thanks."

As I stood, a thought surfaced, unexpected and urgent. "How pregnant is twenty-three weeks, anyway?"

She glanced at me. "That means you're just about six months along."

Six months. Almost there, almost real.

She gave me a polite, practiced smile. "Good luck, Ellie."

"Thanks," I murmured, gripping the pamphlets, unsure if I'd even read them.

As I walked back into the waiting room, I spotted Jennifer and her mom sitting near the entrance. The receptionist barely looked up as she gestured toward a canister on the counter. "Help yourself," she told Jennifer, her tone casual.

Then her eyes flicked to me. "Well, I guess it's a little too late for you."

A tight smile was the only response I could manage. Their words stung not just for their bluntness, but for the ignorance behind them. As if condoms were only about pregnancy. As if the risk of STDs didn't matter.

It wasn't just rude. It was naive. And worse it turned something heavy, something deeply personal, into a joke. Like my pain was a punchline they'd rehearsed before I even walked in the room.

I pushed the thought away as I slid into the car with Jennifer and her mom. The silence held for a few moments until I finally spoke. "I'm about six months pregnant."

Jennifer's mom nodded, reaching into her bag. She pulled out a small bottle and placed it in my hands. "Start taking this right away. Prenatal vitamins. I've had them for a while, but I don't need them anymore."

I turned the bottle over in my palm, studying the label. The gesture was unexpectedly kind, and I wasn't sure how to respond.

"Thanks," I said, my voice quieter than I intended.

She nodded again, like she understood something I didn't.

As soon as I got home, I grabbed my phone and called Steve.

"Can you come over?" I asked, my voice tight with everything I needed to say.

He didn't hesitate. When he arrived, I told him everything about the appointment, the shocking reality of how far along I was. He stared at me, wide-eyed, like the weight of it had just crashed over him.

"Six months?" he said, almost to himself. "I didn't think it had been that long."

I nodded. Somehow, the days had blurred together. It was easy to ignore the passing time when the truth felt too big to face. But now, it was unavoidable.

"We can't tell our parents yet," I said, my words firm.

Steve agreed without hesitation. "And abortion isn't an option."

That part was simple. We didn't even have to say it twice.

Now, all that was left was figuring out where to go from here.

I wasn't sure how much longer we could keep the secret. My clothes strained against me; jeans that refused to button, zippers barely holding together. Soon, there'd be no hiding it. Fatigue pressed down, making mornings harder, each step heavier. The weight of it all consumed my thoughts, leaving little room for anything else.

Chapter Twenty-Five

Buds of Frustration

Word spread fast. Jennifer already knew, but soon Clay, Mel, and a handful of others did too. Of course, Jennifer's mom knew. And after that, the whispers started; low murmurs trailing me through hallways, eyes darting toward my stomach.

I tried to hide it. Oversized flannel shirts swallowed me up, hanging loose over unbuttoned skinny jeans. But fatigue made everything more difficult; keeping up in class, following along, pretending like nothing had changed.

My mind raced through worst-case scenarios. Girls had given birth in bathroom stalls, in bedrooms with no help. Would that be me? Would Steve have to deliver the baby in our basement, our secret kept forever? Was that even possible?

Neither of us had jobs. He was still lost in sports and drinking, while I couldn't touch any of it, not anymore. I had started taking prenatal vitamins, but was it too late? Was the baby growing the way it should? Was I doing any of this right?

Some days, the weight of it all felt crushing, suffocating like I was drowning in bath water murky with mistakes I couldn't undo.

I was trying to keep up at school as best I could. Gym class had shifted into health class, which was a relief no running laps, no sit-ups, just lectures. That, at least, I could handle.

I walked in, taking in the plastic models perched on the teacher's desk; a uterus, a male figure. On the board, in bold, careless handwriting:

"How Babies Are Made." A blunt way to put it for a bunch of fifteen-year-olds, but maybe that was the point.

I sank into my chair as the teacher started taking attendance.

"Ellie Keen."

"Here," I muttered.

Then, an unsettling pause.

"Ellie, would you come here, please?"

I hesitated. "Uh... sure."

That was weird. Why did she want me up front? She watched me step forward, then spoke with a stiff, deliberate tone.

"I'm going to be teaching sex education today. From the looks of things, this will be pointless for you. I think you'd be better off in study hall."

The words hit me like a slap; sharp, deliberate. They were meant to humiliate. A murmur rippled through the classroom. Every head turned. Every pair of eyes locked onto me, scanning my stomach for proof. How did she even know? I swallowed hard. My feet moved; carrying me toward the door, while snickers bubbled up behind me.

I should have fought back. I should have said something. But all I could think about was disappearing, folding myself small enough to fit under a desk and never coming out again.

I didn't go to study hall. I walked straight out the door. Skipping school wasn't part of the plan. I had been trying, really trying, to show up every day; to blend in, to avoid drawing attention. That strategy had failed. And I certainly didn't want to risk my dad slapping me again, like before. I had nowhere to go. Home wasn't an option. So, I walked.

The cemetery felt familiar, grounding. Rob's grave now had a tombstone; his school photo etched into the smooth surface. They had planted bushes on either side; it looked peaceful and well cared for. I sat there for a while, staring, letting the chill settle into my overdressed layers, meant to disguise everything I didn't want seen.

Eventually, I wandered over to the old barn, the place where they stored the lawn equipment. As a kid, this had been home to stray cats and their endless litters of kittens. I had taken some home, more than once. Back then, I hadn't thought about what I was doing ripping them away from their mothers simply because I wanted them. Many had been wild, flea-ridden, and sick. Most hadn't made it. Blackie had, though. He had survived.

There were new kittens now, curled up in the barn, tiny and trusting. I stopped petting them, my hands moving gently this time. I knew better now. I finally understood how much mothers do to keep their babies safe. I stayed until the quiet felt like enough.

Before leaving, I grabbed a bouquet of discarded flowers, tossed aside after adorning a grave earlier. The petals were still bright, still worth something.

At home, my mom and grandma were deep in their usual routine. I stepped inside, holding out the flowers.

"Mom, I brought you these."

She blinked in surprise.

We have barely spoken lately, and certainly not like this. She hadn't expected anything from me.

"Thanks so much, Ellie," she said, taking them carefully. Then, after a pause, "We need to talk. This is perfect timing."

She glanced at my grandmother. "Would you give us a minute?"

My mom went to the doctor today. She hadn't been getting her period for a while and assumed it was just the change of life. But when she sat me down, there was something in her voice that made my stomach drop. Oh no. Is she dying? Cancer? Some horrible disease?

She exhaled, then said, "Ellie, you're never going to believe this, but... I'm pregnant."

"What?"

"Yeah, apparently, it's considered a geriatric pregnancy because I'm forty-two. I had absolutely no idea. Can you believe you're going to be a big sister?"

No. I couldn't.

She was beaming, absolutely glowing. She had always said she wanted a big family but had only been blessed with two kids—until now.

Me and my mom. Pregnant together. Our babies would be the same age. This was insane. I didn't know what to say, so I didn't say anything. Just walked away.

My grandmother returned, and the two of them immediately started fussing over baby stuff, completely wrapped up in the excitement.

Steve was already heading to my house and as usual, Clay was with him. They greeted my mom and grandmom before heading downstairs.

I told them the news that my mom was pregnant.

Steve laughed, finding it ridiculous. His youngest brother was only three months old, so he had a baby brother, and I'd have a sibling too; both of us navigating the chaos of being parents while welcoming new ones into our own families. It was wild. Unreal.

We settled into watching TV, and as expected, Steve took full advantage of our time under the blanket while Clay pretended not to notice.

Eventually, I got up to grab something to drink. That's when I heard it. My grandmother, talking to my mom.

"She shouldn't be allowed in that basement with two boys. She's probably sleeping with them both."

I froze. Did I hear that right? Normally, I stayed quiet. Normally, I let things go. But not this time.

"Grandmom, I am not sleeping with two boys. Steve is my boyfriend. I'm not a slut."

Her expression didn't change. "So, Ellie, are you sleeping with one of them, then?"

"Noooo. And it's none of your business anyway."

"I hear you down there, at all hours, laughing with those boys. If this was my house, I would never let you be down there alone with them."

"Well, it's not your house," I shot back. "And you don't get a say."

She narrowed her eyes, ready to argue.

"Ellie don't talk to your grandmother like that," my mom warned.

"Oh, but it's fine for her to call me a slut? To judge me like I'm doing something wrong just because I have friends who happen to be guys?"

Silence. That's what I thought. I turned on my heel, storming back downstairs, slamming the basement door behind me.

Laughter echoed through the basement as I recounted the confrontation. We joked at my grandmother's ridiculous assumption—sure, she was right about me sneaking around, but two guys? Did she think so little of me? The frustration simmered beneath the amusement.

Then—BANG!

All three of us jumped. We scrambled to the basement door, throwing it open to the backyard.

There she stood—my grandmother, her gun aimed at the sky, smoke curling from the barrel. She fired again, the sound tearing through the quiet evening.

"Don't you dare get my granddaughter pregnant!" she bellowed, her voice sharp enough to slice through our shock. "If you do, I'll take this gun and shoot your balls right off!"

Oh. My. God.

A blur of movement; my dad, already storming toward her, his face twisted in disbelief. "Mom, that's illegal! You can't just fire into the sky like that!"

"I want those boys to know I mean business." She squared her shoulders, completely unfazed.

Dad snatched the gun from her grip. "Get inside. Now."

We didn't argue. We rushed back into the house, our hearts still hammering, the weight of my grandmother's declaration settling in.

The three of us stood frozen, utterly stunned. I never imagined anything like this not from my grandmother. I didn't even know she owned a gun, let alone knew how to fire one.

Then again, maybe I shouldn't have been so surprised. She grew up on a farm in Virginia, where survival meant knowing how to handle things most people wouldn't dream of. She'd told me stories about chasing down chickens, chopping off their heads, and catching them mid-run because that was dinner for the night. About the countless farm cats, how, when a new litter was born, she'd shove them into a bag and toss them into the lake, watching as they sank.

Clay lifted his hands, mimicking a gun, and in his best Southern drawl, repeated, "I'm gonna shoot your balls off!" Each time, he exaggerated it further, adding dramatic pauses, widening his stance like some old Western gunslinger.

Steve was laughing so hard he was practically doubled over, clutching his sides, gasping for breath. I couldn't stop laughing either, especially remembering how my grandmother had warned me that she could hear us earlier. I could only hope she was listening now, catching every ridiculous second of this.

As much as my grandmother's stunt shocked me, what struck me harder was what she thought of me. The fact that she assumed I'd be with two guys was insulting. She had no reason to think so little of me.

At that moment, I decided I wasn't going to just let it slide. Not even for family. If she wanted to treat me that way, she could, but not without an apology. Until then, I wouldn't speak to her again. I refused to let her disrespect me, elderly or not.

Chapter Twenty-Six

Buds of Loss

Days passed, and I kept to my word. I said nothing to my grandmother. Every afternoon when I came home, she sat on the couch with my mom, just like always. And just like always, I pretended she wasn't there.

She wasn't just insulting, she was crazy. Who fires a gun into the sky just to scare off boys? I refused to let her intimidate me. But she wasn't done. Whenever she visited, she'd give nasty looks at me, Steve, and Clay, eyes full of judgment. I hated how she was always in the house; how her presence seeped into every corner, making it impossible to escape her sharp, silent scrutiny.

I was done with it. Done with her.

I woke up in the middle of the night; the familiar urge to pee pulling me from sleep. Lately, it has become a habit, multiple times a night, like clockwork. As I stepped into the hallway, I passed my parents' bedroom. Their door was always shut; their fan humming softly behind it. But tonight, the door stood wide open.

Something felt wrong. I peeked inside. The bed was empty. The blankets and sheets had been ripped away, tossed onto the floor in tangled heaps. I was about to turn away when I saw it.

Blood. A lot of it. My breath hitched. My stomach twisted. What happened?

I called out, "Mom? Dad?" My voice barely broke the silence. No answer. No way to reach them. All I could do was wait.

Three agonizing hours later, the front door finally creaked open. My parents stepped inside. My mom didn't say a word; she just walked straight to her bedroom, tears spilling down her face.

My dad turned to me, his voice hollow. "Your mom lost the baby, Ellie."

I gasped. Words failed me. I had to get ready for school. Dad said Mom needed time alone. He had to go to work. So, we just... resumed our routines. Left her there. Alone. In that room. With the bloody mess.

I was sad for my mom, but I hadn't even fully processed the fact that she had been pregnant. We'd only known for a week. It wasn't planned. It wasn't expected.

I thought she'd be okay. But she wasn't. She was different.

It was as if losing the baby had taken something from her, something she couldn't get back. She would sit in front of the TV, but her eyes weren't watching. They were lost somewhere else, deep in thoughts she never spoke aloud.

I heard her yelling at my father when she thought I wasn't around.

Even though she had only known for a week, she had already built a future in her mind, wondering if it would be a boy or a girl, imagining what music they might love, picturing herself as a mother in her forties. She had been excited. She had been dreaming.

Now, she barely spoke. When my grandmother visited, my mom would nod, hum the responses, pretend to listen but she wasn't there.

She was broken.

She had always taken sleeping pills, but now she slept even more. My dad told her she needed a hobby, that enough time had passed, and that it was time to move on. But she couldn't move on.

And all I could think about was how she had lost the baby she wanted so badly, while I was being given one, I still wasn't sure I wanted.

Chapter Twenty-Seven

Buds of Devastation

I hadn't been feeling well lately, but I kept it to myself. My mom was still drowning in grief, lost in her thoughts, and the last thing I wanted was to add to her pain.

But the ache in my back and side had been growing worse for days. It wasn't just discomfort, it was sharp, relentless, stealing my sleep and making every movement feel heavier.

I told myself it was just the weight of the baby; that my body was adjusting. That it was normal. But deep down, something felt off.

The moment I opened my eyes, I knew I wasn't going to school today. The pain was unbearable, radiating through my back and side like fire. Sitting at a desk all day? Impossible.

I curled up on the floor, trying to breathe through it. My dad walked into the kitchen to grab breakfast when he noticed me. "What's wrong?"

I barely lifted my head. "I can't go to school. My back hurts too much."

He nodded. "Alright, stay home."

Relief washed over me. At least I wouldn't have to force myself through the day. But as the hours passed, the pain only got worse; sharp and relentless, until tears streamed down my face.

Dad watched me struggle, his expression shifting. "I'm taking you to the doctor."

Panic gripped me. I couldn't go. If they ran tests, they might find out I was pregnant, and we still weren't ready to tell our parents. But the pain was unbearable. I wasn't sure how much longer I could take it. I weighed my options, and in the end, decided I had no choice.

The only thing that made it easier was knowing Dad would take me to his emergency doctor, the same one who hadn't figured out I was pregnant last time. Hopefully, he won't figure it out this time either. I agreed to go.

I called Steve to let him know I was going.

I pressed the phone tightly to my ear, forcing patience. "Steve, I must go to the doctor. I can't put this off anymore."

Silence stretched between us, thick with hesitation.

Ellie, the doctor is going to figure out you're pregnant. My parents can't know.

I exhaled sharply; the ache in my back worsening with each second wasted on this conversation. "No. Trust me. This doctor is naive. There's no way he's going to figure it out. I just need him to figure out what's wrong with me and stop this pain." The weight of it pulled at me, an invisible force pressing into my spine, my ribs; every inch of me exhausted.

"I don't think you should go. It's a bad idea."

I hung up. Just like that. Frustrated. Done. Was this really what mattered to him? His parents, their opinions, their judgment? How selfish could he be?

The resentment crept up slowly, like an infection. I was sick, and something was wrong. And yet, in his world, the biggest crisis was exposure. Not me. Never me.

We arrived at the doctor's office. It was quiet; too quiet. No other patients, no distant hum of conversation. He was probably closed for lunch, but since my dad was a regular, he agreed to see me.

Inside, the sterile scent of disinfectant clung to the air. My dad followed as the doctor led me into the examination room. The paper on the table crinkled beneath me as I sat down.

"I've had this sharp pain in my back and side for days now. It's only getting worse." My voice was steady, but the discomfort gnawed at me, relentless.

"Any other symptoms?"

"Not that I know of."

He took my temperature.

"101.6—You do have a fever." His brows pulled together as he checked my ears, my eyes, and my throat. Then, he nodded. "Can you lie down?"

I did. The pressure of his hands as he pressed on my stomach was calculated, searching.

"You might have a bladder infection. Have you been urinating more?"

I hesitated. "Um... yes."

"How about burning when you pee? Anything unusual?"

"Sometimes."

A pause. His eyes flicked up.

"When was the last time you had your period?"

I swallowed. "I don't know. I don't keep track."

He studied me for a beat. Then: "Is there any chance you're pregnant?"

Before I could answer, my dad spoke.

"No, doc. She's a virgin."

The words landed heavily. My breath caught. The doctor looked at me, expectant. His expression was unreadable.

I looked back but said nothing.

Another pause. Then, his professional demeanor returned.

"Okay. Please pee in this cup, and we'll see what's going on. We'll take care of it."

I nodded. "Okay... thanks."

The doctor returned, shutting the door behind him with quiet finality. His face was measured, professional, but something in his eyes held hesitation.

"Mr. Keen," he began, his tone careful, controlled. "I'm sorry to have to tell you this, but your daughter is pregnant."

Silence.

My father's expression barely flickered before twisting into a smirk one that didn't quite reach his eyes. "Really?" His voice was light, but the undertone was anything but. "I wonder how that could be."

Then, he turned to me. His gaze bore down, expectant. "Ellie. Can you explain how that could be?"

Every nerve in my body screamed at me to move, to shift, to do something other than just sit there frozen in the sterile air of the room. But I did nothing. I said nothing.

Finally, I managed to meet his stare and let out a quiet, "No. I'm not sure."

The doctor didn't linger on the exchange. Maybe he sensed the thick tension in the air, or maybe he was simply used to situations like this one; tangled in silent judgment and unspoken truths.

"You also have a severe kidney infection," he continued. "You'll need antibiotics and plenty of fluids to get any relief." He reached for a bottle, handing my dad the medication without ceremony. "Luckily, I have them here."

My father's grip tightened around the medicine, but his gaze remained fixed on the doctor.

"How far along is she, doc?"

The doctor hesitated. "I'd estimate around four months, but I can't say for certain. She really should see a maternity specialist."

Another beat of silence. Then my father nodded once; stiff, and curt. "Okay. Thanks, doc."

The doctor exhaled, as if releasing some unspoken weight. "Good luck to you both. Tell Mrs. Keen I said hello."

And just like that, the conversation ended, but the storm inside me had only just begun. The car ride was silent at first. My dad didn't say a word; his hands gripping the steering wheel, his focus straight ahead. He had mentioned earlier that he had errands to run. Maybe, despite everything, he was still planning to check them off like nothing had changed.

But something had changed. After a few minutes, his voice cut through the quiet; sharp, and unforgiving.

"Wow. I can't believe this, Ellie."

I braced myself.

"I thought you were gonna do so much better than this. I thought you learned a lesson from your sister. She was at least seventeen, at least she graduated. But you? You're just fifteen."

Each word landed like a blow, knocking the breath from my lungs.

"You just had to spread your legs for some guy, huh? Couldn't keep 'em shut?"

My stomach twisted, but I stared straight ahead. The trees blurred past the window, indifferent to my shame.

"This is going to break your mother's heart." His voice darkened. "We raised you better than this. You know you're not supposed to have sex before marriage. There is no way God will bless this baby."

I swallowed hard, my throat thick.

"Does Steve know?" His tone has changed sharper now, cutting through me like glass. "Of course, assuming it's his."

I turned to him, my voice tight. "It is his."

"Does he know?"

"Yes."

A beat of silence. Then: "How long have you known?"

"I... I don't know."

I could feel his disappointment like a weight pressing into me. It filled the space between us, suffocating.

"Well, you're not going to keep it."

My fingers curled into fists. My voice, small but steady.

"Yes, Dad. I am going to keep it."

I scoffed. "Steve and I are going to get married," I continued, my words coming faster now, desperate to hold ground. "We have it all figured out."

A humorless laugh escaped his lips.

"You do, huh?" His grip on the wheel tightened. "We'll see about that."

When we got back to the house, something was odd. My mom wasn't sitting in her usual spot on the couch. Instead, we heard movement, rummaging.

We followed the noise down the hallway. My heart started to beat faster. She was in my room, a trash bag half-full beside her, digging through the space beneath my bed. As soon as we walked in, she pulled out my Ouija board, her fingers curling around it like it had burned her.

"What is this, Ellie?" Her voice was sharp, shaking with something deeper. "Why do you have this? You know this is of the devil. I can't believe this is in our house."

I opened my mouth to say what, I wasn't sure, but it wasn't the time to argue. She shoved it into the trash bag, sealing it away like it would poison the air. Then my dad spoke, his words cutting through the room like glass.

"Your daughter is pregnant."

Mom froze. Her grip tightened around the trash bag as she turned to face me.

Her lips pulled into a tight grimace.

Pregnant?

She barely said the word, more of an acknowledgment than a question.

"I thought you said you were a virgin, Ellie."

The air turned thick, suffocating. I could feel my chest tightening, but I still couldn't speak.

"You were lying to me this entire time. I trusted you, letting you spend time alone in the basement with your friends. And you were just laughing at me for being so stupid, weren't you?"

Her voice cracked, but the anger buried beneath it didn't waver.

"But your grandmom knew, didn't she?" Her mouth twisted into something bitter, something unforgiving. "She wasn't stupid."

She let out a short, humorless laugh; one that didn't hold a trace of warmth.

"Well, you got one over on good old Mom, didn't you?"

Each word landed like a stone, pressing deeper into my skin.

"I was so stupid. You couldn't be trusted."

Silence stretched between us.

"Oh, and Steve; Steve would walk in here, all nice, and we would buy him pizza, treat him like family. And the entire time, he was lying behind our backs."

She exhaled sharply, her eyes narrowing.

"Get out of here."

The words hit harder than I thought they would.

"You disgust me. I can't even look at you right now."

My eyes burned as the tears came, hot and relentless.

I couldn't stop them; couldn't swallow the sob that forced its way past my throat.

But my mother felt nothing.

"Oh, poor Ellie is upset." Her voice dripped with mockery, twisting my pain into something laughable. She dragged her finger down her face, a fake tear, mimicking me. Mocking me.

The humiliation stung more than the words. I couldn't be here. I ran out of my room, down the hallway, but there was nowhere to go. No escape.

Now they know.

And I wasn't sure I would ever have told them if the doctor hadn't figured it out. I had convinced myself he was too stupid to notice; had clung to that false hope like a shield. But it is gone now.

I needed to call Steve. I had to warn him. I reached for the phone; fingers trembling, barely gripping the receiver.

My dad stepped into the room.

"No phone, Ellie." His voice was sharp, final. "Just stay right there for now."

The receiver slipped from my grasp.

Time blurred. Minutes, hours; I couldn't tell. The weight of everything sat heavy on my chest, pressing down, making it hard to think, hard to move.

Then my mother appeared from my room, three large trash bags in her grip. The plastic crinkled under her grasp, swollen with whatever she had decided to throw away.

I stared, waiting for an explanation. None came.

What was in there? Clothes? Books? Pieces of me she no longer wanted in this house. I had no idea. And I had no intention of asking.

She had been telling me for weeks to clean my room. I ignored her; stuffing more beneath the bed, cramming things into the closet, convincing myself that if I didn't deal with it, it wouldn't be a problem. I guess she had gotten sick of waiting. And now, those things, whatever they were, were gone.

The emptiness in my room stretched out before me, a stark contrast to the mess I had hidden for so long. Was she only throwing away the clutter? Or was it meant to be something more symbolic? A warning? A purge? I swallowed hard but said nothing. Because really, what was left to say? Time had lost meaning. Minutes. Hours. The weight of their words had settled into my skin, heavy and suffocating.

When my mom and dad spoke in hushed voices, I barely listened until my dad turned to me, his expression unreadable.

"We're going to take care of the mess you made."

The words were simple. Chilling. Take care of it? What did that mean? I wanted to ask. I didn't get the chance.

"Go into the bathroom," my dad ordered.

I hesitated. Something in his voice made the air feel colder. Slowly, I moved. My mom followed.

The bathroom felt too small with both of them inside. My heartbeat thumped in my ears.

"Get in the tub."

I stared at him.

"What? I'm not getting a bath." The tub was empty; no water, nothing.

His jaw tightened.

"Ellie." His voice sharpened. "Take your pants and underwear off. Sit in the tub. Now."

The sound of him screaming the words made my body lock up. My hands trembled. I couldn't move. I couldn't breathe. What was he going to do to me?

My mom stepped forward, yanking at my waistband.

"Stop!" My voice cracked, but my dad grabbed my wrists, holding me in place while my mom pulled my clothes off.

I was shaking.

"Get into the tub," he ordered. "Sit down. Now."

I climbed in; my movements were jerky and clumsy. I sat. The porcelain was cold against my skin. My breath came in shallow bursts. My mom perched on the edge of the tub, looming over me. My dad handed her something. I couldn't see it.

"What is that?" My voice was barely steady.

"It's a douche."

"For what?"

My dad's voice was eerily calm.

"It's not too late. We can try to wash it out of you."

Wash it out of me?

I felt sick.

"What are you talking about?"

He ignored me, turning to my mom. "Put it inside her," he instructed. "Squeeze hard. Empty the bottle. Hopefully, it gets rid of it."

It.

My stomach twisted violently. I recoiled, pressing my back against the tub.

"Ellie," my dad warned, his voice like steel. "Don't fight your mom. Let her do it. If you don't, you'll sit here until you do."

He paused.

"Or I'll come back and do it myself."

I couldn't believe what was happening.

Are they trying to kill my baby? Are they insane?

My mother's voice was steady, unnervingly calm.

"Okay, Ellie. Push the tip in."

She was still holding the bottle, the fluid inside waiting, like some terrible inevitability.

"No, Mom. I'm not doing that." My voice wavered. My hands trembled in my lap.

"You have to."

"No. I can't."

The words barely left me before the sobs took over hard, ugly, uncontrollable. My chest heaved as I gasped for breath, but nothing came easily. My nose ran, my throat tightened, and I shook so hard I thought I might break apart.

"Please," I begged. "Stop. You can't make me do this."

A shadow fell over the doorway. My dad.

I froze.

I knew what was in the next room. The nightstick. The unspoken threat. I knew he wouldn't stop.

Slowly, I moved my shaking hands. The tip slid inside, and my mother began to squeeze. The cold liquid rushed into me, invading my body.

I stopped. No more screaming. No more crying. Just silence. The bottle emptied, the fluid gone. My mother stood, turned, and walked out. I barely moved.

Standing felt like something I had to force, like gravity had doubled. The cold liquid dripped down my thigh as I climbed out of the tub, my legs weak beneath me. I grabbed my clothes, pulled them on with shaky hands, and walked down the hall.

My bedroom door shut behind me. It didn't look like my room anymore. Most of my things were gone. Was my baby gone too? Did it work? I didn't want to know.

My dad told us stories; scenes burned into his memory from 911 calls, where he walks into rooms just a moment too late. He describes the blood, the panic, the silence that follows a desperate attempt at an at-home abortion. One story keeps coming back: a babysitter he once hired for my brother tries it with a coat hanger, right there in front of him. He says it was considered "less abrasive." I don't even know what that's supposed to mean. Less brutal than what?

But what echoes louder is what just happened when I'm the one who's pregnant. My parents don't scream. They don't try to talk. They just act. They try another "less abrasive" method. On my baby. It's too late for it to work, thank God, but that doesn't matter. They're still trying to erase this part of me; like it's a stain they can scrub out before anyone notices. It's horrifying. It's shattering. And it makes me wonder what else they're willing to do in silence.

I crawled into bed, curled into myself, and let the tears fall silently. Sleep came like a slow pull into darkness.

Chapter Twenty-Eight

Buds of Hope

Morning came too fast. Too sharp. I barely registered the knock before my dad's voice cut through the door.

"You have an appointment at the gynecologist."

I blinked. My body felt heavy, like I hadn't slept at all.

"We need to get you checked out."

Checked out?

My breath hitched.

"Last night, you tried to—" My throat tightened before I could say it. "You tried to kill the baby. And now, now you want me to get checked out?"

His voice was calm. Too calm.

"Well, obviously, it didn't work," he said flatly. "I should have realized you're probably too far along for that to have worked anyway."

Too far along. Like he was discussing timing. Like it was just logistics.

"We need to find out exactly how far along you are."

He paused.

"Get ready. We'll head over."

I stared at the ceiling, unmoving. Like this was normal. Like this was just another appointment. Like last night hadn't happened at all.

The waiting room buzzed with quiet movements; the shuffle of papers, the murmur of voices, the soft rustle of magazines turning in practiced fingers.

I sat next to my mom, who flipped through glossy pages like none of this mattered. My dad was at the counter, signing forms, answering questions, handling things. Like this was routine. Like this was normal.

I looked around, taking in the other women scattered throughout the room. Some looked young but not as young as me, maybe in their early twenties. Others were my mom's age, settled into their chairs with practiced ease. A few had big, round stomachs; the kind that made their movements slower, more deliberate. And then there were others—women who looked fit, toned, like they had just stepped out of a workout.

Why were they here? I shifted in my seat. I didn't belong here. And yet, here I was.

They called my name.

I stood, my legs stiff, and followed without looking back.

The hallway smelled like antiseptic; clean in a way that felt too sharp, too sterile. They handed me a cup. "Pee."

I did because what else was I supposed to do?

They weighed me. Took my blood pressure. Led me down another hallway, into a room with a bed that looked eerily familiar like the ones at Planned Parenthood; like something designed for decisions heavier than I could hold.

"Change into a gown, front open," the nurse said. "Lie down."

I moved slowly, fabric cold against my skin as I pulled the gown over me. The paper crinkled beneath me as I lay back, staring at the ceiling. The door opened. A doctor stepped in, warm-eyed, reassuring.

"Hello, Ellie. I'm Dr. Albright, one of the delivery doctors here at the practice."

Delivery. Like this was happening. Like, there was no more pretending.

"I'm going to do an exam to see how far along you are and check that everything looks good," she continued. "We'll take some blood, run some labs—just to make sure everything is going well and that you and your baby are healthy."

Healthy. She said it like a good thing. Like something to protect. Like something my parents didn't want.

"Sounds good?"

I swallowed.

"Okay."

I tensed, every muscle locked tight, my body refusing to cooperate.

"Relax, Ellie," the doctor urged, her voice steady but firm. "You need to relax."

I tried. I really did. But it was impossible.

"I can't insert the speculum if you're this tense," she said, her hands gentle but insistent.

Relax?

How was I supposed to relax?

"You've had sex before," she continued, like that was supposed to help. "Just relax like you did then."

I almost laughed. She didn't realize that the only sex I'd ever had was missionary style under a blanket; barely moving, barely breathing. I held my breath through the rest of the exam, wanting it to end.

She rubbed gel onto my stomach; the sensation cool at first, then settled into something warm.

A soft, smooth glide as she moved the tool across my skin. Then, a sound. Strange. Hollow. Like an echo from somewhere deep inside me.

"This is your baby's heartbeat," she said.

Good. Strong. I listened. It sounded unlike anything I had ever heard—like a rhythm I wasn't sure I fully understood but somehow knew belonged to me.

My baby's heartbeat. It was amazing.

Then she brought up the screen and rubbed something else across my stomach.

"Can you see that little thing moving?" she asks, her voice light, like this is a moment I'll want to remember. "That's your baby.'"

"I'll print out a picture you can take home."

Steve isn't here with me. Just me in this dim room and a flicker of movement on a screen that no one else seems to look at long enough to understand.

Alone with this image, this grainy, fluttering life and the hollow space where his hand should be. Alone with the quiet knowledge that no one in this room, or outside it, truly sees what it means to me. What it costs.

Finally, she finished, pulling off her gloves.

"You look extremely young."

I hesitated. "I am. I'm only fifteen."

Her eyes flicked between me and my chart, as if double-checking the numbers. As if she didn't quite believe me.

"I think you might be my youngest patient ever," she murmured.

I didn't know how to respond.

She seemed unsure; like she wasn't sure if she should smile, offer reassurance, or say something else entirely.

"I feel, based on what I'm seeing and what you've told me, that you're most likely about thirty weeks, give or take."

Thirty weeks.

I barely registered the number before she continued.

"I'm giving you a due date of March 10th."

March 10th.

A real date. A tangible marker.

"You can get dressed now. When you go out to the lobby, be sure to have your dad schedule the rest of your appointments."

I stared at her.

"At this stage in your pregnancy, you'll need to have a glucose test and come in every two weeks."

Every two weeks.

"These next few weeks will go by pretty fast," she added.

Would they?

"Good luck to you."

I nodded, numb.

My dad held a paper in his hand, thick with appointments and tests; an entire schedule mapped out. It looked overwhelming. Too much. Too real.

"Do I have to go to all these things?"

He didn't look at me.

"Yup."

A pause.

"This is what you get for getting knocked up."

The words landed like stones, sharp and unforgiving. I stared at the paper, the list blurring in my vision. Each appointment, each test—an endless line of things I had to do. For this baby. For myself. For the future I wasn't sure I was ready for. I swallowed hard, but the weight of it didn't go away.

Chapter Twenty-Nine

Buds of Planning

The next morning, I went to school. Like nothing had happened. Pretending I was the same person I had been before. My parents sent me off without a word; without asking if my back felt better, if the medicine was working. Not that I had thought about it. Not after all that happened. After they tried to abort my baby.

I couldn't even speak the words. My Christian parents. My parents, who said they loved me. My mother, who had just lost a baby, who had wept over her miscarriage like the world had shattered. These were the people who were supposed to take care of me. To protect me. To love me. But they didn't. Not in the way love was supposed to feel. Not in a way that made me feel safe.

I ran through the halls, my breath coming fast, my heart hammering in my chest. By the time I reached Steve's locker, I could barely speak.

"Steve, you're never gonna believe what happened."

He turned to me; his expression was flat. "I already know."

I blinked. "What? What do you mean you already know?"

"Your dad called my house last night. Told my parents everything." His voice was tight, frustration simmering beneath it. "What happened at the doctor's?"

My stomach dropped. I hadn't expected that. Hadn't thought they would tell Steve's parents before I could even say the words myself.

"Wait. I had no idea." My voice was quieter now.

"Yeah, well. My parents are pissed." He slammed his locker shut, running a hand through his hair. "I told you the doctor was gonna figure it out. You should never have gone."

I stared at him. "This is all my fault?"

His eyes met mine, hard. "If you had listened to me, this wouldn't have happened."

The words stung, sharp and unforgiving.

Did he think we were going to hide this forever? That we'd just keep pretending and somehow no one would notice. Where exactly did he think we were going to stash a whole baby once it was born? Under a bed? In a drawer?

I look back and realize I have no idea what he's been thinking this entire time. Maybe he hasn't. Maybe that's the point.

I opened my mouth, but he kept going. "And now my parents are coming over tonight. Your dad said we need to figure out a plan. They agreed. I must be there."

The weight of it settled deeper. "Your parents are coming to my house?"

"Yes."

It wasn't a question.

"Well, it makes sense you'll be there, right?" I tried to keep my voice steady. "I mean, it's our baby."

Something flickered in his expression, something guarded.

"I wasn't ready for this, Ellie," he said quietly.

I searched his face for something; reassurance, certainty, anything.

"I thought we were in this together," I whispered.

Steve exhaled, looking away. "My dad couldn't even look at me. My mom cried."

I swallowed hard.

I don't think he ever planned on telling them, I thought.

I wanted to tell him. I had wanted him to know. They forced me into the tub. They tried to kill our baby. But all he cared about—all he ever cared about—was his parents knowing. His consequences. Not me. Not us. Not what I had been through.

I had wanted to tell him how I went to my first real appointment with a baby doctor. How I heard our baby's heartbeat and got a picture. How I got a due date—March 10th. How I had to go alone. How he wasn't there. How he missed out. But I knew. I knew he didn't care. And somehow, that hurt just as much as everything else.

I trudged through the school day, every hour dragging me with unbearable anticipation. I couldn't help but think about Steve and our future. Despite everything, I was in love. I believed we had a future together, and although the timing was off, it felt like this was what was destined to happen. Our love was real, and I held onto the hope that we could make it through this challenging time. My mind spun in circles, replaying everything, replaying Steve's words, replaying the unknown waiting for me at home. But it would be simple. They just didn't know it yet. We would tell them we were getting married. Of course, they'd realize that was the only choice. Of course, they'd support us. Right? Maybe after last night, that was wishful thinking. But what choice did they have? This was our baby.

The doorbell rang. My dad opened the door. They stepped inside. I felt a knot tighten in my stomach. The room was filled with uncomfortable tension, a palpable sense of unease that seemed to hang in the air.

Two couches facing each other across the room; a silent battlefield. My family took one. They took the other. The lines were drawn. I glanced at Steve hoping for some sign of reassurance, but his eyes were fixed on the floor.

My dad spoke first; his voice measured, as if trying to keep control of something that was already slipping away. "Well, I did some research, and there's a place in Florida that Ellie can go to. A Christian ministry that takes in pregnant girls. A good one, I might add. They'd care for her and the baby. She could finish the pregnancy there, away from prying eyes, and then after the baby is born, they'd find a family to adopt it. Then Ellie could come home like nothing ever happened."

Silence. Then Steve's mom stiffened her words were sharp. "Absolutely not. I'm not giving up my grandchild to strangers. Ellie must keep the baby."

My dad leaned forward slightly. "Well, are you planning to take the baby in? Let Steve raise it at your house?"

"I—" She hesitated. "No. We barely have enough room as it is. And Steve needs to stay in school. He'll have to get a job. We still expect him to keep up with sports so he can get a scholarship."

My dad's expression hardened. "I don't think these kids can raise a baby. Your boy didn't even have enough common sense to keep it in his pants."

She flinched. "Well, we're not throwing away our son's future."

Steve sat there, nervously rubbing his hands together, his eyes flicking toward me but never holding my gaze. Mostly, he just stared at the floor.

The adults talked, their voices rising and falling, passing decisions back and forth as if we weren't even in the room. Plans. Solutions. What was best? No one asked us anything. No one even seemed to notice us. I had had enough.

"We've decided we're getting married," I blurted.

Silence. Five heads snapped toward me.

"I heard you can get married at sixteen in Maryland," I pressed on, my voice stronger now. "I'll be sixteen in May. Steve will be right after the baby is born. We can get married, raise the baby. Steve will get a job, and I'll take care of it."

My mom leaned forward, her face unreadable. Then, unexpectedly, she spoke. "I have some extra money. I can buy both bus tickets. You can go down, get married. Maybe we can fix up the basement into a little apartment. I can help with the baby so you can finish school."

A breath of relief escaped me. "Yes. That would be perfect."

But Steve's mom wasn't having it. She stiffened. "Never. Steve is not getting married. He is going to finish high school. He is going to college."

Steve still sat there. Still said nothing. I wanted to scream, to make them understand that this wasn't just a problem to be solved, but a life that needed to be cherished and protected.

The conversation turned again; more back and forth, more talk about futures and responsibilities but not once did Steve speak. Not once did he push back, argue, or agree. He just... folded into himself. He was shrinking, vanishing right there on the couch.

The adults spoke louder now, more decisively, shutting us out completely.

"Be quiet," one of them said. "Let us figure this out. You two can't make wise choices."

I looked at Steve. I waited. But there was nothing left of him. I thought we were going to be in this together. I felt completely alone.

Finally, the decisions were made.

Steve would get a job when he could, balancing it with school and sports. Every paycheck would go toward the baby; his contribution to the life we were about to build. We would both stay in school and graduate as planned.

My mom agreed to watch the baby three days a week. His mom, the other two days at the daycare where she worked. After school and on weekends, the baby was mine to care for; Steve's too, when he wasn't working. Steve's mom insisted the daycare was no big deal; she already brought her youngest to work, so one more child wouldn't matter. My mom hated the idea, saying daycares were chaotic and impersonal. But Steve's mom was firm; this was how it would be. My mom didn't like it, but in the end, there was no choice.

"Oh, and Ellie I expect you'll breastfeed," Steve's mom said, as if it had already been decided. "I breastfed all my kids, and it's best for the baby. Plus, then we won't have to buy formula."

I felt my stomach twist. "No. I'm not doing that. That's gross."

Her eyes locked onto me, unreadable at first. Then slowly she turned to my mom, letting out a quiet sigh. "Yeah. They're too young to understand."

The baby would live with us. My dad would provide health insurance. It was the best plan, maybe the only plan. Giving up my child was never a choice, so I was grateful Steve's mom had spoken up against it. My mom wasn't happy, but it was the closest we'd come to something everyone could live with.

We said our goodbyes, and I exhaled, relief slipping in, if only a little. My dad barely looked at me when he mentioned it. Just a passing comment, as if it wasn't something that could change everything. A school for pregnant girls. A tour. I knew nothing about it. No details, no reasoning; just a statement dropped into the air and left there.

I could have asked. I could have pushed back. But the weight of the evening still hung over me, thick and heavy. So, I let it pass, swallowed the questions that rose to the surface, and said nothing. For now.

I called Steve almost at once, still caught in the whirlwind of everything that had just happened.

"I thought we were getting married," I said, the words tumbling out before I could stop them. "Why didn't you say anything? Why did you agree to college? How are you supposed to raise a baby if you're away? What just happened?"

A pause. Then his voice, quiet, tired. "Ellie, I'm sorry. I just couldn't stand up to them. You have no idea how it's been since they found out. Everyone at my house knows, and they're all on edge. I just must do what they say, you know?"

I swallowed. "I don't know how you're gonna do all of this; school, a job, sports, and still have time left to help me."

"Don't worry. It'll all work out. My mom's great with kids. She'll help. Just trust her."

I hesitated. "Yeah, I guess."

Then, because it was still gnawing at me, I added, "My dad mentioned a school for pregnant girls. He's taking me on a tour. I don't know if I want to go."

Steve sighed. "Maybe check it out. See what they have to offer."

Silence stretched between us. Then, almost as an afterthought...

"I love you."

"I love you, too."

Chapter Thirty

Blossoms of Progress

My dad walked into my room and stood in my doorway, staring at me. "Ellie, I know you may not like the idea, but I want you to consider it. At least go check it out." His voice was calm, but firm.

He sighed. "Your sister went there when she was pregnant, and it helped her get through it. I think you'll find it's a better place to be."

I stayed quiet.

"Let's go together," he added. "Just hear what they have to say." Reluctantly I agreed and we drove over together.

We stepped inside. The building felt like any other school brick exterior, rows of lockers lining the hallways, classrooms tucked behind thick wooden doors. But it had a weight to it; an oldness that lingered on the creaking floors and faded decor.

First, we went to the office to meet the principal.

"Welcome, Mr. Keen. And this must be Ellie." The principal's voice was warm, familiar. "Hello, nice to meet you."

Then, as if this place was already woven into my family's history, she asked, "How is Sarah doing since she graduated?"

"Oh, she's doing great," my dad answered.

"And her baby?"

"Yup, all is well."

The principal nodded, satisfied. "Nice to hear it."

Then she turned to me. "Let me tell you how the program works."

I folded my arms, listening.

"You would come here every day for school. The teacher in charge, Mrs. Blum, collects all your books, assignments, and work from your old school. You'll complete your coursework at your own pace in the mornings, then have lunch in class. In the afternoons, you'll have lessons on infant care, along with crafts, field trips, and other activities. The girls often share their concerns and talk about fears; Mrs. Blum becomes a close friend, a therapist. The students love her."

I nodded slowly, absorbing the structure, the purpose behind it. It wasn't just school, it was preparation. A place built for girls like me.

I glanced at my dad. He was watching me closely, waiting for a reaction. But I wasn't sure what to give him.

We walked down a long hallway, the silence stretching between us. A few students passed by; their footsteps echoing against the old, tiled floors, but the building felt strangely empty. It wasn't like any other school I'd been in no packed halls, no chatter, just a quiet weight pressing in.

"The students here have been expelled from their schools," the principal said as we walked. "Some for behavior, others for grades, and even criminal records. But we don't talk about that. This school is a second chance. We teach them trades, technical skills, things that will help them build lives beyond these walls. When they were told there was no way forward, we made one."

Then, almost as an afterthought, she added, "That's why we created this class for pregnant girls. A space that understands morning sickness, doctor's visits, even naps if needed."

We reached the room, and when we stepped inside, it wasn't just a classroom. It was a suite. A kitchen with a full refrigerator and stove. A sitting area with rocking chairs and a couch. Tables for studying. And tucked in the corner, almost like an afterthought, a small nursery.

"Mrs. Blum, this is Ellie," the principal said.

I turned and froze. I hadn't thought much about who would be teaching this class, but for some reason, I didn't expect her. Grey hair, soft wrinkles, the presence of someone who could easily be someone's grandmother.

She smiled warmly, introducing me to the girls. That's when I spotted Becky.

"Becky?" I blinked. "I didn't know you were pregnant."

"Yeah." She rubbed her belly. "I'm due in a couple of months."

"Wow. I had no idea."

Mrs. Blum gestured to the others. "The girls come from different school districts, different ages. This is Jessie, one of our youngest, she's thirteen. And Joann just turned eighteen. She's about to graduate."

I glanced around at them; each carrying a different story, different circumstances that had led them here.

"We go to the cafeteria together each day, but we eat back in the classroom," Mrs. Blum continued. "We keep to ourselves; give each other space. It's safer, more private. Most of the time, we stay in this room, unless we take a field trip."

I nodded, letting the information settle. This was something I had never imagined. But maybe that was the point.

"You'll learn so much in this program," Mrs. Blum said, her voice warm and steady. "We'll prepare you for delivery, for birth, and then for everything that comes next. You'll learn how to feed, bathe, and care for a baby. How to handle unexpected situations. How to be ready."

She paused, letting that settle.

"It's the best way to get educated before everything changes. And you won't be alone—you'll be surrounded by girls going through the same thing. No judgment. No stares."

Something about that felt heavier than I expected.

I glanced at her and then, almost hesitantly, told her about what had happened in health class. I had been sent to study hall. They had removed me instead of acknowledging me.

Her expression flickered annoyance, maybe frustration but then she just laughed, shaking her head. "See, that's why we have this program," she said. "That wouldn't happen to you here."

She leaned forward slightly, her eyes warm but expectant. "So, what do you think, Ellie? You can start next week."

I didn't want to say yes. I didn't want to leave normal school, to be separated, to be placed in a program for girls like me. I didn't want to walk a different path than Steve; to feel like I was hiding while he went on like nothing had changed.

Why wasn't there a program like this for teen fathers? Didn't they need to learn how to do all these things, too? Why were the girls the ones that were pulled aside, taught how to adjust, while the boys got to keep their lives intact? It didn't feel fair. Not at all.

But at the same time... this program sounded like it would help. There was so much I didn't know, so much I needed to learn. No matter how much I resisted, the truth wouldn't change, this wasn't just about me anymore. Maybe for the first time, I was putting my baby before myself. And this wouldn't be the last time I had to do that.

I exhaled. "Yes. I'll be here next week. Thanks for letting me join."

Mrs. Blum smiled. "We couldn't be more thrilled."

Switching schools felt like stepping into unfamiliar territory, where the routine of seeing Steve every day would suddenly vanish. And if he got a job, that gap would widen even further. Everything was changing, and I wasn't sure how to process it.

He would continue forward as if nothing had happened; free to flirt, to date, to move on. And the worst part? I might not even know. The thought unsettled me, making my stomach twist with discomfort. Not knowing where I stood, not knowing what came next; it all felt too uncertain.

When we stepped through the door at home, my mom and grandmom were in their usual places. The air shifted heavily at once, charged. My grandmom's eyes locked onto me, sweeping up and down before settling on my stomach. Then came the sharp, disapproving click of her tongue.

"I am so disgusted that you are even my granddaughter," she said, her voice dripping with venom. "If Pop-pop were here, he'd be sick just looking at you. You are an absolute disgrace to this family. When your baby is born, I don't even want to see it."

Steve came over after school, and I started leading him toward the basement. Before we could get there, my mom stopped us in our tracks.

"Ellie, Steve, I don't want the two of you down there anymore," she said, her tone firm. "Now that we know you've been having sex, we don't trust you to be alone."

"Mom, that's ridiculous," I shot back. "I'm already pregnant, nothing's going to happen. And the other day, you wanted us to get married! This makes no sense."

"I don't care, Ellie. This is how it is now."

With nowhere else to go, we sat in the kitchen, but the open floor plan made it impossible to escape my grandmother's relentless stare. She just kept gawking at us, making the whole situation even more uncomfortable.

"Can we go outside then, Mom?" I asked.

"Yeah, go ahead," she said.

We bundled up against the cold, the light dusting of snow crunching beneath our boots as we wandered. There was nowhere to go, nothing to do, just the quiet weight of winter pressing in all around us.

As we reached the back of the house, Steve's gaze landed on the two old junk cars my dad kept at the far end of the yard. They sat in the shadows, barely visible under the dim winter sky.

"Hey, are those cars open?" he asked.

"I don't know, but I doubt it," I said. "Let's go check."

We made our way down to them. The first one was locked up tight, but the second truck surprisingly opened.

"Let's climb inside," Steve said. "It won't be as cold."

We slid into the seats, but the chill still clung to the air. I could see my breath hanging in front of me. My stomach twisted when the console lights flickered on. I held my breath, hoping my mom wouldn't notice from the window. After a few tense moments, they finally faded, leaving us in the quiet, frozen dark.

It didn't take long before Steve was tugging at my waistband, his hands moving with familiar urgency. He didn't seem to care how much my stomach had grown, how different things were now. At this point, it felt like the only thing he cared about.

We were crammed into the front of a junky truck, the gear shift pressing against my side, barely enough space to breathe let alone maneuver in a way that made this even remotely comfortable. This wasn't my plan, but I needed to keep Steve happy. I needed him to stay. If I didn't, what would stop him from finding someone else? From leaving me and the baby behind?

Before long, this became our new routine, just like the basement had been before. Sometimes, after, we'd sit and talk about the future, about the baby. But deep down, I wondered if it weren't for this, would he even bother coming over at all?

One small relief was that Clay had stopped tagging along every day. For that, at least, I was grateful.

Chapter Thirty-One
Blossoms of Comfort

The past month was a whirlwind of catching up; test after test, appointment after appointment. I had to do a sugar test to check for gestational diabetes, along with extensive blood work. Thankfully, all my numbers looked good; confirming that I was officially in the final trimester.

One of the best moments was the ultrasound. Seeing the baby on the screen, all the tiny details were surreal. And then they told me I would be having a boy. At first, I wasn't sure if I wanted to know, but the anticipation was unbearable.

I had met several doctors by now, some I liked more than others, but since I didn't know who would be on duty when the time came, they wanted me to be familiar with all of them.

Starting at the new school was another adjustment. At first, my dad made me walk, which was miserable. Trekking through snow and ice in winter while pregnant was no joke. Eventually, he took pity on me and started driving me. Initially, I was mortified when he pulled up in his patrol car; uniform and all, at the so-called "bad kids" school. But after a while, I found it kind of funny and honestly, I was just relieved not to have to walk.

The program itself was interesting. Schoolwork was tough since no one was teaching, but I did my best. The other girls shared their plans; some were getting married, some had fathers who had already disappeared or denied responsibility, and one girl wasn't even sure who the father was.

The practical lessons fascinated me; learning how to swaddle a baby, give a bath, recognize jaundice, and even understand why certain formulas might cause vomiting. It was a lot to take in, but I absorbed every detail, preparing for what was ahead.

One day, we took a field trip to the local hospital, walking together through the cold. Inside, we toured the maternity ward, seeing the rooms where we'd soon be staying and the infant area where our babies would rest. One detail that stuck with us was the special meal for the new parents, something different from regular hospital food, a small celebration. It felt like a glimpse into the future.

We knew that when a girl didn't show up to class for a day or two, it likely meant she had given birth. Soon, Mrs. Blum would return with all the details, both the raw and the beautiful. A few weeks later, the new moms would come back; cradling their babies, sharing their experiences before saying goodbye. Once you gave birth, you were no longer in the program. It was a revolving door, pregnant girls entering, new mothers leaving. Soon, it will be my turn.

One unexpected outcome of the program was that I started sharing everything with my mom. The details, the lessons, the emotions, became something we could talk about, something that connected us in a way I hadn't expected.

Every afternoon, I'd come home from school and sit with my mom, eager to share everything I had learned that day; the things that excited me, the things that scared me. It was our time together; a ritual that made me feel heard. Even though I knew she was still upset about me having sex so young, I could also sense a shift as she was starting to imagine the baby in our lives, and at times, that excitement peeked through.

But there were days when my grandmother was there too, watching me with her silent disapproval. We didn't talk anymore. Whenever I spoke to my mom in her presence, she would get annoyed and leave. I overheard her telling my grandmother a few times to forgive me, to be kind, but my grandmother refused. Her harsh gaze, the cold distance stung. So, I learned to avoid her, to navigate my home in a way that felt less like stepping into judgment and more like carving out small spaces where I was still welcome.

When my mom and Steve's mom decided to host a baby shower at my house, I was floored. The idea of it seemed so out of place, so unexpected; but once I thought about it, I realized how practical it was. A way to gather everything we'd need without breaking the bank. Still, inviting my friends felt strange. A baby shower filled with teenage girls wasn't exactly the kind of event I'd ever pictured my mom throwing for me. Maybe a sweet sixteen, but certainly not this.

Several of my friends came though, including Jennifer and Mel, and even some of Steve's family. It was odd, but it worked. We ended up with so many essentials adorable outfits, stacks of diapers, wipes, blankets, bathing supplies, bottles. My favorite gift? A dark wooden cradle with teal bedding and soft bumpers. It felt real then, like I was truly stepping into this new chapter.

Some of my friends admitted their parents weren't thrilled about buying a baby gift for someone our age. Some weren't even allowed to come, like their parents thought pregnancy might be contagious. I tried not to take it personally, but deep down, I suspected it had less to do with the baby and more to do with how they saw me. As if my choices had somehow marked me as a bad influence. It wasn't easy to sit with that, but I focused on the ones who did show up; the ones who chose to stand by me despite everything.

After the baby shower, we moved everything into my bedroom, carefully arranging each item to make space for both the baby and me. The cradle found its place in the corner, and a small dresser was stocked with all the essentials diapers, wipes, blankets, bottles. Somehow, I managed to fit everything while keeping room for my things; and when it was all set up, it looked nice.

Steve helped me organize, and I was glad to have him there as I showed him all the gifts we had received. He seemed happy with everything, though the weight of responsibility still lingered. He hadn't found a job yet, and I wasn't sure how hard he was trying. The need for money was becoming more real, more urgent.

Through it all, I felt incredibly grateful for my parents' support. Without them, I honestly don't know what I would do. Their help was the foundation holding everything together, giving me the space to prepare for what was coming.

I'm surprised by how much has changed in our relationship. At first, they just wanted me to be gone; no baby, no mess, no reminder. Then came the pressure to give the baby away, like that would somehow erase everything.

But now... now they're here. Not perfectly. Not always gracefully. But they're trying. They're supporting me in only the way they know how, and even though it's messy and late and tangled in all the hurt that came before, it means something.

It means everything.

Chapter Thirty-Two
Blossoms of New Life

After my dad convinced me to apply for Women, Infants, and Children (WIC), I realized how much it could help with providing formula and certain foods each month; easing some of the financial strain on my parents. Steve's mom, however, refused to support it; holding firmly the belief that nursing was the only acceptable way. Maybe if I were older. Maybe if I felt more at home in my body or if I'd ever seen my mom breastfeed, seeing it modeled like something natural and okay, I'd feel different. But I didn't. And I don't.

The program itself was great, but it was income-based, and my dad made too much for me to qualify. He came up with a plan; claiming I paid rent for my room so that his income wouldn't count toward mine, technically putting me in financial need.

I was surprised my parents were comfortable with bending the rules like that, but I understood why as it was a way to make sure the baby had everything necessary without adding too much pressure on them. I went to the office to turn in the paperwork and sign forms. They needed to see me in person maybe to verify I existed, maybe just to take in the obvious reality of my pregnancy. At this point, there was no hiding it. With just a few weeks left, my belly had rounded so much that maternity clothes were the only option; most of which I had received at my baby shower.

Everywhere I went, I felt the weight of people's stares. The unspoken judgment. It made venturing beyond school and home an uncomfortable experience, but I pushed through it, knowing I had more important things to focus on.

As I sat in the office with my mom, an unexpected warmth spread between my legs, almost like I was peeing myself. A sudden gush. I knew from my class that your water could break before any contractions start, and if it did, getting to the hospital quickly was crucial. That protective fluid kept the baby safe, and walking around without it wasn't a clever idea.

"Mom, I'll be right back. I just need to pee."

She nodded, and I rushed to the bathroom. Sitting on the toilet, I noticed the pad I was wearing was soaked. The fluid was clear with no blood. A good sign. But it was still trickling into the toilet, confirming what I suspected. I had to go to the hospital.

I walked back to my mom, my heart racing. "We need to go. My water broke."

She glanced at me, unconvinced. "Ellie, I don't think your water broke. If it did, there'd be more like a puddle. I think you're fine."

Her words hung in the air, but deep down, I knew she wasn't right.

As we stepped outside to wait for my dad, the reality of what was happening started to sink in. The office staff wished me luck; their voices a mix of encouragement and understanding. When my dad pulled up, I wasted no time.

"I need to go to the hospital," I told him, my words firm despite the nerves tightening in my chest.

He frowned. "You're not due for two more weeks."

I knew that. I had counted every single day leading up to this moment. But none of that mattered now. The baby had decided it was time, whether we were ready or not.

At first, he hesitated, weighing the uncertainty, the surprise, the shift in plans. But as he looked at me, really looked at me, something in his face changed.

"Alright," he finally said. "Let's go."

And just like that, we were on our way.

When we arrived at the hospital, we explained everything, and the staff quickly set things in motion. The doctor needed to confirm that my water had broken and check if I was dilated at all. I remembered from my class that ten centimeters was the magic number for delivery, so this exam would decide where I stood.

The doctor arrived and examined me. "Yes, your water has broken," she confirmed, "but not completely. We'll need to release the rest of the fluid."

She inserted a long, hook-like instrument, and suddenly a warm gush spilled onto the bed. It was startling, but I knew this was part of the process. Then, she checked my dilation. Two centimeters. Not nearly enough.

"You're not in active labor yet," she said. "We'll need to induce you."

Thankfully, I learned about induction in class too. Pitocin, the medication they'd administer through an IV, would kickstart my contractions and get things moving. I took a deep breath, bracing myself for what was coming next.

The nurses quickly hooked me up to a baby monitor, securing it around my stomach, while an IV was set up to administer the medication. The plan had always been for my mom to stay with me through everything and for Steve to be there too. But since it was still early, around 9 AM, he was at school and completely unaware of the sudden change in plans.

Originally, my WIC appointment was supposed to be the first event of the day, followed by school. But now, everything had shifted. We needed Steve's parents to get him out of class and bring him to the hospital. This wasn't how I had imagined things unfolding, but there was no turning back now. The day had adopted a new meaning; one that would change everything.

The doctor on duty was one I had met twice before; one of the nicer ones, so I felt relieved knowing she would be taking care of me. Even after weeks of preparation, of hearing the same explanations again, I still had no real grasp of what was coming. You can be told what to expect a hundred times, but until you're living it, the reality is impossible to fully expect.

I wasn't ready. I was scared. Nervous. Apprehensive.

As my heart rate climbed, they gave me something to help me relax. They didn't want me stressing out the baby. I took a deep breath, trying to steady myself, knowing that no matter how unprepared I felt, this was happening. There was no turning back now.

About an hour later, Steve arrived; stepping into the room dressed in a hospital gown and one of those ridiculous hair nets that matched the ones my mom and I were wearing. He looked adorable, and for a moment, the sight of him eased some of my nerves. I was relieved he had made it, and he was here, ready to be part of this moment.

But as much as I loved Steve, I still wanted my mom by my side. No matter how grown-up this situation made me feel, I needed her. I needed the comfort only she could give.

As the relaxation medicine settled in, I started to drift off; my mind slipping into a hazy, dreamlike state. Without thinking, I raised my hand and asked if I could have the peanut butter.

The moment I realized what I had done, I snapped back to reality, my hand still hovering in the air. Steve and my mom stared at me, confusion flickering across their faces. Then, I burst into laughter.

"Sorry," I chuckled, shaking my head. "I thought I was at school, asking Mrs. Blum if I could go to the kitchen to make peanut butter crackers."

For a moment, I had completely forgotten where I was. And then just to make things worse I let out a tiny toot. Steve's face twisted as he fought to hold back his laughter, and my cheeks burned with embarrassment. In two years together, I had somehow managed to keep that part of myself hidden. But now? There was no hiding anything. I was officially bearing it all.

The contractions weren't what I expected. No dramatic screaming like in the movies; just a deep, aching pressure in my lower back, worse than the pain from my kidney infection. It came in waves, relentless but rhythmic. Pain, pain, pain, then relief. The doctor checked in on me regularly, measuring my dilation and asking how I was feeling.

At one point, she asked, "What was your favorite thing about being pregnant?"

I answered honestly: "Not getting my period." She laughed, then turned to my mom and said, "I can tell she's super young."

I guess most women have different answers; feeling their baby move, the excitement of becoming a mom, the so-called pregnancy glow, shopping for tiny outfits. But I had spent so much time trying to hide being pregnant that I missed most of those moments. Or maybe they just weren't meant for me. There were things we didn't do, things we avoided because of the shame hanging over everything.

So, I focused on the most tangible, immediate relief a fifteen-year-old could appreciate; no cramps, no bleeding for nine months. And I meant it.

I drifted in and out of sleep; the exhaustion pulling at me, but the waves of pain made rest impossible. The aching had transformed; no longer just a dull pressure but a fierce, constricting force wrapping around me from my back to my stomach, squeezing like a boa constrictor.

I focused on my breathing, trying to remember the techniques we had practiced. Inhale. Exhale. Stay steady. My mom sat beside me, feeding me ice chips; her presence a tether keeping me grounded. Steve, on the other hand, looked completely panicked; his wide eyes darting between me and the monitors as if wanting them to stop flashing numbers he didn't understand.

Then the anesthesiologist arrived. He barely paused before announcing the epidural. I learned in school about the risks of the procedure, but at this point, none of that mattered. I needed immediate relief.

Then, I saw the needle. It was enormous; the biggest I had ever seen. Fear gripped me. I had to stay completely still as they inserted it; but my body betrayed me, trembling under the weight of anticipation. My mom squeezed my hand, and I squeezed back, harder than I ever had before. I shut my eyes, held my breath, and prayed.

Then, just like that, the pain was gone. Not a slow fading, but an instant, almost unnatural disappearance. The pressure stayed, anchoring me in reality, but agony had vanished.

Relief. Finally.

The doctor did one last check, then looked up. "It's time."

I wasn't ready. I couldn't be ready. The words sent a shock through me, and suddenly, the weight of everything crashed down. I can't do this. I can't be a mom. I'm too afraid.

My mom squeezed my hand. "Trust me honey, you can do this. We're going to do it together. All of us."

I swallowed hard, trying to steady my breath. The doctor tilted her head. "Would you like a mirror placed overhead so you can watch?"

"No." The answer came fast, sharp. The thought of seeing my body torn open, of seeing something so raw and irreversible was too much. "Definitely no mirror."

I couldn't believe I was about to let Steve see me like this. He positioned himself at the foot of the bed, where he had the best view. My mom stayed near my head, her fingers brushing my hair back, her eyes filled with worry.

Then, without hesitation, the doctor said it again.

"It's time."

I leaned forward, bracing myself, and started to push. I bore down with everything I had, but the numbness from the epidural made it feel like I was disconnected from my own body. Was I even doing it right? I couldn't tell.

Then a new fear crept in; what if I pooped the bed? I had heard the stories, the warnings, the jokes that weren't jokes. And Steve—he was right there. Watching. The thought of him seeing something like that made my stomach twist.

"Okay, keep pushing," the doctor urged.

I shook my head, tears spilling over. "I can't." My voice cracked. I looked her straight in the eyes, desperate for her to understand. "I can't push anymore. I can't push any harder. I can't do it."

She didn't hesitate. "Try, Ellie. Just one more. One final push."

I gritted my teeth, grabbed the sides of the bed, and summoned everything I had left. My body trembled with the effort, every muscle straining. Then, sudden relief.

A baby. A boy, just like they said.

The doctor turned to Steve, offering him the scissors. He hesitated for only a second before cutting the cord. Then they whisked him away, moving with practiced efficiency. I watched as they cleaned him, checked him over, and did all the things Mrs. Blum had talked about—eye drops, a hearing test, identification, umbilical cord care.

It felt like forever.

Finally, they brought him to me, wrapped snugly in a soft blanket; a tiny, knitted cap perched on his head. He was here.

The first thing my mom did when I was born was count my fingers and toes, so that's what I decided to do too. Ten tiny fingers. Ten tiny toes. All there.

He had light blue eyes just like Steve and wisps of light blonde hair. I was relieved he wasn't bald like most newborns. But what struck me most wasn't his features, it was his size. He was so incredibly small. I wasn't ready for how tiny he was.

I cradled him carefully; afraid I might hold him too tight or somehow hurt him. My hands felt clumsy, uncertain. I passed him to Steve. He held him with ease, with confidence; like he had done this before. It was obvious; he was used to holding babies.

The doctor walked in with a stack of papers in hand. She placed them in front of us; forms to review, signatures to make official. Then she handed us the birth certificate.

Steven Scott. Born March 6, 1990, at 1:19 PM. 7 pounds, 3 ounces. 19 inches long. Mother: Ellie Keen. Father: Steven Law.

We had always known his name. There was never a question he would be named after his dad. But seeing it written, printed in ink, made it real.

The doctor continued; going over the vitals, explaining the routine checks. But my focus had narrowed. My son's name was on paper. His existence was official.

The next day, Steve and I sat down for the hospital's celebration dinner for two. It was strangely nice but also deeply unsettling. I could understand why parents who had spent nine months preparing for their baby would need this moment; a quiet pause before stepping into their new life. But for us? We were just kids. And while we technically had something to celebrate, nothing about this journey had felt celebratory. Sitting there, pretending this was some kind of milestone, I felt almost hypocritical. Still, we decided to take it for what it was. A meal. A moment. Maybe even the closest thing to a real date we had ever shared.

The next few hours blurred together in a whirlwind. Steve's parents came to see the baby, followed by my dad and sister. My mom finally went home to get some much-needed rest, and Steve had to return to school.

The nurses walked me through the basics of how to bathe him, how to care for his umbilical cord, and fresh circumcision. I nodded, listened, and tried to absorb it all. Then, it was time to go home.

Fear gripped me. Despite everything I had read, everything I had been shown, I felt completely incapable. How was I supposed to take care of this tiny, fragile human? He would need me for everything. Every cry, every whimper. How would I know what he needed? Was he cold? Hot? Hungry? Full? What if I couldn't burp him? What if he stopped breathing?

Panic swelled inside me, tightening my chest. I wasn't sure how I was going to do this.

I felt helpless.

Chapter Thirty-Three
Blossoms of Home

My dad opened the door for me since my hands were full. Inside, my mom sat on the couch with my grandmother. I set Steven down in his carrier, moving carefully, still sore from the stitches.

Then, my grandmother saw him for the first time. Her gaze was the same as it had been for months; cold, sharp, filled with resentment. She didn't soften, didn't smile. Just stared.

I swallowed hard. "You know, Grandmom, he's just an innocent baby. He didn't ask for this. It would be nice if you didn't look at him like you hated him."

She didn't respond. Didn't blink. Just kept staring.

I felt the weight of it pressing down, suffocating. Without another word, I scooped Steven up and walked to my room, shutting the door behind us.

It was hard to fathom how a woman who claimed to live by faith, who attended church every Sunday and sang in the choir, could be so cruel. Her disdain was sharp, cutting through the air like an unspoken curse. It wasn't just toward me; it extended to my son, an innocent baby, as though he carried some invisible stain that she refused to overlook.

What stung more was that my mom let her into our home, knowing full well the way she saw us. The judgment lingered, thick and suffocating, turning our own space into something unrecognizable. Whenever she was near, it felt like our very presence was unwelcome, as if we were intruders in our own home. She treated Steve the same way; her eyes narrowing whenever he stepped through the door. The weight of it pressed down on both of us, making even the simplest moments feel like walking through a battlefield of quiet rejection.

I had learned so much in the school program, but now I would have to apply all the swaddling techniques, the feeding schedules, the little tricks to soothe a crying baby. The realization hit me with a quiet weight: I was about to do this, to step fully into motherhood.

I was grateful for the six weeks' maternity leave from school. It gave me time to settle in; to figure out the rhythm of caring for my son, to build some kind of routine. But the relief was overshadowed by the nagging frustration that Steve still had to go to school every day. His visits would be short, just evenings and weekends and for now; most of the responsibility would fall on me.

And when he finally got a job, it would only get harder. Less time, more distance, more moments spent navigating this new reality on my own. The weight of that truth pressed in, but I had no choice except to adapt and to keep moving forward, even when it felt overwhelming.

The first few days blurred together; a rush of voices, hands reaching, hushed admiration. People kept stopping by, eager to see the baby. Steve's parents visited more than once; passing him back and forth, marveling at how much he resembled Steve or his siblings. Never me. Aunts, uncles, brothers and sisters filtered in and out; their presence turning the house into something almost unfamiliar. It felt like I had bought something brand new; something everyone wanted to inspect, to touch, to admire.

My sister came, and even a few friends I hadn't expected. But with them, it was different. They didn't reach for him, didn't press their fingers against his tiny hands or cradle him close. To them, he was like a delicate artifact; something meant to be seen from a distance, admired but untouched. I couldn't blame them. They were curious, maybe even trying to be supportive, but there was no denying how out of place they felt; like visitors in a world they had never stepped into before. After all, none of their bedrooms had a cradle in the corner.

I had so many cute little outfits for him; tiny onesies with playful patterns and soft pajamas that felt like clouds, but none of them stood a chance against the inevitable blowouts. It was almost comical how quickly they met disaster. I'd heard about blowouts before but experiencing them firsthand was a different thing entirely. Diaper changes were still a learning curve, and more than once my fumbling hands had cost another outfit its life.

Most of my days blurred together in the quiet of my room. It was safer there; away from my grandma's sharp gaze, where I could figure things out on my terms. I wanted to do as much as possible myself, knowing that once school started back soon, a lot of this responsibility would shift to my mom. She already had her hands full with my nephew; he was growing up, which helped, but he still had his moments.

For now though, I have time. Time to learn, to adjust, to carve out my rhythm before everything changes again.

When we left the hospital, my dad surprised me by letting me buy a photo package of the baby. I hadn't expected it, especially since before, he had been distant; almost like a shadow that barely touched this new reality. But now, here we were, picking out prints as if everything had shifted.

I chose a package that included a poster-sized photo, imagining it alongside all the posters already lining my bedroom walls. It felt fitting; like the biggest change in my life deserved to take up space.

I gave pictures to a lot of family. He was a beautiful baby; delicate skin and crystal-blue eyes that stood in contrast to the green ones my family all shared. But those eyes weren't unfamiliar. They were Steve's; the same shade that ran through his whole family. His hair, a light brownish blonde, was a perfect mix of both of ours. I had been coloring mine blonde since I was twelve; first with Sun-In and then eventually dyeing, but in the end, it matched my natural color.

The funniest part was his hair itself. Long for a newborn, it spiked in the middle like it had a personality of its own. Even in the photo, it stuck up just enough to make him look playful, lively. It was impossibly cute.

I learned how to make his formula; grateful that WIC had approved it for me. Each measured scoop, each careful swirl in the bottle felt like a small victory; another piece of knowledge clicking into place.

His pacifier became a lifesaver; his tiny fingers curling around it, the quick sigh of relief when it settled in his mouth. It was amazing how something so simple could calm him when nothing else worked. Slowly, I was piecing together all his little habits, the unique traits that made him who he was.

Even changing diapers had started to feel easier, more natural. The initial fear of being too delicate, too unsure, had faded. My hands moved with more confidence; no longer hesitating at every shift, every fastening.

And maybe just maybe-I was beginning to get the hang of this. Even if only a little.

Chapter Thirty-Four

Blossoms of Responsibility

Steven's first well visit felt like stepping into unfamiliar territory. My parents had chosen a doctor based on what the insurance covered; a practical decision, nothing more. Usually, mothers swap pediatrician recommendations; discussing bedside manners and philosophies, but I had no reference point. We were walking in the dark.

I wasn't even sure what the appointment was for. "Well Check" means not sick, right? I only went to the doctor when I was sick. Still, my dad drove and my mom joined; their presence steady even if unspoken.

The visit itself was smooth. Steven was weighed, measured, and checked over. They asked all the expected questions: how much he ate, how he slept, whether he was a happy baby or fussy. That last question stuck with me. How would I know if he was happy? I guessed he was. But could he be, knowing his mom was still just a kid herself and his dad had to miss the appointment because school still demanded his time? Or what about the fact that his world, at least for now, was a teenage girl's bedroom, falling asleep each night beneath the unwavering gaze of Ozzy Osbourne? If he had a choice, would he want that?

The doctor seemed sure Steven was happy and healthy but recommended switching his formula to help with the spit-up and improve his weight gain. My mom and dad told me I was doing a decent job, and for a moment, that assurance settled over me like a quiet relief.

After picking up the new formula, we stopped at school. I wanted Mrs. Blum to see my baby, and I wanted to step into a place where I knew I would fit in. The waiting room had been its own world, filled with seasoned mothers who had glanced at me like I was lost. I guess I looked more like a sister than a mom.

Mrs. Blum greeted me with a hug; not just asking about my baby but about me how I was feeling, what labor had been like. She saw me, not just the baby. That meant something.

Most of the girls I had known were gone, already past this phase and off navigating motherhood elsewhere. One friend had given birth to a sick baby and was still in the hospital, still fighting for his life. The weight of that sat heavy. I couldn't imagine what she was going through.

The newer girls, the ones still waiting for their turn, asked questions I had expected. Was the hospital meal special? Did the epidural numb all the pain? They didn't know me, not really, so their curiosity was polite but distant.

Mrs. Blum took Steven in her arms, her face lighting up. And then, something small but important she said he looked like me. No one had said that before. I appreciated her for it.

Returning home and stepping through the door, I let out a quiet breath; our first outing was behind us, and it had gone smoothly. The nerves that had clung to me all day finally loosened, at least a little. I had worried about the germs, the invisible threats lingering on every surface; but more than that, I had dreaded the stares. The ones that weren't just curious but weighed something heavier, something that felt like judgment.

Fortunately, Steven had received his first set of vaccinations; a small shield against the unseen dangers. That brought some relief, knowing he was protected in a way I couldn't always control. Still, he was so small, and the world was so impossibly vast, filled with things I wasn't ready to face. Not yet.

But I wasn't even allowed to avoid some battles. The cruelty wasn't just outside; it sat within the walls of home, lingering in glances, unspoken words, the way certain people saw me, saw him. That part I still had to live with.

Steve was on his way over and I was eager to tell him all about the appointment, but before that, I decided to call Jennifer. The last time we talked was right after the baby shower. It felt strange that she hadn't reached out in so long; maybe she was just waiting for me to call first.

Her phone rang, and her mom answered.

"Hi, it's me, Ellie. Is Jennifer home?"

"Oh, Ellie... I'm sorry, she's not here."

That wasn't the answer I expected. "Oh... Do you know when she'll be back? I haven't talked to her in forever and just wanted to see how she's doing."

A pause. Then, a careful answer. "Sorry, Ellie, but I'm not sure when she'll be back."

Something in her tone made my stomach tighten. "Well... could you ask her to call me when she gets a chance?"

Another pause, heavier this time. "Ellie... we've been having some problems, and things got bad here. I had to send Jennifer away for a while to a girls' group home. It's about an hour away. I can visit her on weekends, but they said we need some time apart first."

The words sank in like a slow weight. "Oh... I'm sorry. Can I have her number? Or an address so I can reach her?"

"No, Ellie... I'm sorry, but she needs to work through some things and can't be contacted right now. Maybe later, if she's doing better. But not now."

I swallowed, unsure how to respond to that. Instead, her voice shifted, softer. "Did you have the baby?"

"Oh yeah, I did. His name is Steven, and he's adorable. Thanks again for all your help."

"Take care of yourself, Ellie."

"Thanks. I will. And please tell Jennifer I called."

I kept wondering what had happened. What could Jennifer have possibly done that made it impossible for her to stay? I knew she felt like her mom's new boyfriend didn't want her around. Maybe that was all it took. Maybe he had decided, and that was enough.

I didn't know then that the baby shower would be the last time I'd ever see her. Her mom moved, and just like that, she was gone with no phone call, no letter, no chance to say goodbye. Some friendships end like that; slipping through your fingers before you even realize you were supposed to hold on tighter.

I would have liked to have said goodbye. I would have liked to have told her how much she meant to me; that no matter where she ended up, I'd never forget her. And I never will.

I'll always remember that first day, watching her come up over the hill, dressed for battle, ready to put me in my place but somehow walking away my best friend instead.

Steve arrived and went straight to the crib, picking up Steven with effortless care. He had been sound asleep, but Steve knew exactly how to cradle him, how to move in a way that wouldn't startle him. Watching him like that; so natural and gentle, it was hard not to think that maybe, in some way, he was born to do this.

He handled diaper changes too; even remembering to cover up, so he wouldn't get splashed in the face with pee. He was excited to hear about the doctor's visit; grimacing when I mentioned the shots, wincing as if he could feel the sting himself.

Then the conversation shifted; he told me about school, about how people had been asking about me. Some knew I was pregnant, some knew I had switched schools, some knew I was now a mom. Steve said he had been catching people up, filling in the gaps of my absence.

One girl had asked if he was still dating me or if he was available. The words made something tighten, coiling in my chest. He was a father; why would someone even ask that? Wouldn't they want someone else; someone without responsibility, without the weight of a baby in the background? It seemed ridiculous to me, like when I had found out Ed was a dad, I hadn't wanted to be with him. Who wants to take on that kind of baggage at our age?

I couldn't help but wonder if Steve had encouraged this kind of talk? Did he just let the conversation drift that way? Or worse, did he make it up to get a reaction out of me? Either way, it was working. I felt irritated, restless; the warmth of earlier moments fading fast.

I asked him if he had gotten a job yet and told him maybe he should focus on that instead of wasting time entertaining girls who had no business asking about his relationship status.

His expression shifted. Anger flickered in his eyes, and then, just like that, he stormed out. He hadn't even been here for thirty minutes.

I stood there, frustration crackling beneath my skin; the silence in the house swallowing the moment whole. It felt like an excuse, like a way out. Like he had been looking for any reason to leave before the real weight of responsibility settled in. And just like the night before, I was alone again. I hadn't pictured this.

I had always imagined us as a little family; together, happy, figuring things out as we went. We had made a mistake; but if we were married, if we had a real home, then it wouldn't feel like a mistake. It would just be an early start.

I saw myself as a stay-at-home mom, just like mine had been. Steve would find a job doing something steady, something he was good at. His masonry training in tech school seemed perfect; a career that could support us, give us a foundation to build on. But this wasn't the plan.

I wasn't supposed to be here, stuck in my room all day, while he carried on with his normal teenage life. I am different now. My stomach bore the proof; bright pink stretch marks stretching across skin that used to be smooth. My breasts ached; veins rising beneath the surface like roadmaps of something I didn't fully recognize. My hair, once something I fussed over every morning, was limp and unwashed because I no longer had time to style it.

Sweatpants were my uniform because my jeans didn't fit anymore. I felt ugly. I felt heavy. I felt like something had shifted inside me that I couldn't quite fix. Maybe I had convinced myself we were building a life that was never within reach. Or maybe I had been blind to reality; too wrapped up in the idea of us to see what was happening all along. Or maybe, just maybe this was the depression they had warned me about; the kind that creeps in after birth, making everything feel hollow.

I just needed Steve to be here with me right now. But he wasn't.

The phone rang, pulling me from the quiet routine of the day.

"Ellie, phone."

I picked it up.

"Hey Ellie, it's Michelle. What are you doing?"

"Just taking care of Steven. Steve was here, but we got into a fight."

"Well... do you wanna hang out?"

I hesitated. "I would, but I don't know if I can. Let me ask."

I turned toward my mom. "Mom, can I go to Michelle's for a little bit?"

"No. You have to take care of Steven."

Her answer was firm, but before I could respond, my dad chimed in.

"Why don't you let her go? She hasn't been out at all since Steven was born. She could use a break."

A pause. Then, a sigh.

"Okay, I guess, but just for a couple of hours. No longer, understand?"

"Yes. Thanks."

I pressed the phone back to my ear. "Michelle, I can come over, but just for a little while."

"Awesome! See you in a bit."

Excitement bubbled up as I quickly did my hair, pulled on something a little more put-together, and ran out the door. My mom would take great care of Steven, and Steve was off doing whatever he wanted. Why shouldn't I be able to go out and have some fun too?

I headed to Michelle's house, but her mom was passed out on the couch, the house thick with the kind of silence that comes after too much drinking. So, we decided to go to her boyfriend's place instead.

Michelle wasn't expected. That was the point. She suspected something, suspected him, and wanted to catch him off guard.

When we got there, she went straight upstairs to talk to him, leaving me downstairs in the chaos. This house was wild parties every night; people constantly drinking, acting like responsibilities didn't exist. I had no idea how any of them kept jobs when they were always drunk.

I sat on the couch, watching TV, waiting. In the brief time I was there, I was offered everything: cigarettes, beer, hard liquor, pot, and coke. I said no to all of it. I was tempted. Really tempted.

I was feeling down, frustrated, and for a moment, it seemed like maybe something could lift the weight off my chest. Maybe it would make me forget how angry I was with Steve, how isolated I felt. But in the back of my mind, I knew I was a mom now. And that meant something.

Michelle took forever, but eventually she came back and told me everything was fine. We left, walked around town and caught up, letting the cool air clear our heads.

"So, how is it? Having a baby?" she asked.

"It's different. I mean, I know I'm a mom and all, but I still feel like a teenager. My life has changed so much, but I don't fit anywhere. I'm not about to start hanging out with the stay-at-home moms at the mommy-and-me classes, but I can't party with you either. Steve acts like life hasn't changed for him at all, and my grandma thinks I'm the scum of the earth. So yeah… It's not exactly what I envisioned."

She glanced over. "You know, it's not too late to give him up for adoption."

"No." I shook my head. "I want to keep him. I just need time to adjust, but it's gonna work out."

"At least your parents are being supportive." She gestured toward me. "I mean, they let you come out tonight, so that's something."

"Yeah, I guess it is."

I arrived back home and walked through the door and there she was my grandma; her glare sharp and unwavering, fixed on Steven. I barely had to strain to hear their conversation.

"I don't think you should've let her go out," my grandma said, voice edged with disapproval. "It's her job to raise this baby. Why should you have to babysit just so she can go out and have fun?"

My mom glanced toward the door as I stepped inside. Her tone was light, like she was trying to keep the moment from shifting any further.

"Hi, Ellie. How was your time?"

"It was good," I said quickly, setting my bag down. "Thanks again."

"Steven was fine he spit up a little, but the new formula seems to be working."

"Great."

I crossed the room, scooping Steven into my arms, holding him close. I could feel my grandma's stare still burning, waiting for an opening. Before she could say another word, I turned and walked straight to my room, closing the door behind me.

I was glad to be home. I hadn't thought about leaving him and having him sit in the room with my grandmom. I hated the way she stared at us, but especially him. None of this was his fault, and she was punishing an innocent baby for my mistake. I was just getting so angry with her. I was starting to feel a hatred towards her that I never really felt for anyone else before, except maybe my brother. It was energy I didn't care to waste. I needed it all right now.

That night, Steven wouldn't sleep. He cried endlessly, refusing his cradle, whether rocking or still. I tried everything; the pacifier, feeding, changing, but nothing helped. His tiny fists curled, his face scrunching in frustration; I felt my helplessness creeping in.

Finally, I swaddled him and tucked him beside me in bed. I knew they warned against it saying I could roll over and that it wasn't safe, but I knew myself. I would never sleep deeply enough to let that happen. And besides, my mom had already complained about his crying keeping her awake. With her door shut and fan humming, she wouldn't hear a thing.

I held him close; his warmth pressing into me. He gazed up, locking his impossibly bright eyes onto mine. And in that moment, the weight of responsibility settled. He was entirely dependent on me. Every need, every comfort, every ounce of care was mine to provide cleaning, bathing, dressing, feeding, soothing. The list stretched long, endless, and yet I realized some of those things I still needed too. But now, my job was to give them to someone else.

The love I felt for him was different. It wasn't something I had carried with me all along; it was something that had formed, built itself in the spaces where it was needed. Almost as if becoming a parent creates love, manifesting at the exact moment it must exist.

I didn't know yet what he truly needed me to be. I only knew that I would do everything in my power to become it.

His weight was so light; almost nothing in my arms. And yet the duty of him, the sheer responsibility, was the heaviest thing I had ever carried. I must have drifted off at some point because I woke up to the clicking sound of my dad's Polaroid.

He smiled, shaking the picture as it developed. "You looked so cute sleeping, both of you with the same expression. I had to take one."

He handed it to me, still warm from the flash. He was right. We did have the same expression. I pressed the picture onto my mirror, letting it settle into its place, a quiet reflection of a moment I never wanted to forget.

Chapter Thirty-Five

Blossoms of Spring

I was settling into a routine. Taking care of Steven mostly by myself had become the norm. His family, once eager to visit, had slowly stopped coming around. And Steve showed up occasionally, but it never felt like enough. Most of the time, we argued, or he found excuses to sneak down to my dad's truck, avoiding responsibility like it was optional.

I was getting tired of it. He didn't seem to care about the consequences, like the possibility that I could get pregnant again. It was like he only thought with impulse, never with reason. How could he not see that we could end up right back where we started? How could he not grasp what this all truly meant?

But maybe it wasn't the same for him. He was still going to school, still caught up in his activities. He was excited about getting his permit and his dad teaching him how to drive. He still didn't have a job, but that didn't seem to bother him. Every few days, he would show up, put in his time, and then slip right back into his normal teenage life. Mine looked nothing like that. It didn't seem fair. Why was it so unbalanced? Why was it so sexist?

Steven had attended multiple well checks and had just received another set of vaccinations. The doctor was pleased that his weight was improving since switching formulas and everything looked good.

Then it was my turn. My follow-up appointment with the gynecologist felt routine, just another box to check after delivery. She examined me, said everything looked great, and all my stitches were gone.

I didn't tell her I had already started having sex again. I wasn't supposed to, not yet, but explaining that to someone who wouldn't understand felt pointless. She would've only reminded me why I should wait, as if Steve's impatience was something I could control.

Steven was in my arms when she turned her attention to him, smiling at how much he had grown in just six weeks. She asked if I was feeling blue, and I told her nothing outside the norm. It was not entirely a lie, but not the full truth either.

Then, the inevitable question. "Are you still with the father?"

"Yes."

Her eyebrows lifted slightly, surprise flickering across her face before settling into relief.

She signed off on my discharge paperwork and cleared me to return to school. "Best of luck," she said, then added lightly, "and I hope I don't see you again anytime soon."

We both smiled, but I didn't find it very funny.

Going back to school felt like stepping into two different worlds. In some ways, I was excited. It meant seeing Steve and my friends outside the confines of my bedroom, being part of something beyond the four walls that had started to feel more like a cage. It meant glimpsing the world again, maybe even taking part in it. And it meant figuring out if Steve was doing right by us.

But I also knew I was different now. I wasn't just another student; I was a teenage mom trying to finish school, balancing more than most people around me could understand. I would have to go straight home after school, relieve my mom, and stay on top of my work. There was no flexibility, no room to slack off. Sleep would be unpredictable if I even got any, but I would still need to wake up on time.

This was going to be hard.

Chapter Thirty-Six
Blossoms of Adulting

The morning came too soon, but I woke up extra early, slipping out of bed while Steven was still asleep. I had showered the night before, knowing I wouldn't have time in the morning. My mom had asked me not to wake her, so I carefully carried Steven into her room, settling him into the crib that my nephew used to sleep in. She didn't want to get up until she had to, and honestly, I understood that feeling now more than ever.

I wrestled my way into a pair of jeans, not easily. I had barely eaten in weeks; desperate to fit into the clothes every other teenage girl was still wearing. I wasn't going back to school in "mom clothes." That wasn't happening.

Carrying my backpack, I stepped onto the bus, where Mel greeted me with her usual excitement. I barely spoke, but I liked sitting there, listening to her catch me up on all the gossip. I didn't want to talk baby talk. She told me she was still visiting the cemetery every week to see Rob but was finally starting to let go. Of course, she brought him up. It wouldn't have been Mel if she hadn't.

When we got to school, Steve was waiting for me at the entrance. He wanted to walk me to my locker, wanted to welcome me back like this was some grand reunion. And just when I think he's a complete jerk, he does something like that, something that reminds me why I liked him in the first place.

Navigating the hallways wasn't easy. I had forgotten where most of my classes were; after all, I had only been in school for half the year before switching. Now, with barely two and a half months left, everything felt unfamiliar.

Some kids asked where I had been. Some had no idea I was ever pregnant. Some had heard I left but thought I went far away, not realizing it was just the school across town. Others simply stared, eyes darting between my face and my stomach, whispering behind cupped hands. I tried to block it out, tried to just get through the day. Even the teachers were confused, mistaking me for a new student. Too bad I couldn't just stay home and finish school that way. I hated being back.

More than that, I hated being away from Steven. My mind kept wondering if he cried, would my mom hear him? Would she know he needed his favorite stuffed animal? Would she recognize when he was hungry, or would she wait too long? It felt wrong being here, like I belonged at home instead. By the time the final bell rang, I was relieved.

Walking through the door, I found my grandmother sitting with my mom.

I ignored her, directing my questions only at my mom. "How was your day? How did things go?"

She smiled. "It was great. I loved being with Steven. I enjoyed his company."

That eased something inside me. He was dressed, bathed, and happy. She had taken care of him the way I needed her to. I kept my answer short; just a summary of my first day back, before heading to my room. There was so much to do.

Tomorrow, Steven will be going with Steve's mom to her daycare for the first time. She had handed me a sheet of instructions and a list of everything I needed to pack; all of it labeled, all of it accounted for. It was exhausting just looking at it. Diapers, wipes, bottles, pacifiers. Towels, blankets. Extras of *everything*.

I needed his vaccination records, had to print his name, birthdate, and *my* name on every single item. I spent the night preparing bottles, stacking them neatly into a special cold bag so they'd be ready for the day.

My mom walked in as I was still gathering everything.

"Ellie, you know he doesn't *have* to go," she said. "I loved having him home with me. I'd be fine if he stayed every day."

I sighed, trying not to get frustrated. "I know, Mom. But they offered to help, and you need a break too. They *should* help. Right now, they're barely doing anything. This is *their* chance to step in."

She hesitated. "I know, but those places have a lot of germs. Babies get sick more often in daycare. He'd be better off staying home with me."

I shook my head. "Mom, they *need* to help. Just let them help, okay?"

Another pause. Then, a quiet sigh.

"I guess, Ellie."

I felt bad. My mom was right; keeping Steven at home with her would be safer and easier, but it wasn't fair for her to do everything. His family needed to step in, needed to show support in the ways they could. This was something.

Still, it felt like *a lot*. Packing every item, labeling everything, and double-checking the list was exhausting. And the worry lingered.

Steve kept reminding me that his mom was experienced; that she had *eight kids* of her own and that she had worked at the daycare for *twenty years*. She was a baby expert. She would be in the same room as Steven the whole time. I had *no* reason to worry. He said I should worry *less*.

Morning arrived and Steve's mom showed up right on time. I had everything packed, bottles stored, labels in place. It was early, an hour before I even needed to wake up, and she reminded me she wouldn't be back until almost six. I nodded, waved goodbye, then crawled back into bed, catching a little more sleep before heading off myself.

The day dragged on, long and exhausting.

I had no idea what was happening in any of my classes. At my old school, I had done my work and stayed on task, but these past six weeks had been about healing and about being a mother. I hadn't touched a book.

Now, sitting in a classroom again, I felt completely out of place. I had missed *so* much.

My grades were already low, failing in most subjects. There were only a few weeks left in the school year; I wasn't sure if catching up was even possible.

At lunch, I saw Steve and asked if he could help me with some assignments after school.

"No, sorry. I'm going out with my buddy, I think I found a job opportunity."

"Oh. Well, that's great! What is it?"

"I'm not sure yet, but it seems promising."

I forced a smile. "That's great. Good luck. I hope you get it."

"Yeah, me too," Steve said, already distracted, already thinking ahead to something else.

At least there was *some* good news.

The day finally ended, but when I walked through the front door, the house felt wrong. *Empty.* Steven wasn't there, and I felt like something was missing, like I had lost him.

I had a couple of hours before he came home, so I tried to focus, tried to study. English was first, but it was about the Renaissance, and I had *no* idea what that even was. I switched to math, but I was still struggling with repeating ninth-grade algebra, completely forgetting how to work through a parabola function.

Science seemed like a safe choice. I opened my book, hoping for something simple. Nothing made sense. I stared at the page, then at my notebooks, then at the desk in front of me, frustration twisting in my chest. I was *so* behind. The work was overwhelming, and without help, there was no way I could catch up.

It felt too late. I just wanted Steven home. Finally, he arrived.

It felt like the longest wait of my life. The sky had already deepened into twilight, and soon, he'd be ready for bed. The hours at daycare stretched longer than I had expected. I knew some families had no choice, but I did. My mom was right here, willing, and able. Still, I needed them to help, and this was the help they could offer. We had to accept it.

The moment I brought him inside, relief washed over me.

A small card was tucked into his bag, carefully handwritten with details from his day; when he ate and how much, when he slept, how long he was held, when he was alert. It was a sweet touch; a little glimpse into the hours I had missed, something to bridge the gap between us.

After tossing the old bottles and clearing away the unused ones, it was time for my favorite part of the day bath time. There was something so pure about it; the warmth of the water, the way his tiny fists splashed with excitement. I kissed his soft skin, letting myself soak in the little squeals of joy as his mouth opened wide in delight. The lavender-scented soap filled the air, wrapping the room in its gentle calm.

Once his bath was done, I bundled him in a cozy blanket—the one with tiny dragons scattered across it—then rubbed lavender lotion into his delicate skin. He smelled *perfect*. I took my time; running my fingers over his little feet, tracing each tiny toe, watching him watch me.

For a moment, we locked our eyes, and something quiet passed between us. He *knew*. He knew I was his mommy.

By then, the lavender had worked its magic, easing both of us toward sleep. I pulled him into bed with me—it had become our routine. It was easier this way, avoiding the constant need to get up for feeding. Now, all I had to do was grab a bottle, keep him close, and keep him comforted.

Chapter Thirty-Seven
Blossoms of Destruction

Steve sat on the bed, bouncing his knee impatiently. His presence was a relief, especially now. Diapers were running low, and other than formula, I needed money for everything. My parents had been covering most of the expenses, but I hoped Steve had good news about a job.

"How did that opportunity go last week?" I asked, trying to keep my voice hopeful.

He leaned back, arms crossed. "It worked out. I brought you some cash. Fifty bucks."

My breath caught. "That's great! I want to hear all about it."

"There's not much to tell." He shifted, looking away. "Just be glad I got the money."

"I am. This will cover diapers and maybe some wipes, but that's about it. They'll be gone in a week."

"I'll get more," he said, rubbing his face. "It's just gonna take time."

I hesitated. "Where are you working?"

He let out a short laugh. "It's not a place… more like a job. I'm an entrepreneur."

I frowned. "An entrepreneur? What does that mean?"

He sighed and leaned forward. "Ellie, can't you just be happy I found a way to bring in money?"

"I am," I insisted. "But I want to know what you're doing."

He glanced toward the hallway, as if checking for eavesdroppers. "Okay, but you must keep it to yourself. No telling; Mel, your parents, nobody. Promise?"

I swallowed, uneasy. "Yeah. I promise."

He rubbed his hands together like he was preparing to confess something big. "So, me and James you know, James, right? The one always messing around with drugs."

I stiffened. "Yeah. Go on."

"Well, he takes some weed from here, rides the bus to the city, and sells it for a profit. Barely took anything, and after the bus fare, I still had fifty bucks. I couldn't make that in a day working minimum wage."

I blinked. "So… this is drug money?"

Steve scoffed. "Ellie, it's gonna get bought anyway. Why shouldn't I be the one making the money?"

My stomach twisted. "It's not safe. Going into the city, being around those people, you could get mugged. Or worse."

"It's fine," he insisted. "We need money, and this is a straightforward way to get it. Next time, we're bringing double. You'll see it's worth it."

This was the worst idea I had ever heard. Yes, I was grateful that he finally brought back some money, but not like this. When I imagined ways he might earn, I pictured mowing lawns, picking up odd jobs, anything that wasn't criminal. But this?

I could hardly believe it. He had spent years wrestling, running, pushing his body to be stronger, always warning people about how drugs ruined lives. He never let Clay smoke without lecturing him. He had even thrown full packs of cigarettes out behind his back, refusing to let addiction touch him. And now, suddenly, he's earning a living by enabling the very thing he despised?

Drug money. That's what was supposed to keep our baby fed, clothed, and cared for. The thought made me sick. I didn't want to take it. I didn't want to encourage him. But Steven needed things, and diapers wouldn't buy themselves. The baby shower had helped, but the needs wouldn't stop, they'd only grow. And so would the cost.

I stared at the cash, knowing I couldn't turn it away. But deep inside, I wished I could.

After Steve left, Clay knocked at the door, and I felt a small wave of relief. Any company was welcome these days, especially someone my age.

He settled onto the couch, stretching his legs out with a tired sigh. "How's life treating you?"

"Same as always." I glanced at Steven, who was dozing in his bassinet. Clay had stopped by a few times to see him before but not much has changed.

I told him about Steve and his new job.

He nodded, rubbing the back of his neck. "Yeah… I already knew about Steve."

I sat up straighter. "You're not surprised?"

Clay snorted. "Not really. Doesn't mean I'm not disappointed, though."

I let out a slow breath, shaking my head. "It goes against everything I thought he believed in."

Silence settled between us. Clay stared at the baby, his fingers tapping absently against his knee. I could feel the weight of something unsaid hanging in the air.

"Ellie," he finally said, his voice quieter, more serious. "Is Steve treating you alright?"

I hesitated. "Yeah… I mean, I guess." I wasn't sure what he was asking. What did 'alright' even mean at this point?

"Okay." He nodded once but didn't look convinced. "I just wanted to make sure. I know this isn't easy."

"No. It's not." I swallowed. I wasn't sure why hearing him say it made it feel even more real.

He shifted, stretching his arms. "Glad you're back at school. How's that going?"

I let out a humorless laugh. "Honestly? I'm failing at everything."

His expression tightened. "That sucks. Hopefully, it will get better." He pushed himself up, giving Steven one last look. "Let me know if Steve isn't manning up."

And then he was gone.

Clay's visit felt… off. It wasn't that I didn't appreciate the company. I did. Talking to someone my age was a rare break from the routine. But there was something in the way he sat, in the way he asked about Steve, that made me wonder if this wasn't just a casual check-in.

Maybe he wanted to see if I knew what Steve was involved in. Maybe he wanted to gauge my reaction. Either way, we were both confused, and I was still trying to make sense of it.

I couldn't shake the feeling that Clay was worried, not just about Steve but about me. And that unsettled me more than I wanted to admit.

It had been two weeks since I went back to school, and I was finally settling into the rhythm of things. My mom watched Steven some days, and on others, he went with Steve's mom to daycare. The schedule was tight, the juggling constant but somehow it was working. Maybe even better than I had expected.

For the first time in a while, I felt like I had space to breathe. My mom even let me hang out with my friends after school a few days a week, and those moments felt like pieces of my old life slipping back into place. Like I was reclaiming a part of myself.

Steve was still working, keeping his word about doubling the money. Things were falling into place. And after everything, that was a relief.

My parents were planning a weekend trip to the mountains. They wanted me to come with Steven, but the idea of traveling with a baby, especially to a place as remote as our mountain home felt overwhelming. I told them it was too much, and thankfully, they didn't push.

Instead, they agreed to let me stay home alone. The only condition? No visitors. That meant an entire weekend in the house, just me and Steven. No escape, no distraction, no help. The thought made me uneasy, but still not as uneasy as the idea of going to the mountains.

So, this was the better choice. Right?

When I told Steve, his face lit up instantly.

"What?" I asked, leaning in.

His grin widened. "That's crazy—you're not gonna believe this, but my sister Joanne and a few friends are heading to their mountain house too. They invited us to come!"

"Really?"

"Yeah. And they said it could just be the two of us. My mom even offered to watch Steven for the weekend—she's been wanting more time with him anyway, since he's always at your house."

I hesitated. It did sound nice. A break. Time alone with Steve. We hadn't had that in so long.

"That sounds like a lot of fun," I admitted. "I'll ask my parents and let you know."

My parents weren't thrilled about the idea, but after some back-and-forth, they agreed on one condition. Steve and I had to sleep in separate rooms, and they wanted confirmation from Joanne. She agreed without hesitation.

My mom was still uneasy, insisting that Steven should come with them to the mountains. But my dad sided with me. "It'd be good for her to have a break," he said. "And it's time Steve's family takes more responsibility."

I hadn't expected them to say yes. But they did. I could barely hold my excitement. A weekend away. A chance to have fun. To just be a teenager, even if only for a little while.

Last week, I came home from school earlier than expected. My mom hadn't noticed me walking in; she was alone with Steven, bathing him.

I paused in the doorway, watching as she gently poured water over his tiny hands. Her voice was soft, affectionate. "Do you like when Mommy gives you a bath?" she asked. "Come to Mommy."

I froze. *Mommy.*

At first, I told myself she was just caught up in the moment, saying it without thinking. I knew she understood that she wasn't his mother. But lately, she'd been wanting to spend more time with him even when I was home. She encouraged me to go out, to let her take care of him, as if she needed that time more than I did.

It was starting to feel like some lines were blurring, like she was stepping into a role that wasn't hers.

I told my dad what I had seen and heard. He listened, then shook his head gently.

"It's innocent," he assured me. "You don't need to worry."

He explained that after my mom's miscarriage, she had struggled with a deep sadness. When Steven was born, it filled a gap giving her something to hold onto when that loss felt unbearable. She knew she wasn't his mother but having him close made the grief feel less heavy. I understood. But even so, it didn't erase the unease settling in my chest. Maybe the weekend apart would help. Maybe it would remind her that *she isn't his mom.*

I decided to take Steven over to Steve's house, even though I didn't have a stroller. Carrying him in the carrier would make the walk long, but the afternoon was gorgeous, and I needed to drop off what he'd need for the weekend. Tomorrow, after school, we'd be leaving, and everything had to be in place.

I packed up the essentials and headed out. The sun was warm against my skin, and for the first time in a while, I felt a little lighter.

When I got to Steve's house, I had an idea. "Let's have a picnic," I said. "It's too nice out to stay inside."

We spread a blanket in the yard and snacked as we talked about our trip, about how much fun it was going to be. For a while, it felt easy, effortless, like nothing was weighing on us. But the heat crept in faster than I expected, and I could tell Steven was getting too warm.

"It's probably time to head back," I said.

I left everything Steven would need for the weekend, and as we walked home, Steve carried the carrier for me. My arm throbbed with relief.

"I can't wait for this weekend," I said.

"Me too," he replied.

I smiled. "Love you."

"Love you too."

Chapter Thirty-Eight
Blossoms of Warning

My parents were all packed for their weekend trip, and so was I. It was funny how all of us were going away to the mountains, but to separate areas. I would be in an area that was more of an actual town with phones and running water; where my parents went there was no one, just woods and bears. No phones and isolated. My parents liked it that way.

My mom reminded me how important it was for her to get a good night's sleep. She needed to be well-rested to watch Steven while I was at school and to prepare for the four-hour drive ahead.

I needed rest too. School was already exhausting, and tomorrow I'd have to push through the day before stepping into a weekend surrounded by a group of strangers. Still, the thought of time alone with Steve made it worth it. A break from everything. A chance to breathe. Just for a little while.

The bedtime routine went as usual; Steven tucked in, lights dimmed, quiet settling over the room. He dozed off for a while, but at 1 a.m., the silence shattered.

A sharp, piercing cry ripped through the air. His tiny face was red, scrunched with frustration. I scooped him up, walking through the room with slow, bouncing steps. His screams didn't fade. I tried the bottle, but he pushed it away. I held out his pacifier, but he spat it out. His diaper was dry, but I changed him anyway. Still nothing.

Panic crept in. My mom needed sleep for tomorrow's trip, I needed sleep. Why tonight, of all nights?

By 3 a.m., exhaustion gnawed at me. My arms ached and my head pulsed with a dull headache. Steven was getting hotter from crying so much; his tiny body tense and overheated.

I needed a break. Just a moment.

I placed him in his cradle, stepping back as his cries still rang through the room. My fingers hovered over the doorknob, stomach twisting as I debated waking my mom. My fist rose, ready to knock but I stopped short.

She needed rest. She had asked me not to wake her.

Tears burned my eyes. The frustration, the exhaustion; it all crashed over me at once. Nothing worked. Nothing. Steven kept screaming, his tiny body tense and restless, and I had no idea what else to try. I had walked him, fed him, changed him, rocked him, and pleaded with him.

Nothing.

And I couldn't ask for help. Not tonight. Not when my mom had made it clear she needed sleep. I sank, my whole-body aching, my mind foggy with exhaustion. I was too tired to think. Too tired to fight. I pressed my forehead against my knees, letting the quiet sobs slip out. I just needed a break. A moment. But even that felt impossible.

I backed away, standing outside my bedroom door, breathing in the muffled sound of his crying from the other side. He was safe. He had everything he needed.

I curled myself on the floor, arms wrapped around my knees, exhaustion pulling me under. Sleep took me before the crying stopped.

I woke up hours later, stiff, my body aching from sleeping on the floor. A glance at my digital clock sent a rush of panic through me because I had overslept. If I didn't move fast, I'd be late for school.

I scrambled to my feet and stepped into my room. Steven was exactly where I had left him, staring up at my posters, completely still. The quiet felt almost unnatural. After hours of crying, he must have finally exhausted himself.

I moved quickly, checking his diaper, trying to feed him. Nothing. He wasn't hungry. He wasn't uncomfortable. Just content, like last night never happened. I shook off the lingering frustration and hurried to get dressed. My mom would be up soon so she could feed him when he was ready. I grabbed my things, took one last look at Steven, then headed out for school.

Every class felt like a countdown. Each period was just another step closer to my weekend escape, and I couldn't get through them fast enough.

I hadn't been this excited about anything in months. Steve had promised fun, games, drinks, and time together. Joanne had reassured my parents we'd be sleeping in separate beds, but he had different plans.

The day blurred past in a haze. First period. Second. Third. The clock dragged, each minute crawling slower than the last. But finally, the bell rang.

I was free.

I walked through the door, and just like any other day, my mom was sitting with my grandmother, chatting. The second my grandmom saw me, though, her expression shifted—her usual death stare locking onto me.

"Ellie, Hun, I think something's wrong with the baby," my mom said.

I sighed, already bracing myself.

"He hasn't eaten all day. No wet diapers. Not even a cry."

I glanced at Steven in his carrier. He looked fine; quiet, but fine. "Mom, he was up crying most of the night. He probably just wore himself out."

"That's not normal," she insisted. "I think you had him out in the sun too long yesterday."

I frowned. "He's okay."

"No, Ellie. I think something's wrong." She inhaled sharply. "Maybe we should stay home and not go to the mountains."

I shook my head. "No, Mom. He's fine. I'm bringing him to Steve's mom; she's great with babies. If there's anything wrong, she'll catch it."

She still didn't look convinced, but I was done arguing. "Don't worry," I added, trying to keep my tone steady. "You're being dramatic."

She wasn't listening. But it wasn't just worrying, it was something deeper. And it was starting to bother me more than I wanted to admit.

I figured she just needed an excuse not to leave him for the weekend. She was getting used to the rhythm of feeding him, changing him, rocking him to sleep. It had become her normal, her comfort.

She didn't want him out of her sight. And somewhere along the way, she'd stopped thinking of him as mine. She was starting to believe he was hers.

I packed up my things and walked over to Steve's house, Steven snug in his carrier. The minute I stepped inside, I went straight to Steve's mom.

"My mom says the baby might be sick," I told her. "He didn't sleep well last night, he cried for hours. When he finally stopped, he barely ate, and he hasn't had any wet diapers all day. She thinks I had him out in the sun too long yesterday and that something's wrong."

She didn't hesitate; carefully looking him over, feeling his skin, inspecting every detail.

"No, I don't think he's sick," she finally said. "He looks perfectly fine. Maybe he was tired from the heat; yesterday was unusually hot. I wouldn't worry."

Relief washed over me. *She raised eight kids. She works in daycare.* She knows what sick babies look like. If she said Steven was fine, then he was fine. My mom was overreacting; probably just struggling with the idea of being separated from him for an entire weekend. Assured, I let the worry go, packed up what I needed, and headed out for the trip.

Chapter Thirty-Nine

Blossoms of Shock

After a long, winding drive through dense forest roads, we finally arrived at a secluded log cabin, nestled deep among the trees. The air was crisp, carrying the scent of pine and damp earth, and the warm glow from inside hinted at a lively gathering. When we stepped in, three couples greeted us; older than us, clearly adults, already laughing, drinking, and settled into the evening's festivities. Despite the age gap, their welcome was warm and effortless.

We were led to our room, a cozy space with a large bed and a private bathroom. The moment we entered, Steve grinned mischievously. "Try it out," he said. I pulled back the blankets, expecting softness and warmth but instead, *ahhh*! My scream shattered the quiet as I jumped back, heart pounding. Nestled beneath the covers was a fake snake, its lifeless stare frozen in place.

Laughter erupted. Steve was doubled over, practically gasping for air. "Got you so good!" he howled, pride radiating from him. I stared, still catching my breath, before breaking into reluctant laughter. Turns out, they had planned this ahead of time, and Steve had been in on it from the start. The night had officially begun.

Joanne told us to unpack and get comfortable. The living room was warm and inviting; the coffee table crowded with snacks and drinks. We grabbed a bowl of chips and dip and settled in as we pulled out Monopoly, ready for what we hoped would be a full-length game for once.

We were just starting to set up when the phone rang. Joanne picked up, her tone sharp from the start. I could only catch fragments of her conversation, but the irritation in her voice was unmistakable.

"...Really necessary?" she said, sighing loudly. "I must drive all the way back? Why can't they just—?

A pause. She barely waited for the other person's response before exhaling sharply again. Then, without a goodbye, she hung up, shaking her head.

Joanne's voice cut through the air, firm and impatient. "We have to drive back," she said, already grabbing her keys.

I froze mid-step. "What do you mean? What's happening?"

She exhaled sharply, looking irritated. "My mom said Steven is sick. She had to take him to the hospital, but they won't administer care without your signatures because you're his parents."

"Sick?" My stomach twisted. "She told me he was fine."

"Well, apparently he's not." Joanne crossed her arms. "And since you guys must go back, I have to drive two hours there and two hours back. My night is officially ruined." She rolled her eyes before turning on her heel.

There was no time to argue. We scrambled to throw our belongings into bags; stuffing clothes and toiletries into whatever space we could find before hauling everything into the car. The trunk slammed shut and we climbed into the backseat, the weight of the situation pressing down on us.

The tension that had been simmering finally boiled over. The Monopoly board sat half-assembled on the table, abandoned. The snacks we had barely touched seemed irrelevant now. There was no point in arguing or asking for details, her tone told us everything.

The ride back was silent. I stared out my window, the passing trees blurring together. Beside me, Steve did the same. Joanne gripped the wheel, her foot heavy on the gas, her annoyance etched across her face. The atmosphere felt thick, tense; like a storm was brewing but there was nothing either of us could say to make it better.

Joanne barely slowed the car as she pulled up to the hospital entrance. "Out," she muttered before speeding away, tires squealing.

Stevens' parents were already waiting, their faces tight with worry. We barely had a moment to process before we were ushered inside. The next few minutes blurred together, flashes of bright overhead lights, the sterile smell of disinfectants, the hushed urgency in their voices. A nurse handed me a paper, and before I could even ask questions, I signed it.

The words *spinal tap* hung in the air. I didn't know exactly what it meant, but the way they said it sent ice through my veins. We hadn't even seen Steven yet.

His parents explained everything in low, hurried tones. After we left, the baby had just sat there, staring. No crying, no feedings, no wet diapers, no eye contact. Something was *wrong*, and when they called the pediatrician, the instructions were clear: get to the ER *at once*.

I have been here before. This was my birthplace. But at this moment, it felt unfamiliar; like a place I never imagined being in for *this*.

Time stretched into something unrecognizable as we sat and waited; the minutes slipped by without definition. When they finally let us into the room, my breath caught in my throat.

Steven was inside a transparent plastic box; small and fragile, separated from us by a barrier with circular openings for our gloved hands. The hum of machines surrounded him; their quiet rhythms punctuated by the occasional beep. Wires snaked from his tiny body; needles, tubes, blinking monitors. He wasn't crying. He wasn't moving. His eyes were open, but they were vacant; unfocused, staring past everything.

The doctor gestured to the incubator. "You can sit here," they said. "You can reach inside to touch him, but he needs to stay enclosed." Their voices blurred into a string of words, terms, and explanations I didn't understand. The sentences ran together like static, empty of meaning. The only thing I grasped was the final statement: *he needs more care than this hospital can provide*. He was being transferred to the city.

The ambulance would take him. We had to follow. Again, we found ourselves in the back seat of a car, staring silently out the windows. Nothing felt real anymore.

We pulled up to the Children's Hospital of Philadelphia—CHOP. It was massive, towering over our local hospital like a city within a city. The sheer scale of it was overwhelming, stretching upward with countless floors.

The hospital felt different at this hour, dimly lit, eerily quiet, its towering presence suddenly intimidating. This was my first time here, and even though several doctors and nurses came to give updates, they would give them to Steve's parents, not directly to us. I am not sure if it was because they didn't realize we were the parents or if it was because we were so young, they figured we wouldn't understand what they were saying anyway. I did not understand anything they were saying. All I knew was they had run a battery of tests, and they were just waiting to review all the results before they explained everything to us in detail. They told us it might take a few hours before they had any updates. They showed us to a parent suite where we would be able to wait for more answers. I just sat on the couch and waited. Steve and I had yet to say a word to each other. All I kept thinking to myself was that my mom knew he was sick, and I didn't believe her because the baby expert said he was ok.

I had heard about CHOP before, but walking into its halls under these circumstances made it feel unfamiliar, almost surreal. The play areas stood still, their bright colors clashing with silence. The outpatient clinics were dark, doors locked, and no families shuffling in and out. Even McDonald's so often a place of movement and noise was closed, its chairs stacked neatly; an empty shell of what I imagined it would be during the day.

There was nothing to distract from the reason we were here. Every step echoed as we moved toward the elevator, winding through sterile hallways that seemed to stretch longer than they should. The weight of the situation sat heavy in my chest as we finally reached the department that would be caring for Steven. My exhaustion fought against my nerves, but there was no way sleep would come easily tonight.

The sun rose, casting golden light through the hospital windows. The once-quiet halls filled with movement; doctors, nurses, and families weaving through corridors, voices overlapping in the morning rush. The first floor bustled with energy; footsteps echoing against the polished floors as people hurried to different destinations.

Finally, we were allowed into Steven's room. As we stepped inside, the sight of him stopped me in my tracks. He was in a full-sized hospital bed now, but he looked impossibly small against the crisp white sheets. His little diaper was his only clothing, his head resting on a pillow that seemed too large for him. He wasn't crying, just lying still beneath the blankets, surrounded by monitors, tubes, and wires.

We were told we could visit for a while, but none of us knew what to say or do. Steve's parents sat quietly, their faces etched with uncertainty. I knew Steven was being cared for, but I still didn't understand what was happening. He looked so helpless.

I couldn't hold him, not with everything attached to him, but I could reach for his hand. I slid my fingers through his tiny ones, wrapping them gently around mine. As I leaned in to kiss him, I caught a faint scent on his breath one I recognized instantly. The smell of sickness. It's hard to describe, but once you know it, you never forget.

I still didn't know exactly what was happening, but I knew one thing for sure, this was one of the best hospitals in the country, and whatever he needed, he would receive it here.

The doctor closed the door behind him, his expression heavy with something I couldn't quite place. "My name is Dr. Rob, and I've been caring for your son since he arrived," he began, his voice calm but serious.

He listed off the tests they had performed: a spinal tap, a CT scan, and multiple labs. Then came the words that shifted everything. *Your son has contracted a form of meningitis.*

I tried to grasp what he was saying, but the weight of it was heavy and unfamiliar. *Meningitis.* I had never heard that word before.

"What is that?" I asked, my voice quieter than I expected.

"In simple terms, it's a bacterium in the air," he explained. "For most of us, our immune systems fight it off. But if you're incredibly young or already sick, your body may not be strong enough. That's why we vaccinate against it, but the first dose is given at eight weeks, and your son is just shy of that."

"So, you're saying it was just… a germ in the air?" The words felt absurd; too simple for something so devastating.

"Yes, that's the easiest way to explain it."

I swallowed hard. "He was supposed to get his next shots on Wednesday."

Dr. Rob sighed. "Unfortunately, he won't need that shot anymore."

Panic pressed against my chest. "So, what are you going to do? Is there a cure? Can you give him medicine? Does he just need time to recover?"

His answer came too gently, too carefully. "No, Ellie. It's more complicated than that. The medicine we gave him is reducing the swelling, but the damage has already been done."

I didn't know what to say, what to think. Everything blurred.

"A social worker will be in to talk with you soon," he continued. "After that, a support team will help you process everything and discuss how you want to proceed."

Steve's dad shook the doctor's hand, but his mom was already breaking down, sobbing quietly beside him.

I just sat there, stunned. My mind refused to catch up.

I needed my parents. It was already Saturday, and they were still in the mountains with no phone, no way to reach them. The thought of explaining their location to the police made my chest tighten. Their home wasn't marked by street signs or house numbers; it was buried deep in the woods, beyond the gravel roads that swallowed the wheels of any car that dared to pass.

I had no phone numbers, no directory, no easy solution. My only hope was my grandmother. I hurried to the payphone; the metal cold against my palm as I gripped it tighter than I needed to. The scent of damp concrete and faint cigarette smoke lingered in the air.

"I need to make a collect call," I told the operator, my voice steady despite the storm brewing inside me.

"Yes, we have a collect call from Ellie. Would you like to accept the charges?"

"Yes, hello?" My grandmother's voice came through, familiar but distant.

"Hi, Grandmom. Listen, I'm at CHOP in Philadelphia. The baby is sick, and it's bad. I need you to find a way to get in touch with Mom and Dad. Please. I don't care how. Just tell them it's an emergency."

A pause. The weight of doubt hung heavily between us.

"Well, I don't know how I can do that. You know they don't have a phone," she said, her voice calm in a way that felt unbearable. "They are coming home Monday night. I'm sure it can wait."

"No, Grandmom, it can't." My breath caught in my throat. "I don't understand everything that's happening, but I *know* this is bad. Please. Call the police. Have them find Mom and Dad and send them here."

Another silence. Then finally, "I'll do my best."

"Okay. Thanks."

I hung up, pressing my forehead against the payphone for just a moment before stepping away. The world moved around me; strangers passing, monitors beeping, but all I could hear was the racing pulse in my ears.

I was going to have to trust that my grandmother could somehow reach them, get word to them, and convince them to come. The uncertainty gnawed at me. What if she was still too angry and didn't even try? There was no way for her to call me back; I wouldn't even know if she had managed to contact them or if they were already on their way.

The thought of waiting in this hospital without answers made my chest feel tight. Steve's family was there, hovering, offering words of support but it wasn't the same. I needed my parents. Their absence made everything feel colder, harsher. The fluorescent lights above cast an unkind glow, buzzing faintly, like an added layer of discomfort pressing down on me. The hospital smelled of antiseptic and something stale, a scent that had already begun clinging to my clothes.

I wrapped my arms around myself, as if that could ease the loneliness. Machines beeped rhythmically in the distance, each sound reminding me of why I was here. I tried to push away the fear, but it kept crawling back.

The only thing I could do now was wait and hope.

Out of the corner of my eye, I spotted a familiar face, someone I hadn't seen since the pregnancy program. A rush of memory hit me as I recalled Mrs. Blum mentioning that my friend's baby had been sick and hospitalized.

Without hesitation, I hurried over. "What are you doing here?"

She turned, her eyes exhausted but steady. "My baby was born sick."

A sharp pang of sympathy struck me. "I'm so sorry... Are things any better?"

She hesitated before answering, her voice subdued. "No, unfortunately, he might not make it."

My heart clenched. "What's wrong?"

"He was born premature, and some of his organs were on the outside. They're doing everything they can, but... I don't know if they can save him."

The weight of her words pressed down on me. I struggled to find something meaningful to say. "Why are you here?" she asked.

"My baby got sick. I don't even fully understand it yet. I just got here yesterday."

"I'm sorry."

"Thanks."

An awkward silence lingered between us. There was nothing either of us could say to change the situation. "Well... best of luck to you."

"Yeah. You, too."

As I walked away, I felt the pain settling deep. The image of her standing there, holding onto nothing but hope, stuck with me. She had been in this hospital for weeks, just waiting to see if they could fix him, waiting to know if she would get to keep him.

I couldn't even imagine the kind of heartbreak she was carrying.

Chapter Forty

Petals of Turmoil

We were put in a private room with a group of doctors. The space felt too small, the walls pressing in as they introduced themselves as an infectious disease specialist, a neurologist, and a pediatrician. Their titles sounded important, but in that moment, they were just voices with answers I wasn't sure I wanted to hear.

Steve and his parents sat beside me. I barely registered their presence, too consumed by the crushing weight of uncertainty.

"It seems your baby contracted bacterial meningitis," one of the doctors began, his voice steady, clinical. "This disease moves through the body very quickly and can have serious, sometimes fatal results in less than twenty-four hours. Because your son is so young and his body is so small, it likely happened in an extremely brief time."

A sharp chill ran through me. I wanted to interrupt to say, *no, there must be some mistake*. But I stayed silent, fingers curling tightly in my lap.

The doctor continued, his words growing heavier. "Once this illness enters the body, it causes swelling mostly in the spine and brain, which can lead to severe brain injury and even death. We took some scans and confirmed that the level of inflammation in his brain is severe. This caused irreversible damage. We've treated him with medication, but the swelling that already occurred has left lasting effects."

Steve's parents asked so many questions. Their voices rose and fell around me, words twisting into meaningless sounds. I tried to listen. I *wanted* to understand, but it was like trying to grasp water in my hands. Impossible.

"Ellie, do you have any questions?"

I blinked, suddenly aware of the silence. My mind raced, searching for something to say. But to ask questions, I would need to understand. And I didn't.

"So… how exactly did he get sick?" My voice felt detached, smaller than I wanted it to be.

"It's a bacterial infection, not a virus," the specialist explained. "It isn't airborne. Most healthy people can fight it off, but babies, the elderly, or unvaccinated individuals are vulnerable."

I latched onto one piece of information. "He wasn't vaccinated?"

"No. The vaccine is given at eight weeks. He was scheduled to receive it next."

A fresh wave of nausea rolled through me. He had been so close, just days away.

I was so confused. I thought one doctor said it was airborne and the other said it wasn't. I started to wonder if I was hearing them correctly because my ears were ringing and I felt lightheaded and dizzy.

"How would I have known he was sick?" My chest tightened as I thought back, searching for signs I had missed. *He wasn't vomiting, didn't have diarrhea—nothing obvious. How was I supposed to know?*

"It typically begins with a headache, then leads to a stiff neck. Fever, irritability, lethargy—those are common symptoms. But with a baby this young, there's no tangible way to communicate discomfort. And unfortunately, in cases like this, the illness progresses so quickly that parents don't always have time to notice."

I nodded, though the motion felt hollow.

The sterile hospital air felt thicker, heavier. The hum of machines filled the silence between us. And at that moment, I realized I wasn't just afraid. I was drowning in guilt, in helplessness, in a kind of grief that didn't even have words yet.

How could I have known? His skin was warm, but the day before, the sun had been on him, heat wrapping around us like a heavy blanket. I told myself he was just a little overheated. That night, he cried, sharp and restless, his tiny body twisting against sleep. I rocked him, whispered to him, but nothing settled him. I thought he was just overtired.

I tried to read the signs, but none of the warnings from my classes fit. No fever that I could tell. No cough. No telltale symptoms. My mom wondered if he might be sick, but when I asked Steve's mom, the one who had done this before she said he was fine. I trusted her. I wanted to trust her. I never would have left if I thought he was sick. I would have done something. I would have known. Wouldn't I? The thought lodged itself in my chest, sharp and suffocating. Was I trying to explain or convince myself? The doctor's voice was steady, clinical, but his words shattered everything.

"Due to the inflammation and swelling, his brain has suffered irreversible damage." A pause, as if he hated saying it. "I'm sorry to tell you this, but your baby is brain-dead. The machines are keeping him alive. Without them, he may breathe on his own for maybe thirty minutes. If we continue life support, he could pass at any time or live for years but he will never wake up. He will remain in a vegetative state."

The world tilted. The air in the room thickened, suffocating, pressing against my chest. My mind struggled to process the words, to make them real, but they couldn't be real. They couldn't.

Steve's parents fought against their tears, but they came anyway, silent and unstoppable. Steve sat hunched forward, shoulders curled inward, his fingers gripping his knees as if holding himself together. The tears slipped down his face, but he never looked up.

I couldn't move. I couldn't think. Life support. Brain dead. A vegetative state. The words echoed, hollow and impossible.

"That's all we can tell you for now." The doctor's voice was measured but heavy. "The social workers will be in shortly; they'll explain what happens next, how to move forward from here."

A pause, brief but unbearable.

"We're truly sorry," he added. "If you need anything, please let us know."

And then he was gone. The room, once filled with voices and movement, felt hollow, shrinking in around us.

The four of us sat in silence, trying to absorb the weight of it, trying to make sense of something that refused to make sense. I was drowning in confusion. How could this happen? How could a single night change everything?

He had been born perfect. I remembered counting his fingers and toes, marveling at every tiny, flawless detail. At every appointment, the pediatrician smiled, reassuring me that he was thriving, happy, and healthy. He had his shots, each on time, just as they said. I had sanitized his bottles, labeled every belonging, and followed every instruction.

I had done everything right. So, what happened?

Silence hung over us heavily, suffocating. There was nothing left to say.

Then, the door opened. Two people stepped in, dressed in casual clothes rather than medical scrubs. The contrast made them stand out. The social workers; a man and a woman.

"Hi," the woman began, her voice gentle but steady. "We're here to help explain things now that the doctors have spoken to you from a medical standpoint. We know this is a deeply challenging time, and we want to support you, to guide you in the best direction for what comes next."

She hesitated for just a moment, as if bracing for the weight of what she had to ask.

"Ellie, where are your parents?"

I swallowed, the words tight in my throat. "They went to the mountains. There's no phone service where they stay. I called my grandmother to try to reach them, but I don't know if she was able to or not."

"Would you prefer to wait for them before we continue?"

The question barely registered. The thought of waiting—of pausing in this unbearable limbo felt impossible.

"Honestly... no."

The social worker shifted slightly, her voice calm but firm. "Since Steve's parents are here, we can continue."

A breath. A pause.

"Your son is on life support. You have a choice. If you leave him on the machines, his body will continue to function but as the doctors explained, he is brain-dead. He won't wake up. He won't open his eyes or respond. He will remain in a vegetative state for an unknown length of time days, weeks, possibly even years. There's no way to predict."

She glanced at each of us, gauging the silence that had settled in.

"Or... you can remove him from the machines. If you do, you'll be able to hold him. Eventually, his breathing will slow until it stops. He won't feel pain. He won't be aware."

The weight in the room was suffocating.

"This is an incredibly difficult decision," the man added gently. "You don't have to decide this second, but we will need an answer soon. It will determine how we continue."

I forced out a whisper, a shred of hope clawing at my chest. "If he had medicine, could he get better? If we leave him on the machines, could there be a chance?"

The woman shook her head, her gaze soft with sympathy. "No, Hun. The damage to his brain is irreversible. There's nothing anyone can do."

I swallowed hard, the words pressing against my ribs. "And if we remove everything?"

Her voice remained steady, but I barely heard it. "He will breathe on his own for a little while, maybe thirty minutes... but then he will stop. His brain won't be able to tell his body to continue. He will stop."

Stop.

"But you will be able to hold him. You can say goodbye."

Everything blurred for a moment. Then, the thought tumbled; out one I hadn't expected.

"My friend's baby is just down the hall. He's sick." I hesitated, my voice shaking. "Could we donate his organs? Maybe he could save her baby."

The woman's brows lifted slightly, something unreadable flickering across her face. "We can certainly talk with the doctors," she said slowly. "That's... a very bold suggestion, Ellie."

She turned to the others. "Would all of you be on board if that were an option?"

Steve's parents nodded, their faces tight with emotion. Then, slowly, Steve did too.

And so, I did.

"We also want you to know that we have grief support and counseling services available if any of you would like to take advantage of them," the woman said gently. "When you're ready, we can also help with the next steps whatever you decide."

Her tone was steady, reassuring, but it didn't make the weight in my chest any lighter.

"We'll give you all some time to talk things through," she continued. "Please know that we're here for you."

She reached into her bag, pulling out a small stack of cards, and placed them carefully on the bedside table.

"If you need anything, don't hesitate to call."

And then they were gone.

Steve's mom looked at both of us; once at Steve, once at me. Then again, as if searching for the right moment.

"Would you like my opinion?"

We exchanged a glance, then nodded.

She took a breath. "I would remove him from life support. He's already gone. Why would anyone want to leave him attached to machines, stuck in a bed for God knows how long, when he'll never get better? That's not life. That's torture."

Her words settled over us, heavy and sharp. But how could we let him go? He was just a baby. My baby. How did this even happen? Nothing made sense.

Steve turned to me, his eyes wet with tears, his hand reaching for mine. "I agree with my mom, Ellie. We can't just leave him like this. We must let him go."

I swallowed hard. "I just don't know if I can. What if they're wrong? Maybe we should get a second opinion."

Steve's dad spoke, his voice firm but gentle. "This is one of the best children's hospitals in the country. If there was even a chance, they would have found it."

The finality of it pressed against me, suffocating.

"You have to let him go," he added. "It is the best decision."

Steve's mom exhaled, rubbing her hands together. "We need to go home. The other kids need us. We need to eat, change clothes."

She turned to Steve. "You need to come too. We'll be back later."

They offered to take me with them, but they weren't my family. And I couldn't leave. Not now. Not when my son was still here.

"No, thanks," I said, voice barely above a whisper. "I'm going to stay."

Maybe my parents will show up soon. Maybe they already knew. Maybe.

Chapter Forty-One

Petals of Dreams

I made my way across the hospital to my son's room, the hallways stretching endlessly ahead of me.

We had to garb up before entering; mask, gown, gloves, even a hair net. A quiet precaution, a necessary barrier between us and whatever lingered unseen. Maybe he was contagious. Maybe it was protocol. I wasn't sure.

At the last hospital, he had been inside the plastic enclosure, sealed away. Here, he wasn't. But still, the layers between us remained. I pulled on the gown, the fabric stiff against my skin, the gloves foreign and clinical. The mask hid everything except my eyes. Then, I stepped inside. The silence was deafening.

The room, once filled with voices, decisions, and movement, was now still. It felt too big, too empty. My mind raced, but the weight in my chest kept me anchored, heavy and unmoving.

Alone.

With the machines, the quiet hum of their function. With the steady beeping that measured time, breath, and existence.

With him.

The world outside continued. People walked, spoke, lived. But here, everything had stopped.

And I was alone.

I stared at his tiny body, so still except for the rhythmic rise and fall of his chest, guided by the breathing tube down his throat. A needle rested in his arm, the bag of fluids dripping steadily, methodically, keeping time in a world that had suddenly stopped. Another machine monitored his heartbeat, a quiet pulse against the silence.

His eyes remained closed. He looked peaceful. He looked like he was sleeping. I wondered what he was dreaming. No, he couldn't be. Not really. But I let myself imagine. Maybe he was chasing butterflies, laughing as they fluttered just out of reach. Maybe he was splashing in the bath, his tiny fist smacking the water, his giggles filling the room. Or maybe he was curled against me, the way he always had, his little body tucked close, safe in the rhythm of our breathing as sleep finally took us both.

He didn't look sick. He looked like my baby. Like he was simply sleeping.

I held his tiny hand in mine, the glove a fragile barrier between warmth and loss. For seven weeks I had watched him, searching for glimpses of the life he might have; his first steps, his first words, the way he might laugh or love. But today, I saw only absence.

There would be no crawling, no school, no reckless teenage adventures. No prom, no wedding, no future. Just this bed, this room, this moment. The sadness settled deep, a relentless storm without reprieve. No rainbow would follow this rain; only destruction, consuming everything in its path.

My grandmother had spoken of punishment, of consequences for sins I hadn't known were sins until I became a mother. Was this fate's judgment? A debt paid in sorrow. Or just a cruel, indifferent twist of fate? I couldn't know. I could only sit, watching the steady rhythm of the machines, feeling the weight of unseen eyes.

The nurses moved with practiced grace, adjusting monitors and swapping fluid bags. Their expressions were gentle, their smiles soft but hollow. Did they see me as a mother drowning in grief? Or as a foolish girl reaping what she'd sown? I would never know. I only hoped they would see the love deep and boundlessly woven into every moment I stayed.

Time stretched. Hunger gnawed at the edges of my awareness, and exhaustion pressed heavy against me. But I didn't move. Didn't speak. Because leaving felt like another ending, and I wasn't ready to face that yet.

Eventually, the doctors urged me to leave the room; to move, to eat, to do something. I stepped out, but I had nowhere to go. My clothes were the same ones I wore when I left Friday night for the mountains, unchanged. I hadn't showered, hadn't brushed my teeth. Going home wasn't a choice; I had no keys, no way in.

Had my parents gotten my message yet? Were they coming? I needed help. I needed something to guide me forward.

Steve's family had made their decision, but it was still mine to make too. And I wasn't ready yet.

I just had to hold on. A little bit longer.

Steve and his parents arrived later in the evening. They brought a small bag of snacks and drinks. I was grateful. His parents stayed with Steven for a while before heading home, leaving Steve to stay with me. We sat on opposite sides of our son's bed, silent. There were no words, just the weight of guilt pressing down on both of us. We had left for a weekend getaway. We thought it would be fun.

We were naïve.

He was sick, and we didn't know. But of all people, we should have known. We sat. We cried. This wasn't how any of it was supposed to happen. This wasn't the life we imagined, not even in our worst fears.

Later, we lay together on the couch in the parents' room. Eventually, exhaustion won. Sleep came in broken pieces. But each time I woke, I found myself drawn to the window, the one that looked toward my heart.

Chapter Forty-Two
Petals of Loneliness

Sunday morning arrived with quiet footsteps. The visits had already begun. A doctor from the organ transplant team entered the room, his face composed but kind. "I'm sorry," he said gently. "We won't be able to use your baby's organs for donation. The bacteria in his body… it wouldn't be safe."

I swallowed hard, nodding.

"I know you wanted to do this," he continued. "It's an admirable thing. But in this case, it just won't work."

"I understand." My voice was small. "I was just hoping… my friend's baby is sick. The one down the hall. I thought if my baby could help her, then maybe all of this would make sense somehow. Maybe it wouldn't feel so…" I trailed off.

The doctor hesitated. "You mean baby Reagan?"

I nodded.

"I'm sorry," he said softly. "He passed yesterday. His mother has gone home."

"Oh."

The word felt hollow. I thought of her in the hallway just days ago; how she had looked at her son the way I looked at mine. How she had hoped, just as I had. But now he is gone. And soon, my son will be too.

The social workers arrived, and by then Steve's parents were back with us. They asked if we had weighed our options. If a decision had been made.

Steve and his parents turned to me. The weight of the answer was mine alone. They had decided. I didn't. What if it was wrong? I needed my parents, but they weren't there. What was I supposed to say?

"Ellie, have you made a decision?" Steve's mother's voice was gentle but firm.

She looked at me, waiting. "It is the right thing to do. It would be selfish to keep him alive like this."

The right thing. Let him go.

I stared at the social worker. My voice felt distant. "I guess… remove him from life support."

"Are you certain?"

Silence pressed against me.

"Yes," I whispered. "I'm certain."

"We'll need you to sign some paperwork confirming your decision. That you understand once life support is removed, your son will eventually stop breathing and…"

"I understand."

I signed.

"Nothing will happen until tomorrow," the social worker said gently. "There are legal steps to complete and medical preparations to finalize. We're aiming for the morning."

The words felt distant, almost unreal.

"In the meantime," they continued, "please don't hesitate to ask questions or seek support. Our grief counseling team is available. Let us know if you need anything."

Need?

What could I possibly need?

Steve and his parents planned to head home, returning tomorrow when everything would take place. They needed to reach out to the rest of the family, explain things to the younger kids and help them understand.

I didn't want to be alone again. But at the same time, what difference did it make? The decision had already been made. Nothing anyone did now would change that.

Steve had barely spoken for days. His parents handled everything. Pushed every decision. Maybe that was why, in some quiet way, their leaving felt like a relief.

I sat in silence, replaying the decision repeatedly. Had I done the right thing? How could a fifteen-year-old make a choice like this? Was it ever truly mine? Or had Steve's parents already decided, letting me believe I had control?

None of this made sense. I barely understood half of what was happening; how it had all spiraled to this moment. My mind pulled me back, unraveling every memory; the picnic, the night Steven cried, the way exhaustion won, forcing me to sleep in the hallway, being afraid of waking my mom.

If I had done something different, would it have mattered? Or was it already too late? I would never know. No one had answers.

As I sat lost in thought, my parents walked through the door.

"Mom! Dad!" My voice broke in relief. "You're finally here."

My mother scanned the room frantic. "Ellie, where is the baby?"

"Across the hallway," I said softly.

"We need to speak to the doctors," she said. "We don't know anything. What's going on?"

I hesitated. "I don't understand it all… but I can get the doctors. They can explain."

So, I sat. I listened.

The doctor spoke, his voice steady, but the words cut deep. I watched my parents' faces; saw the grief settle in, saw the weight of each sentence reshape them. My father's jaw tightened, holding back tears that refused to stay hidden. My mother crumbled, sobbing aloud, raw, unfiltered.

They asked every question we had already asked. And they got every answer we had already received.

Then they asked to see him.

I let them go alone.

They needed to see for themselves, needed to understand, in their way, that he was already gone.

Through the window, I could see them. My parents sat in the room across the hall, curtains open, nothing to hide the grief unfolding.

My dad sat by the bed, hands resting on my mother's shoulders, trying to ground her. Trying to offer something that might hold her together.

She shattered anyway.

Her sobs came in full-body thrusts, shaking her head, pleading with the doctors. As if begging hard enough might undo the inevitable.

It was painful to watch. To see her this way. To see my father try so desperately to comfort her, only to be pushed aside. She held my baby's hand. Stared at him. Loss and unrelenting pain spilling from her eyes.

I wondered if her grief was deeper than mine. If she loved him more because, somehow, she still saw him as hers. Maybe she did.

I wanted to comfort her. To tell her something, anything. But I had no comfort to give. And I had none to get. Finally, my parents returned to me.

My mother's voice broke the silence first. "Ellie, why did you sign that paper?"

Her words were heavy, pleading. "Haven't you seen those stories? The ones on TV? People in comas for eighteen years and then one day, just like that, they wake up. That could be him. If you don't give up, God can do anything. He could give us a miracle."

"Mom," I whispered. "We can't just leave him like this for eighteen years. The doctors said that he's brain dead. He won't come back from that."

She shook her head, her eyes wild. "Ellie, I told you he was sick, and you didn't listen to me. Oh, but you listened to *her*, didn't you? You believed Steve's mom over your own. And guess what?" Her voice cracked. "Your *old mom* was right. And she was wrong."

The words struck deep.

"If you had listened to me," she went on, "he could've gotten to the hospital sooner. Could've gotten help sooner. And then—then he wouldn't be like this now. This *is your* fault, Ellie. Because you refused to listen."

I swallowed hard. My voice was barely there. "Mom, if you *knew* he was that sick... why did you go to the mountains?"

Her breath caught.

"Why didn't you stay? Why didn't *you* take him to the doctors?"

Silence pressed in.

I looked at her. "She took him to the doctors. *Not you.* So that makes this *your* fault."

Her mouth opened, but before she could speak, my father cut in. His voice was firm, strained. "Just stop it. This isn't going to fix anything."

We stared at each other; at the grief, the anger, the wounds that would never fully heal.

"I made up my mind," I finally said. "I had days to think about it, and I signed the papers. I'm not changing my mind."

My mother's voice was sharp. "Well, *you* had days. *We* just got here."

"Well, whose fault is that?"

"Ellie, it took two days for the state police to find us. But as soon as they did, we *rushed* here."

The air was thick with words that couldn't be taken back. My mother stormed out of the room. My father followed. Through the window, I saw them again, standing with my son.

I stayed where I was. Watched. But now, the sadness was gone. Anger settled in its place. She blamed me. She thought this was *my* fault. And maybe, maybe she was right.

When they arrived, I thought they would hold me. Tell me they understood. Offer some shred of compassion. But they hadn't even looked at me that way. I got it, I did. But they were *my* parents. And I needed them. They were finally here. And still, I was alone.

I curled up on the couch, letting the weight of everything crash over me. How could I live knowing my mother blamed me? What if she was right? How could I live with *that?* The doctors told me it wasn't my fault. But their words didn't matter. My mother mattered.

I looked across the hall repeatedly through the night. Sleep barely came. My parents stayed in his room, never leaving. Anger twisted inside me. She blamed me.

I would never, *never* hurt my child. I had never even heard of this illness before. I couldn't have gotten the vaccine faster. I didn't *do* this. But maybe I waited too long. The first cries. Maybe if I had taken him to the doctor. Maybe if I hadn't cared so much about sleep; mine, my mom's. Maybe time could have made a difference.

Maybe.

I drifted into uneasy sleep. When I woke up, it was Monday morning.

Today was the day they would remove everything.

I wasn't ready.

Chapter Forty-Three
Petals of Remorse

My mother approached me one last time, her hands trembling, her voice raw. She begged me to reconsider. To leave my son on life support.

I met her pleading eyes but held firmly. "No, Mom," I said. "I can't."

She sobbed, shaking her head, refusing to let go of the hope that no one else shared. If the doctors had given even the faintest sign that things could change, I would have agreed. But they hadn't. This wasn't a coma. He was gone.

Her grief twisted into something sharper: blame. "You're only doing this because Steve's family says it's what's best," she spat. "They said he wasn't sick before and look at what happened. Did you learn nothing from trusting them?"

I flinched but didn't waver. "I'm following what the doctors said, Mom. This isn't about them."

She looked at me then, the pain in her face shifting, darkening. As if I were the one taking him from her. As if I were doing this out of cruelty, not love.

"I am not changing my mind," I said, my voice cold, final. The words hurt to say, but they had to be said. She had to understand—it was over.

My mom looked at me like I was choosing to kill my child, as if there was still some flicker of hope, and I was the one snuffing it out.

She could not or would not understand that nothing could change what was already set in motion. No miracle, no bargaining. The outcome had been written long before that moment. But to her, I was the one holding the pen.

The doctors sat down with us; me and Steve, my parents and his. Their expressions were steady, practiced, yet heavy with the weight of what they had to say.

"Only two people can go in at a time," one of them explained; his voice measured, careful. "Ellie and Steve, you'll go first. We'll remove everything, and then you can stay. As we mentioned, he will continue breathing for some time. After you both say goodbye, the grandparents can take turns."

Silence hung between us; thick and unyielding.

"Does anyone have any questions?"

My mom leaned forward. "Doctor," she whispered, barely audible. "Can't we just—just leave him on support? Hope for a miracle? They happen all the time. Maybe he'll wake up." Her voice cracked like something fragile, something breaking apart.

A pause. A glance was exchanged between the doctors.

"I'm sorry, ma'am," one finally said, his voice gentle but firm. "He will remain in a vegetative state indefinitely. He will never wake up."

She inhaled sharply; a small, unsteady breath. Then she looked down, staring at the ground as though searching for something-some answer, some reasoning that could undo it all. But there was nothing. Nothing but the cold reality was settling in.

The nurse ushered Steve and me into the room when the time came. We sat down, hesitant; as if crossing a threshold, we could never return from. This time, no personal protective equipment was needed; nothing to create distance between us and what was about to unfold.

She moved methodically, explaining each step as she removed the machines and tubes that had sustained him. First, the feeding tube. Then the breathing apparatus, heart monitors, IVs; each piece detached carefully, her movements gentle, practiced. But it felt like the unraveling of something much larger.

"This was helping regulate nutrition," she murmured. "This assisted his breathing."

One by one, she dismantled the lifelines, and soon, there was nothing left but him.

"You can hold him if you'd like," she offered, her voice soft, as if cradling the weight of the moment herself. "When he eventually stops breathing, just note the time and let me know."

She moved to the window, drawing the blinds shut. Then with a quiet nod, she stepped out, closing the door behind her.

The silence pressed in.

I cradled him in my arms, his soft little body still warm, still familiar. For a moment, he looked like he did on so many other nights curled against me; peaceful, as if only sleeping.

I watched the slow rise and fall of his chest, the delicate rhythm that still clung to life. Bringing him closer, I pressed his cheek against mine, letting the softness linger, memorizing it. I breathed him in the scent of his hair, his skin, the faint sweetness still there beneath the sickness. Tears slipped down my face; silent, heavy, but there were no words. Only his aching presence.

Then I handed him to Steve. Steve held him gently; his grip firm but reverent, as though holding onto the pieces of what should have been. "I love you, little man," he whispered. His voice cracked, breaking on the weight of it. "I wish we could have gone fishing together, hunting" His breath shuddered. "All the things I thought we'd get to do."

He pressed his lips to our son's forehead. "Goodbye, buddy," he murmured, and then tears came. Slow, unrelenting.

The grief between us was unbearable, unlike anything we had ever known. I had lost loved ones before, but they had lived long, full lives. This was different. This was unnatural.

I thought of Rob's parents. Of the unbearable choice they had once faced. Of how this weighs the decision; letting go was never supposed to belong to us.

Steve handed our son back to me. We watched and waited. Each breath was borrowed time, ticking away before our eyes. These last moments so brief and so fragile were everything.

Then we noticed the clock. More time had passed than expected. More than an hour.

"Steve..." I whispered. "Do you think the doctors were wrong? They said maybe half an hour, but it's already been over an hour. Maybe he's stronger than they thought, maybe he can breathe on his own."

The flicker of hope startled me, dangerous and desperate.

Steve exhaled, his eyes fixed on our son. "It was just an estimate," he said, cautiously. "Not a guarantee. Let's wait a little longer, then we'll let them know. Okay?"

I nodded. "Okay."

I clung to him, pressing my lips against his soft skin. "I love you, little guy," I whispered. "You were a precious gift; one I wasn't sure I could take care of, but I tried. I tried so hard. I'm so sorry. I'm so sorry if this is my fault. I'm so sorry I didn't know you were sick. I'm so sorry I wasn't the mom you needed. I'm just so, so sorry."

At that moment, he took in his final breath; a small, sudden gasp and then stopped.

I waited, hoping. But nothing more came. I pulled him close, holding him one last time, letting my grief spill into the silence.

1:34 PM. Monday, April 30, 1990.

Steve held him again, one last time, his tears falling freely. We told the nurse.

Then, we left. And the grief followed.

Steve's parents entered the room next. They were in the room for only a few moments; just long enough to say goodbye. A priest went with them, murmuring prayers; his voice steady and solemn as he performed the last rites.

The ritual was unfamiliar to me, but I watched as Steve's parents bowed their heads, hands clasped, drawing comfort from the words meant to guide their grandson's soul to rest.

When they appeared, their faces were streaked with silent tears.

There was nothing to say.

Then my parents went in.

Time became strange. Elastic. I wasn't watching the clock, but their absence felt endless. My mother refused to leave. I could hear muffled voices, then my father's quiet pleading, then something more urgent pulling her away.

I felt the irritation rise, sharp and bitter. *Her grief shouldn't be harder than mine.* It wasn't fair. It wasn't hers to carry like this; like she was his mother, not me. But exhaustion dulled the edges of my frustration. Maybe she wasn't thinking either. Maybe none of us were.

Then the staff approached. Their voices were soft, measured. "There's nothing left to do," one of them said. "You're free to leave."

Leave.

The word settled in, strange and wrong. I had been there for four days. Now, I was walking away. Leaving. But he wasn't. He was staying.

I couldn't go home with my parents. Not yet. Watching my mother consumed by grief was too much, too overwhelming on top of everything I already carried. I asked if I could go home with Steve instead. They agreed.

When we arrived, his siblings were waiting. One by one, they came to us, offering quiet condolences. Hugs. Soft words. One of them handed me a small drawing picture of the three of us; a tiny family preserved in pencil lines. Another simply held onto me, wrapping me in an endless embrace, as if trying to absorb the sorrow for me.

It was the first time anyone had truly offered me something.

Steve and I retreated upstairs. We laid down on his bed, side by side, the weight of everything pressing down. We didn't speak. There were no words left.

We just existed in grief, exhaustion and silence until I finally decided I was ready to go home.

Chapter Forty-Four
Petals of Greif

I walked through the door. My mom sat with my grandmom; their quiet conversation filling the space. I murmured a hello, barely stopping before retreating to my bedroom.

I haven't been home since Friday. I just needed to be in my own space; to breathe, to exist without eyes on me. I was exhausted. My body ached for a shower, for clean clothes, for something familiar.

I wanted to hold my son. But he was gone.

Instead, I searched for something like an outfit, his baby blanket, anything to keep him close. Then I stopped. The room was empty. The cradle. His dresser. His diapers, his wipes; everything was gone.

I stared at the hollow space where his things had been, my breath caught in my throat. The emptiness swallowed me whole.

Then my father spoke behind me, his voice steady, subdued. "I packed it all away," he said. "I didn't get rid of anything, just put it away. I thought seeing it would be too hard."

Then, he left.

I turned, scanning the room, my mind racing. *The poster. Where did he put the poster?*

I opened my closet. There it was. The life-sized photo from the hospital. I pulled it out, pinned it inside the closet door. Then I lay down on the floor and closed the door, sealing myself in with the only piece of him I had left.

After a few hours and a long nap in the closet, my dad woke me.

"We have to plan the funeral," he said gently.

I blinked, disoriented. *The funeral.* I hadn't even thought about that, hadn't realized it was something that needed doing. I hadn't looked beyond the past few days; hadn't considered what was next.

We didn't belong to a church. We had no minister. And everything had to move fast.

"They don't embalm babies," my dad explained, his tone careful, measured. I didn't know the specifics, only that this meant we had to arrange everything sooner than most.

"I understand," I murmured.

I sat down as he made calls, listening but not engaging. He spoke with Steve's dad, trying to sort out the details, taking the lead. They agreed on things; piecing together arrangements based on what he'd already learned, funeral costs, logistics, who would pay for what.

I couldn't process it. I couldn't pay for anything. I couldn't make sense of what mattered, what needed deciding. It was overwhelming, and I was grateful that our parents were handling it. But at the same time, I felt oddly absent like something crucial was happening, and I wasn't a part of it.

I wasn't making decisions. But I also had no idea *how* to decide. I was both relieved and saddened.

My dad asked if I wanted to go with him to the flower shop and help pick out flowers.

"Sure," I said. I was grateful—finally, there was something I could do.

The shop smelled beautiful, an overwhelming mixture of blooms; soft, sweet, fresh. The florist handed us a book filled with arrangements, each page a carefully crafted display of petals and meaning.

As my dad flipped through, my eyes landed on one that stopped me. A *bleeding-heart*, white carnations shaped into a heart, red roses cascading down the center like falling blood.

My dad hesitated. "It's a bit dark," he said.

But it wasn't. It was exactly how I felt, beautiful in its' sorrow, perfect in its grief.

He showed me others gentle whites, soft pastels; but my heart had already decided. That was the one.

We chose a spray for the casket top; elegant, full. Then I spotted a small cross pillow with a singular rose and knew that I wanted it for the inside of the casket.

My dad spoke with the florist, arranging delivery, discussing costs. I tried to focus, but my mind kept drifting back to everything that had happened; back to the impossible days leading to this moment.

Flowers almost felt like an afterthought. But still, I was grateful my dad had found a way for me to be included.

"Ellie, Steven will be buried at Riverside Cemetery. There are two options available, the original baby section near the old mausoleum or the newer area along the river. Do you have a preference?"

I barely hesitated. "Please, don't put him in the old section."

I at once pictured the chipped statues, the broken-headed lambs, the worn-down space teenagers used for drinking and escape. That wasn't right. It wasn't where he belonged.

I exhaled as the weight of it settled in. *He was going to be buried here.* Here, in the cemetery where I had spent my childhood riding my bike, wandering through the quiet rows, visiting the cats at the barn. Here, where I had traced my steps so many times, stopping at Rob's grave, thinking, remembering. Now, part of me would stay here forever.

The headstone.

My parents said this was the final task, and once we picked it, everything would be done.

We drove a few towns over to a monument store, stepping into a quiet showroom filled with polished stones. Just like the flower shop, there were so many options; pages and displays filled with traditional choices, safe choices. I wasn't interested in what was standard, only in something that felt right; something bright, something *his*.

Not a lamb. Nothing fragile. Nothing that could be broken.

We flipped through pages together, scanning the rows of gray and black stones, the occasional marble. Then, I saw *a pinkish hue, soft and rose-colored*, standing out against the dark.

That one. That's what I want.

My dad hesitated. "Are you sure, Ellie? That stone's a bit big."

It wasn't massive, just a little larger than the rest but *it wasn't depressing*, and that mattered.

"Yes," I said. "That's the one."

Then came the details, the name, the dates. He took my last name because I wasn't married. But it only felt right to include Steve's, too. We hyphenated the two together.

Next, engravings. The salesman showed us options; symbols, figures, images etched into the stone. I remembered Rob's headstone; his school photo perfectly preserved in granite.

Then I saw it. A little boy with praying hands. It spoke to me, a glimpse of what might have been. If my son had had a chance to grow up, maybe he would have looked like this kneeling beside his bed, hands clasped, whispering a prayer.

I nodded. *Yes.*

My mom agreed. "It's perfect."

Then, I noticed the rosary.

"Can I include this too?" I asked.

The salesman said yes.

"But we're not Catholic," my mom reminded me.

"No," I said, "but Steve's family is. I think they would appreciate it."

A pause.

"I don't think it's appropriate."

"Dad, can we please do it? I think it would be nice to recognize their beliefs."

Another pause.

Then finally he nodded. "Yes, Ellie. It's fine."

He filled out the paperwork, paid, and we drove back home.

Silence. Again. There was nothing left to say.

My parents dropped me off at Steve's house. I needed to tell him about the flowers, the burial location. I needed to be *with* him. I needed someone to comfort me.

The day had been consumed by planning, decisions, and details. It had been all business. No one had hugged me; no one had asked how I was holding up. Maybe they were too lost in their pain, maybe they blamed me and couldn't bear to offer anything.

I just wanted someone to hold me. Someone to tell me it would be okay.

When I stepped inside, Steve's mom was waiting. She held up a delicate white satin outfit.

"I think this would be perfect for Steven," she said. "It was from one of our christenings."

It was formal, pristine, like a dress, though it wasn't. I hesitated. I had planned to bury him in one of *his* onesies, something familiar, something soft, something *his*.

"No, I think this would be better," she continued. "It's already been to the dry cleaner." Her voice was steady, decisive.

She wanted *this*. And really, what was I going to say? She hadn't chosen the gravesite, the flowers, the tombstone—*this* was hers to give.

"Okay," I said. "Sure."

Still, it felt strange dressing him in something he had never worn before, something that wasn't his. But she hadn't asked, only decided. And I let her.

Steve and I spoke briefly about everything. He had told Clay and some of the others. The funeral was on a weekday, meaning most of our friends would be in school. I didn't mind. I wasn't even sure I wanted to be there.

The next morning, we got ready and headed to the funeral home. My dad ushered me inside, past rows of empty chairs. Then I saw it. The smallest casket I had ever seen. I hadn't known they made them so small.

Everything inside me collapsed. My legs buckled, my body froze mid-fall, locked between motion and paralysis. My dad caught me before I hit the ground.

"I can't do this," I pleaded, my voice breaking. "I can't go forward. I can't see him like that."

"You have to," he said. "You can."

I shook my head, but he was already guiding me forward, past the final row.

Steve's family stood around the casket; already there, already waiting. As I approached, the white satin outfit came into view, perfect and untouched. Then his face. *Frozen in time. Lifeless. Beautiful.*

I knelt, reaching in. My arms wrapped around him, pressing him close; but his body was cold, stiff. The shock rattled through me. I should have known, but nothing had prepared me. I stayed there; silent, unmoving.

People came and went; my sister, my brother, my parents' friends. Aunts and uncles, extended family. Whispers surrounded me; hushed condolences, words I couldn't grasp.

"I'm so sorry."

"It's such a shame."

"He looks beautiful."

The words wheezed past, weightless and meaningless, ringing in my ears like a distant hum. I knew I was supposed to stand, supposed to greet them, supposed to acknowledge their grief.

But I *couldn't.*

Then the drive to Riverside.

The cemetery so familiar, once filled with childhood memories, now hollowed out by sorrow. We followed the little loop, stepping out onto the uneven earth, where the ground had been carved away for him to sleep *forever.*

The words came soft, final. The casket lowered. I stood there, drowning. Like swimming underwater, gasping, reaching, sinking deeper, deeper. No one pulled me back. No one reached for me. Before I knew it, everyone was leaving. Cars pulling away, voices fading.

I turned to walk, then noticed the fresh dirt beside his grave. A plastic marker stood at the next plot—*Reagan.* My friend's baby.

Down the hall from one another in the hospital.

Now, side by side forever.

Two innocent babies, born into impossibility, buried in eternity.

Steve's family hosted the after-lunch. I couldn't tell you who was there.

Steve and I slipped upstairs without a word. We laid down on his bed, side by side, the silence stretching heavy between us.

We stared at the picture of our son, still and small and perfect, and it's like the air leaves the room. Steve doesn't know what I'm thinking. I don't know what's in his head either. But the grief? The grief is mutual. It's earth-shattering. It swallows the words before they even form.

There's nothing to say that would make any of it easier. So, we say nothing. Hours later, I returned home and went to my room.

A quiet knock at the door. I hesitated, then opened it. It was my grandmother.

She looked at me, her expression unreadable. Then, softly, she said, "Ellie, I am so sorry your baby died."

Before I could react, she wrapped her arms around me. For a moment, I wanted to hug her back. To say *thank you*. But then I remembered. The stares. The judgment. The way her words once stuck like daggers calling me a sinner, telling me my baby deserved to die, just like David and Bathsheba's in the Bible.

I remembered the hatred in her eyes. And so, I stood still. I did not move. Did not return the embrace. She released me. Without another word, she walked away.

I shut my door.

Chapter Forty-Five
Petals of Blame

Returning to school felt like stepping into a world that had kept moving while I had been frozen in time.

It was May. The school year is almost over. I had missed so much due to transferring schools, six weeks of maternity leave and the funeral. I was completely lost. I didn't even know what classes I was supposed to be in or where I was supposed to go.

And then, the questions.

"Aren't you pregnant?"

"I thought you left."

"I heard you had a baby."

"Is it true that your baby died?"

It was overwhelming. Did they care? Or was it just gossip; just something to whisper about, something shocking to tell each other?

They stared. Some murmured sympathy. Others said it was *for the best;* that I was too young to be a mother anyway. Noise. Voices. Opinions I never asked for. I felt like I was going to explode.

I walked out. Just left. I made my way to the cemetery and sat by my son's grave. The flowers from previous days stayed, slightly wilted, but still there. I could smell them, and it reminded me of the funeral parlor. A sadness gnawed at my soul; relentless, consuming.

I wanted to lie down, to sink into the dirt beneath the earth where it was quiet, where the questions couldn't reach me, where the opinions would finally disappear. I knew I couldn't stay. But it was the only place I wanted to be.

When I got home, my parents were waiting. A white-frosted cake sat on the kitchen table, speckled with sprinkles.

"Happy 16th birthday, Ellie."

I hadn't forgotten, but I had no intention of celebrating. How could I? My son died five days ago. This was supposed to be a milestone, the year I could finally drive, the big sweet sixteen party. But none of that mattered now. What was there to celebrate?

The earth had shattered beneath me. If I could have traded places, I would have. I would have left, and he would have stayed.

Still, my parents were trying. They sang to me hesitantly, unsure. Their faces said everything. They still blamed me.

"You guys didn't have to do this," I murmured.

"We weren't sure if you'd want us to," my dad admitted. "But we felt like we should at least try."

"Thanks."

"Here, have some cake."

"No, I'm not hungry."

My mom stiffened, frustration flickering across her face. "I appreciate it," I said quickly, trying to soften the rejection. "I do. I just don't feel like celebrating right now."

Her lips pressed into a thin line. "Well, *I* didn't feel like celebrating either, but I still made you a cake. The least you could do is eat a slice."

"Mom, I *don't* want it."

"Ellie, don't you know you should be *grateful?* Everything doesn't revolve around you."

I hesitated. "Are you mad at me?"

"Why should I be?"

I swallowed. "Do you think I've done something worth being mad about?"

"No."

"Then why do you think I'm mad?"

"Because you're being short with me."

265

She exhaled sharply, crossing her arms. "Maybe if you stopped being so selfish, things would be a lot better. Like if you hadn't let Steven go to that stupid daycare."

The words hit like a slap.

"You know that's where he got sick, don't you?"

My chest tightened.

"All those germs," she continued, voice rising. "I knew it wasn't a good idea, but you insisted on *doing what you wanted.* Then, when he got sick, I told you, and again you refused to listen. Because his mom knows so much better than *yours*, right?"

I stared at her, speechless.

"And guess what? Again, I was right. And now he's gone."

Anger clawed its way up my throat. "Mom, you acted like he was your baby. The way you cried at the hospital, the way you clung to him—."

She recoiled.

"It was ridiculous to think he wasn't going to be brain-dead anymore," I said, my voice shaking. "How crazy is that?"

Her eyes darkened.

"So, I'm crazy now?" she snapped.

I didn't answer.

"But I knew better the whole time, didn't I?" she seethed. "If you had just listened to me, he would still be here. But instead, he's dead."

She exhaled sharply.

"I hate you," I whispered.

The words sliced through her.

"Leave me alone."

Did she believe this was my fault?

I sent him to daycare so she wouldn't have to carry it all. To give her a break. Babies go to daycare every single day, and they don't just die. That's not how it's supposed to happen.

But now he's gone. And I'm drowning in anger; I can't hold back anymore. Anger at her. At myself. The entire world for not warning me.

I'm furious for a thousand varied reasons, and none of them make it easier. I can't control it. It's boiling over. I feel like I'm going to explode.

I turned and ran out the door, down the street; hot tears spilling as rage and sorrow tangled inside me. I didn't stop. I kept running straight to Steve's house.

When I arrived, it didn't take long to realize Steve was drunk.

He sat on the porch, a beer in hand, Clay beside him. As soon as he saw me, he staggered up, wrapping me in a sloppy hug. His breath reeked of alcohol, and his skin was damp with sweat. He pressed his lips against mine, sloppy, forceful.

Clay shifted uncomfortably. "Sorry, Ellie. I've been trying to get him to slow down, but he won't listen."

Steve grinned, wobbling on his feet. "Come on, Ellie, sit down. Have a beer."

"No thanks, I don't want one." I hesitated. "I was hoping to talk. I just got into a fight with my mom, and I needed to talk."

Steve nodded. "Okay, Ellie, here you can talk to me and Clay. Right, Clay?"

Clay exhaled, glancing away. "Uh… sure, Steve."

Then Steve laughed sharply, bitterly. "I was just telling Clay here what a loser of a father I am. Did you know that, Ellie? Did you know I'm a worthless dad?" He gestured vaguely at the beer in his hand. "Can't take my son fishing. Can't take him hunting. Not like a real dad."

I swallowed, my pulse quickening.

"Steve, I think you've had enough to drink," I said carefully. "Please. Take a break."

He looked at me, eyes unfocused. "What happened with your mom?"

"We fought. Because she made me a birthday cake."

Steve blinked, swaying. "That's right, your birthday." His words slurred together. "I knew that. I got a present for you too. You just gotta come inside to get it."

For a moment, excitement flickered inside me. He had not forgotten. Just maybe he knew today mattered.

I followed him inside. He led me to his parents' bedroom, the only room in the house with air conditioning. The only room with a lock.

Steve stumbled closer, breath hot against my skin. Then, he pushed me down on the bed. His mouth swallowed me, his teeth scraping my lips until I tasted blood.

"Steve—get off me."

"Come on, Ellie," he murmured. "I'm sad. I just want to have a little fun."

"No, Steve. I am not doing this right now."

But he wasn't listening. He was on top of me, yanking at my clothes, forcing them down.

"Steve, stop," I gasped, panic rising. "Seriously. I'm not kidding. You're drunk; you need to stop."

He ignored me.

"Come on, Ellie," he murmured. "I just want to feel better, even for a minute, please."

Then before I could process, before I could fight harder it was over.

Steve staggered, tripped as he pulled away, laughing hollowly.

"Sorry, Ellie," he mumbled. "I just wanted to feel something, ya know?"

Then, just like that, he was gone.

Back outside. Back to Clay. Back to another beer. I lay there, staring at the ceiling. What the hell just happened? Slowly, I pulled my clothes back on; shaking, stunned. Then I ran to the bathroom.

"I'm leaving. I need to go home."

Clay looked at me, concern flickering in his eyes. "Are you okay, Ellie? You don't look right."

"I'm fine, Clay." The words felt hollow. "I just need to go home."

"Come on Ellie, have a beer," Steve slurred, grinning.

"No. I need to go now."

I walked away. *Alone.* The air felt thick, my steps were unsteady. I couldn't understand what had just happened. I had asked him to stop. I had said no. But he ignored me. He didn't care. But he was drunk. He wasn't thinking straight. He's hurting. We all are. He didn't mean it. He's still my boyfriend. So—it wasn't rape, right? It's not like he hurt me.

My mind raced, tangled in contradictions. What was happening? Then, fear struck, sudden and suffocating. Oh my God. What if I get pregnant again? I cannot get pregnant again. I needed birth control pills. I needed to protect myself. But my parents could never know. I couldn't go home. I hated it there. So instead, I went to Michelle's house.

Michelle was thrilled to see me, practically beaming when I showed up at her door. She could drive, so I asked her if she'd take me to Planned Parenthood the next day.

"I need to get on the pill," I told her. "I can't risk getting pregnant again."

She didn't hesitate. "Of course."

Then I told her what happened with Steve.

"You should dump him," she said at once.

But I still loved him. We had just gone through something traumatic, tragic—how could I abandon him now? He was hurting. We all were.

I asked Michelle if I could stay over.

Her mom said yes. My dad said okay.

That night, we blasted music, painted each other's fingernails and toes; messy colors smudged across skin. Michelle had a bottle of vodka, swiped from her mom, who had already passed out.

We drank. And for the first time in what felt like forever, I was laughing. Not thinking. Being a teenager. Not drowning in everything that had just happened.

The next morning, she drove me to Planned Parenthood. I got on the pill. Relief. I couldn't go through another teenage pregnancy.

Now, I just had to hope, hope it wasn't already too late.

Chapter Forty-Six
Petals of Insanity

Steve never apologized. He didn't even remember. Lately, he's been drowning himself, always drunk or trying to be. And he's still making his runs to the city, still selling, even though there's no reason to. We don't have a child to support anymore. He doesn't need the money. So why risk everything? It's like he's spiraling, pulled into a darkness he doesn't know how to escape. But I can't pull him back. I can't even pull myself back.

He's doing everything he can to feel something, to drown out the guilt. I'm doing everything I can to make sure I don't feel at all. The carving started again. I stopped while I was pregnant, but now, I just don't care. His name is etched into my skin, carved repeatedly, as if making it deeper could bring him back. And eating? What's the point? My body is different now; unfamiliar hips widened, stomach soft and scarred with stretch marks, with proof of something that no longer exists. A body that carried life but holds nothing now.

Mother's Day is days away. But am I a mother? I gave birth. My body changed for him. But my arms are empty. I failed him. I failed at the one thing that mattered, keeping him safe. And my grandmother was right. Maybe this is justice for my sins. Maybe this was always meant to happen.

Would he still be alive if we had given him up? If we had made a different choice? Would Steve still be whole? Would he still be drinking for the joy of it, instead of silencing whatever's eating him alive? We were different before. But now, we're shattered in a way that can't be undone. There's no going back. Everything is different now.

I feel lost. Empty. And there's no one to turn to. My mom is drowning in her own grief, barely looking at me except to remind me that it's my fault. My dad is absent more than he's present. Steve is always drunk. No one wants to talk about what happened, and when they do, it's just a fight, full of words that slice deeper than silence ever could.

And school? That's its own kind of torture. The questions never stop. *What happened? How did it happen? Why?* As if I have answers, as if I understand, as if explaining would change anything. But I don't waste my breath. They don't care. They just want something to talk about.

I'm desperate. Alone. And I want it to end.

Mom made it clear this grief is mine to bear. If I had never brought him into this world, she wouldn't be suffering now. When she looks at me, she doesn't see her daughter. She sees the reason she lost him.

So, I should take that pain away. Hers. Mine.

I went downstairs to my dad's gun cabinet. He's a cop, has plenty, but these guns are old, locked away like something forgotten. I don't even know if they work. But the bullets are there.

I grab a pack. A gun.

Then I ran upstairs to my bedroom. The door slammed behind me. The weight sits in my hands. Heavy. Cold. And finally, for the first time in too long, everything is quiet.

I could do it right here in my room. But then my mom and dad would have to see, would have to deal with it. No. That's not enough. Steve should see. He should *know*.

All I ever did was love him. And all he ever did was hurt me. He used me, over and over; taking what he wanted and leaving nothing behind. I could be pregnant again, and he wouldn't even remember.

He should go with me. This is his fault as much as mine. I can't stand the idea of him moving on; living his life like none of this ever happened. It's not *fair*. It's not *right*. We were supposed to be together with our son forever. That's it. I'll bring it to school. I'll take him with me. And all those people, the ones who have mocked me, whispered about me, spread their rumors like a disease they'll see. They'll *finally* see. I'll give them something to talk about. Something better than my poor baby.

I woke up the next morning and packed the gun and bullets into my backpack like it was any other day. No one else knew. No one could guess what I was carrying.

At school, I placed my backpack in my locker, locked the door, and thought about the perfect moment. It had to be right. It had to matter.

I wondered if my mom would finally miss me. If she'd finally realized she loved me. She hadn't hugged me. Not once. Not since Steven died. Not since the day she decided this loss belonged to me. She blamed me from the very beginning.

I didn't know how to say what I felt. How could I untangle it all? The layers were too deep; buried under years of hiding, years of silence. And when I finally told the truth, when I stood up for what was right, they still didn't see me.

They tried to erase him before he was even born. They wanted him to disappear. Now, suddenly, he's the most important thing in their world. *But what about me?* I am still here. I am hurting. And I need somebody. Anybody. Please.

I saw Steve in the hallway and walked up to him.

"Hey, what's up?"

He turned, smiling. "Hey, Ellie. You look pretty today."

"Thanks," I said, voice steady.

Steve then said, "I thought maybe we could do something fun together this weekend, since it's Mother's Day and all. Figured you wouldn't want to just sit at home."

I considered it for a second, then nodded. "Yeah, that sounds nice."

"Okay. Let me know if you have any ideas."

Then, just like that, he leaned in and kissed me. It was so simple. So normal. But I felt nothing. Not the warmth of his lips. Not the weight of his touch. Just the steady rhythm of my heartbeat. And the quiet certainty of what would come next.

The first half of the school day passed in a blur. I moved through the halls, through the classes, but I wasn't really *there*. The plan played on a loop in my mind; each detail sharpening, each step becoming more certain. This was the only way. The only way either of us could have peace.

We were both suffering, both tarnished. At least, *I* was. A girl already used up; my body marked by a child that no longer existed. A body that carried proof but held nothing now.

Everything felt distant. The noise around me was muffled, like I was hearing it from underwater. The people walking past seeing me but looking right through me. Was I even *here* or was this some half-formed dream?

What if none of this was real? What if I woke up right now and everything was different? This *wasn't* the solution. This *wasn't* the answer. Maybe just maybe I needed help. But there was no help. Who could help me? *I* was supposed to help myself. But how could I trust myself?

I turned down the hallway, feet moving before my mind could stop them. I walked through the doors of the guidance office.

"Do you have an appointment?"

"No," I said, voice steady. "But it's an emergency. I need to see a counselor. Right away."

I didn't even know who my counselor was. I had never been here before. Now, at the very end of the school year, I sat in the waiting room for the first time. And for the first time, I let myself hope that just maybe someone would listen.

"Hello, Ellie. I'm Mr. Juno. How can I help you today? I was told you couldn't wait for an appointment."

"Yes, sir, that's correct," I said, voice steady, but barely hanging on. "I need help, and I wasn't sure where else to go."

I hesitated for a second, then forced the words out. "My backpack is in my locker, and right now, there's a gun and a box of bullets in it."

The air in the room shifted.

"A real gun? A real, working gun?"

"It's real," I admitted. "But honestly, I have no idea if it works. I don't even know if the bullets I brought are the right ones for it."

His expression remained calm, but something in his posture changed; something quiet, careful.

"You said it's in your locker right now?"

"Yes, that's correct."

He nodded slightly, then stood up. "Ellie, can you hang on just a second? I need to grab something from the other room."

"Sure."

I sat there, staring at my hands, at the edge of his desk, at the door that had closed behind him. The seconds stretched. Then, finally, he returned.

"I'm going to need you to write down your locker number and combination, please."

"It's 50—no, here, just take it."

I scribbled the numbers onto the paper, slid it across the desk. He picked up his phone.

"Lisa, can you send maintenance up? I need help retrieving a student's backpack from their locker."

A moment later, Lisa entered, took the slip of paper, and disappeared.

Mr. Juno folded his hands. "Ellie, what were you planning to do? Why did you bring that to school?"

I swallowed hard. "It's... complicated. It doesn't even make much sense to me right now. But I wanted to kill myself and my boyfriend."

His eyes flickered with concern, quiet and understanding, but he let me keep going.

"It's a long story, and I don't want to get into it. But I changed my mind. I realized it was a dumb idea. I don't want to hurt anyone."

I hesitated. "Well... maybe myself. But not now. Not like that."

His phone rang.

"Mr. Juno, Mr. Keen is here for his daughter."

I turned as my dad stepped into the room, still in his police uniform. My backpack sat in his hands. They had called him.

"Mr. Keen," Mr. Juno said carefully. "Ellie brought a gun to school today and we're very concerned. She has homicidal and suicidal thoughts. She needs to be removed from the school and seek immediate emergency help."

My dad sighed, apologized to them all, then guided me out of the room. Away from the school. Into his patrol car.

"Ellie, what in the world were you thinking?"

I stared ahead, avoiding his eyes. "I don't know. I wasn't."

The patrol car moved through the streets, each turn bringing me closer to a place I didn't want to be.

"I'm taking you for an emergency evaluation," Dad continued, his voice tight with controlled frustration. "They need to make sure you're safe to come home. Depending on what you say, they might admit you for 48 hours."

I gripped my seatbelt, the weight of it pressing into my chest. "Dad, I don't need to go. I didn't even do anything. I realized it was stupid, that's why I told them."

He didn't respond.

When we arrived, I saw the bars on the front doors and on the windows. It wasn't the state hospital, but it was close enough.

He signed me in, explaining everything; his voice measured, controlled. I watched him fill out form after form, each one cementing the fact that I was *here*.

Eventually, a woman came to get me, and led me back into a quiet, void room.

I don't remember much of what she said. She asked me the same questions, over and over.

"Have you hurt yourself?"

"Have you hurt anyone?"

"Do you plan to hurt yourself or someone else?"

I knew what answers she needed to hear. I wasn't staying here. Not for 48 hours. Not for any amount of time.

"I had an irrational thought," I told her. "But I realized it was stupid, and I told someone."

"So, you never intended to follow through?"

"Never," I said firmly. "I would never hurt anyone."

My dad agreed to secure the guns in a place I couldn't access.

They discussed it, measured my responses and weighed their options.

In the end, they decided I was safe to go home. They didn't force me to stay.

"You do have the option to remain here if you want to," the woman said.

I barely let her finish before shaking my head.

There was no chance in hell.

Dad led me out, back into the car, back toward home. I sat in silence, wondering if I had escaped or if I had only postponed the inevitable. Dad brought me home and told my mom everything.

She looked at me like I wasn't just the murderer of her grandchild, but something worse. Something unrecognizable. Something she might need to protect herself from. A locked door. A light left on. Even a weapon under her pillow. I couldn't stand that look.

I called Steve and begged him to come over. He showed up with Clay. My parents let us go into the basement, just like they always had. They didn't seem to care anymore. Not about me. Not about whether I was alone with him. Maybe that was their punishment; letting me rot in the choices I made.

I told Steve and Clay what happened at school. I didn't tell Steve that I had planned to take *him* with me. Just that I had planned to hurt myself.

I cried. Told him everything; how I still couldn't believe it, how I was drowning in it, how none of it made sense. I asked all my questions. But like everyone else, they had no answers.

I couldn't believe I had showed up at school with a gun. I've never done anything that reckless before never even come close. But it's grief. This unbearable loss claws at me from the inside. Trying to imagine a future without him, while also failing school, hearing my mom say this was my fault, carrying all this heat and fury toward my grandmother.

I'm drowning in blame from others, from myself. And there's no one offering comfort. No one is even trying to help me breathe through it. It's too much. And I don't know how to survive it. Steve just wanted to drink.

"Are you still selling?" I asked him.

"Yeah."

"Why?"

"I've got prior commitments."

He said he'd be gone most weekends, finishing up whatever deals he had left.

Then he talked about drinking. So, we did. We grabbed Michelle and Clay. We went to the local bar, waited outside, and begged strangers to buy us something. Forty ounces.

It takes time, but if you ask enough people, you always find someone willing, for a few bucks or a cheap feel.

Michelle didn't mind keeping up our end of the deal. And then, we drank. We drank at the state hospital, in abandoned buildings, in cars of people willing to drive us around for a little fun. Drinking, drinking. Until it was the only thing that mattered. I stopped eating. I drank all day.

Then Michelle offered me pot. Steve wouldn't approve. He hated drugs, said they ruined athletes, ruined people. But me? I had nothing left to lose. So, I tried it. And it was better than drinking. No constant bathroom trips, no throwing up. No moments when I drank so much, I felt even sadder. This made me laugh. Everything was funny. For the first time in too long, I wasn't suffocating. I wanted to feel free. I wanted to stop caring. And that's exactly what I did. Day after day. Drinking. Getting high. Spending more time with Michelle. Less time with Steve. He was always gone on weekends, keeping secrets that I didn't ask about.

But it didn't matter. Because I was keeping my own.

Forty-Seven

Petals of Fury

Dad announced it as a decision already made. "We're going to start family counseling."

I wanted no part of it. I already knew where my mom stood on *everything*.

"We need this," Dad insisted. "Our family is falling apart. We need to work through things since Steven's death."

It didn't matter what I thought. He had already set it up.

We walked into the office and met Janice. Just Janice no Miss, no Mrs. Just the name, said plainly, as if it was supposed to make us trust her more.

Dad caught her up on everything. She nodded, taking it all in, then stared—long and deliberate—before asking the question that made my skin crawl.

"How does that make you feel?"

And then she waited, like whatever came next would be the most earth-shattering thing she'd ever heard. Her intensity unsettled me. I didn't like her. I didn't understand why she *cared* about my feelings or why I was supposed to spill them out to a stranger. We only went a handful of times. And every time, me and Mom ended up fighting. She was still resentful that I had listened to Steve's mom over her when Steven was sick. I was still furious that she acted like she was his mother, not me.

We kept dragging up the same arguments. The same anger. We always ended up in the same place, nowhere. Nothing resolved. I always left feeling worse than when I came. So, I decided I wasn't going back.

Mom said she'd keep going for a while—said she needed someone to listen. Someone who could *understand*.

I was barely home anymore. I hated being there. I hated seeing my grandmom. I hated seeing my mom even more. The house felt foreign, like it didn't belong to me anymore. I didn't belong. Unwanted. Unloved. The enemy.

Whenever I walked past my mom, it felt like stepping into a cold breeze, like something unseen was pushing me away. Her silence carried blame. Her stare carried disappointment. Finally, one day, I asked.

"Mom, why do you hate me so much?"

She blinked, taken aback. "I don't hate you. Why would you think such a thing?"

I scoffed. "Because you still blame me for what happened. You're cold towards me. I feel uncomfortable around you."

Her expression hardened. "Ellie, you're just making things up to be mean. You're trying to be a martyr now. I don't do any of that."

"Oh? That's funny, because Janice said I am handling everything very well."

I clenched my fists. "Well, is Janice helping you work through realizing that Steven was *my* baby, not yours?"

Her face barely moved. "Ellie, I don't think that way."

Then she exhaled slowly, like she was about to reveal some great truth.

"Actually, Janice said my daughter is a real B-I-T-C-H."

She spelled it out carefully, like she wanted me to hear every single letter.

I laughed sharply, bitterly. "Oh, did she now? That sounds like a great counselor. Calling your daughter that."

My voice rose. "Does that make you feel good, Mom? That she said that about me. Does that make you happy?"

She didn't answer. I didn't wait.

"She's the real bitch."

I stormed out, refusing to hear another word.

Chapter Forty-Eight

Petals of Want

I barely saw Steve anymore. He was always in the city, always somewhere else. I tried to reach him, tried to understand, but nothing was the same. He had slipped away. And I was slipping away from myself. Smoking, hiding it. Knowing he was hiding something too. I didn't trust him. I didn't know what he was doing, but I knew he was doing something behind my back.

Whenever we were together, it was always the same: sex, drinking, nothing real. We never did anything fun. Not that we ever really had.

Still, there had been something about him in the beginning; the way he thought so little of himself and put me on a pedestal. Or just how sweet he seemed before the lies started piling up. And they had started early. Jennifer. The mall hookups. Pretending he was just there for *moral support*. Feeling up friends during flag football, staying late after practice to flirt, lingering.

Then when everything fell apart, when I was drowning in a pregnancy, in a different school, in all the uncertainty, he had just tried to *hide* it. Hide me. Hide *our* baby. He never put me first. He never took responsibility. And now, he was doing God only knows what. And I was supposed to just accept it. To stop asking questions. No. Things weren't right. I couldn't do this anymore. I had to step away. I had to tell him it was over.

So, I called. "Steve, I think we're done."

"Why?"

"You've built this whole life around secrets, and none of it includes me. You're drunk more often than you're sober. And when you do show up, it's just for sex like that's all I'm worth to you.

You hurt me. You don't remember that night, but I do. I remember everything.

And this drug business in the city? It's a disaster waiting to happen. Reckless. Thoughtless. Like you've decided to torch your future and drag everyone else down with it.

After everything... I'm done watching you vanish piece by piece. I'm done waiting for someone who stopped choosing me a long time ago."

Silence.

Then, just like that "Fine. You'll be back. You always are."

And he hung up.

I cried. I wanted him to say no. I wanted him to say he *loved* me, that he couldn't live without me. I wanted him to tell me our time together was the best he had ever known. That everything we shared, everything we survived had bound us together in a way nothing could break. I wanted him to convince me I was wrong. I wanted him to change my mind. I wanted him.

I wanted to die. I wanted it all to be over. I wanted to take it back; every kiss, every touch, every whispered promise, every look that had only ever belonged to him. What had I ever really meant to him? All I became at the end was a guarantee. A certainty. A place to land. Because he knew I would come back.

I always did. But not this time. No. Not anymore. This is over.

Chapter Forty-Nine

Petals Of Goodbye

Michelle and I were inseparable. If I wasn't at her house, we would be out driving her car or someone else's car, it didn't matter. We were drunk, high or both. Trying to get more or finishing what we had.

She had a boyfriend, but her parents hated the relationship. Always fighting. Always tense. Her mom was usually passed out.

Somehow despite her mess, I felt comfortable in it. It wasn't my mess. And for me, it was easier to exist in hers than my own.

Without my mom talking much, without Steve in the picture, life moved forward like I had never been pregnant. Like I had never lost my baby. No one mentioned it anymore. The topic itself had become taboo.

"She seems happy, so don't bring it up."

"She's doing well—no need to remind her."

How naive. Like I could ever forget. Like I wasn't constantly thinking about it, about him. But there was no one to talk to. No one understood. So, the world decided it *hadn't* happened. I was supposed to move on, take my second chance and start fresh. But I wasn't fresh. I was tarnished. I hurt. I suffered a loss. And the weight of it—unbearable.

People thought that by never bringing it up, they were helping. But all they did was bury me deeper—deeper in my facade, pretending that life was fine. That I was fine. I wasn't.

I was drinking. Smoking. Doing whatever I wanted. And no one stepped in my way. No one tried to stop me.

Michelle's boyfriend's house had become my second home. A party house. No begging for beer. No desperate deals in parking lots. Everything we wanted; alcohol, weed, it was all there, all the time. And we took it. We started going there constantly.

It didn't take long before the guys started hitting on me. It felt good to be wanted again, even if for the wrong reasons. To be able to hide behind nice clothes, behind their drunken haze, behind whatever version of myself I chose to show.

I knew what they wanted. Sex. So, I dragged it out if I could make them work for it, made them *care* for just a little while. Because once I gave in, once they got what they wanted, everything else stopped.

One night, a commotion outside pulled us from the house. Steve and Clay sat on the curb; both drunk, both pathetic. Steve saw me and started begging me to go with them. I didn't even hesitate.

"These are my friends now. I'm not leaving."

He laughed, turning to one of the guys beside me.

"She'll leave. She always does."

Then he lifted his hand, twisting his fingers in the air, like wrapping an invisible thread around them.

"I've got her wrapped around my finger."

It hit me. Hard. We were done. For real. For good.

The arrogance in his voice, the certainty in his movements like he could *snap*, and I would just *run* back.

That was honestly what he thought. That was *who* he thought I was. So, I turned to the guy beside me.

"Carry me inside," I said.

And he did—threw me over his shoulder, carried me through the door.

I knew Steve was watching. I *wanted* him to. I wanted *his* last memory of me to be this; my body carried away by someone else.

I was done.

I don't even know why I wanted to hurt him. Maybe because he did it to me first, over and over, until the pain felt like the only language we shared. Or it was just the ache talking; that hollow, shapeless grief that shows up when someone uses you and calls it love. He only ever wanted one thing, and I knew that. But part of me still wanted to show him I wasn't his to keep. That I could walk away. That I already had.

I threw myself into the crowd, into the music, into the haze of alcohol; anything to drown out the gnawing thoughts of Steve and the promises he never kept. Had he ever really meant to marry me? Or had it all been a game, a calculated deception from the start? Maybe he knew about my reputation, saw an easy mark, someone too willing to believe in love. Maybe it had never been more than sex for him. Maybe he had never loved me at all.

The vodka burned going down, but not enough. Not enough to silence the downward spiral pulling me deeper. Shot after shot, the night blurred, my body moving without intention, without care. When I woke, the morning light stabbed through the window, revealing the unfamiliar room, the stranger beside me, the hollow ache in my chest. It wasn't the first time. It wouldn't be the last.

I was losing myself, slipping into something I'd always feared becoming. And for the past few weekends, I hadn't even tried to stop it.

I was lost and no one was looking for me. It was as if my child had never existed, as if I had never carried life inside me. If you give birth but your child dies, are you even a mother? I suppose it depends on who you ask. Everyone around me pretended it never happened. As though silence could erase it. My parents called it kindness not wanting to upset me, but it only made everything feel less real, like a dream slipping through my fingers.

It was like I had been swept away to a foreign place; a version of my life where the past no longer existed. My old world, its people, its promises vanished. I was in a new story; one I never wanted to be in, and I didn't even know who I was anymore.

The days blurred into nights, into cigarettes and vodka. The smoke curled in my lungs, heavy and bitter. The alcohol burned, but it didn't cauterize the wounds. It was just a mask, a disguise for the inferno inside. And I needed help to put out the flames, but no one saw them. No one tried.

I hated myself. I hated what had happened to me. The regrets stacked up; suffocating, pressing down like hands around my throat. I felt used and dirty; as if every mistake clung to me like a second skin, impossible to shed. And no matter what I did, nothing could undo what had already been done.

How could I meet someone new and tell them the truth? That I had carried life, only to lose it. That maybe it was my fault but probably not, but how could I ever be sure? That I wasn't a virgin, that my reputation was ruined, even if the first one had never been true. That this new reputation, the one built from nights that I barely remembered, was real. That my mother hated me. My grandmother, too.

I was a disaster. A mess. A ruin. I spent weeks trapped in a downward spiral; numbing myself with substances, drowning in the ache of everything I didn't want to feel. Steve wasn't done with me though. He left notes on my doorstep; desperate scribbles that begged for a second chance. He even sent his siblings to find me, as if their presence could soften the edges of his betrayal.

I wanted to believe it meant something; that he loved me, that he wanted me back, but deep down I knew the truth. He didn't miss me. He missed the ease, the familiarity, the way I had always been available. That was all I had ever been to him, a convenience.

His notes trembled with desperation, telling me he couldn't survive without me. I pictured myself wrapped around his little finger again, falling back into the cycle. I wasn't going back. Not this time. He never loved me. There were too many memories, too much evidence. It had never been love.

I walked to his house; my hands clenched tighter than I meant to. I needed to explain myself. To his sister, at least. I hated how I had just disappeared, how I had left them without a word. They deserved to know that it wasn't about them. But I couldn't stay tethered to Steve; not even through them.

I knocked, and his mother answered. Her face was tight, unreadable.

"I need to talk to Jenny," I said. She was the one leaving all the notes, the one who wouldn't stop reaching out.

But before I could say another word, his mother's voice sliced through the air.

"Ellie, you hurt my kids so much. They loved you, and you just walked away from them like they were nothing. They cried for weeks, and they're just now starting to move past it. The last thing I want is for them to have to go through it all over again. You need to leave before they see you. And don't ever come back."

The world blurred. I couldn't even look at her.

The pain I caused her kids. *Her* kids?

What about the pain *her son* caused *me*? What about the years of being used, of being lied to? I wasn't a person to him; I was a convenience, a plaything, something to toss aside when it no longer served him. And yet, she didn't care. She only saw what hurt her kids.

I walked away slowly and steadily, trying to hold myself together. The air outside was thick, suffocating. The weight of everything pressing down, pressing in. I was done explaining myself.

My report card arrived in the mail, and I barely needed to open it to know what it would say. Failed. Everything, except art. No surprises there. Two schools, barely any attendance. After everything, school had been the least of my concerns.

But now I had to face it. Face the reality of going back. The thought made my stomach twist.

How could I walk those halls again? Sit in those classrooms, surrounded by kids who had whispered about me since third grade? The ones who had taunted me with cruel names? The ones who thought I was pregnant. The ones who assumed I had been sent away, or had a baby waiting for me at home? And the worst ones, the ones who knew my baby had died.

And now, on top of everything, I'd have to deal with all the rumors about Steve. The ones who thought we were still together. The ones who knew we weren't. What if I ran into him? What if he had a new girlfriend, laughing with him, kissing him near his locker? The thought made my pulse pound. It was too much. I couldn't go back.

I turned to my dad. "I want to drop out. I'm sixteen now. I can't go there anymore." He had left school at sixteen surely, he'd understand. "I can get my GED instead, just like you did. It'll be better for me. If I must go back, I think—" My voice caught, the weight of it pressing down. I think I'll kill myself. "Please don't make me go back."

He hesitated, eyes searching my face, reluctant. "Ellie, I think you should try to stick it out. You might regret it if you don't."

Regret? I had never planned beyond high school. No one had ever mentioned college, never asked what I wanted to do. The only future I had ever imagined was marriage, being a wife, being a mother. But that life had been ripped away. Now, I had nothing. No plan. No future. Just the unbearable thought of walking through those doors again.

I knew I needed a job, something, but I hadn't thought that far ahead. I only knew one thing. I couldn't go back.

My dad finally sighed, reluctant but resigned. He signed off on the papers. Relief settled over me, though it wasn't the kind that felt like freedom.

It just felt like nothing.

Chapter Fifty

Petals of Falling

There was a stretch of time where everything unraveled. Drinking, smoking, doing things just to feel something, or nothing. The days blurred as I leaned harder into chaos, as if living recklessly could somehow make the emptiness feel less permanent. Love, purpose, even family... they all felt like echoes from a past life. I had no partner, no child, and every glance from my grandmother reminded me of how much I'd changed. Even my parents, still submerged in their quiet grief, couldn't reach me where I was.

And yet, in the same breath, I knew I was different. I had grown; stretched painfully into someone new, but I still felt like a child pretending at adulthood. Lost in the in-between.

So, I searched for things that made me feel. Music that rattled my chest, time alone with carving my skin as if the cuts could absorb some of my sadness. And sometimes, I found brief solace in the company of others, whose pain dwarfed mine. Their stories made mine feel small. Manageable. Almost survivable.

There were days when I couldn't stop imagining how I might hurt myself. Not because I really wanted to die, but because I wanted someone to notice. To grieve. I played it out in my mind, again: their regret, their sorrow, the sudden weight of everything they'd failed to say or do. It became a bitter comfort; a fantasy where pain became proof that I mattered.

But in chasing that grief, I was losing pieces of myself. I couldn't trust my own hands, my silence. I was slipping up living recklessly, hoping something would catch me before I disappeared entirely.

"Steve used to laugh at people like this; slumped on stoops, smoke curling from their fingers like they were burning their lives in slow motion. We said we'd never be them. Never numb ourselves. Never run.

But here I was, flicking a cigarette like I meant it. Doing all the things Steve and I once swore off. And you know what? I didn't care. Maybe I wanted it to hurt him. Maybe I wanted him to picture me choking on the same smoke he left me in. Because if he could forget so easily, maybe pain was the only language we had left in common."

I finally agreed to see a therapist. I didn't want to. I didn't want to recount it all again, didn't want to watch someone else flinch at my pain. But I was running out of ways to keep myself safe. The therapist suggested I try an antidepressant called Prozac. It was new, still shadowed by mixed reviews, but at that point, I wasn't sure anything could make me feel worse. One pill a day. Give it a few weeks. It seemed simple enough.

I told my mom.

Her voice was sharp the second I mentioned the name. "Ellie, that medicine is horrible. You can't take it. I just saw it on TV; it causes teens to get more depressed. Some even take their own lives."

I blinked. "Why would a doctor prescribe it for depression if it causes more depression, Mom?"

"I don't know. But you can't take it."

"You don't get to decide that. I feel horrible every day. I think about dying more than living. I need something, anything that might help me crawl out of this."

She didn't look at me. "Why are you so sad?"

"Because of everything: Steve leaving, Steven dying, school... life."

She exhaled slowly. "I feel like that too. But you just need to pray more."

That did it.

"Mom, I don't think you're in any position to give advice. You've been depressed for years."

There was a pause, then something sharp cracked through her voice. "Well, I lost my grandson. And before that, my child. If you had just listened to me, he would still be alive."

The room stopped breathing.

"What are you talking about?"

"I told you not to take him to that daycare. That's where he got sick. When I said he was getting worse, you didn't listen. You should've kept him on life support. None of this would've happened if you hadn't gotten pregnant to begin with. It's your fault that we're suffering."

I couldn't speak. Couldn't breathe. Anger hit me like a sudden wave; not because I wanted to fight her, but because I knew nothing I said would fix it. Not for her. Not for me.

So, I walked out. And I didn't look back.

I didn't suddenly start feeling better. The Prozac dulled the edges, but the sadness was still there; just softer now, like a storm humming low instead of roaring. I spent most days avoiding people, walking the same streets until the cracks in the sidewalk felt familiar.

Then Michelle invited me out.

She kept calling until I said yes and said a bunch of people were getting pizza and walking around the mall. I didn't want to go, but I also didn't want to keep rotting in my bedroom. So, I went.

That's when I met him. Jonah.

He wasn't loud like the others. Just kind of... steady. He said Hi when Michelle introduced us. He smiled like I wasn't the girl who'd barely spoken all summer. He didn't ask what school I went to or make a joke to fill the silence. He just walked beside me, sipping his drink, like being quiet wasn't uncomfortable for him. He has just graduated. Wide-eyed. Unscarred. He didn't know Steve, or the way that name still curled like smoke in my chest. He didn't know my reputation either; the whispers, the stories, the pieces of myself I'd left scattered behind.

He was a clean slate. And standing next to him, I almost believed I could be too.

Later, when the group scattered, he hung back with me. He talked about how he had gotten fired from his summer job for not showing up, how his older brother danced to all the latest songs, and how they both liked pop music. Nothing deep. Nothing loaded. And that felt nice. And that mattered more than I thought it would.

I didn't expect to fall into anything that summer. Especially not with someone like Jonah. But once he was in my life, it felt like he'd always been there. Within a couple of days of meeting, we were talking every day; late-night calls, random voice messages that made me laugh when I didn't think I could anymore. He didn't smoke and didn't do drugs. He carried himself like someone who hadn't needed to numb anything yet. Something was maddening and magnetic about that; as if he was proof, it was still possible to live clean. Untouched. Next to him, I felt every bruise I'd ever tried to hide.

He started coming over, not even asking anymore, just showing up with chocolate milk or a fun adventure to take me on. We'd sit in his car or on the floor of my bedroom and just exist. Sometimes we kissed. Sometimes we didn't. But when he looked at me, I felt like a whole person again, not just the sad girl with too much history.

I told him about Steven one night when the power went out in a storm. The house was dark except for the flicker of lightning behind the curtains. I didn't plan to say it. But it slipped out, soft and shaky. My son died.

Jonah didn't freak out. He didn't say "I'm so sorry" or ask a million questions. He just reached over and held my hand; his thumb tracing slow circles like it was the most natural thing in the world.

He started calling me "El." said it like a secret, like it meant something only he got to say.

We were official. He kept a hoodie in my room, and I knew how he liked his coffee. I played old songs I used to love before everything broke, and he listened like they were sacred.

It was fast. It was too fast. But after everything, I didn't want to be slow. I wanted to feel like the world could still surprise me.

And Jonah did.

I didn't mean to fall for Jonah; not in the thick of the mess I was still crawling through. But it was happening fast. And that scared me.

He called to say good morning, like it was a promise. He wanted to know what I ate, what songs I was listening to, and how my heart was holding up. For the first time in forever, someone looked at me like I wasn't broken, just bruised.

It wasn't perfect. It was impulsive and messy and full of nights we stayed up too late, wondering what the hell we were doing. But it was real. And after everything, real felt like it was enough.

We'd spend hours in his room; legs tangled, CDs looping, windows open to the sticky summer heat. His thumb would trace circles on my wrist, and I'd think, *I can do this, I can still feel something good.*

But the more he gave, the more I panicked. I panicked because he was kind, and I was still grieving. Still haunted. Still holding a sadness, I didn't know how to share without making him run. So instead, I kept parts of myself quiet. The worst parts. The ones that still whispered dark things when the lights were off and the music stopped.

I was starting to feel better, not whole but steadier. Life began to settle into something resembling rhythm: work, laughter, shared dinners with more quiet than tension. I wasn't waking up afraid every day.

One morning, Jonah dropped me off after an overnight adventure, the sun already rising, the air soft and still. As I stepped out of the car, I saw my grandmother sitting outside in her old chair, legs tucked under her, eyes closed like she was listening to the breeze.

I haven't spoken to her much lately. Things between us had grown strained from old words and old wounds, but something in me pulled me toward her. No plan. No speech.

I walked up, kissed her cheek, and told her I loved her.

She blinked, surprised. Smiled, but didn't say much. Neither did I. It was quiet and a little awkward, but it felt right. Like my heart knew something I hadn't caught up to yet.

Less than a week later, she passed away in her sleep.

I don't know if that moment changed anything between us. But I'm grateful I listened to the part of me that reached out—because even in all the mess, even in the unspoken, there was still something that felt like hope.

Another afternoon, I came home and found several black trash bags sitting on the porch like they were waiting to be claimed. I stepped inside, confused, and asked my mom what was going on. She didn't even turn around when she said, "Since you're at Jonah's all the time, you might as well live there."

I hadn't asked to move in. I hadn't even thought about it. We'd only been together for an abbreviated time, and we weren't ready, not really. But when she said that, and I saw that everything I owned had already been packed up and placed outside like some quiet eviction, I just... stopped thinking.

I walked to Jonah's car, heart thudding, and said with a smile that didn't quite reach, "So... want a roommate?" Like it was a joke. Like I wasn't sixteen and scared and suddenly without a home.

It wasn't really a question. There wasn't enough space to decide. There wasn't even time to ask his mom.

He looked at me for a second long enough to register what this meant but then he just nodded. No hesitation. We loaded the bags into the trunk like we'd planned it, like we'd chosen it. But the truth is, we hadn't. We were just kids caught in a moment that moved faster than we could.

We would've ended up there eventually. Maybe. But that day, it wasn't about readiness, love, or choice.

And just like that, my whole life got hauled away in the back of a Plymouth Reliant K.

Jonah had a way of making the world feel a little less dangerous; like it wasn't reckless to believe that something good could last, even in a half-furnished apartment with chipped paint and a leaky ceiling.

We were teenagers playing house with old plates and secondhand emotions, but there was tenderness there—real tenderness. A kind of love that came from being seen at your worst and still being handed the last clean towel or the bigger half of a grilled cheese sandwich.

We didn't even make it to the front door before his mom stepped onto the porch and said, "Finally." She smiled; not the tight kind people give when they're tolerating something, but the kind that carries relief. "I've been thinking of moving in with my boyfriend for a while now. Figured I'd wait until Jonah had someone to look after him."

I blinked. So did Jonah.

She hugged me, handed us the key, and said she'd be out by the end of the week.

Just like that, we weren't just crashing in someone else's space, we were inheriting a life someone else was ready to leave behind. The apartment still smelled like her floral hand soap. Her coffee mug was still in the sink. But it was ours now, whether we were ready or not.

By Monday morning, reality had settled in like dust in the corners of the apartment. The fridge hummed too loudly. The ceiling still dripped. And rent was due in three weeks.

Neither of us had a plan; just a drawer full of takeout menus, half a tank of gas, and a handwritten list scrawled on notebook paper that read: grocery store, café, bookstore, maybe gas station.

I borrowed Jonah's hoodie and tied my hair back, trying to look older, steadier. He printed out his resume at the library and crossed his fingers when the printer jammed.

We spent the day walking strip malls, smiling too widely at managers who barely looked up. I filled out an application at a smoothie place that smelled like bleach and strawberries. Jonah got a call back from a local diner where the owner said, "We don't hire kids, but I'm short on dishwashers." He said yes before she finished the sentence.

That night, we sat on the floor again; no cereal this time, just toast and the stale end of a peanut butter jar and whispered our fears like kids at a sleepover. What if this doesn't work? What if we screw it all up? What if loving each other isn't enough?

We were young, scared and broke.

But the lights stayed on. The apartment didn't fall apart. And for the first time in a long time, we had something to build from, even if we had to build it with minimum wage and secondhand everything.

Jonah landed a job as a line cook at a place just off the highway; nothing fancy, but the kind of spot that never slept. Burgers, wings, eggs over easy at two a.m. He came home smelling like grease and rosemary; his collar damp from steam, face flushed from the heat. I'd kiss him on the cheek and taste the salt of a double shift.

I got a job at a deli on Main, where the cold cuts were stacked like playing cards and customers barked their orders without looking up. I learned fast how to wrap a sandwich in under ten seconds, how to smile through someone's bad mood, how to count change without thinking too hard about how little we had left.

We left sticky notes on the fridge to keep track of who was working when. Some nights we didn't see each other at all; just brushed past one another in the hallway, trading aprons and half-eaten granola bars.

But when we met in the in-between, when he got home early or I had the morning off, we made a point to be soft with each other. Shared pop-tarts over the sink. Took turns reading grocery receipts like they were letters from another life.

It was exhausting. It was growing up too fast.

But it was ours.

There were nights that we didn't speak. There were weeks where bills came faster than paychecks and our fights echoed off the apartment walls louder than the laughter ever did. We lost time, sleep, and patience. Some days it felt like we were two kids in grown-up clothes, pretending we knew what we were doing.

But we learned.

We learned how to hold space for each other without always fixing things, how to say 'I'm scared' in silence, how to fight fair and make up softer. We grew around the cracks, instead of trying to patch them.

And somehow, against the odds, the us-that-wasn't-supposed-to-last kept showing up.

We didn't choose this life in the beginning; not really. But eventually, we did. We chose each other again and again in the small ways that mattered: Hamburger Helper at midnight, shared headphones at the laundromat, whispered apologies under warm blankets.

We got married in a rental hall near the edge of town. The kind with drop ceilings and folding chairs, a floor scuffed by decades of awkward dancing and community potlucks. I wore a pink dress from an outlet store because my parents said it wasn't right for me to wear white. Jonah borrowed a suit from a rental shop. We hired a DJ from the yellow pages, and the buffet was mostly trays of pasta and fake flowers that we arranged ourselves.

It wasn't fancy. But it was enough.

When we said *I do*, it was quiet, certain, the kind of promise forged in cluttered apartments, in late shifts and tired hands, in shared resilience. We danced until our cheeks hurt from smiling

Years passed. We worked. Saved. Moved out of the apartment and into a home with a crooked walkway and enough light in the mornings to make coffee feel like a ceremony. The cherry tree in the yard was stubborn; it didn't bloom for the first three years—but when it finally did, I cried. The kids came later. Much later. When the fear had loosened its grip enough for me to believe I could hold something fragile and not lose it. Two children, with Jonah's dimples and my curiosity. Their laughter filled the corners of the house I once thought might stay quiet forever. Some nights, the old fears still surface; grief doesn't vanish, it just softens. But when I looked across the dinner table and saw Jonah grinning through mashed potatoes, when the kids bickered over crayons or climbed into my lap without asking, I knew: this unexpected, unplanned life was the one we built. Brick by brick. Choice by choice. It wasn't easy.

Before the house, before the mornings soaked in light and the cherry tree that refused to bloom, I went back. First, for my GED. Then beauty school, where I learned how to shape and soften, not just hair, but a bit of the ache I carried. And then because I still haven't finished college, Jonah worked doubles so I could study. I graduated at the top of my class. It wasn't loud or triumphant. It was steady, like placing the first brick of a home you hope will last.

It was a Sunday afternoon, sunlight pooling across the living room floor, Legos scattered like confetti, the smell of something baking drifting in from the kitchen. Our youngest, five and full of questions, climbed onto my lap holding a crayon-scribbled family tree. "How did you and Dad meet?" he asked. Jonah looked up from the couch, amused. "Do you want the short version or the real one?" I smiled, kissed the top of his head, and said, "Well… it started with some trash bags on a porch and no plan at all. Just two scared kids who had no idea what they were doing." Our son frowned. "That's a weird way to fall in love." I laughed. "Yeah. But it worked." Jonah reached over, lacing his fingers through mine. "It more than worked." The house was small but full of noise, of warmth, of second chances. And for the first time, I didn't worry about the future pulling away what we had. We were still choosing each other. Every day.

Epilogue

The Cherry Tree

Cherry trees bloom everywhere, but each one belongs to him. Not just the one in my yard, rooted in the soil I once turned alone, but all of them. Every March, when pink begins to whisper from bare branches, I feel him again. He came with the first buds. He left with the last.

Seven weeks. That's all the time we were given. But he filled it with soft cries, sleepy sighs, the shape of his fingers curling around just one of mine. He didn't make it to summer. But while the trees bloom, he is everywhere.

I slip off my shoes. Let the petals gather against my bare feet like tiny prayers. Soft. Cool. Weightless. The scent in the air is faint, sweet, tentative; gone if I don't stop to notice. Just like him. Still, I notice.

The blossoms shift with the light: pale blush at sunrise, almost white by midday, deep rose by dusk. Each hue is a breath. A heartbeat. A moment I got to have. Each petal proves that something so fragile can still leave a mark.

I know they'll fall. I know the wind will carry them off. But I want people to remember. I want them to see cherry blossoms and think not just of beauty, not just of spring, but of him. Because he was here. He mattered. And if his name isn't spoken, if his story isn't carried, how will he remain?

So, this is what I ask: When you pass a blooming tree whether it's in a city park, a quiet backyard, or tucked between crumbling sidewalks, think of a child who never saw summer. Let every blossom be a remembrance. A name whispered in color and light. A promise that someone loved and still loves. Let him return each year— not just through me, but through you.

The events in this story are true. All names have been changed. What remains unchanged is the love; the kind that lingers, blooms again, and is never forgotten.

Acknowledgments

This book bloomed from grief, hope, and deep love—and would not exist without those who helped me tend its roots.

To my husband: thank you for your patience, quiet encouragement, and the space to create. Your support made this story of renewal possible.

To my children: those I hold in my arms and the one I hold in my heart— you are my greatest teachers. Your courage, laughter, and love remind me why stories matter.

To my dear friend Lisa: your insight, encouragement, and unwavering support gave me the courage to keep going. I'm endlessly grateful for your heart and faith in me.

To Megan: whose artistry brought my vision to life thank you for crafting a cover that speaks in petals and silence. Your work is a gift.

To my cherished friends and early readers: thank you for your honesty, encouragement, and willingness to sit with the hard parts. You helped me find the clarity this story needed.

To the teens who feel unseen, unheard, or unsure, you are the heartbeat of this book. I wrote this for you. May you find comfort in its pages and know you are never alone.

And to the cherry blossoms—symbols of impermanence, beauty, and renewal—you reminded me that even in goodbye, there is grace.

Author's Note

This story is a work of creative nonfiction. Though names and identifying details have been changed to protect privacy, every moment was lived. Every emotion remains.

It happened many years ago, yet its shape never fully left me. Time has softened the sharp edges, but not the meaning. Writing this now is both a memorial and a release; a way to honor the lives touched, the ones lost, and the strength that grew in between.

Some parts were hard to write. Some were harder to live with. But I believe in telling stories that bear witness in making space for grief and hope to coexist.

There was pain beyond what's on these pages. My parents and I couldn't understand each other at that time. They didn't want this baby, and when I lost him, their grief came out as anger. Mine did, too. For a long time, we stood on opposite sides of something we didn't have language for. But over the years, we returned to one another; not all at once, but gently. Like everything else in this story, our relationship was rebuilt.

What I've come to understand is that I wasn't angry at my mom for mourning my son I was hurting because she didn't comfort *me*. In all my pain, what I needed most was compassion. Some part of me was still a child needing her mother's arms. But that tenderness went to him, not me. And that's why it broke me. I didn't know how to ask for it then. I just needed to be seen.

I sometimes wonder about Steve. He never went to college. Never became the man his family hoped he'd be. Over the years, he slipped into a different kind of absence: addiction, arrests, long stretches of silence. I don't know if what happened between us helped set that course or simply met him where he was already heading. I don't offer that as an excuse. But I no longer carry it as a judgment either. Some people grow out of their wounds. Others keep living inside them.

And for a while, I was heading down that road too. There was a period when I couldn't tell if I was escaping the past or becoming it. I pulled Jonah into that with me into late nights and hazy mornings and people who mistook pain for fun. But that life wasn't who I was. And deep down, I think I knew it. It vanished as quickly as it had arrived, taking with it the friends who had been walking me further from myself. To those who've carried joy and sorrow in the same breath, this is for you. To those still healing, still reaching, still choosing love: you are not alone. And to the one who stayed for seven fleeting weeks but changed everything, your name is not printed here, but it blooms in every petal.

Thank you for reading.

Please contact me in the following ways:

Zannepascale@gmail.com

Resources

Resources for Teens (U.S.)

According to experts, you should seek help immediately if you or someone you know is thinking about self-harm or suicide.

National Suicide Hotline: 1-800-SUICIDE (784-2433) or the National Suicide Prevention Lifeline: 1-800-273-TALK (8255) [988lifeline.org] (https://988lifeline.org.

Safe Place: 1-888-290-7233
Project Safe Place provides access to immediate help and supportive resources for young people in crisis through a network of qualified agencies, trained volunteers, and businesses in 32 states.

The Trevor Project: 866-4-U-TREVOR
The Trevor Project operates the only nationwide, around-the-clock crisis and suicide prevention helpline for lesbian, gay, bisexual, transgender, and questioning (LGBTQ) youth LGBTQ+ youth crisis help The Trevor Project 1-866-488-7386 or text "START" to 678678 · [thetrevorproject.org](https://www.thetrevorproject.org)

Sexual assault or abuse RAINN 1-800-656-HOPE (4673) · [rainn.org] (https://www.rainn.org)

Dating or family violence National Domestic Violence Hotline 1-800-799-SAFE (7233) · [thehotline.org] (https://www.thehotline.org)

Self-harm or peer support Teen Line Call 1-800-852-8336 or text "TEEN" to 839863 · [teenline.org] (https://www.teenline.org)

Pregnancy resources Planned Parenthood → 1-800-230-PLAN (7526) · [plannedparenthood.org] (https://www.plannedparenthood.org)

Bullying or school-based harassment StopBullying.gov[stopbullying.gov] (https://www.stopbullying.gov)

www.ingramcontent.com/pod-product-compliance
Lightning Source LLC
Chambersburg PA
CBHW050026120726
47903CB00006B/1932